Conjuror

Advance Praise for Conjuror

A monster serpent, amulets of power, secret societies, ancient legends—
the perfect recipe for tension and turmoil that adds up to high-stakes
entertainment. *Conjurer.* Just the title itself is enticing, but the entire
story resonates with spirit, blending myth with reality, tragedy with
triumph. A banquet of adventure.
—Steve Berry, *New York Times* bestselling author of *The Patriot Threat*

Cherokee prophecy runs like deep-veined gold through *Conjuror*, a book
true to the promise of its title. McClure weaves a potent tale here, ancient
as the mountains and timeless as story itself. Dark with striving and
bright with destiny, *Conjuror* lays bare both the history and the heart of a
people, and in doing so, proves that the power of our tales lies in their
telling.
— Tina Whittle, author of the Tai Randolph/Trey Seaver series

A compelling tale of secret relics, betrayal, and blood ties.
—Maggie Toussaint, author of *Bubba Done It*, a Dreamwalker Mystery

The world of Native Americans is as rich and alien to most readers as any
fantasy landscape, and Holly Sullivan McClure brings the land, the lore,
and tribal conflicts to life. Using Cherokee myths and beliefs, she has
created a modern day tragedy that explores the power of good and evil.
Conjuror is a story of powerful beliefs and a supernatural element capable
of bending man to its will—except for those strong and brave enough to
fight. Wise men listen to history and learn. The unwise pay the price.
— Carolyn Haines, author of the acclaimed Sarah Booth Delaney
mystery series

In *Conjurer*, Holly Sullivan McClure has created a vivid tale of mystery
and peril, filled with characters enriched by internal conflicts and
complex motivations. McClure weaves Cherokee history and
philosophies deftly into the narrative, drawing the reader ever deeper into
a world where the greatest danger is not the ever-present threat of death
but the destruction of the soul.
—Jaden Terrell, Shamus award finalist and author of *River of Glass*

Conjuror

A Novel

Holly Sullivan McClure

[handwritten inscription: "05.17.0 To Jonathon Wado H S McClure"]

Mercer University Press | MACON, GEORGIA

MUP/ P512

9 8 7 6 5 4 3 2 1

Books published by Mercer University Press are printed on
acid-free paper that meets the requirements of the
American National Standard for Information Sciences—
Permanence of Paper for Printed Library Materials.

ISBN   978-0-88146-537-2
Cataloging-in-Publication Data is available from the
Library of Congress

Conjuror

A Novel

Holly Sullivan McClure

0520

To Jonathon Wade

HSMcClure

Mercer University Press | MACON, GEORGIA

MUP/ P512

© 2015 by Mercer University Press
Published by Mercer University Press
1501 Mercer University Press
Macon, Georgia 31207

9 8 7 6 5 4 3 2 1

Books published by Mercer University Press are printed on
acid-free paper that meets the requirements of the
American National Standard for Information Sciences—
Permanence of Paper for Printed Library Materials.

ISBN   978-0-88146-537-2
Cataloging-in-Publication Data is available from the
Library of Congress

Acknowledgments

Thanks to The Eastern Band of the Cherokee Indians, especially the Snowbird Community. Listening to the elders speak the language on the streets of Robbinsville, gave a little mixed blood girl a taste of how it used to be.

Thanks to my grandpa who taught me to love a good story, especially one that scared me to death.

In appreciation for the Cherokee artist who inspired the character, David Wayanettah. Your work spoke louder than many voices.

To my brothers who gave me all kinds of ideas for this book, thanks for having my back while we were roaming the hills and climbing the mountains in Graham County NC. Hope you don't mind if you recognize yourself on these pages. You'll show up again in the sequel. Wren couldn't handle it without you.

MERCER
UNIVERSITY PRESS

Endowed by
TOM WATSON BROWN
and
THE WATSON-BROWN FOUNDATION, INC.

Conjuror

When They Were Boys

Qualla Boundary

The white boy sat apart, watching a red-tail hawk circle above the beech tree and a fox slinking under the hedge at the edge of the yard. Like the rabbit feeding unaware, the other boys ignored the predators, too preoccupied to take notice. Eyes wide and fixed on the grandfather, they listened.

Two boys, so alike in size and features they could pass for brothers, sprawled on the steps. The smallest of the five sat coiled like a spring, his skinny arms clasped around bony knees. The eldest stood behind the grandfather, listening. The white boy kept his distance at the end of the porch, his eyes on the diving hawk. Red hair and freckles marked him as different, but his attitude toward the storyteller put him outside the circle. While the other boys hung on every word the grandfather said, he waited impatiently for the old man to end his story and take them home. He feigned disinterest, refusing to admit how much the story scared him, or how his fear confused him. Why should the myths of a people not his own matter to him?

The grandfather made no concession to his anxiety. "If you're going to run with the Copperheads, you need to know our history," he said.

A big price to pay for his friendship with Yona Copperhead. The redhead turned back to the fox and the hawk. The rabbit lifted his nose and sniffed, the first sign of alarm. The grandfather continued with his myth of an impossible evil he called history.

The eldest boy, not yet in his teens and already the caretaker and protector of the younger kids, went to sit beside the redhead. The boy asked him the question he didn't want to ask the grandfather. "Was it here, Buck? Did he keep it in this house?"

"Tell him, Buck," the grandfather said.

Buck answered his question. "Kanegwa'ti lived over three hundred years ago, Johnny. The great conjuror's house was long gone before the Smokers built this one."

Buck's answer seemed to relieve the other boys, but not the redhead. He considered questions they wouldn't dare ask. With a hint of challenge in his voice, he said, "Looks to me like something that could kill us all ought to be done away with. Why didn't Kanegwa'ti destroy it before he died, instead of going to all that trouble to keep it safe?"

In a voice that summoned up images of a future the boys would rather not know, the grandfather said, "It could show a man things to come, Johnny. It showed the great conjuror, Kanegwa'ti, a time when we would face something bad enough to make us violate everything we believe in to risk using it again. Then, a Suye'ta would come, a chosen one who could control Uktena's evil and harness the power of Ulunsu'ti to save us."

The redhead broke free of the old man's gaze, wondering why he put himself through these sessions with the skinny kid's grandfather. Eli knew Grady Smoker's stories well enough to quote them word for word and still wanted more of the bullshit the old people dished out. Yona believed, just like the rest of his family.

Buck asked, "Why didn't the Suye'ta come during the removal? Our people could have used some help on the Trail of Tears."

The grandfather and the white boy watched the hawk swoop down and soar off with the hapless rabbit in his talons. Then, looking into the distance in a way that made the boys wonder if he saw the conjuror's vision, the old man said, "Kanegwa'ti saw those times, Buck, and he watched us survive them. Then the Ulunsu'ti showed him something worse."

His voice dropped so low they wondered if he meant them to hear. "I think I see it coming, boys, the thing the great conjuror knew would take the last one of us out of this world. You and all the others could see it too if you would pay attention. It won't be long now. I hope one of you will have the guts to do something about it before it's too late."

He gave the white boy a cold, lingering stare that sent chills down his spine, then got up and went inside. The screen door clattered shut behind him.

The skinny boy called out to the old man but his grandfather didn't answer. The white boy laughed a bit too loud. "Come on, Eli. You guys believe that crap? A snake's spirit in a crystal, eating souls and killing everything in sight? Your grandpa's just trying to creep us out."

The others didn't laugh. The two boys on the steps looked worried. "Why is he telling us this now, David? What are we supposed to do about it?"

"I don't know, Yona. Could be he thinks one of us is the Suye'ta."

Buck, the eldest, straightened and put his hands in the pockets of his faded jeans. He didn't sound very sure of himself when he said, "Couldn't be one of us. The Suye'ta is an outsider. We're all full-bloods, except Johnny." The four boys turned their attention to the white boy, expecting him to say something. He ignored them.

The fox slunk away into the woods behind the old house. Only the white boy watched him go away hungry to seek new prey.

3

Present Day

Sunday Evening

Ataga'hi

The digger drove the sharp blade of a shovel through rocky soil, shattering a silence that reigned through centuries in the hidden burial ground. The elder stood aside, grim-faced, watching desecration that broke his heart. He had no right to be here, breaking every law that mattered to him, violating the trust of friends, and defiling sacred land, but he saw no other way. The future of his people depended on him.

Thin rays of evening sunlight filtered through sparse foliage, casting shadows across the rocky bones of the mountain. His sculpted muscles rippled as the big white man tossed shovels full of black earth from the grave. Standing apart from the other two, propped against one of the straggly pine trees that survived at this elevation, the third member of the party watched the digger with an air of acceptance, even for the desecration of an ancestor's grave. He could do no wrong.

The elder directed the digger to move further uphill, then bent close to the excavation, straining his eyes to see anything the shovel might unearth. "Easy, easy," he said when he heard the rasp of metal against stone. "Can't risk breaking anything now. Best use the trowel." The years lent a roughened edge to his voice. He stood to fetch the trowel, his back as straight and strong as the digger's.

"It would be in a coffin, wouldn't it?" the digger asked him.

"Nope. Didn't use them back then." The elder dropped to his belly and reached down into the hole with the trowel. When a smooth surface appeared, he cleared the soil with his hands, exposing an ancient soapstone pot, sealed tight against the ages.

"Here, help me with this." The elder's voice broke, betraying his dread. The digger stepped into the hole with him. It strained both of them to lift the heavy pot free of the grave and set it down on a patch of mossy ground. The third member of the party left the tree and came to peer over the digger's shoulder at their find.

The elder ordered them both to stand back while he squatted beside the ancient pot and cleaned it with a red cotton bandana. He could feel their eyes on him as he ran his finger around the rim until he found a seam. With a hunting knife the digger handed him, he worked at it until he loosened the seal. Laying it aside, he shielded the pot with his body so only he could see inside.

Ancient buckskin, dry and brittle with age, filled the interior. Holding his breath he inched it free of the container and laid it on the ground, then teased the bundle apart to reveal the grave goods the tanned hide and stone pot had protected for hundreds of years.

Centuries spent lying buried with the mortal remains of their owner left the relics in much better shape than he expected. Taking out an ancient war axe, he tested its heft in his hands. It fit his grip like it belonged to him. He admired the skill of its creator evident in every detail, from the finely knapped stone to the intricate markings on the handle. It belonged in the hands of a warrior, not a holy man.

He heard hope in the digger's voice. "This is what you needed, right?"

The elder examined the relics. Lifting them one by one he searched for the marks that told him what he needed to know. Two graves lay hidden here in their high mountain burial ground. One held what they came for. The occupant of the other died to protect a secret he couldn't be trusted to keep. His goods meant nothing. It took only a cursory look at the contents of the opened grave to know they opened the wrong one.

The elder's resolve weakened. The grave held a man who had nothing more to offer his descendants, no debts to pay. He earned the right to uninterrupted rest.

With his face averted so the digger couldn't see how much his mistake troubled him, he said, "Wrong grave. Help me put the pot back in the ground with its owner, then I'll cover up him and his goods and let him go back to his rest."

The digger had to ask, "Who was he?"

The elder didn't answer. The digger put down the shovel and helped the old man maneuver the heavy pot back into the grave beside its owner.

"Start digging where I showed you, before we lose the light."

The elder stood in the open grave and watched the digger pick up the shovel and trudge up the incline. He wiped sweat and dirt off his face on the tail of his T-shirt as he examined the piled stones that marked the second burial site. "Are you sure this is even a grave? Looks to me like it could be a natural rock formation."

The elder answered, "It was meant to look that way. Two men came to bury their dead in that grave. One left the mountain alive and the other sleeps in the grave we opened. Since that time, only one man in any generation knows what they buried here, or why. Start digging now, boy. The sun's sinking low."

The digger drove his shovel into the second grave.

The elder crouched in the open grave and positioned the relics and buckskin in the empty pot. With everything returned to its place but the war axe, he ran his thumb across the razor-sharp obsidian of the blade. A sudden impulse made him set the axe aside while he replaced the seal on the pot. He climbed out of the grave and went to the canvas knapsack he left propped against a lichen-covered boulder, taking the axe with him.

He waited until the digger bent to his work on the second grave and couldn't see him slip the axe in the knapsack.

The third accomplice came to help cover the pot and saw what he did. Shame made him want to explain, but how could he? And what did it matter? He shrugged away his guilt. With the transgressions already on his conscience, stealing from the dead ranked low on his list of sins. The dead man didn't need the axe any more. All his battles ended a long time ago.

The elder accepted the offered help and the two of them worked in silence, scraping the loose earth back into the grave and tamping down the soil. They scattered handfuls of pine needles over the raw earth to erase the evidence of desecration. It did nothing to ease the guilt in the elder's heart or lessen the confusion and accusation in the eyes of his helper. He wished again that the digger had not insisted on bringing along the last person in the world he wanted to involve, but he had his reasons and wouldn't have it another way. When it got dangerous, they'd go it alone, but not yet.

The elder picked up a shovel and went to help the digger. At about three feet down, his shovel met resistance. When the digger spoke, it startled him.

"Must not have buried him real deep."

The elder agreed. He put his foot to the edge of his shovel and leaned into it. Something hard met the blade. He tossed the shovel aside and reached for the trowel. The digger took a second trowel and went to work on the other end of the grave.

They scraped away black loam to reveal a dark outline that emerged into shape as he worked. The digger stood back, amazed. "Three men, you say?"

The elder grunted an affirmative.

"They must have had the strength of a team of bull elephants to lug this thing all the way up here." The digger wiped his brow on his sleeve and bent over the full-sized canoe that served as a coffin.

The elder inspected it. Treated with fire to preserve the wood, the canoe provided protection for the man and his grave goods.

The sun sank to a dim glow leaking behind a distant mountain. Shadows lengthened across the burial ground. The third partner took a flashlight from his duffle bag and directed its beam into the excavation.

The elder worked alone now, hesitant to reveal to their companion what he expected to find.

The digger sat on a fallen log, then got up and paced beside the grave.

The elder understood. This was enough to unnerve the strongest man. "Settle down, son," he said. "Won't be long now."

The digger said, "It's not just the graves. It's this whole mountain. There's not a living thing here but us. That's not normal."

The elder let him pace. He understood how the white man felt. Every sound they made exploded in the silence like a firecracker at a funeral. He knew the reason for the absence of life in places like this, but it still unnerved him. Everywhere else in the Smoky Mountains, bird songs, crickets, frogs, and all the voices of nature filled the woods with sound.

"You know what it is, boy. Nature won't intrude on the places where the Nunne'hi live."

The possibility the immortals might be watching did nothing to comfort any of them. It made it even harder to go through with what they came to do.

The elder put aside the thought of the Nunne'hi, and all the ways he broke harmony with them and his people, and went to work on layers of cured hides that gave way under his careful hands. Remnants of a bearskin robe beneath the hides fell apart. The round dome of a skull appeared amid the fragments. The digger lay on his belly, reaching in to clear away the surrounding earth, then worked the wrappings away from the ancient bones, sparing the elder the need to touch the dead. The white man didn't have to struggle against taboos that made it unthinkable.

The exposed skeleton lay intact in the shielding curve of the canoe, confirming the truth of a legend even the elder doubted at times. How could a rational man believe the stories told about the man buried in this grave, and the secret to his power?

All his doubts vanished as he examined the grave goods buried with the man.

Beside the bones sat a round pottery bowl, somewhat smaller than the one in the first grave.

The digger saw. "Please, Old Man. Don't tell me you picked the wrong grave again."

The elder ignored him and bent to encircle the bowl in his arms. His whole body trembled with the effort to maneuver it to the graveside. The digger took it off his hands and set it on the pile of grave dirt, then helped the elder climb out of the hole.

In the glow of the flashlight, he wiped away the dirt from the pot with his bare hands. His hands felt the markings before his aging eyes could see them, winding around the pot from the bottom, circling the neck, even the scales of the snake remained intact. This is what he came for. In a quaking voice he muttered something in his own tongue that could have been a prayer, or the primal utterance of a man lost in emotion that threw him back to the days before he learned to speak English.

A round disc sealed the mouth of the soapstone bowl, meant to keep its contents safe until the rightful owner came to claim it. He worked it loose with his Barlow knife but couldn't remove the cover alone. He needed the digger's help. He wrapped his arms around the pot and let the digger twist and tug. With a sound like an inhalation, the seal broke. A puff of dust— or was it smoke?—escaped and drifted toward the sky.

The elder said, "I'll take it from here."

The big white man squatted on his haunches beside the pot, watching.

The elder took out the first bundle, checking for markings that confirmed what he needed to know. He found them and, for a fleeting moment, wished with all his soul that his fingers didn't detect the etched outline of the serpent that identified the man in the grave. If this grave held an ordinary man and nothing more, he could call the whole thing off and go home. But this was no ordinary grave, and its occupant, no ordinary man. And he couldn't turn back the clock to a time before he committed himself and the digger to something that would kill them both if he got it wrong. Only the sure knowledge that it was the only way made him do it.

The elder felt the digger's gaze on his neck as he worried the bindings loose from the bundle. Exposing the grave's contents to an outsider compounded the desecration, but only an outsider could do what had to be done. He stalled as long as he could, questioning one last time if there might have been some other option, some path that led him away from this act of desperation and back into the circle. He'd gone through it all before and always arrived at the same conclusion. He was on his own, with only the digger to help.

With trembling hands, he opened the bundles one by one and examined the relics. His accomplices watched in awed silence.

Not a word passed among them as he secured the grave goods in their wrappings and laid the bundle beside the age-darkened skeleton.

When the elder spoke, he saw them startle. Even to his own ears, his voice sounded as brittle as the bones. "Bring the bags. This is what we came for."

The third partner obediently retrieved a couple of crushed canvas bags from the digger's duffle bag and brought them to him. He smoothed them out against his thighs and handed them to the elder. "This is all I had handy, but if we use them both, there should be room to hold it all," he said.

Distaste provoked an uncharacteristic mild profanity from the elder. After all the years of planning this day, he brought nothing better than a couple of old gym bags to hold something that would change the world. Years of spying on his closest friends, violating the trust of the Snake Dancers, involving a man who trusted him in something he could never fully understand, and he overlooked the simple detail of appropriate containers. The gym bags had to do.

He put the wrapped relic bundles back in the bowl and eased it into the largest bag. It filled the canvas, making an awkward, heavy burden. The white man gathered the bones. The elder watched him line the second gym bag with a dingy towel and place the bones inside. He didn't touch them, and he averted his eyes to avoid looking at them.

These were the bones of a man who expected his descendants to open his grave and remove everything in it. He passed that down to them through the generations, leaving instructions for the one who would take his bones, and what he must do with them. The elder came to complete what the dead man started. That should have made it easier.

The elder gave a reluctant perusal when the digger commented on how well the bones had weathered the ages. Strands of black hair still clung to mummified flesh on the skull.

The digger folded the towel over the skull. It bulged against the terrycloth as he closed the gym bag.

The third companion walked away and bent over behind a pine, sickened by the violation of this sacred place, the last resting place of the mortal remains of a holy man. The elder choked back his own nausea. He hated the desecration, even when it was preordained by the dead man. As for the digger, he understood why he needed them, and cared enough to take the risk. The white man adopted his wife's ways when he married in. He had reasons for wanting to protect the homeland and their people, and the child he took as his own.

If this worked the way he planned, they could celebrate in a few days. He didn't dare think about the results of failure.

11

Evening shadows mingled with the eerie silence to make the old burial ground feel too threatening to endure much longer. The digger wanted to abandon the scarred earth and the opened grave and head back down the trail. The elder handed him a shovel and the two of them went to work. They didn't stop until no trace of damage remained. The elder worked as hard as the digger.

One more thing to do, then they could leave. It might be a useless gesture, but the elder hoped it would relieve the foreboding they all three felt. He took an abalone shell from his pack and filled it with herbs from a leather pouch, then held it out to the third partner who struck a match to the herbs. When the flame died and fragrant smoke swirled from the shell, he waved it toward his face and around his body, and then held the shell for the others.

The feeling of cleansing that usually followed smudging eluded them. The smoke drifted away without leaving so much as a trace of fragrance to offer solace. The digger and their companion waited impatiently while he made offerings of tobacco to the Nunne'hi believed to inhabit this mountain. He doubted their presence, fearing the immortal guardians long ago deserted their vigil, but it eased his guilt to leave a gift for them. The silence that lingered around their dwelling places remained, but he saw no sign of their presence. And if they left this secret mountain where no one ever came, how could he hope they still lived anywhere else in the homeland? When they left, the last of his people would go too. Even the men in his circle didn't understand the truth that resided in the heart of the legend of the departing immortals, and what that meant to their people. That's why he had to act without them.

With sadness so profound it pierced his soul, the elder walked away from the graves. He spied on a friend who was closer than a brother to find this place, and betrayed that friend with theft and desecration, and if he failed, it was all for nothing.He pushed the growing pangs of remorse from his mind with the thought of the vanishing Nunne'hi and steeled himself to go through with the plan he had worked on since he came back from the war. He might be too late, but he had to try.

The others followed, staying close enough to give him the benefit of the flashlight's glow in the gathering darkness. An hour's walk through the pathless forest brought them to an old Ford Pinto waiting at the end of a road that was barely more than two ruts through the brush. The old compact car didn't look capable of making it up the steep incline, or maneuvering hairpin curves on the way down.

The elder held the door and flipped the driver's seat forward so the third partner, the only one small enough to fit, could crawl into the backseat, then got behind the wheel.

The white man stashed the bags in the back and folded his long legs into the passenger's seat. Slamming the door, he asked, "Where to now?"

So tired he found it difficult to speak, the elder told him only what he needed to know. "We're going home. I need a good night's sleep. First thing in the morning, I'll do what I have to do at Tatham Gap, and then I'll come for you so we can start the preparations. Tuesday, we'll be ready. Stay on your fast, and don't eat anything or drink anything but water before that."

"I've been fasting like you told me to," the digger said, then as if an afterthought, "I'll keep the bags with me till Tuesday. They'll be safer."

The elder's voice came cold as ice in the darkness. "They stay with me."

Even the contents of the grave had the power to change a man. The digger didn't know how to resist yet. *Why did he ask to keep the grave goods?* A trace of doubt wormed its way into the elder's consciousness. The white man had an ambitious streak. And he liked to think of himself as a shaman. Would the promise of power sway him?

13

The winding dirt road demanded his attention and took his mind off troubling, unwelcome thoughts that crept into his consciousness. He maneuvered the old Ford Pinto around the curves, the brakes squealing on the steep incline. It would be easier once he reached the parkway. Here, the mist that gave the Smoky Mountains their name obscured hairpin turns so thoroughly, he had to be careful not to slip off the sheer drop along the narrow shoulder.

Down the Blue Ridge Parkway and on the other side of the mountain, he pulled into the parking lot of Mingus Mill. The restored old gristmill attracted a fair number of tourists, even this early in the year. The Sunday crowd was long gone. An old truck sat by itself near the trail, its headlights outlining a couple of teenaged kids on the footbridge swinging their legs over the mill stream.

He drove past the truck and parked beside the dark green Mitsubishi Montero his passengers left there when they met up in the parking lot.

The digger flipped the front seat up so their companion could crawl out of the back. "Where do you want us to meet you tomorrow?" he asked the elder.

"I'll go to Tatham Gap by myself. No need for you to come with me." The elder kept his eyes averted to hide the unwanted stirring of mistrust he feared would show. "I'll get back to you when I'm done."

From the corner of his eye, he saw the white man look at the bags in the backseat. He shifted into first gear and stomped on the accelerator.

He drove down the parkway, trying not to dwell on what he carried in the two gym bags. A month ago, he tried one last time to persuade the Snake Dancers, but they stood together, refusing to do anything but wait. He couldn't wait any longer. He was prepared to take action when they refused to acknowledge the peril they faced. It took him years to follow the guardians of the relics the Snake Dancer Society protected and learn their secrets.

The white man stood by him the whole time, even when his own people refused.

His grandfather told him about the Nunne'hi and their relationship to the Cherokee when he first brought him into the Snake Dancer's Circle. The number of the immortals and the number of the Cherokee in the world stayed the same, he said. When the Nunne'hi left the world, the Cherokee would soon follow. The Snake Dancers all heard the same story from their grandfathers. They knew, but they refused to believe.

The guardian of the grave at Ataga'hi led him unawares to the conjuror's resting place. Surely he felt the absence of the immortals when he visited the grave. The silence that lingered around the doorways to their world bore witness to their passing. No evidence of their presence remained.

One by one, he found their ancient places deserted. Who could blame them for leaving? With pollution drifting from the cities leaving the air unfit to breathe, poison rain killing the trees, too many people crowded into the mountains, trampling through lands where they didn't belong, the Nunne'hi didn't feel at home anymore. If this kept up, it soon wouldn't be fit for human beings, much less the Nunne'hi.

It saddened him that the young people considered the immortals only mythic beings, kept alive in old stories told by their superstitious elders. He knew better, and so did the Snake Dancers, but they still wasted time talking. While they talked, the immortals left their despoiled homeland, and the Tsalagi went with them. His heart ached to think about it.

He drove past flashing neon lights advertising motels with names like Redskin Inn or Warrior Lodge. This whole tourist town was part of the trouble. The Snake Dancers had the power to change it all and take back what rightfully belonged to the people they existed to protect, but the years made them soft. Always too afraid of what would happen if things went wrong.

Well, it couldn't get much worse than this. With time running out, they kept saying wait. He waited as long as he could.

If his plan killed him, he vowed to go down fighting. His very nature demanded action. His clan supplied many of the great war-chiefs of old and their blood ran strong in him. This Wolf Clan Warrior wasn't born for talking and waiting. He honored the duty to protect the Ulunsu'ti and the place where it lay hidden on Tatham Gap, but the guardianship of the crystal included the responsibility to use it when the time came. His ancestor who first accepted that sacred duty, and all his fathers who followed, would do it in his place. He felt sure of it. Why else would Kanegwa'ti leave it in their care?

Fear and hunger combined to bring on a bout of nausea. He swallowed hard and spoke aloud into the darkness. "I have to do it, before everything is gone. If I don't, somebody else will, somebody who's too weak to handle it." He knew who that would be, and it pissed him off that the old fool conspired with the others against him, agreeing to wait and see. When did Walker Copperhead, the one dancer he thought he could count on, turn old and soft? Why didn't he understand they couldn't leave it for the next generation to deal with? By the time their grandsons took over, they could say goodbye to the last of the Nunne'hi. Then there wouldn't be any Cherokee people to save. When the big white man came into his life, he saw it as a sign. Like a chosen son, he listened to the stories and observed the sacred ways the elder taught him. He had his faults, but not as many as that lazy-assed weakling of a white boy Walker Copperhead had his eye on ever since he married into the Copperhead family, maybe even since he started hanging around with his grandson back when they were boys. What right did Walker have to judge the white man for teaching their ways to a few of his followers? There were things about the white man Walker didn't know.

A hint of suspicion teased at the back of his mind. Walker

might be up to something, keeping it secret from the dancers. Wouldn't that be just like the sneaky old fart? He hated to admit it, but for all their differences, he and Walker thought alike about the traditions. Walker kept things closer.

He drove past the Qualla Boundary sign on 441 and steered the Pinto off to a side road for a few miles, then up a gravel driveway for the half-mile to his trailer. The house he lived in since the night he came into the world stood behind it, leaning precariously against rotting porch posts. His wife wanted something more modern to live in so he bought her the trailer. Two years later she went and died and he still owed monthly payments. He parked under the big beech tree that shaded his old house and went inside the trailer. Tired to the bone, he stashed the gym bags under his bed and laid down for a couple hours of sleep. A nightmare stretched before him in the days ahead, and only the white man faced it with him. Against his will, every flaw in the white man's personality ticked off one by one in his memory. He fretted about Walker Copperhead, wondering if he might come around if he gave him another try. Or if he might be way ahead of him with his own Suye'ta. His mind refused to let him rest.

Smokey, his wife's old cat, cuddled up beside him. He got used to talking out his troubles with her since Sally walked over. Smokey purred while he fretted about an old Snake Dancer who lived on Snowbird Creek, and a white boy who married into the family. He confided his opinion to Sally's cat. "If that white boy knew what Walker had in mind for him, he'd haul ass out of Graham County and as far away from all them Copperheads as he could get."

An owl hooted somebody's death call outside in the beech tree. It took his mind off the rest of his worries long enough for sleep to overtake him. His dreams tormented him worse than his waking thoughts. A snake as big around as his leg surfaced from the shadows of a mountain creek and looked straight into his eyes, forcing him to return the gaze. He had no choice but to stare deep into the very human eyes of the serpent and try like hell to wake up.

Saturday Night

The Round House

The door opened, letting the cigarette smoke out and the cool night air in. The man who entered moved like a shadow, his black eyes darting around the room, settling on the fiddle player as he tucked his instrument under his chin and began to play. The first note echoed the fiddler's startled groan when he saw who followed the big Indian through the door of the Round House Supper Club. She looked harmless enough, so petite the top of her head would barely reach his chin. She stared straight at him and smiled. The smile froze his blood. It curled her full red lips and stopped before it reached her eyes. Those eyes smoldered like black pools of lava that could roll over the soul of any man fool enough to cross her. He cursed himself for being that kind of fool.

His fingers acted on their own, playing from habit with no input from his brain. The fiddle sang under the bow and the woman listened, standing beside the Indian at the door. She still smiled. The Indian didn't, just folded his arms across his chest like a parody from a Western movie, his face impassive.

"Sing it, Johnny!" the mandolin player yelled.

A woman wearing a cowboy hat echoed the yell. He cleared his throat and tried to remember the words. As the lead singer of his band, he had to sing. He lowered the fiddle and tried. His voice broke and came out way off key but the boys covered for him. They saw the woman at the door, and the big Indian with her. This was John McLeymore's last song of the night. The banjo player gave him a look that said, *I'd help if I could but you're on your own tonight, friend.*

He understood. Nobody could help him now. He had to

face this tune alone.

"Shady Grove my little Love,
Shady Grove my darlin',
Shady Grove my little love,
Going back to Harlen."

While the mandolin wailed the last few notes, the fiddle player put the fiddle across his knee and reached under his chair. He needed a sip of courage. The unlabeled Mason jar he came up with held the only measure of comfort he could expect to find in this room. His eyes watered as he drank. One sip, and he lowered the jar. He knew better than to resist when the woman came on the stage and took it from his hand.

"He won't be needing any more of this tonight." She handed the jar to Will.

Will put down his mandolin to take the jar and knocked back a quick sip before passing it on to the bass player.

The Indian towered over him, handing him his fiddle case. He took it and stowed his fiddle. The woman looked him square in the eye with that unflinching gaze. "John, you've got two kids at home that want to say goodnight to their daddy, and a woman that ain't gonna sleep alone tonight. Yona and I think it would be a good idea if you'd come on home now."

It sounded like a good idea to John too. He rescued what little dignity he could by sweeping his hat low in a bow to his fans when his brother-in-law lifted him out of his chair by the elbow and eased him toward the door. Some cheered but more laughed.

Lightning Creek Bluegrass Band lit into playing without the fiddler. It didn't sound as good, but the Round House patrons understood. A few got up to dance. It beat listening to a bluegrass band without a fiddle or a tenor.

They didn't blame him for leaving. Nobody wanted to see his wife get mad. Faron Copperhead McLeymore could raise some holy hell if he set her off. He learned that back when she was a kid four years younger than him, following John and her brother Yona around like a little puppy, bossing both of them around like she had a right. He had a lot of years to get used to it.

Yona carried the fiddle. John walked with his arm draped around Faron's waist. She smiled up at him sweet as sugar. He breathed easier knowing he hadn't made her mad. He couldn't ask for a better wife, and it didn't take much to make her happy. Just keep the all-night sessions to a minimum, like when her mom could watch the kids and she could come along, be a good daddy, and not cuss or drink in front of his daughter and son. He had the rules down and, for the most part, he toed the line. He shuddered when he remembered the few times he screwed up. Will and the other guys in the band ragged him about those times. "You're whupped, man," they said.

"Yeah, like an egg-sucking hound." John didn't mind admitting it. He knew Will and every man in the band—hell, in the whole state of North Carolina—would trade places with him in a New York minute if they could.

"Had to bring the bulldog," Yona said. "Charlie's got my Blazer and Mama Kate and Faron drive those little cars that make you feel like a sardine." Yona's big, red Mack truck sat parked across the road, sporting the polished hood ornament that inspired its name. He had a fleet of them, all just alike. The logo on the door depicted a snake coiled among the words "Copperhead Logging." John helped his brother-in-law design it when they still went to Robbinsville High. Inside the cab he could see a dark form.

"Old Walker?" John asked.

"Yeah," Yona grinned. "He wanted to come along to say 'osiyo,' brother."

"I doubt it was greeting me he had in mind. More likely he wanted to come along to watch, in case Faron kicked my ass."

"More likely he did." Yona slid behind the wheel.

John climbed in beside Walker Copperhead and lifted

Faron up next to him. One good thing about Yona's truck, it was as roomy as a limo. "Evening, Grandpa," he said, without looking at Faron's grandfather.

"Osiyo, son," Walker greeted him in Cherokee. "How's the crowd?"

"Good crowd tonight. Kinda rowdy, but then they usually are on a Saturday night." John looked at his watch in the glow of the dashboard lights. "It's late, though, after midnight. High time we cleared out and went home. I appreciate you and Faron and Yona coming to pick me up."

"Bullshit," Walker said.

John didn't say anything else, just hugged Faron as she cuddled closer to him. Walker had said all he planned to tonight. Yona never did much talking, not even when they were kids. Besides, he had to keep his eyes on the road. Tatham Gap cut several miles off the trip home, but the road ranked only slightly higher than a logging trail, twisting and turning around the mountain.

Near the top, an even more primitive road veered off to the right toward the fire tower on Joanna Bald, reminding John that he'd be coming this way early Monday morning to take supplies and hang out with Eli Smoker for a while.

The lights of the truck fell briefly on a state park historical marker. He didn't need to read it to know it said Tatham Gap Road was a section of the Trail of Tears. Just passing it always made him think of the stories he heard all his life about how they rounded up his wife's people and marched them away to the west, tearing them from their homeland and robbing them of their homes. How many of the thousands of Cherokee people who died on the trail lay in unmarked graves on this very mountain?

The three Cherokees in the truck with him said nothing, but the silence resonated with unspoken feelings.

At almost one o'clock, they turned into what could loosely be termed a driveway. Gravel covered the single lane but weeds sprouted through and puddles formed every time it rained. The door on Yona's side scraped against thick huckleberry bushes. He slowed to ease the big truck into the creek and up to the turn-around below the house.

"Need to build you a bridge over that creek, brother," Yona said.

"Never seemed to need one before," John said. "We've got the footbridge, and it's no problem to just drive through the creek."

"That's okay for your pick-up, but Faron's Mustang and Mama Kate's Trans Am sit mighty low in the water," Yona said. "While little brother Charlie's home from Appalachian State, we'll get to work on it. We'll be over first thing in the morning with a load of lumber and the three of us will build her a good bridge. Should have done it years ago. One of these days, we need to look into paving your driveway too."

Wouldn't do any good to object. Seemed like one of his in-laws had something in mind for his property every time he turned around. Well, as long as they came up with the supplies and most of the labor, it wasn't such a bad deal.

As soon as the truck came to a stop, Faron climbed down and went to the house. Yona and Walker stayed in the truck, waiting for Mama Kate to come out. John loitered at the door, stalling so he could avoid Faron's mom.

Walker scooted over to the door and prodded John in the ribs with his walking stick. "Need to get some rest, boy. Never know when you might need it." He chuckled like what he said was real funny.

"Yeah, sure, Grandpa." John followed Faron up the porch steps. She stopped to pat Red Dog on the head. He knew the sound of Yona's truck well enough not to waste his energy barking at it. Black Dog came around from his post at the back door to check. "Go back to sleep, old buddy," John said. "It's just us." Black Dog trotted back around the house.

Kate greeted him on her way out the door, making no attempt to conceal how she felt about staying up till the wee hours of the morning babysitting John's kids. "The babies went to sleep on the couch. I promised them their daddy would carry them to bed if he ever got home."

John tried not to flinch. Having a mother-in-law who stood four inches taller than he, and outweighed him by a good twenty pounds, intimidated the hell out of him. By the time he turned ten years old, he gave up trying to figure out whether Faron's mom loved him or hated his guts. "Thanks for looking after Wren and Diamond, Mama Kate," he said. She patted his arm as she sashayed past him, then said to Faron, "I'll ride over tomorrow with the men when they come to make you a bridge. You'll need help cooking for all that bunch." She didn't say anything to John. Funny how everybody knew about this bridge project but him.

Diamond hardly stirred when John picked him up and carried him to bed. John kissed his son's cheek and tucked the covers around him. He was a big boy for a two-year-old. Took after his uncle Yona, or his Grandma Kate. John watched him sleeping for a moment, then went back to the living room for his daughter.

Wren stretched and opened her eyes. Her sleepy smile warmed his heart as she reached her arms up to him. She looked as dainty as the tiny bird Kate named her for, just like her mama.

With the kids tucked in and sleeping, he could get a couple hours of shut-eye before time to wake up for the bridge building. When Yona said "first thing in the morning," John learned from experience he meant well before sunrise.

The stairs to the loft bedroom felt steeper than usual. The Copperheads helped build the room in the attic after Faron got pregnant with Diamond. "Need some more room with another kid coming along," Yona had said. The memory of the weeks following that decision drained the last of the energy left in him.

He ducked into the shower, only because he knew Faron

would kick him out of bed if he came in reeking of smoke, moonshine, and sweat. He made it quick and staggered into the bedroom ready to fall asleep as soon as his head hit the pillow. Faron had other ideas. Every inch of her soft skin shined like the finest warm, coppery silk as she welcomed him to bed.

"Looks like I'm not gonna get much sleep tonight," he said.

"Probably not," Faron tangled her fingers in his red curls and drew his mouth to hers. Damn! How did he get so lucky? Faron set about removing any lingering traces of doubt about his immense good fortune.

When she finished with him for the night, Faron slept the sleep of a satisfied woman while John lay wide awake. He couldn't shake a vague feeling of unease that kept him tossing and turning. Maybe thinking of all the work the Copperheads had lined up for him kept him from sleeping. These projects of theirs had a way of running his ass off, and he dreaded it like a toothache. He almost dozed off when Walker Copperhead's farewell words surfaced in his mind. "Get some sleep while you can"? What the hell did the old goat mean by that?

The Copperheads arrived and woke him up about the time he fell asleep. Little brother Charlie hung around and helped with the bridge building all morning, but he had better things to do with a Sunday afternoon. He left in Yona's blazer, hinting about a tourist girl at the lake with a picnic basket packed and ready for a hike in the woods. Mama Kate let her baby boy get away with a lot more than Faron and Yona ever did.

John held his own, working like a mule until Kate and Faron called them in for supper. Mama Kate bandaged the blisters on his palms, making comments about how a man needed a few calluses so he didn't have hands like a girl. Black Dog and Red Dog returned from their check of the perimeters of his land and sat on the porch waiting for Faron's family to leave so they could settle in for the night. John stifled yawns until they said goodnight and went on their way. He liked taking it easy on the weekend, not slaving on a bridge while his in-laws cracked the whip. A few more days like today would just about kill him. They made an early evening of it and went to bed as soon as the kids allowed.

Faron snuggled next to him and went to sleep. He lay awake, resisting the urge to toss and turn, looking for a position that didn't hurt. Aches and pains tormented every muscle and joint in his body. Hard manual labor took its toll. He got up and ate a couple of aspirin. They took the edge off the pain but they didn't stop the dreams that woke him every time he dozed off. Damn, he never had such dreams in his life. Might need to talk to Walker about it tomorrow. Being married into the Copperhead family all these years infected him with their tendency toward dreams and visions.

He knew they considered snake dreams a sign of something, especially when you dreamt of the same one all night and he talked to you. Unfortunately the snake spoke Cherokee and John's limited grasp of the language made communication difficult. He understood enough to know the snake didn't want anyone to bother his grave, and that something bad happened. Something that would cause a lot of trouble.

Sometime before dawn, the snake went away and let him get some sleep and forget.

Monday Morning

Qualla Boundary

A thin crescent moon hung over the beech tree, silhouetting newly sprouting leaves in its pale light. Sally's old cat got tired of his tossing and turning and jumped on his chest to wake him. According to the clock on his nightstand, less than two hours had passed since he crawled into bed. He thanked the cat for freeing him from one of the worst dreams he ever had.

The elder stretched stiff limbs, reached under the bed, and pulled out the bags that held proof of his night of grave-robbery. He needed a hot shower to loosen up sore muscles and wash away the dream image that clung to his mind. After he double-checked the locks and propped a chair under the doorknob, he carried the bags with him to the bathroom.

The fast he began seven days ago didn't allow for breakfast, not until after he went to water at sunrise. He could eat when he completed the part of the purification ritual that prepared him for tomorrow. He hoped it put him back in harmony with the Above Beings. Estrangement from them caused a depth of loneliness almost too intense to bear. It hurt when Walker Copperhead and the Snake Dancers turned against him, but feeling unworthy of the Immortals broke his heart. Desecrating an ancestor's grave might have been enough to put him beyond redemption, even when he did it for a good cause.

He brewed a pot of coffee and filled a thermos, then stuffed a loaf of bread and a wedge of hoop cheese into a paper bag—a meager meal with which to break a seven-day fast, but he had nothing else. Sally kept a well-stocked kitchen before she walked over to the above world. Now that he had to do his own grocery shopping, he lived on sandwiches and the few meals he ate when his son's bossy wife or the white girl his grandson married cooked for him. Or when he went to Walker Copperhead's house and Kate invited him to stay for supper. The thought of Kate's cooking tempted him but he couldn't face the Copperheads now. Every one of them could look right through a man and see anything he tried to hide. He couldn't risk Kate's intuition. The way she protected her father-in-law, she would pick up that he betrayed Walker the minute she laid eyes on him. She could smell guilt and treachery like a hound dog caught the scent of a rabbit.

He pulled the sheet off his bed and tore it into squares, then took the soapstone bowl out of the gym bag. He didn't need the bowl, and its weight and bulky shape made it impractical. He took the grave goods from the bowl and arranged them on his bed. One by one, he wrapped them carefully in the squares of linen. Padding a gym bag with the rest of the sheet, he gently packed each bundle inside it and zipped up the bag. With luck, he might live long enough to clear Walker Copperhead of any blame for the disappearance of the relics and bones he guarded. Walker could be proud of the way he honored his duty. It took years to catch him going to check on the site, and follow.

In the back of a storage closet he found an old canvas duffle bag. Both gym bags fit inside it with room to spare. They would be easier to carry like this, and the two other things he needed would fit when the time came.

He dreaded what he had to do at Tatham Gap even more than robbing the grave at Ataga'hi. His grandfather took him there as a young man, just before he went away to war, and told him about their family's duty to guard the Ulunsu'ti. Nothing on the battlefield scared him half as much as what lay hidden behind that big stone. Two years after he came home, the old man walked over, leaving him the sole guardian of the powerful crystal. He filled those two years with a lifetime of education, teaching him about his duties, the history of the Ulunsu'ti, and what it could do. It took another five years to get up the nerve to go check on the place alone. When he left Tatham Gap this time, the crystal would come with him.

Only one more item remained, hidden behind an ancient mound up the Cheoah River. Many years ago an Englishman got wind of it and wrote about it in a book. He called it the Cherokee Ark of the Covenant, and the name stuck. The ark held the only objects that could control the power of the Ulunsu'ti once it awakened. For years he believed Driver Wayanettah guarded the ark, and wasted years spying on him. Driver caught him while following him through a cave on Wolf Mountain and gave him holy hell for sneaking around, then explained how his family hid out in the cave to avoid being rounded up and marched off to Oklahoma during the removal. It sounded like the truth. The Wayanettahs managed to stay in the homeland back then, even got some of their land back when the dust settled. He gave up on Driver and went on to Del Locust, the only other Snake Dancer left with the status to be a guardian. He spied on Del until he died, then watched his grandson Buck, until he led him to the ark. The boy learned well, but in time, he too slipped and gave his secret away. Out beyond the old burial ground called Degal gun'yi, the Locusts guarded the ark almost in sight of the Council House Mound. Since that marked the only place a sane man would dare wake up the crystal, it made sense to keep it there, near where the Nunne'hi still lived like they did when the first guardians concealed the ark. They would need the immortals when the Ulunsu'ti came to life. He hoped the big white man lived up to his part, but if he didn't, the intervention of the immortals would be crucial.

With every minute, his dread intensified. The thought of touching the crystal made his gut clinch. In all the centuries it laid hidden away, not one of his ancestors dared check to make sure it still existed. Not even when their people hovered on the brink of extinction during the removal did they consider using it to save them. Like the Snake Dancers of today, they waited. If he could be sure it stayed hidden, he might agree with them, but his hiding place no longer guaranteed its safety. In the wrong hands, the Ulunsu'ti threatened their very existence. Kanegwa'ti warned them the time would come when they must be willing to violate everything they believed in. He started with spying on his friends and ended with desecrating the conjuror's grave.

His warrior nature didn't allow him to stand by and risk the end of his people if he saw a chance to save them. He watched the young move away and forget who they were. The elders died out taking their wisdom with them. Many families didn't speak the language, or know the names of the Above Beings, much less invoke them. Worst of all, the dwelling places of the Nunne'hi became home to subdivisions and shopping centers. Houses and towns encroached on the very doorways to their land.

One by one, the immortals abandoned sacred sites, leaving them silent and dead. He feared his people would follow. He couldn't let that happen. Waking up the Ulunsu'ti might be a drastic measure but it beat standing aside and waiting for the end.

He braced himself for the hardest job he ever did and hefted the duffle bag into the front seat of his Ford Pinto. No more waiting. Time to put the conjuror's tools to work, while they could still do some good.

On the way to Tatham Gap he passed darkened houses where all the night owls were in bed and all the early birds still slept. At the top of the gap, he turned up Joanna Bald Road toward the tower, then after a few miles, off onto a new logging trail. It took him within half a mile of where he needed to go.

For centuries this place lay as undisturbed as the graves on Ataga'hi. Now, loggers spread out everywhere. While they didn't clear-cut like loggers did in other old-growth forests, they still worked all over the mountains. Sooner or later one would decide to extend the logging trail. The boulder blocking the hollow stood in the way. His grandfather described the niche behind the boulder and what it concealed. His family watched over it since Kanegwa'ti entrusted it to his forefather. His grandfather feared it might one day end up in a museum or some pothunter's private collection. The elder expected a far worse outcome.

If the others could only see it as clearly as he did, they'd be helping him now and he wouldn't feel like a traitor to everything he believed in.

He drove as far as he could and parked the Pinto. The top of the boulder rose above a pile of discarded branches and debris at the end of the logging trail. With the prime virgin timber spread out in that direction, less than a week remained before they cut the trail a few yards more to reach it.

Ten minutes later, he stood beside the boulder wishing he never started this. His hands shook. The first time he came here, he considered the Ulunsu'ti nothing more than a story to scare kids. He learned better after his initiation into the Snake Dancer Society. His elders proved the truth of the legend and changed him forever. He rolled a big rock into place beside the boulder and found a sturdy sapling among the logger's debris to complete his fulcrum. Inch by inch he worked the boulder aside, enlarging the gap between it and the excavation it concealed. After almost an hour of toil, it toppled forward, rolling down the slope, crashing through the undergrowth, and coming to rest against a giant poplar tree. A cascade of rocks and earth followed it, leaving a path of wreckage in their wake.

When the noise and dust subsided, he dropped to his knees and reached into the fissure that now gaped open, unprotected. His hand met emptiness. Lying prone, his head inside the opening, he shined a flashlight into the dark interior. He expected the Ulunsu'ti to be waiting for him just behind the boulder, but the fracture went deeper than he anticipated. It took every ounce of determination he had in him to crawl into the shadows. The smell of moist, ancient earth comforted him. He

31

closed his eyes and breathed it in, reaching forward.

His fingers touched something smooth and cold.

Things went gray then. He retained consciousness but his attention shifted, detached from his body, watching. He saw his hand reach around the crystal, drawing it into the crook of his arm, and watched himself wiggle backward out of the hole cradling the cold, hard orb to his chest. He made it to the Pinto and slumped across the hood. His ears rang a high-pitched tone that vibrated in his head and left him disoriented and lightheaded. He shivered, chilled deep to the core of his body. Staggering to the car, he wrenched open the door and dragged the duffle bag out. With numb hands he opened the bag and dropped the Ulunsu'ti inside. The duffle bag fell against the car when he let it go. Slowly, warmth returned to his body and his shivering abated. The ringing in his ears ebbed to a soft whine. His head still throbbed with pain and confusion. An irrational desire to look at the crystal, to touch it once more, seized him. He bent over the duffle bag and pulled the neck open. One peek inside and the ringing intensified to an unbearable keen. He staggered backward, feeling something dark and hungry reaching for his soul. He willed himself to draw the cord tight around the neck of the bag and stow it in the backseat.

With his ears still ringing and his head throbbing, he crawled into the car. The familiar comfort of the Pinto's worn seat gave a measure of ease to legs too weak to support him. He sagged against the steering wheel, resting his head against his hands until a measure of strength returned. Drawing a deep breath of clear, cool air, he steeled himself against the aftereffects of his brush with the Ulunsu'ti. His insides quivered. He attributed it to seven days of fasting, a long time without food for a man his age, but fear played a bigger part. The crystal scared him, but his friends posed a threat that ate away at his nerves. To betray the Snake Dancers invited the vengeance of powerful men who would make him pay for his deceit. He had only the white

32

man on his side. What if he wasn't all he claimed to be?

The duffle bag rattled in the backseat, settling into place, he hoped. He refused to allow his mind to consider other possibilities. His old Pinto held everything he needed except the ark, and he would have that before noon. For the first time, he allowed himself a trace of pride. He outsmarted all the guardians and located the grave and the ark, something nobody else had accomplished since the days of Kanegwa'ti. It didn't seem fair that he must turn it over to a white man who didn't contribute anything but an evening of digging, and his status as an outsider. But only an outsider who wanted in could wake up the Ulunsu'ti.

The wave of possessiveness swept over him with the thought of the Ulunsu'ti in the white man's hands. It caught him off guard, coming on so hard and sudden it took his breath away. Why should he turn all this power over to a man who did nothing to earn it? Why not keep it for himself? The acts he committed, and intended to commit, made him as much an outsider as the white man.

His mind played with the concept of what it would be like to become the most powerful man in the world. How would it feel to know anything you wanted to know, from any time? To be able to make things happen the way you wanted them to? He could be like Kanegwa'ti, the great conjuror, so powerful his fame lived through generations yet to come. But that power would go to the white man, not him. The injustice of it gnawed at him.

He reached inside his shirt and grasped the leather pouch hanging around his neck. A firm squeeze released the fragrance of sage, cedar, and wild tobacco. He breathed it in and found the strength to resist the kind of thinking that could get him into real trouble. It bothered him that doubts about the white man kept intruding on his thoughts. For sixteen years, he knew him as a good man. Some considered him odd because he tried so hard to become an Indian, and placed so much store on the old ways. He had his reasons.

Thoughts of personal power and suspicions about the white man had to go. The man who had control of the crystal and its power didn't matter, whether that man was him or the outsider. He had to think of the good of all his people. After purification, it would be easier. He needed to get to Snowbird Creek in a hurry.

He turned the key and the Pinto's starter ground weakly. He let it rest a moment and tried again. The engine rattled to life, sputtered, and died. The third time, it caught. He shifted into reverse and backed up to a clearing wide enough to turn around. The old car bounced over the rough logging trail, inching along until he reached Tatham Gap, then went as fast as he dared to the Snowbird.

The sheltered cove on Snowbird Creek held memories that spanned generations of his people, going back long before the removal. His father and grandfather first brought him when he was too young to understand the ancient ritual that kept them in harmony with their people. He took his place beside the stream, touched fire to a shell of herbs, and watched smoke ascend toward the treetops. Chants and prayers came unprompted to his lips, so familiar they required no thought.

When the first rays of sunlight broke through the treetops, he stepped into the icy water to begin the seven immersions. He prayed harder than he ever prayed before, calling on every Above Being he could think of, anyone who might still be willing to listen to him, imploring them to restore him to harmony and empower him to finish his task. He called them by name and invoked their presence to give him the strength to complete what he started, then went under the cold water, staying down until his lungs hungered for air, praying to beings who always listened and made themselves known before. Seven immersions and he rose to silence. No comforting presence appeared; no voice spoke in his mind. Not a trace of harmony remained to him.

He stood beside the stream, alone and deserted.

As a young soldier in the middle of the war to end war, he didn't feel this scared. Not even when he marched through blood and bombs, earning medals and a battlefield promotion. They called him a hero then, but in those days, other men fought at his side and he knew harmony with the Above Beings. Nobody walked with him now, not even the spirit guides he took for granted all his life.

His seven days of fasting came to an end when he stepped out of the water, but his insides rebelled at the thought of food. With the brown paper bag containing his bread and hoop cheese untouched in his knapsack, he dried off, put on his clothes, and got back in the car. He prayed every prayer he knew as he drove up the Cheoah and on into the hills, needing that brush of Spirit against his mind, that awareness of guidance beyond the mortal realm. When they eluded him, he gave up and accepted that he walked a solitary trail this time. The digger expected him. He headed for their designated meeting place. The thought of the Ulunsu'ti in the white man's possession filled him with hostility that shocked him in its intensity. He fought the urge to leave the white man out of his plan. Everything he knew said he couldn't go ahead without him, that the outsider had to be the one. What if an old man's body couldn't stand the strain? He'd need the white man's muscles then. He called up memories that diminished his doubts and reminded him of all the reasons he trusted his accomplice, and drove to the meeting place.

The white man waited at the end of the drive leading to the rustic circle of little log houses where he held his retreats. The way he looked through the lowered window, searching for the gym bags, hit the elder all wrong. He looked into those ice-blue eyes and saw something that made him want to get the Ulunsu'ti out of his sight.

Before the white man could reach for the door, he called out instructions to meet him near the mound where they could wake the crystal, then sped away so fast he left behind a smear of rubber the old tires could ill afford to lose. He didn't tell him about the road that ran within half a mile of their destination. The white man had a long hike ahead of him.

He drove too fast on the narrow gravel road, grateful that he had it to himself, wishing for a way out of the partnership he created. He tried to attribute it to a desire to protect their unwitting companion, but there was more. Distrust of the white man mingled with a growing possessiveness toward the crystal and the power it promised. Nothing he could do now but keep a close watch and maintain control until his partner went to water. If the white man harbored self-centered motives, the ritual would bring them to the surface. He couldn't turn back, and he couldn't do it without the white man.

A few miles along the road that paralleled the Cheoah, then up a gravel country road. Through woods so deep and dark nothing but green showed on all sides, he kept watch for the almost invisible trail through the woods. Not much more than a couple of ruts worn into the ground, and so rough it rattled the old car until it threatened to come apart, it brought him closer to the place where the Locusts guarded the ark. When the trail proved steeper and rougher than the Pinto could handle, he quit trying to force the spinning tires up the incline and left it concealed under a stand of pines. He slung his knapsack over his shoulder and got the duffle bag from the backseat and started walking. Within sight of the mound, he put the duffle bag on the ground and opened the neck. With his mind cleared by his hike, he remembered something important he overlooked before. The Ulunsu'ti shouldn't be in there with the bones. That invited disaster.

Preparing himself for the effects of the crystal's touch, he reached into the duffle bag. The cold orb weighed heavy in his hand. Ice spread up his arm. Moving quickly, he dropped it into his knapsack where it settled beside the war axe. Cold numbed his hands. The ringing in his ears sounded like a swarm of locusts

36

and nausea rose in his throat.

And still he craved one more look at the crystal.

He clutched the knapsack against his chest, fighting the irrational need to peek inside. He thought he had prepared himself to resist the power of the crystal, but the bond between the Ulunsu'ti and its guardian proved stronger than he expected. The strength of the desire to claim it terrified him. He shoved the knapsack behind a tree out of sight, and waited while the effects wore off.

With his back against the tree, he let the silence of the woods steal over him. His eyes grew heavy and he slipped into the edge of sleep. Heavy footsteps shattered the stillness. He stood up and waited beside the tree, making no attempt to conceal his presence. The white man didn't see him until he spoke. Their third partner acknowledged him with a nod and walked off into the woods alone.

When the white man squatted across from him, he pulled both gym bags out of the duffle bag and set them on the ground, leaving the knapsack that held the crystal out of sight behind the tree. He fought the possessive feelings and pushed the first one toward him.

"I've told you what we're gonna do. Now I want you to see what we'll be doing it with."

"Is this everything?"

"Everything but the ark. I'll have it before the day is over, then, first thing in the morning, we have to prepare you."

"What do I do now?"

"Take out the bones."

The white man hesitated. "You never explained to me why we need the skeleton."

"It has to be held in the conjuror's own hands for it to work. We only need his hands, but it wouldn't be respectful to separate them from the rest of him. After we're done, we have to put him in a proper grave intact, so the earth can claim his body and free

37

his spirit. Find the hands and then I'll tell you how it works."

The white man lifted the dingy towel out of the gym bag and unwrapped it, spreading the bones across it. The elder turned away.

"What the hell?" The white man's face registered confusion.

The elder made himself look at the skeleton lying spread out on the towel, fragile and ancient. The skull's empty eyes stared accusations at him. A pile of ribs lay stacked beside it. Spinal discs, femurs, tibias, fibulas, and feet—but no hands, or parts of hands. Not a single digit.

Squatting down beside the pile of bones, he lifted the intact arm bones and examined them in the morning sunlight. They ended abruptly at the wrists. The marks on the bones told the story. The hands had been cleanly severed by something very sharp.

Desperation can cloud the mind, but there are times when it brings clarity. This time it swept away the cobwebs, leaving his thoughts sharp and clear. He understood something that nagged at the back of his mind for years.

Driver Wayanettah was a Snake Dancer Guardian, just as he thought, but he didn't guard the ark on Wolf Mountain. He didn't lie about that. He guarded the conjuror's hands in his cave. The hands didn't lie buried in the grave at Ataga'hi. Driver stood guard over them deep in that crevice he watched him kneeling beside. He gave up on him too soon.

With something akin to relief, he told the white man, "We can't do anything without the hands. Come to my house at dawn tomorrow. I'll need your help to get them."

Suspicion clouded the white man's face. "Where are you going?"

"To get the ark. Go on home now, and meet me in the morning."

"And you plan to keep everything with you till then?"

He didn't answer. Ignoring the white man, he gathered the

bones and wrapped them in the towel. He put them back in the gym bags, put the gym bags in the duffle, and hoisted it to his shoulder. He reached behind the tree for the knapsack and slung it over the other shoulder and turned to go.

"Be there around sunup tomorrow," he said, and walked off into the woods. He could feel eyes on his back until he got well out of sight behind a stand of spruce.His mind sorted through the facts. The great conjuror handpicked the first Snake Dancers and prepared them to keep the wisdom of the elders alive through the generations. To the elite among them, he entrusted the guardianship of the Ulunsu'ti and all the tools for waking and using it, then bound them all to an order of power and secrecy. The Snake Dancers all knew each other, but as for the guardian, only he and his chosen heir knew of their status and what they watched over. The elder guarded the Ulunsu'ti, but it took most of his adult life to learn the name of the other guardians and what they protected. After all that effort, he never learned that the hands didn't get buried with the body, or that a different guardian watched over them. That part of the Ulunsu'ti's story didn't come down to all the Snake Dancers. He suspected that only the man the conjuror appointed to take care of the hands knew it. And only the heir he passed the duty down to needed to be told. Driver's story convinced him he wasted time on Wolf Mountain. He understood now, Driver Wayanettah told a hell of a tale. The hands lay deep inside the cave and he knew where to find them.

The more he thought about it, the clearer it became to him that the Above Beings guided him in his work. Otherwise, he would never suspect the location of the conjuror's hands, and without them, he couldn't wake the Ulunsu'ti.

The trip up Wolf Mountain to get them moved his plans up one more day, no more. He considered going to Driver's cave after he retrieved the ark, but his legs and back rebelled. A long hike up the steep, rocky side of yet another mountain seemed more than he could take. And he couldn't do it alone. The big white man possessed the physical strength for the grunt work.

He struck out for the Locusts' hiding place behind the mound at Degal gun'yi. Old age and the stress of violating more taboos than he could count drained the strength out of him. Half an hour's hike and he saw what could be mistaken for a natural hill rising out of the trees.

His stomach rumbled. He needed to break his fast before he attempted breaching the Locusts' hiding place. He sat on a flat rock and ate his meager lunch. A nearby stream provided water, and the bread and hoop cheese gave him the energy to go on.

He brushed the crumbs from his jacket and trudged a few feet up the mound to retrieve a shovel and axe from the cache of tools he left secreted under a laurel thicket in preparation for this day. Too bad he hadn't brought the white man along to do all the hard labor. This job threatened to be too much for a tired old man.

A jagged slab of granite protruded from the earth halfway up the mound, marking the place the Locusts' ancestors tunneled out a hiding place for their part of a legend. He climbed up and began the search. Shallow roots clung to the layer of earth underneath the granite slab. He chopped and shoveled the scrub brush away and drove the shovel deep. It clunked against an obstruction. An hour later, he had cleared away the soil that concealed a log barrier. Now to chop through and create an opening.

An afternoon of toil added another set of aches and pains to his arthritic joints, more blisters to his calloused hands, and another artifact to his collection. This one claimed as much fame as the Ulunsu'ti, but few suspected it really existed. Only he and the generations of Locust men who guarded it knew it lay hidden deep within a tunnel, concealed behind a false wall.

He emerged from the cavity in the hillside and blinked in the bright light. When his eyes adjusted, he examined his find.

The ancient buckskin that protected it through the centuries fell apart in his hands as he pulled it away, revealing the prize that took him years to find. He expected it to be bigger. He turned it in his hands, examining a container about the size and shape of the box his boots came in. Some claimed the Nunne'hi fashioned it from wood grown in the Above World, and gave it to Kanegwa'ti to hold a great treasure until the next Suye'ta claimed it.

The Cherokee Ark of the Covenant, they called it, and the name fit as well as any. He looked it over, caressing the graceful markings that spiraled the lid. He lingered over it awhile, admiring the handiwork of the long dead ancestors who created it, or if the stories were true, the artistry of the immortal Nunne'hi. Curiosity tempted him to look for a latch, or a way to open it. No one knew what it held, only that whatever it contained was necessary to control the Ulunsu'ti once it woke up. He inspected the snake that twisted around the ark, its mouth closed tight at the lid. He resisted the urge to part the fangs and look inside. Best not risk opening it while alone in the woods. He might need the white man for that.

With the buckskin covering crumbling in his hands, he looked for something else to protect the ark. He used his jacket to wrap it tightly, tying the sleeves to secure it, then added it to the collection in the duffle bag. He trudged back toward his car, feeling the weight of the duffle bag cutting into his shoulder. His back ached and his legs trembled with exhaustion. Shifting the load to ease the dull pain in his shoulder, he remembered the feel of the white man's eyes on his back. He couldn't afford to trust anyone, not even his partner. The crystal could work on a man's mind, making even the most loyal friends turn on each other. Taking it from the secluded woods to the insecurity of his house trailer worried him, and his back rebelled against carrying it much farther.

He looked around as he walked, searching for a place where

he could leave it for a while, somewhere nobody ever came.

A cool breeze carried the scent of early blooming wild flame azaleas. Sally always loved those flowers. Their aroma reminded him of coming home to a house full of the smells of good food and wildflowers on the table. He went toward them, just for the comfort they offered.

Beyond the blossoms he spied a big hickory tree uprooted by one of last winter's storms. He made his way to it and scooped a hollow under the trunk, then stuffed the duffle bag into it.

He kept the knapsack with him. Nothing could make him leave the crystal behind. He found comfort thinking of it resting there atop the war axe he took from the grave.

With night falling in the darkening woods, he climbed into the Pinto and made his weary way home to his trailer. The Pinto struggled on the steep mountain grade. Maybe after a good night's rest they'd both be ready for another day tomorrow.

The climb up Wolf Mountain loomed ahead like a threat.

His trailer offered no welcome, sitting under the beech tree in total darkness, its flimsy metal doors vulnerable to anyone who wanted to kick them in. He thought of the white man and the crystal, and decided not to sleep in the trailer.

He drove the Pinto behind a tangle of laurel bushes beyond the house and parked it well out of sight.

The night chill gnawed at his aching bones. He ducked into the trailer long enough to retrieve one of Sally's quilts from his bed and carried it into his old house. It felt good to be there, warm and safe, with memories of good times gone. His son, Thomas, wanted to tear the old house down but he couldn't bring himself to do it.

He wrapped up in the quilt and slumped into the old recliner Sally banished from the living room of her new trailer. The worn brown chair served him well for many years and fit the curves and angles of his body better than his bed. Sally's old Smokey Cat curled up beside him and they both fell asleep.

Monday Morning

Snowbird

Monday morning came way too early for Johnny McLeymore. When Wren woke him with a gentle shake, he would have shooed her away and slept another hour if not for the smell of bacon and eggs wafting up from the kitchen. That made getting out of bed worthwhile.

Wren trotted downstairs yelling, "Daddy's up, Mama! He'll be down in a minute."

Johnny took the gauze from his blistered palms and flexed his fingers. If he could hold a toothbrush, he should be able to handle a steering wheel. "No problem," he muttered through a mouth full of toothpaste. His hands still functioned and the pain was bearable.

Wren waited in the kitchen, impatient to get started. John pretended he remembered his promise to take her with him to the tower, since she had a day off from school for a teacher's workday. He took time for a hot breakfast, then, armed with a paper bag full of sausage biscuits and a thermos of good, strong coffee, he headed for his pickup truck. Wren tagged along behind with her school lunchbox. He didn't tell Faron, but he saw their daughter switch the carton of milk she put in the cooler for a couple bottles of Coke. Faron packed extras for Eli Smoker.

"You watch out for her climbing up that tower, John," Faron ordered after she kissed them both goodbye. "And don't hang around with Eli Smoker all day. You know his language isn't fit for a child to hear."

"Don't worry about her, honey. I've always brought her home in one piece before, ain't I? And she's never said a cuss word in her life. Eli knows to watch his mouth in front of a kid.

You know that, Faron."

"He'd better watch his mouth."

He watched Faron in the rearview mirror, waving goodbye as the Dodge Ram eased up onto her new bridge.

John loved taking Wren with him when he could get away with it. She wasn't the kind of kid to bounce around and carry on like most eight-year-olds, but he could tell how much she liked these outings. Her eyes searched the trees along the lake. He didn't blame her. The road to the ranger station went through some of the prettiest country in the world.

She raised her hand for him to slow down, just like her mama did when she saw something she wanted to look at. He followed her eyes and saw the red-tailed hawk soar up from the shore with something small and furry squirming in his talons.

"He caught him some breakfast." Wren sat back on the seat ready to talk to him. She saw what she was looking for. Both Wren and Faron liked to catch sight of some special bird at the beginning of an adventure. The good time started when the bird showed up. Probably had something to do with the fact they belonged to the Bird Clan.

He watched the hawk soar away and felt the same twinge of apprehension that nagged him the past couple of days. Is that what Faron and her folks meant when they said they got a "feeling" about something? If so, he got a feeling the hawk foretold more of an adventure than he cared for. He felt a sudden urge to turn around and take Wren home. The urge and the feeling passed quickly. He chalked them both up to the influence of the Copperheads and their superstitions.

He checked in at the ranger station and exchanged greetings with the few men still around. Most were already out on duty.

Wren waited patiently while he loaded supplies to take to Eli in the tower. He liked taking Wren along when he could, and she loved going with him. From the time she started walking, Faron called her "Daddy's little shadow."

He wheeled the truck out onto the blacktop, drove alongside the Snowbird a few miles, then turned up Tatham Gap Road. The pavement ran out just before they passed the last house, a wood-frame cottage set back in the woods, hardly noticeable. A mile or so on, he had to pull over to let a dusty Honda Civic pass from the opposite direction, the only other car they saw.

"Amanda Hooper coming over from Andrews to see her Mama and Daddy up on Sweetgum Creek," John said. He and Wren both called "hello" when she braked to greet them.

"Saw your Mama at the store Friday," John yelled. "She said she was feeling a lot better after her operation."

"Yeah," Amanda answered. "Doctor says she's gonna be just fine. She's got a valve from a pig in her heart now. Can you believe that?"

"Not hardly," John answered, "but you never know what they'll be doing next. Tell her me and Wren said hey, and if she and your daddy need us for anything, just let us know."

"Thanks, Johnny." She shifted the Honda into gear and drove away.

"Wonder why she doesn't take the highway in that Honda?" he said to Wren as they drove off. "This is a mighty rough road for a car that small."

"'Cause this way is prettier," Wren said. "And you and Uncle Yona say it's the shortest way over the mountain."

He turned off toward Joanna Bald and around the twisting road to the fire tower until he reached the locked metal gate that marked the end of the road for public motor travel. He got out and unlocked the gate, drove through, and parked under the tower. From the deck around the living quarters atop the steel tower, Eli called out a greeting. The sharp, high-pitched yapping of his rat-sized Chihuahua, Yippi, reached all the way to the truck. His wife, Hilda, gave him the silly little thing to keep him company in the tower. It practically lived in his jacket pocket.

Wren ran up the steel steps.

John yelled at her to slow down. "You know your mama said you had to walk up with me. You want to get us both in trouble?"

She waited for him on the first landing and kept his slower pace up the four steep flights. Faron's orders stated he had to stay right behind her, making sure she didn't fall off the tower. Yippi barked his little head off until Eli handed him over to Wren. She always brought treats. This time, her lunchbox held a bag of chicken bits and cubes of cheese for his breakfast.

Eli welcomed the leftovers Faron sent. "Best biscuits I ever tasted. If Hilda could cook like Faron, I probably would spend more time at home." He poked a bite of sausage into the dog's mouth. "Here ya go, Yippi."

Hilda used to be a shapely blonde cheerleader for the Black Knights back when they were in high school. She topped the scales at around one-fifty now but still looked cute as a button. She didn't have any trouble eating her own cooking. Eli, on the other hand, stayed skinny as when he, John, and Yona were boys running wild in the woods. Hard to believe he descended from the famed Wolf Clan Warriors. Not only did he look scrawny as a green willow twig, he took pride in being an outspoken pacifist and a dedicated environmentalist.

"Shouldn't have married out, Eli," John said. "Your grandpa tried to tell you to find you a good Cherokee wife like I did. Old Grady Smoker knows white women can't cook."

"Faron's mama and grandpa tried to tell her the same thing, not to marry out of the tribe." Eli punched John playfully on the arm as he sat down with his coffee. "Wonder what Walker Copperhead told her white men can't do."

"Whatever it was, she knows by now whether I can or can't." A wicked grin spread across John's face. "Anything she ever asked for so far, I've managed to handle. No problem."

Eli laughed. He stroked the skimpy mustache he kept trying to grow. John recognized the gesture. Eli did that any time he had something serious to say. Looked like the lighthearted part of this visit was over. "One thing you're real good at, John, that I want you to check on for me. Come over here. I want you to take a look at something."

"Sure, Eli." John followed him out to the deck that circled the 14-by-14-foot structure atop the tower. Wren picked up Yippi and trailed behind without a word. Eli pointed the telescope toward the northwest and focused it. "Look here, Johnny, and tell me what you see."

John put his eye to the glass. He could see for miles, nothing but a vast sea of green, the kind of green only seen in spring and early summer. "It's a beautiful sight, man," he said. "You just wanted to show me the scenery?"

"Keep looking right where I've got it pointed. Tell me what you see."

John let his eyes roam across the expanse the glass magnified. He saw dark green stretches where pine and hemlock grew, lighter greens shading into each other among the hardwoods, and then, something that just didn't look right. That must be what he was supposed to see. Eli would have been the first to notice. Years of searching the forests for any sign of fire made every mile that fell within range of his telescope as familiar to him as the tower cab he virtually lived in.

"You see it, don't you?" Eli asked.

"Uh-huh, but I'm not sure exactly what I see. It just doesn't look like the right color, but not like a die-back or blight or anything. You filed a report on this yet?"

"No. Wanted you to see it first. I figured you could check it out for me. There's nobody else at the station, except maybe Buck Locust, that I'd want to send up there." Eli turned to look toward the place he showed John, as if he could see it without the telescope. "You know where that is, don't you, Johnny?"

"Well, I'd guess somewhere south of the Cheoah. If it's where I'm thinking, there's not a decent road or trail for miles around. A man would have to do some serious walking to get to it. That's not in the state park system, is it?"

"It's our land. Belongs to the Cherokees. You've heard of it." Eli's voice dropped, as if hearing echoes of the tales they listened to at the feet of the old people all through their childhood. "Degal gun'yi."

"Sorry, buddy." John rolled the word around on his tongue: "Degal gun'yi." It was familiar but he couldn't remember why, and the words, when he tried to translate them, didn't add up. "I'm not that good with your language."

"Degal gun'yi," Eli repeated. "Means something like, where they are piled up. It's a burial ground. A big one, and old. The kind with mounds."

"That's why you want me to take a look at it, huh? So we don't risk any outsiders finding the graveyard." They both looked toward the Cheoah without the scope. "How long do you think it would take before a bunch of archaeologists started digging the whole place up if word got out?"

"Archaeologists, *National Geographic*, the Smithsonian. Everybody wanting some bones and pots and stories of the indigenous people." Eli looked like he wanted to spit.

"Tell you what, Eli," John said. "I've got some things to do first, but when I finish, I'll run on up there. I'll talk to Buck about it first chance I get." For some reason, the discoloration made John uneasy. It wasn't something he would usually talk to Buck Locust about, but he would feel better to bring him in on this. Not only because Buck was his supervisor, but if Eli wanted somebody he trusted, they couldn't do any better than Buck. John and Eli went through a rebellious stage back in their younger days, but Buck set them straight before they got too wild. They looked up to him ever since.

"Thanks, John." After a thoughtful moment, Eli added, "Take Walker Copperhead with you."

"Hey, man. We'll be walking for an hour at least. Walker

might not be up to it."

"You tell him where you're going, and why, and the old man will be up to it." Eli took Yippi from Wren and scratched the dog's head with one finger.

He didn't know why Eli wanted Walker along, and he didn't ask. He learned that sometimes with Faron's people, it was best to keep his mouth shut and do what they told him to. That way, he occasionally got an answer. He sure didn't get one by asking questions.

He nodded toward the dog. "Hey, buddy, how long since that mutt's feet last touched the ground? I wonder sometimes if he can still walk at all."

Eli looked offended. Yippi just nodded off to sleep in Wren's arms.

John drove in silence back down the mountain, wondering what could cause the changes to the foliage in just that one spot. Whatever it was, it had to be in the early stages or Eli would have called him sooner. Eli knew John could tell him more about these mountains and their flora and fauna than just about anybody. John grew up in them. His dad, Duncan McLeymore, worked with the forestry service most of his life and took John along even more often than John took Wren. He learned a lot that way. Then there was his degree. He actually studied this stuff in college.

Wren interrupted his reverie. "Daddy, what's wrong at Degal gun'yi?"

The only thing he remembered about the mound from the old stories was that even the powerful Nunne'hi stayed away from it. "What do you know about that place, honey?"

"I've been there," she answered. "With Uncle Yona and Mama Kate. They take me to a lot of places in the stories. They want me to learn the real history, so I won't get confused by the stuff we learn in school."

There were times when John felt left out when it came to

the education of his daughter. Faron's family taught her things he never knew. Maybe Wren could answer some of his questions. "So, sugar, what did you learn about Degal gun'yi?"

"It's real old, older than anybody knows for sure. Grandpa says it goes back to the days of the Ani'Kuta'Ni." She sounded like she knew what she was talking about.

John hesitated. He hated to show his ignorance to his own kid, but who else would tell him? "Who are these Ani'Kuta'Ni, and what were they doing at Degal gun'yi?"

"Oh, they lived a long time ago, Daddy, but they're all gone now and that's good, 'cause they thought they were the boss of everything." She warmed to the role of the one with the answers and he didn't interrupt. "They did mean things to everybody 'cause the people were all afraid of them, 'cause they had all the power, and they got it from the Above Beings, 'cause the Ani'Kuta'Ni thought they were born to be the boss and had magic power."

He wasn't used to his quiet-natured daughter talking this much or this fast.

Wren took a deep breath and went on. "One day they got what they deserved for all the bad things they did. They made a warrior's wife go with them to their lodge on the top of a mound and did very bad things to her. The warrior got so mad he didn't care about their magic and power, so he killed them all dead."

John remembered that story, now that she brought it back to his mind. "Is Degal gun'yi where they killed the Ani'Kuta'Ni?"

His luck ran out. Wren had told him all she knew of the story.

"I guess so." She flipped her black hair back in that way that said, "don't ask me any more about it," then added, "What's wrong at Degal gun'yi?"

"I don't know for sure that anything is, honey. Eli just noticed that the leaves were a bit off-color around that area. Sometimes that can mean an infestation of borers or other insects, or a blight or disease. Trees can get sick just like people."

"Like what happened to the chestnut trees?" she asked.

"Yeah, like that." John hoped it wasn't like what happened to the chestnut trees. He still occasionally ran across the remains of one of the massive trunks, rotting away, the last trace of a forest that provided a major food supply to the Cherokee people for thousands of years. Now, not one single tree still lived.

"Grandpa Walker will know what to do," Wren said. She quickly added, "And you too, Daddy."

John smiled at her to let her know he didn't mind. He was used to coming in second to Walker Copperhead. Faron's grandpa probably would know what to do. People for miles around came to him for answers, calling him "the conjuror." He hoped at least one of them would know.

Back at the station, he got stuck with paperwork and an errand that took him around the lake. It ate up more of the day than he liked, and it was after four when he got in touch with Walker. Walker volunteered to explain to Faron that Wren might be late getting home. They needed all the daylight left, and he didn't want to waste the half hour it would take to drop her off at home.

When they reached the Copperhead place on Little Snowbird Creek, Walker stood waiting at the end of the neat, tree-shaded drive to the house where he lived with Kate, Yona, and Charlie. He claimed he moved in to look after Kate and his two grandsons when his son, Kate's husband, died in a logging accident about ten years ago. It looked to John like it was the other way around. Kate bossed and pampered Walker nearly to death ever since. She practically took over running the family logging company.

That's how all the Copperhead women were, and Faron learned it from her mother. A man couldn't complain, as long as he didn't harbor any illusions about being the boss around the house. The women had things well in hand and didn't like the

51

men interfering. John didn't mind, but his father made it clear to him he thought the way he let Faron run his life was downright unnatural. Duncan McLeymore believed a man should be the head of his household. His wife was kind enough to let him maintain that illusion. John smiled as he thought of all the reasons he wouldn't change a thing.

Wren opened the door for Walker and scooted over next to John to make room. Walker got into the truck and propped his walking stick between them. The eagle carved on the head of the walking stick rested against her leg. She traced the curved beak with her finger. "He looks like he's alive, Grandpa," she said. "Like he could just fly away."

"Well, he hasn't done it yet, honey. Not in my father's lifetime, nor his father's, or mine. "He'll probably stay around to keep Diamond company when he's an old man."

John looked at the walking stick and wondered again what it was made of. Walker called it locust wood, but he'd seen some very old locust wood, and it looked different. In fact, he never saw wood like that walking stick. It amazed him that an old man like Walker could lug around something that heavy. It looked like more of a hindrance than a help, but Walker would never go anywhere without it. He always kept it within easy reach, even when he slept. John suspected it had something to do with his "conjure work." He asked Walker about it. All he got was some nonsense about how the walking stick came in handy for spirit walking, whatever that meant. It was about as good an answer as he ever got from the old man.

"So, Johnny, how big of an area are we talking about checking out before dark?" Walker asked.

"We don't need to look at much to figure out what's going on," John said. "My guess is it's just some kind of borer. We deal with that kind of sh–...stuff all the time. No problem."

"If it covers enough ground for Eli to spot it from the tower, must be a lot of borers," Walker said.

"Lord, Grandpa, Eli could spot just a single one of those pests from his tower," John said. "I don't think he even needs that telescope. The man knows every tree in Graham County by heart. If there's a lick of change in one, those little beady eyes of his are gonna spot it."

Walker nodded. "And just as stubborn as his grandfather. If he thinks there's a problem, he'll aggravate you to death till you do something about it."

"You and Daddy can fix whatever it is," Wren said. "No problem."

John smiled at her as he turned off the pavement onto the graveled road that edged along the river. The trees beside the road were already ancient back in Walker Copperhead's boyhood. Their branches met to form a canopy above the truck. Through the open windows came the sound of the Cheoah rushing over the falls beyond the laurels. Unseen birds called high among the leaves. The crunch of gravel beneath the tires provided the background soundtrack. John was accustomed to the quiet nature of Faron's folks, only talking when they had something worth saying. When he spent time with his own family, they kept asking him why he was so quiet. He soon tired of all the chatter.

After a few miles, Walker pointed to a cut-off John missed completely. It couldn't be called a road, just a pair of ruts with fewer bushes growing between them than the rest of the forest. John shifted down to second gear and eased in.

He closed the window after a branch whipped through it and slapped him in the face. "How did you know this road was here, Old Man?" he asked.

Walker didn't answer, just leaned over and checked Wren's seatbelt like he hadn't heard the question. Even though they hardly topped twenty miles an hour, she bounced around on the rough road.

John didn't ask any more questions. One of these days, his in-laws might stop thinking of him as an outsider and let him in on a few things. Like why they maintained these "roads to nowhere" in such out-of-the-way places on their lands. He knew from experience that this one would end abruptly with no discernable purpose. Now, if it just took them close to the die-back before it ended.

"Anything you want to tell me, Grandpa?" John expected Walker to ignore him like he usually did.

Walker surprised him with an answer that sounded almost respectful. "Many things I want to tell you, son. Troubles and worries you don't want to know about. Soon, John. When the time is right."

Walker's attitude made him nervous.

When the road ended at the top of a steep incline, he saw nothing around but more woods. Nothing explained the reason the road existed or who maintained it. He got out of the truck and looked back the way they came. Tracks threaded among the prints left by his truck, like a little car traveled this way recently. Walker saw them too but didn't say a word about it. Must not mean anything. The old man probably knew about every vehicle that came this way.

John walked ahead while Walker lifted Wren down out of the truck. He scanned the trees for any sign of the discoloration he saw from the tower. So far, nothing looked out of the ordinary. A squirrel chittered on a limb above and got a good scolding by a blue-jay when he got a little too close to her perch.

Wren held Walker's hand until they caught up with her daddy, then she let go and ran ahead into the trees. John didn't try to stop her. She knew these woods better than he did. He watched her through the foliage in the distance and saw where she headed. The first buds of a bank of wild flame azaleas flashed a vivid orange in the underbrush. Faron loved the way their scent filled the kitchen when she put a vase of them on the table. Wren liked surprising her mom with a wildflower bouquet, and these would be a rare treat this early in the year.

He kept Wren in sight while he and Walker discussed the healthy appearance of the foliage in the area. She clambered over a fallen hickory tree, heading for the wild azaleas when she stopped, still hanging over the dead tree trunk with her feet on the other side, and yelled, "Daddy, come here. Quick!"

John leapt over the log and lifted her down. "What's wrong, baby?"

She dropped to her knees, raking away leaves with her hands. "I felt something with my foot." She cleared the leaves from a mound of gray-green canvas. "See, I told you I felt something." She grasped a cord in her hands and tugged as hard as she could, her feet against the log for leverage. It didn't budge.

Walker stooped down and gently moved Wren out of the way and took over. John could feel the old man's tension as he pulled an old duffle bag from under the tree trunk. A drawstring closed the neck tightly and a metal latch secured it.

Walker held up the latch to show John. "No rust on the metal, and no sign of exposure to the elements on the canvas. This hasn't been here long."

"What do you reckon this is, Grandpa?" John asked.

Walker looked grim. "Danged if I know, boy. One thing's for sure. Ain't nobody got any business around here hiding stuff." He set the duffle bag on end and unfastened the latch and worked the neck open. He held it while John reached in and pulled out something wrapped in an old windbreaker jacket. He placed it on the leaves at Walker's feet, then reached back in for a black nylon gym bag. A blue one about the same size came next. The three objects looked completely out of place there on the forest floor.

Walker unzipped one of the bags and spread it open. Aged linen fabric covered a collection of carefully wrapped bundles of various sizes. "Somebody went to a lot of trouble packing this," he said. "Must be something fragile." He took out a couple of the bundles and laid them on the leaves.

Walker gently removed the wrapping from the first bundle, exposing its contents. He looked at it for a moment like he couldn't believe what he saw, then said a word he didn't usually say in front of Wren. She didn't hear it. Her eyes wide with shock, she stared at the object in her grandpa's hands.

John opened another bundle and thought he understood what bothered Wren and Walker. "Grave goods?" he asked.

"More than that." Walker opened a package and removed an ancient, long-stemmed clay pipe. He laid it aside and unwrapped a second bundle that held a turtle-shell rattle. Another held a fragile doeskin pouch, its contents showing through the frayed leather. The dried sinew that held the neck closed disintegrated when he opened the pouch and removed a small hollow bone with tiny holes drilled along its length. "Eagle bone," he said. "The one who owned this whistle walked over to the other world about the time the first white people started settling around here."

He put the whistle back in the pouch and laid it on the sheet, then reached for the package wrapped in the windbreaker. When he untied the sleeves, the jacket fell away from a rectangular chest bound with mummified hide and marked with faded symbols. Walker quickly wrapped it up, muttering something in Cherokee that John couldn't understand. Wren paled but she didn't say a word.

John resisted the urge to ask questions. Walker motioned toward the other bag and John unzipped it. A dingy white towel wrapped something else. He laid it down beside the rest and pulled away the corners. "Goddamn," he said.

Wren and Walker both looked like they couldn't move. They just sat on the forest floor, frozen in a moment of pain and anger.

Walker folded the towel back over the ancient brown skull and the pile of bones beneath it. "Johnny, zip him up and let's go. We'll have to check on these trees later. Right now, we need to take Kanegwa'ti back over to Swain County where he belongs."

John repeated the name. "Kanegwa'ti. The Water Moccasin?" A memory from an old legend teased at his mind. Why would Walker connect the collection of old bones to a mythical conjuror?

Wren held the blue gym bag while John zipped it closed. Walker carefully bundled the grave goods in their wrappings and packed them in the black bag. He kept the mysterious chest close to his side the whole time, wrapped in the jacket. John tried to get another look at it but Walker was too wary. His furtive behavior made John even more curious. Was it part of the Water Moccasin's burial goods? Did Walker want to bury it with the rest in his grave?

Shadows deepened among the trees. Sunset came quickly in the mountains. The fading light made it hard to see the way back to the car. Wren clung to John's hand and tried to keep up. Poor kid had to be tired. He picked her up to carry her to the car.

"Grandpa, I'd say we ought to wait till morning to take this stuff back to the burial ground. I've had Wren out all day, and Faron's gonna be mad as hell if I don't get her home."

When Walker insisted they needed to take care of this problem right away, John tried using logic. It didn't usually work with any of the Copperheads, including his wife, but it was worth a try. "We need to see the place in broad daylight, so we can check for any clues that would lead us to whoever is digging up old Cherokee graves. At best, it'll be pitch dark before we even make it to Swain County. Besides, if we put him back in his grave, what's to stop the same guys who dug him up from digging him up again? Anyway, I have no idea how to find the burial ground you're looking for after we get there."

"Ataga'hi. That's where we need to go. On Thunderhead Mountain right near the county line. Don't have to be in the same grave, but his bones have to stay in Ataga'hi." Walker drew a deep breath to calm himself. "Don't say a word about this to anybody, either of you. We gotta keep this in the family."

The thing that finally convinced Walker to wait until morning was not logic so much as the dread of Faron's wrath. If they kept her daughter out any later on a school night, they would both catch hell. That was John's closing argument, and it worked.

John didn't expect Wren to give him trouble, but sometimes his kid could be as stubborn as the rest of the Copperheads. She planted her feet on the ground, crossed her arms, and insisted, "I found Kanagwa'ti's bones and grave goods, and I have to go with you to take them back where they belong. It's my responsibility."

"I understand, baby," John said. "But it's too late tonight."

"Then, it's settled," she said. "We'll leave really early in the morning so we can get there by daylight."

"You've got school tomorrow," John told her. "Grandpa Walker and I will see that everything gets taken care of, and remember, we don't talk about this to anybody."

Wren came as close to pouting as she ever did. "It's not fair, Daddy. I should go to Ataga'hi with you. The great conjuror would want me to."

"We'll have to leave that up to your mama, honey." John shook his head to clear the cloud of confusion that became his constant companion as his daughter got older. The great conjuror, huh? What else did Wren know that he had no clue about?

He dropped Walker off at his house and drove home, still questioning the reality of the Water Moccasin. If he was real, and not just an old story, he died a few hundred years ago. Who would know the location of two of the sacred burial grounds the Cherokee managed to keep hidden all this time, and why would they dig up a grave in one and bring its contents to another at least ninety miles away? And why did his eight-year-old little girl know so damn much he didn't know? He put that last question to Wren as they crossed her mama's new bridge and parked in

58

front of the house.

"'Cause I listen, Daddy."

Damn! "So, since you know so much, who was this great conjuror you and your great-grandpa seem to know all about?"

"Some people think he was an Ada'wehi," she said.

Well, that helped a lot.

Faron met them at the door. She looked at John expecting an explanation for why he left home before seven o'clock in the morning with their daughter and was just now getting home when it was already past her bedtime. He stammered, trying to frame an acceptable description of the day's events, when Wren calmly spoke up.

"Mama, we've got a lot to tell you."

"You two go wash up while I put supper on the table." Faron gave them both a quick hug. She wasn't as mad as John feared.

Faron carved slices from a steaming venison roast and spooned up servings of potatoes and steamed greens. A stack of Mama Kate's fry bread finished the meal. She took her place at the table and said, "Walker says you had quite an evening."

Wren said, "Mama, did Grandpa Walker tell you why we went up to Degal gun'yi?"

Faron nodded. "That's where you've been all evening?"

"Uh huh, and we found a terrible thing there."

"Is it like what happened to the chestnut trees?" Faron's grim expression reflected the sorrow her people still harbored over the passing of a treasured denizen of the forest.

Wren shook her head as John answered, "We didn't get a chance to look at the trees, honey. Still don't know what's going on there. Wren's talking about something she found before we even got to where the trouble is."

He and Wren filled Faron in on what Wren found.

"Is it in the truck now, John?" Faron asked. "I almost wish you had gone on over to Swain County and put everything back in the grave where it belongs. I don't like this."

"Walker didn't trust me with it, I guess," John said. "He took it with him. Said he wanted to show the stuff they dug up with the bones to Mama Kate."

Faron nodded. "Yes, Mama would know for sure."

Wren nodded. "Yep. She'd get a feeling if it is."

"Know what for sure?" John asked.

"It's time you were in bed, young lady," Faron said, clearing Wren's empty plate away. "Go tuck her in John, while I clean up in here."

John and Wren both complied. "What will Mama Kate know for sure, honey?" he asked as he pulled the blanket around her chin.

"Whether it really is the great conjuror. But I already know."

"And is it?"

"Oh, yeah. It is for sure, Daddy."

"How do you know?"

"Because of the ark. Grandpa Walker thought he hid it real quick, but I saw enough of it. It was the ark, alright. He knew it too, 'cause of what he said when he saw it."

"What was it that he said?" John asked.

"Ulunsu'ti." She cuddled down under the covers, already half asleep. "Goodnight, Daddy."

John went into Diamond's room to say goodnight to his son. He was still awake. "Sorry, buddy, about not getting home before you went to bed." Diamond just reached up to be held. John picked him up and carried him back to the kitchen and sat down at the table. Faron handed John a cup of coffee. He was funny about coffee. Didn't care for it in the morning, preferring to start his day with a cold Coke straight from the bottle. At night he could drink all the coffee he wanted and still sleep like a baby. This was the best. Extra strong, scalding hot Luzianne. The chicory in it took the edge off and made it taste extra good.

Diamond snuggled against John's chest, ready to fall asleep now that he was safe in his daddy's arms.

"Darlin', I kinda need some straight answers here," John said.

Faron put the last plate in the dishwasher and sat down beside him with her own cup of Luzianne. "I thought you might, Johnny. Where do you want to start?"

"Well, let's start with you telling me who the hell is the great conjuror named Water Moccasin, and how Walker could tell those were his bones from looking at the stuff from that grave, and why our daughter knew it from seeing that box thing and hearing her Grandpa say one word when he saw it."

"And what one word did he say?"

John made a stab at pronouncing the word. It was close enough for Faron to understand.

"And you didn't guess what that meant?" she asked. "Think, John. You spent a lot of time hanging around with me and Yona and Eli and Dave when we were kids. You heard the tales our folks told us same as we did, and you must have realized by now that our grandpas knew things most folks don't."

John cupped his free hand around the hot mug of coffee and leaned back, looking away from his wife. "I don't think I listened the same way y'all did. I thought they were just telling stories, the same way my folks used to tell me Jack tales. Now, according to Wren, you guys consider them history, and old Walker is acting plumb weird."

"He's got his reasons, and, no, not all of them are historical, honey." She rubbed his thigh. It felt good. "There's history in the stories, some of them at least. Some are just tales, like your Jack tales. Some are legends built up around real people and events. A lot of the stories go way beyond history. Those are as sacred to us as your grandma's Bible is to her. You want me to tell you again about the great conjuror?"

Finally, some answers. "I'd appreciate the hell out of that, honey. But first, what category does this story fall into? Was the great conjuror a real person?"

"He was real. That part we know for sure. The rest, well, I believe it's true." She hesitated long enough for John to begin to wonder if she changed her mind about filling him in. "He lived a long time ago. Back about the time we started seeing a lot of your people settling around here. He was a great man, some people say more than a man."

"Ada'wehi?" John asked.

"Uh-huh," she nodded. "You remembered some of what you heard from the old folks."

"With a bit of help from our daughter," he said. "They were magicians, weren't they? Or supernaturals of some sort?"

"Something like that. We learned the word 'conjuror' from your people. It doesn't do justice to what Kanegwa'ti was, but it's the title he has been given. The great conjuror, they called him, because he was the most powerful man of his day. His power came from the Ulunsu'ti."

"That thing that came from the snake's head?"

"The great crystal from the head of Uktena," she answered. "And, yes, he was a snake of sorts. A snake so big he could coil around Bald Mountain with his head resting on the top. He was a monster that devoured anything that lived for miles around. You remember the story about how the Cherokee captured a Shawnee and sent him out to slay Uktena. Many others had tried, but no one was ever expected to succeed. The Shawnee was brave and sly, and using trickery, he killed the monster. Uktena's blood and poison caused the mountain to be bald. Nothing will ever grow there again."

John hesitated before he asked his next question. "Honey, aren't we getting too old to believe in monsters and magic crystals?"

Faron sipped from her cup and put it on the table. Leaning away from John, she looked him in the eye. "Somebody still believes. Somebody believes enough to gather up everything they need to bring the Ulunsu'ti back to life. Then they brought it all to the only place it can be done. I doubt they did it for any childish reason."

"Darlin'..." John was still trying to adjust to his practical, down-to-earth wife's belief in the old legends. "If it's been buried more than three hundred years, I don't think it's gonna be easy to bring it to life. I'm afraid the Ulunsu'ti is just as dead as old Water Moccasin, and if those are his bones in that Adidas gym bag at your grandpa's house, he's pretty dang dead."

She hardly blinked. It was disconcerting the way she could hold his gaze that way. "I hope you're right on both counts. Kanegwa'ti took a lot of precautions to make sure the Ulunsu'ti slept till we needed it most, and until someone came along who commanded the power to control it. We've had a lot of times when we sure could have used it, but no one dared wake it. Looks like there's somebody around here who thinks he can handle it. The Suye'ta, or Chosen One."

"Chosen for what, and who does the choosing?" John asked.

"Chosen to be the master of the Ulunsu'ti. As for who does the choosing, I don't know. Could be the guardians. Could be the Ulunsu'ti himself. Anyway, Kanegwa'ti inherited the crystal from the conjuror, who had it before him. He used it wisely and the people respected its power. Those who held it before him never had to fear that someone would try to take it from them. Native people knew what it could do, but they also knew the danger it brought to a man who didn't have what it took to be its master. In the wrong hands, there could be hell to pay."

"Anything with that much power must be real valuable," John said. "How come it ended up buried with its owner? Sounds like one of those things that used to get passed down to the next conjuror in line for it."

"It always did before, but like I said, our people knew enough about it not to mess with it. When the white people heard about Ulunsu'ti, they wanted it. They thought it was kept in the box they called the Cherokee Ark of the Covenant. They were wrong. The ark only held the ceremonial objects used to wake it up and control it. Kanegwa'ti had to post guards around his lodge to keep them from taking it, but he knew they would keep trying. They didn't understand the danger of owning a talisman with a mind of its own."

"Wait a minute, honey. It's a piece of crystal, or something, from a dead snake's head." John needed to remind Faron, and himself, that they were talking about an old myth. "My ancestors were sensible types like me and didn't think inanimate objects had minds."

"Well, whether they believed it or not, it did."

She sounded like his third-grade teacher. It almost made him feel like he was the unreasonable one. He resisted the temptation to tease her about it since that might keep her from telling him anything else. Instead, he kept quiet and let her go on.

"The Ulunsu'ti had a mind of its own, and a hunger. It had to be fed."

"Whoa, sugar. This is getting too weird. The thing was a piece of rock. Rocks don't eat." When she said nothing more, he said, "Okay. What did the rock have to be fed?"

"Blood." She dropped the word in his lap and got up to rinse out their empty coffee cups.

"Damn, Faron. Who writes this shit for you guys? Stephen freakin' King?" This was too much. Vampire crystals from a snake's head. And she was the level-headed one in the family!

"You gonna put the baby to bed, honey?" she asked as she wiped the countertop. "He's sound asleep now."

John stalled, hoping for more information. When she made it obvious she wasn't going to volunteer anything further, he had to ask, afraid of the answer, "Honey, what kind of blood did the rock like?"

She ruffled his curls and kissed his earlobe. "That of skeptical husbands," she grinned. "Preferably cute, redheaded ones. Now where could we find us one of those?"

He was not amused. "Really, Faron. Did the conjuror give that crystal thing human blood?"

"Of course not, John. He killed a poor little bunny rabbit and bled it on the crystal. Once in a while, if Ulunsu'ti had been working hard, he needed something stronger. Then he got the blood of a whole deer."

"And if he didn't get it, what happened? Did he starve to death and just lie there like, say, a rock?"

Faron's playful mood disappeared. "No Johnny, he didn't. He went out and found him some dinner. When he had to fend for himself, he usually didn't settle for rabbits and deer. People are much easier to catch."

John got a chill down his spine. "Now, Faron. How's a crystal gonna go anywhere, let alone go catch somebody and drink his blood?"

"It's not just a crystal, and it consumes more than a man's blood. What they don't tell you in the story is that you can't ever kill the Uktena. He just goes into the Ulunsu'ti to live, but he doesn't always stay there. If he needs to, he can take up residence in somebody's head. Somebody who has touched the crystal. He just needs a taste of their blood to give him strength."

"And they have to do his killing for him?"

Faron nodded. "And once he gets a taste of human blood, he learns to like it better than any other kind. That's why they had to get the Shawnee to kill Uktena in the first place. He was eating up everybody for miles around—not just their bodies, but everything that made them who they were. Their very being, their souls."

"Sugar," John said, "I think I'll go put Diamond to bed now. He's sound asleep."

"Yeah, I know." She stroked Diamond's hair, black like hers

and curly like his daddy's, and kissed his forehead, then slipped her arm around John's waist. "I'll come with you, Johnny. It's high time you and I got into bed too."

John was fine with that. He'd had about all the weirdness he could stand for one night. "No problem," he said.

Monday Night

Qualla Boundary

The sound of a car engine coming up the drive to the trailer roused the elder before he got to sleep. He sat up in the recliner and listened. Sally's cat lifted her head and stood at attention. He reached under the chair and pushed the knapsack further out of sight.

"I knew he couldn't be trusted." He hugged the cat against his side to keep her quiet. Smokey understood and froze without a sound.

Loud, insistent knocks rang against the trailer door and a voice called his name. Not the white man, but that made it worse. This was someone he trusted, someone who could help. He wanted to answer, but that wouldn't do. Did the man outside know about the violation of the mound at Degal gun'yi? He forced himself to stay still, even when he heard the crunch of footsteps on the gravel behind the trailer where he usually parked his car.

He could almost see him outside looking around at the empty parking space and the dark windows of the trailer. He didn't breathe until the grass on the patch of lawn he kept cleared in front of the trailer muffled the footsteps. A door closed, and the engine started. He heard the powerful purr of a working man's truck back up, turn around, and head toward the highway. Loneliness closed around him. Smokey curled up on his lap and purred him to sleep.

He didn't wake again until almost dawn, when the sound of pounding on the trailer door roused him. This time, the voice he expected to hear called his name. He took his time stretching his stiff back and listening to his joints crack and pop. A long nap in the chair could be refreshing, but a whole night's sleep left him twisted and aching all over. He grabbed the knapsack and hefted its weight, a mighty heavy load to carry where he had to go, and the influence of the Ulunsu'ti already wormed into his mind. Carrying it around on his back before he claimed control of it wasn't good for him or the white man. Best to stow it away before he saw it.

The old well on the back porch still supplied his water. The bucket and pulley he used in the old days still hung there, but now an electric pump brought it into the trailer through shiny copper plumbing. He wiggled a loose stone in the well's wall, inching it free to reveal a roomy niche secreted behind it. Sally came up with the idea of making a safe there when they remodeled the porch twenty-five years ago. Only the two of them knew about it. It held the few valuables they owned. He wished he had let Thomas in on his secret. He might never get the chance to tell his son about it if things went wrong.

He took the Ulunsu'ti from the knapsack and slipped it into the niche. It lay atop the deed to his land, the title to the Pinto, a handful of military medals, a couple of U.S. savings bonds, and twelve $100 bills that comprised his life savings. He fitted the stone back in place, slung the knapsack over his shoulder, and went to meet his visitors. The stone war axe settled into place, a heavy but reassuring weight against his back.

The pounding on the trailer's front door became more insistent about the time he entered the back door. "Coming," he called.

The white man entered and took a seat at the kitchen table. He didn't come alone. His constant companion went straight to the coffee pot and started it perking.

The elder objected. "Your fast isn't over till we go to water. You can have your coffee then. We'll take care of that after we get the conjuror's hands."

"Hey, man. You look like you could use a cup. I'm still

fasting like you told me to." The white man took two cups out of the cabinet like he owned the place.

The coffee smelled good. He went to his bedroom and got a faded flannel shirt from the closet while it perked. The shirt wasn't as warm as his jacket, but it would help keep out the chill. A cup of black coffee waited for him when he got back to the kitchen. It was strong, hot, and just what he needed. He and the third partner sipped their coffee in silence. The white man breathed in the aroma until it became too much of a temptation. He went down the hall toward the bathroom in the back.

The elder set his half-empty cup on the table and said, "Tell him I'm going on ahead. We'll meet up on Lightning Creek. Go up Big Cove Road till you come to Lightning Creek Road. Drive as far as you can till the road ends. Turn onto that dirt road that crosses the creek, then go about a mile past Lynelle Wayanettah's place and park and wait for me. I'll meet you there."

He didn't hang around for the white man to return from the bathroom, just adjusted the knapsack and ducked out the back door and through the laurel thicket to his car. He saw them getting into the Montero when he pulled around and drove down his driveway toward the road. Before they could catch up, he pulled behind the Holiday Inn on the highway, then watched from the hill above the motel until he saw them go by. He needed nourishment before he could face the hike up Wolf Mountain. The fast-food drive-thru across the road usually provided his breakfast.

From the drive-thru, he ordered a couple of ham-and-egg sandwiches and a second cup of coffee. After a seven-day fast, he needed to get his strength back.

The first tinge of dawn lit the sky as he turned onto Big Cove Road. He had the road to himself when he angled off to Lightning Creek. A well-tended gravel road curved along beside the creek. The few houses on the far side of the water revealed nothing more than a glimpse of lighted windows through the trees. In full daylight, most people would never notice them. They liked their privacy.

He rattled along for a few miles until the road ended abruptly against a thick stand of hemlock.

He pulled the Pinto as far as he could get it under the trees and parked. Thick, low-hanging branches concealed it from sight.

To his left, a dirt road crossed an aging wooden bridge over Lightning Creek and curved around out of sight. Less than a mile ahead, the Montero sat waiting. The two inside were completely unaware of him until he opened the back door. "Start driving," he said, climbing into the backseat. "I'll tell you where to go."

Winter left its mark on the road, freezing, thawing, and eroding the thin layer of gravel that made it passable. The Montero negotiated the washed-out potholes and made it farther than his Pinto would. He watched the roadside till he saw the remains of an old logging trail disappearing among the trees as it wound its way up the mountainside.

"Turn here," he said. The white man did as he was told. The elder felt a twinge of regret for the suspicions he allowed to enter his mind. The work of the Ulunsu'ti, no doubt. "Go as far as you can, then park this thing. We'll have to walk the rest of the way."

A stand of hemlocks once again served as a good place to park when the logging trail petered out. Chances were, nobody would be around to see the Montero. There were only two houses on this road and practically no traffic. The logging trail was abandoned last year when the timber ran out, but just in case, he thought it best to leave their vehicle out of sight.

He struck out up the steep slope of Wolf Mountain, carefully scanning for markers he committed to memory when he tailed Driver Wayanettah to the cave, back when he thought Driver and his family guarded the ark somewhere on this mountain. Driver was gone now, walked over to the other world like most of his old friends. Even if he were still around, it wouldn't matter. Driver wouldn't want anything to do with a man who could betray the Snake Dancers and everyone else who trusted him.

He set a brisk pace and his two companions matched it.

The stolen war axe weighed heavy in the knapsack over his shoulder, but it felt lighter than the Ulunsu'ti would. He thought of it in the niche under the well and a cold presence brushed against his mind. He shouldn't have left it behind. It belonged with him.

A couple of times he had to backtrack to relocate a landmark he missed. Years passed and the terrain changed since he followed Driver up this way, paying close attention to everything and fixing all the details in his mind for later. After he learned Del Locust and his grandson guarded the ark, he lost interest in the cave. Driver's story about how his ancestors hid out there to avoid the removal and the Trail of Tears had the ring of truth. They'd talked about how places like the cave made it possible for a few of the Cherokees to avoid the long march west, or one of the shallow graves along the way, and stay in the ancestral homeland. Yes, Driver knew how to make his story convincing.

He doubled back to reconsider his directions when he got confused. They tagged behind without a word to him, just spoke quietly to each other. He went ahead, feeling like he was the one on the outside.

After a while the trees gave way to a steep expanse of granite interspersed with sparse scrub laurel and boulders. The entrance to the cave he followed Driver into lay behind one of the great boulders He couldn't seem to remember which one. He threaded his way through the forest of stones with his companions close on his heels. One tall boulder stood out from the rest, pitted with age and leaning against its neighbor. He slipped behind it and found himself in a hollow formed by the stones. The cave stretched ahead into the darkness.

The white man accompanied him into the hollow under the slab of granite, after instructing their companion to stay behind and watch the trail. He took the same cheap plastic flashlight he used on Ataga'hi out of his backpack and pointed it into the cave. It cast a weak light against the darkness. The elder fished a better one out of the knapsack, clicked it on, and strode into the cave, signaling the white man to follow.

The flashlights illuminated only a few feet of the cave ahead before the dark stone devoured the light. An oppressive silence cut them off from the outside world. He heard the white man humming something that sounded like a hymn. Driver whistled when he got to the dark part of the cave. That's the only time he ever heard his old friend whistle. This shadowy hole in the mountain probably spooked him too.

The white man made a confession. "I don't do too well in confined spaces. This better not take long, or I can't stand it. How much further?"

"Up ahead, we'll come to a waterfall," the elder said. "I watched Driver duck into a passage just this side of it and followed him as far as I could without getting caught. I hid in a crevice and he went on ahead, but I never lost sight of his light, and he never got out of hearing. I heard his prayers. That's where we'll find the hands."

The white man went ahead and lit out in the direction of the distant roar of a waterfall. The elder fell in behind. The sound of water got louder, just the way he remembered. He and the white man used their lights to search the cavern walls for the jagged cleft he remembered. When he saw one that looked right, he nodded to the white man and ducked inside. The white man had to stoop over to manage the cramped passage. His breath came loud and labored.

Gaps in his memory left the elder uncertain and confused

about the distance to the niche he hid in back then. It was in earshot of the place Driver stood and called on the ancestral spirits to guard the sacred relics he watched over. If he could find his hiding place, he could find Driver's.

The ceiling sloped down, becoming even lower than before. He inched forward in an awkward stoop; that gait sent spasms through his legs until he emerged into a cavern that expanded into a spacious chamber. He remembered this chamber. Somewhere ahead, Driver shone his light against the far wall, dropped to his belly, and reached into an opening that engulfed his head and shoulders. He waited for the white man, struggling through the narrow passage.

Inching against the wall, he explored with an outstretched hand until a roughened split in the rock met his touch. He slipped into the niche it formed and sent the beam of his flashlight ahead until it met darkness. "It will be there, about twenty feet ahead. Go look for a hole that's right on the floor. You should be able to stick your head in and look around."

"Old Man, I've come this far, but that's more than I can stand. If I don't get out of here soon, I'm going to lose it."

The edge of panic in the white man's voice convinced the elder. "Stay here where you have room to stand up, and I'll check it out." He stretched his knotted muscles and felt his way along the wall looking for Driver's hiding place. Fissures and crevices marked the granite walls. He didn't come this far when he followed Driver. He stayed in his hidey hole and waited for Driver to pass him, then followed him and his light out of the cave.

He dropped to his knees and searched for openings along the floor. The first one he found to be less than a foot deep. He sent light inside and found nothing but a void. He had hope for the next one. He could get his head and shoulders in, like Driver did, but blank stone met him less than three feet away from the opening. He had to admit his mistake. This was not the hole where Driver stashed the conjuror's hands.

A few feet on, he found a more promising crevice. He flashed his light inside and saw a little cavern that disappeared at the end of his flashlight's reach. He crawled in and found that the ceiling soared out of sight. After he examined every promising crevice he could reach, he found nothing. He needed help. He backed out of the hole and described it to his partner. "I checked everything I could reach. Driver was a big man. He might have stashed them on a high ledge. You will have to go in."

The white man gasped an oath—or was it a prayer? "Oh, holy God." His breath came in wheezy gasps. A sharp ammonia odor wafted from the crevice. He took a white handkerchief from his hip pocket and tied it across his nose and mouth and crept into the cavity. The elder inched in behind him, encouraging him when he faltered.

An ominous, fluttering rush sent a breath of stinking air through the cavern. They hit the floor while a swarm of tiny black bats poured over them and out the opening. That explained the smell, and the filth that caked the floor and walls.

The white man groaned. His hands shook when he stretched up to search ledges and crevices beyond the elder's reach. "There's nothing here," he said.

The elder shined the light deeper into the cavern, back where the bats came from. "Could have been deeper in here," he said. "We have to go in."

The white man had reached the end of his endurance. "Old Man, I've done everything you asked of me, but I'd rather go into hell than search that bat roost." He turned around and rushed out into the more bearable expanse of the cavern outside.

The elder came out behind him and heard the big man wheeze, his chest rattling. "What's wrong with you?" he asked.

"I can't breathe in here." The white man slumped against the cave wall, recovering his breath. "I'll take over if you can find the hands, but I have to get out of this cave."

The elder's sudden anger came on strong. "You'll take over after I do all the grunt work, huh? Do you think I'm going to trust you to control the Ulunsu'ti when you can't even help me find the conjuror's hands? You've got the muscle for it, but it's going to take more than physical strength to keep from becoming the tool of Uktena, instead of his master. You don't have it."

He pushed past the white man and headed toward the crevice leading to the main cavern. The white man struggled to his feet and caught up, catching him by the shoulder and spinning him around. "You put me through all this, after feeding me promises for the last fifteen years, now you're cutting me out. What the hell, Old Man? You found them, didn't you? While I was up to my eyeballs in bat shit, you found the hands. You used me, now what are you going to do, bring in somebody else to claim the prize? Did you team up with Walker Copperhead to turn everything over to his granddaughter's husband? Come on, I'll look for the hands, after I make sure you don't have them in that knapsack you hang onto like it's part of your body."

The white man jammed his flashlight into a crack in the stone. Its weak beam shone on the elder, clutching the knapsack, daring the white man to touch it. The white man took the dare and made a grab. The elder spun away and went down, fading into oblivion for a moment when his head cracked on the stone. He recovered and drew the knapsack beneath him.

The flashlight in the crevice dimmed and went dark, taking the fight out of the white man. In desperation, he banged the dead flashlight against the cave as if that might bring it back to life. It shattered the lens and bulb and sent sharp fragments flying. Enough of them connected with his face and forearms to draw blood. He flung the useless plastic shell down the cavern.

He had all he could stand. The only light in the cave lay a few feet away from the elder, who lay prone on the cave floor. The white man grasped it and gave a desperate lunge into the niche that led to the main cavern.

The elder dragged himself to his feet and staggered after him. Fifteen years ago, the white man took a little girl and her mother into his heart, and brought them home to him and Sally. That made him part of his family and worthy of trust. He confided in him his worries about the future of his people and the only way he knew to save them. He told him about Walker Copperhead's suspicion that John McLeymore might be the Suye'ta. Then, to his shame, he trusted him with the story of the Ulunsu'ti and how men in the Snake Dancer Circle guarded it and the tools to control it. The white man claimed he had an Indian soul and wanted to do anything he could for the tribe. That's why he taught the old ways to his followers, married a Native woman, and adopted her child.

It was enough to make the elder bring him in—or was it wishful thinking on his part?

The white man stumbled ahead with the light. The elder didn't need the light to keep up with him. His panicked panting and praying echoed through the cave. He plunged ahead, showing no concern for the elder, who, as far as he knew, lay wounded or dead on the cave floor.

Blood trickled down the elder's face from a gash on his forehead. He brushed it away with his sleeve, feeling disoriented. His head throbbed with every beat of his heart. He fell behind the light ahead. Sickness and shame knotted in his belly for all the wrongs he committed against the Snake Dancers. He desecrated sacred sites, robbed the graves of his ancestors, and revealed knowledge of things so powerful that even some of the Snake Dancers didn't know it. The desire to curl up in a ball and pass out from the pain possessed him. He fought the urge and allowed the full force of his guilt to wash over him. It drove him toward the dim light fleeing into the darkness.

He had to make it to the mouth of the cave and find a way to fix the mess he created. The thought of what would happen if he didn't gave him the will to keep moving. He kept the light in view and stayed far enough behind to stay out of the white man's hearing.

Blood oozed from his mouth and a loosened molar wiggled when he breathed. The fall left him bleeding and weak, but it must have knocked some sense into him. His thinking cleared. He knew what he had to do and felt a shred of hope. Nobody but the white man and the one who waited outside knew what he had done. If he put everything back in its place and swore them to secrecy, everything could go back to normal.

In the back of his mind, he knew it wasn't that simple. The white man knew enough to crave the power the Ulunsu'ti held. It promised to give him the status he led his followers to think he possessed. And, the Snake Dancers couldn't have a rogue outsider with the knowledge of the guardians and what they protected. By telling him their secrets, the elder sealed the white man's fate.

He crept out of the cave a few feet behind the white man and eased over behind a boulder, biding his time.

"Where is he? Is he alright?" The voice of the one who waited sounded concerned.

"Doesn't matter," the white man said. "He lied to us. We don't need him anyway. I know as much as he knows now."

"He's in there alone? Go back for him."

The elder flattened himself against the rock and listened to the white man complaining that they were used by the Snake Dancers. Lying, saying the elder found the conjuror's hands and stashed them in his knapsack. That he planned to give everything to John McLeymore and cheat them out of everything he promised.

"I wanted to do this for you," he said. "It's rightfully yours. He owes you."

"I never wanted it. It's what you wanted and I went along. I'm going inside for him. You left him in there alone."

The white man wouldn't give up. "I didn't come this far for

nothing. I've prepared for this all my life, and I've earned the right. I can't let it go to a man who doesn't even want it, and you have to help me. You know the way back to the truck. We need some new flashlights, food, and water, so we can wait him out. When he gets tired of hiding out in there, he'll come to us."

He listened, hoping the white man got his way.

"No. I'm going to look for him. He might be hurt."

The white man raised his voice. "Do as I tell you. I can't leave, so you have to go down for the things we need." He went closer. The elder listened in disbelief. "Go now, or he'll rot in that cave. Nobody knows where he is but us, and if you don't do as you're told, nobody will ever see him again."

He couldn't stay quiet any longer. The minute he moved, he saw his mistake. The white man came after him, making threats, reaching for the knapsack.

The elder ran. Boots pounded behind him.

He raced toward the path down the mountainside. The weight of the knapsack pounded against his back, the war axe heavy enough to cause a bruise. He carried a weapon that served his ancestor well. On his best day he couldn't outrun the white man, and his old legs trembled with fatigue. He ducked behind a rock and fumbled in the knapsack. The white man neared, demanding he turn over the hands and the Ulunsu'ti.

He stopped and turned, facing a man who had been like a son, but now had to become an enemy. Their companion tried to help, grasping the white man's raised fist, pleading. He slung the small form aside to land with a bruising impact against a boulder.

The elder's warrior blood rushed in his veins. He had to stand and fight for both of them. His fingers closed around the handle of the axe. It fit his hand like he used it all his life. It felt good.

With a cry that would make his war chief ancestor proud, he raised the axe and took aim. Every ounce of strength he had in his body went into the throw. Time stopped as the war axe arced through the air. He saw the white man duck as the axe whistled past his head.

A clean miss.

An eternity passed while he watched. The axe hit the cliff face behind the white man and gained momentum glancing off the stone. What happened next drew a curtain of darkness across his soul. He sensed his own spirit leave him as surely as the spirit left the one the axe struck. He saw blood spatter against the cliff, then watched his last defender crumple and fall to the gray stone, motionless.

The white man fell to his knees beside the lifeless form and lifted it in his arms. The body hung limp and lifeless. Blood streamed from a jagged gash in the skull and pooled in the crevices of the rock.

His anguished cry echoed off the hillsides as he laid the body on the stone and turned his rage on the elder.

No trace of sanity remained in the white man's eyes. The innate instinct to survive propelled the elder toward the only escape route available. He sprinted toward the mouth of the cave and ran into the darkness, unaware of anything but the need to flee. The last trace of light vanished, but he stumbled on, driven by the afterimage of the body lying on the rocks. It filled his mind, leaving only a faint awareness of the pounding of boots behind him and the hammering of his heart in his chest.

His legs failed. He collapsed on the cold stone, gasping for air. His chest heaved and every breath burned like acid in his lungs.

The thud of boots and maddened shouts neared. He held his breath and lay still, listening as the shouts dwindled off into echoes as the white man passed in the darkness and continued into the deeper recesses of the cave.

He listened, dreading the sound of the white man's return. His heartbeat stilled. Silence settled over him. Curled into a ball of pain beyond anything a man could endure, he retreated into a place even darker than the cave. His spirit sank into the depths of despair to wander with other lost souls in a gray, hopeless land, while his body lay unmoving on the cold granite of the cave floor.

The soft echo of the waterfall came from somewhere in the distance, but it didn't matter anymore. Nothing mattered now.

Tuesday Morning

Snowbird

John rolled over and sandwiched his head between two pillows to block out the murmur of voices drifting up from the kitchen. Morning already? Since he didn't open his eyes, the fact that it was still pitch dark didn't penetrate his sleep-logged brain.

He snuggled in for a few more minutes of sleep before Faron or Wren came to wake him. They usually let him doze until the last second, giving him just enough time for a quick grooming and breakfast before he rushed off to the ranger station. He hoped Faron woke him this time. The way she kissed him awake geared him up for the day. Wren usually yanked on the covers and yelled in his ear.

Footsteps approached his bed, but it didn't sound like Wren or Faron. And the hand prodding between his shoulder blades made no attempt to be gentle. In fact, it didn't feel like a hand at all. He opened his eyes and peeked from beneath the pillow. A round eagle eye returned his gaze.

"What the hell?" The pillow flew over the foot of the bed as John bolted upright.

"Time to get up, son," Walker said, withdrawing his walking stick. "Can't lay here in bed all day when we've got things to do."

"All day?" John glanced at the night pressing against the bedroom window. "Day won't be here for another five or six hours at least. What time is it, midnight?"

"Nearly five o'clock," Walker said. "High time we got started, Johnny." He turned on the bedside lamp.

The glow from the hall lamp gave more light than John could stand. He sure didn't need any more. "Five o'freakin' clock.

Damn, Old Man. I just got in bed."

"You got in bed at eleven and slept all night. Faron told me. Now haul ass, boy." Walker turned and left the room.

John smelled coffee. Thank God. With a strong pot of coffee, he might be able to handle waking up. With Walker here for breakfast, he knew the Luzianne would be strong enough to float a horseshoe and hot enough to melt one. A cup or two might help him keep his eyes open. He pulled on a sweatshirt and boxer shorts and staggered barefoot to the kitchen, grunting his breakfast order as he collapsed on his chair. "Coffee, darlin', and could I have a biscuit and jelly to get me going?"

Faron didn't say a word, though she did give him a sympathetic look, then just sat there sipping her own coffee. John noticed Yona and Walker both sitting at their usual place at the table without coffee or biscuits. And Mama Kate was there, drinking coffee with Faron.

"You might as well go upstairs and put your britches on, son," Walker said. "I'm afraid your belly's gonna have to stay empty for a while longer."

Understanding dawned. "Oh, shit," John groaned. "Please tell me he's only gonna make me do a sweat with him."

"'Fraid not, brother," Yona grinned. "You can skip your hot shower this morning. By the time we get out of Big Santetla, you're gonna be plenty clean."

He went to water before, just to please Faron. The first time, the day before their wedding, and then twice more after the birth of their babies. Doing it first thing in the morning was a good-news, bad-news kind of thing. The good news, it wasn't as hard to fast while you were asleep. The bad news, every river in these hills was cold enough to freeze a man's balls off. Climbing out of the water into the morning chill made him feel like a sack of ice cubes all day. Damn! He hated being cold. Hell had to be a place where they dipped you in ice water on a cold morning. He shivered at the thought of dipping himself seven times in Big

Santetla.

"Grandpa, look. I have a job that I'm expected to show up at. No reason for me to traipse off with you to that burial ground. And if I'm not gonna be a part of this, no reason for me to go to water."

Walker laughed. "Good try, Johnny, but I already talked to Buck Locust at the station. You got all the leeway you need to handle this. Buck says it's really part of your job anyway. You work for a good man, son."

Why did he even try? And Buck claimed to be his friend. "Thought you said to keep this in the family. How come you told Buck?"

"Buck is family, son. The kind that counts when it comes to this kind of thing."

"I'll get you a towel and a blanket, honey." Faron got up and kissed him. "You better go get dressed now."

There was nothing to do but follow orders. He started back up the stairs to the loft to dress.

"John," Mama Kate called after him, "Faron and I will come on over to the river with some breakfast for when you're done. We'll have a fire ready to thaw you out."

He detected a note of compassion in her voice. Perhaps she liked him after all.

It didn't take long to get ready to leave the house in the morning if he skipped breakfast and showering. Within ten minutes he sat slumped in the back seat of Yona's Blazer, feeling like he completely lost control of his life. It was not a new feeling. Seemed like the Copperheads had been leading him around by the nose since he and Faron were kids. It started back around the time she told Kate she planned to marry him when they grew up. She couldn't have been more than ten years old at the time. It freaked him out, but he got used to it by the time she turned old enough to be legal.

Fog lay so thick on the road he couldn't see ten feet ahead.

Yona had to be driving from memory. His Mustang Blazer was made for mountain roads, and he appreciated it after a weekend driving a Mack truck. Little brother Charlie always confiscated the Blazer when he came home from school, leaving Yona no choice but to drive one of the company trucks, or borrow Kate's shiny black Trans Am.

Yona drove with his window down. The cold didn't bother him but the damp chill cut right through John. It would be a good month before it warmed up enough to get Johnny McLeymore into the river at midday. Here it was, early enough in the spring that you still needed to wear a jacket most mornings, and he was on his way to plunge his white, freckled ass into the Big Santetla River. Walker laughed like he could read his mind. More likely his moaning and grumbling gave him away.

"You know, Old Man, that I'm a plain ol' Presbyterian Christian boy. We don't have to get dunked in the water. If I wanted that, I'da been a Baptist, but even then, I sure wouldn't get baptized on a cold morning. Why in hell do you people put yourselves through this? More important, why do you put *me* through it?"

"For a good reason, Johnny," Walker answered. "We need to be purified before we go messing around with some of the things we're gonna be messing with. If you've got any desires to be the big boss man, better get ready to let them go. Gotta get rid of any cravings for power, or you might get it, and son, you don't want it." Walker sounded dead serious. "Need a clean spirit and a mind on service to the greatest good of the people. Anything that would break harmony has to go."

The mist coming through the windows got colder. "Old Man," John asked, "is the Ulunsu'ti in that box we found?"

"I wish it was, Johnny. At least then we'd know it didn't fall into the wrong hands. This could get bad."

"The thing Faron called 'the ark,' they used to say that's

what it was for, to hold the Ulunsu'ti." John couldn't stop shivering.

"Ain't nothing can hold the Ulunsu'ti," Walker said. "Lots of people thought it was in the ark but it never was. The ark just holds some of the tools you need if you try to use it, and it looks like somebody was planning to use it. They had the ark and Kanegwa'ti's bones and medicine bundle."

"Grandpa, if I'm gonna go through all this craziness, I think I've got some answers coming," John said.

Walker looked back at him, his eyes as innocent as a lamb's. "Why didn't you ask me if you've got questions, boy? You know I'd tell you anything you need to know."

Now it was John's turn. "Bullshit." He folded his arms across his chest and went silent. Yona laughed out loud at the perfect parody of his grandfather. The mood in the Blazer lightened.

Yona braked and eased into one of those cut-offs nobody seemed to be able to see but the Copperheads, then bounced along until the river appeared right in front of the wheels.

"Think you could wait a while for those answers, brother?" Yona asked. "Like after we puke and go for a swim?"

John didn't respond. His stomach already churned in anticipation when Walker unscrewed the lid on his thermos. The liquid he poured into the plastic cup was hot and black, but it wasn't Luzianne. He could smell it from the backseat as Yona took a cup and gulped it down, then hurried away to disappear into the trees. Walker poured again and reached the cup back to John. "You know why you do this, boy. You've been through it before. Gotta be clean, inside and out. Hit the woods now and do what you gotta do."

John gagged more than once, but it was not as hard to swallow as the last time he went through purification. If he'd been a woman, he could have skipped this step. Women didn't need to purge.

The black drink wanted to come up faster than it went down, but he gagged it back and ran for the woods. There was an order to this, if he could only remember it with his whole insides heaving. He leaned against a tree and let the draught do its work. He hated puking. This was a hell of a way to start something that was supposed to be spiritual.

When the emetic finished cleaning his insides out, he found what felt like the right place under a big oak and addressed the four directions, calling on the guardians of each to help him. They must have heard because, this time, it wasn't quite as hard as before. The prayers Walker taught him came back to his memory without a hitch, and he surprised himself by adding some of his own. He felt thirty pounds lighter, probably because there wasn't a trace of anything left in his stomach. That had to be what made him so lightheaded and floaty. Kinda made a man think he had hallucinations sometimes.

Walker and Yona waited by the river. So far, he saw no sign of Kate and Faron. Walker hunkered on his haunches on a flat stone. Flames flickered into sight as he nurtured a small fire to life.

John stopped and waited while Yona disrobed. He wanted to delay that step for as long as possible. When Yona's sweatshirt and pants lay in a neat stack on the rock, he followed and added his own jeans, shirt, and jacket to the pile.

Walker stood, wearing nothing but a leather pouch around his neck. He nodded at Yona, then at the mound of green cedar branches beside the rock. Yona picked up the branches and scattered them to enclose the three of them in a protective circle of green, then threw the rest on the smoldering fire. The smoke spread the warding fragrance of cedar up and out beyond the circle. John remembered the story; nothing evil could cross the cedar circle.

Walker lifted his hands toward the dawning light in the east and began to chant so softly his voice barely reached beyond the fire's warmth. The language was Cherokee, but in an older form, a form that went all the way back to the time when his people were still known as the Ani'yun Wiya, the Principal People. John's limited grasp of the language served no use at all. Yona looked like he didn't understand any more than John did. When the chant ended, only the rushing of Big Santetla broke the silence. Not so much as a birdcall could be heard.

Walker took the pouch from around his neck and opened it. Wild native tobacco was not easy to come by anymore. This must be a special occasion for him to use the precious supply he hoarded. He took out enough of the crumpled leaves to fill the hollow of his left hand, added some sage leaves, and something John didn't recognize. He then rolled it between his palms until it formed a tight cylindrical bundle. He lit it from a burning cedar twig Yona retrieved from the fire and blew on the bundle till the smoke swirled from it just right. He handed it to Yona and, with closed eyes, accepted the cleansing of the sweet-smelling smoke. Yona circled him, directing the smoke to flow over his skin from his feet to his skinny gray braid. Walker took the smoking bundle and repeated the smudging for Yona and John, chanting something in a whisper.

The smoke reached John's face and he breathed deeply, drawing it into his lungs. He felt warmer now, like the smoke itself provided a barrier against the chilling mist. Surely he imagined it, but he could feel it, like something alive, writhing up his body. He could even hear it. No. That must be the river—or the snake. The snake that curled up his legs and around his belly, then across his chest, its fanged head lifting just inches from his glazed eyes. The forked tongue flicked and John stared into the gaping mouth. Cottony white.

The tongue flicked again, then dissolved and drifted upward to float away, followed by the rest of the serpent. Smoke blending into mist, and disappearing into the morning.

"John. Time to go, brother." Yona's voice sounded like it

came from far away. John watched him wade into the river, and followed without hesitation, stepping over the rocky shore and into the cold water. Strange, it didn't feel all that cold. Without the usual prompting from Walker, he remembered the prayers. Seven times under, and each time the prayer entered his thoughts and he prayed without effort, and added more prayers that Walker didn't teach him.

Well, he had been in the family nearly ten years. About time their Above Beings decided to accept him.

Yona and Walker stood waiting on the bank when he came out of the water. Yona put his jeans on and pulled a sweatshirt over the kind of body some men work out for years to get. Being a logger had its benefits.

Walker donned his clothing and doused the fire. "Put your clothes on, boy, and we'll go get us some breakfast," he said.

John dried off and dressed. The fragrance of scented smoke lingered on the morning air, the only evidence of the fire. He followed Yona and Walker. They headed up the riverbank, not toward the Blazer like he expected.

He smelled coffee, blending with the aroma of sausage on an open fire. Around the bend in the river he saw Faron. A smoky old percolator bubbled away over the coals of a cooking fire, and Faron stirred something in a big iron skillet. Nothing smelled as good as breakfast cooking on a campfire.

"Hey, Daddy. You done already?"

Wren? She had to be in school in a couple of hours. "Faron, honey. What's Wren doing here at the river wearing nothing but a blanket with her hair soaking wet?"

Wren answered him. "I'm doing the same thing as you, Daddy. We've got important things to do and we needed to get ready."

"Faron, you wanna tell me what's going on here?" John asked.

"She already told you, honey." Faron speared sausage links

with a fork from the smoking skillet and transferred them to a paper plate.

Kate wrapped Wren's blanket tighter around her and sat her down on a rock, then perched behind her with a comb and began to smooth the tangles from her wet hair. "Stay here by the fire and let it dry a while," she said, "then we'll braid it." Wren did as she was told while she sipped on a Coke.

John squatted beside his wife. She added a pile of scrambled eggs to the plate of sausage links and handed it to him. He put it down on the same rock with his coffee cup.

"Faron," he said, "you get pissed off at me if I get Wren home twenty minutes after bedtime, or feed her something that's not on the approved list, or say a cuss word or two in front of her. Now, you drag our baby girl out of bed before daylight on a school day and let your mama dunk her in the freezing cold river. Am I missing something here?"

"Eat your breakfast, John." Faron spoke in that soft, sweet voice that didn't tell John anything. "You don't want it to get cold."

Across on their side of the fire, Kate and Wren were singing something. John listened, wondering what kind of ritual his little girl observed and what prayers she would say. Their voices drifted softly on the mist.

"Feeling good was easy, Lord, when Bobby sang the blues.
Feeling good was good enough for me.
Good enough for me and Bobby McGee.
La te da te da da da da di."

Could this possibly get any more surreal? "If Janice Joplin herself walked out of that river butt-naked, I'd just hand her a cup of coffee."

"She's dead, you know," Yona said.

John sat flat on the damp ground, his head between his hands.

"Faron, you better get some food into your man," Kate

called. "Looks like he might be about to pass out. That happens to the men sometimes."

Faron held the coffee cup to his lips like she was feeding a baby. The mischief in her eyes suggested less solicitation than teasing. He sipped, and it did make him feel better. "Here, honey. Eat these eggs now. Mama's right. You look kinda pale."

"You want some of my Coke, Daddy?" Wren asked, coming around to his side.

"Yeah, Johnny," Kate said. "That might be just what you need. It's got plenty of sugar in it, and you're probably just slightly hypoglycemic." She took the bottle from Wren and held it to his lips. He downed the whole thing, then started in on the eggs while the women talked about his habitual early morning lethargy and its possible causes. Yona and Walker just grinned and ate.

John looked at Walker, the grin on his face as wicked as theirs. "I hope you brought a can of that Metamucil with you, Old Man. You know you're supposed to take a dose after every meal. A man your age has to take care of his bowels."

Walker's grin faded instantly. Yona almost choked on his coffee, not daring to laugh, because even he was not immune to the women's preoccupation with the health of their men. John felt relieved to direct their attention away from himself. While they fussed over Walker, handing him a cup of water to mix his Metamucil in, John opened a carton of heavy whipping cream and added a generous portion to his steaming cup of Luzianne. If he really was hypoglycemic, a couple spoons full of sugar might be a good idea too.

His son stirred in the backseat of the Mustang where he finished up his night's sleep. John heard him, but the rest were too involved with Walker's digestive tract. "Faron, honey, I think Diamond is awake. Sounded like I heard him." Guess he owed it to Walker to call them off.

Faron left them to get Diamond. Kate took Wren's blanket and helped her into a pair of jeans and a T-shirt. "Wear these socks, sweetie. You're gonna be doing lots of walking today over some rough ground, and you don't want your feet to blister."

"How come she's walking so much today, Mama Kate?" John asked. "They got a fieldtrip at school?"

Kate didn't answer till after she tied Wren's high-topped Reeboks. "She won't be going to school today. She needs to go with you and Dad and Yona." Kate reached for a pair of jeans and unwrapped her own blanket from her ample breasts, then stood there, to all appearances wearing nothing but her son Charlie's Black Knights football jersey.

Kate looked damn good in that jersey. John couldn't help noticing she had a nice, shapely set of legs. In fact, it came as no surprise that she had such a cute daughter. Kate Copperhead was a good-looking old girl. Big as an Amazon, but firm and solid and with a fine shape to her. Not an ounce of fat anywhere. She'd sure be worth consideration if a man was looking.

Damn. He must be under the influence of some kind of herb to be thinking such things about his nearly fifty-year-old mother-in-law.

Faron came back to the fire with Diamond toddling behind, still wearing his Bugs Bunny pajamas. "Mama," she said, "spray some of that Deep Woods Cutters on her clothes. I don't want her coming home covered up with ticks and chiggers."

"I don't think there are many ticks around this time of the year, honey. And I know it's too early for chiggers." Kate took the can of insect repellent from her backpack. "But I'll spray some on her clothes just in case."

"Faron, why is Wren laying out of school and traipsing around the Smoky Mountains all day?" John asked, resigned to the reality that the decision had already been made.

"'Cause she had a dream, honey," Faron answered, like it was the most logical thing in the world. "Kanegwa'ti thinks she

91

needs to go along."

He looked at his daughter, not even trying to conceal his suspicion. "So, the great conjuror needs you, huh?" he asked. "And I reckon he told you this himself."

"Sure did, Daddy. I'll let Mama tell you about it. I've gotta put my stuff in Uncle Yona's Blazer." She slung her backpack across her shoulder, pulled an Atlanta Braves cap over braids still damp from her purification in Big Santetla, and, jumping from boulder to boulder, went upriver to the Blazer.

"She had a dream?" John asked. "Must have been a hell of a dream to convince you to let her do just what she's been angling for all along. Sometimes I worry that she has too damn much imagination."

Faron and Kate ignored him and got busy cleaning up the breakfast gear.

John watched his daughter duck through the underbrush and disappear. So innocent. He couldn't see any reason for the pang of apprehension that gripped his gut. She was safe with him. Every living soul here cared more about the safety and well-being of his two kids than anything else in the world. They wouldn't let her do anything that wasn't good for her. Could it be that he didn't want her to be there when they buried Kanegwa'ti's bones? He didn't like her thinking about death. She was too young for that.

The bones in the back of the Blazer didn't scare her. It made her mad that somebody desecrated the grave of one of her ancestors, but she believed the old stories about how the spirit walked over to the above world. The dead held no fear for his daughter.

A vague image from last night's dreams drifted across his mind, and for the first time, he understood what the Copperheads meant when they said they had a bad feeling. He remembered dreaming of a dead body. Not just dried-out old bones, but flesh and blood, lying cold and still on a flat rock atop a mountain. It felt like a premonition.

Seeing that would bother Wren a lot.

Tuesday Morning

On the Road

"Can you believe we've got a traffic jam on Stecoah Mountain?" Yona came to a dead stop. "This used to be the middle of nowhere."

"People working over in Bryson City, I guess," John said. "They have to leave home mighty early to get to work on time."

They moved in spurts, inching along for the next half mile until they came to the source of the hold-up, a white mini-bus with a blown-out tire that didn't quite make it off the road. A knot of people stood off to the side of the road, watching while the driver changed the tire. Walker read the logo on the side of the vehicle's front door: "Sacred Circle Medicine Way. Bullsh–."

It pleased John to see he wasn't the only one Faron trained not to cuss in front of Wren and Diamond. Even Walker knew better than to cross her when it came to the kids.

"I've seen that thing up on the Cheoah a good bit lately," John said. "I take it the Sacred Circle Medicine crap is not sanctioned by the tribe."

"Just another bunch of Indian wannabes," Walker said. "Some big, blonde honcho that claims he's a half-blood Cherokee and the descendant of shamans on both sides of his family. Brings a bunch of white people up here for what he calls 'shamanic training and initiation.' He's got them convinced there's a power place at the head of the river, and he can take them to it."

Yona laughed. "They came in over at Phillips Café last week. Funniest thing you ever saw. Every one of them dressed up like TV Indians with their medicine bags around their necks. One of them asked me if I knew any elders they could apprentice with."

"And what did you tell them?" Walker asked.

"Oh, that my grandpa was a genuine Native American elder who would train them all. Gave them your name and told them how to find your house. I figured you could get with them and dance around awhile and teach them how to make good medicine." Yona acted dead serious until Walker raised his walking stick, then he laughed.

Walker put down the walking stick and chuckled. The old man had a sense of humor. "Son, they're just trying to find some way to feel connected to Creator. Their own ways have let them down and they're searching. I hope they can find what they're looking for. I just wish they'd look somewhere other than up on Cheoah. That's getting too close to some places they don't need to be."

"I've seen the blonde guy at the station. He came in one day to ask directions to some of the hidden ceremonial grounds where you guys used to meet when it wasn't safe to do it out in the open." John remembered something else that hadn't seemed important at the time. "A young girl was with him. She looked Indian but I don't think she was Cherokee. Not Eastern Band anyway. At least I've never seen her around here. Buck talked to them."

"Yeah," Walker said. "Buck called me later and told me about that. Said they knew about how we had places where we used to hold ceremony back when it was against the law to practice our religion. The blonde man calls himself Eagle Feather."

It embarrassed John when white people tried to turn Indian. He gave a derisive snort. "Of course that's the name his blonde mama and daddy gave him at birth."

"No. They named him Carl. Carl Johnson," Walker said. "He used to be a Methodist preacher. Now he runs these shaman schools like they ran the old Methodist camp meetings. He has camps set up in Graham County, and one down in Mississippi near the Choctaws, and near the Catawbas in South Carolina."

"Buck Locust told you all that?" John asked. "How did he find out so much about Mr. Eagle Feather?"

"Not much gets by Buck Locust," Walker said. "And we like to keep an eye on these people that show up with their disciples. Most are fairly harmless, but some are not. We need to know who's who."

"And is the blonde Indian one of the harmless ones?" John asked.

"Don't know yet," Walker answered. "But he sure is making a heap of money off his followers. He seems to have a lot of control over them, even after they go home from the camps. Keeps them coming back for the next level of initiation."

"I don't guess we can be too critical of his pigeons," Yona said. "Look at how many of our people pay tithes to Christian churches or send money to television preachers. Like you say, Old Man, everybody's looking for something. It's just funny how so many have trouble finding it in their own ways."

"Count your blessings, boy," Walker chuckled.

"What seems funny to me," John leaned over the front seat, "is that you've got a perfectly happy Presbyterian white boy back here that you've done everything to but appoint head high muckety-muck in your traditional religion. Sounds to me like somebody might be speaking with a forked tongue around here. I've been smoked and smudged and sweated and purged and half drowned for the past ten years, and nobody complained about how I ought to be sticking to my own ways."

Walker had the decency to look uncomfortable for a few seconds. Yona just turned on the radio and asked John what station was most likely to play that reggae version of "Ring of Fire."

"Damned if I know," John said. "I'm way too purified to listen to that shit."

Wren stirred and adjusted the pillow she had scrunched under her head against the corner of the Blazer and settled back down to sleep. John could almost hear Faron saying, "Watch your mouth, Johnny." Yeah, she trained him well. He reached behind the seat to get Wren a blanket. The blanket caught on the tangled roots of a tree stump packed in beside the tarp that covered the duffle bag. He caught himself before he asked Yona why he had a tree stump with the roots still attached in his Blazer. Why bother? He wouldn't get an answer anyway.

After the traffic eased, they hurried through downtown Cherokee with its souvenir stores selling genuine Indian moccasins with their made-in-China labels and real Indian headdresses and plastic bows and arrows. It was too early in the season for the live Indian chiefs with their feathers and breechcloths, like they just rode in off the plains. Hollywood did such a good job teaching people how Indians looked that even some of their own people didn't remember; Cherokees wore turbans, tunics, and pants, while the Plains Indians were in those headdresses.

Walker must have read his thoughts again. Before John could comment on what he thought of the whole thing, he broke in, "Lot of people don't understand why we tolerate this, but having a major highway through reservation land was the best thing that could have happened to us. This crap brings in enough tourism money to finance a lot of good things. Long as we educate our kids about who they are, we can live with it. And our people make enough genuine historical stuff to make up for the junk."

Yona grinned. "Besides, they won't let us scalp 'em no other way anymore."

Right in the middle of the main tourist trap, Yona took a right turn, like he was going to the bingo hall, or doubling back toward Highway 19 and the brand new casino, then swung left and drove along the Oconoluftee River on Big Cove Road.

"Hey, Yona," John began, "is this a detour? Thunderhead is straight ahead off the Blue Ridge Parkway."

"We're going to visit some of the kinfolks in Big Cove," Yona said.

"Is it any of my business who it is and why we're going there?"

"I already asked, brother, and he won't tell me either," Yona said. "All he tells me is that he has to get some facts straight."

Walker shifted in his seat to look at both Yona and John. "Just a few things I need to understand better. Whoever robbed the conjuror's grave knew exactly what he was doing. He knew where to find the ark, and he must have known what it was and what it contained and why it was important."

"Wait a minute, Old Man," John said. "I thought the ark was part of the conjuror's grave goods. How did the grave-robber know where to find it?"

Walker had that look he got when he tried to decide how much he could tell somebody who wasn't a Cherokee. John was used to it but still annoyed him sometimes. When Walker made up his mind, he spoke slowly, like it went against his instincts to talk about such things. "The ark was in its own place. Everything got separated long before Kanegwa'ti died. He planned it that way. No one person knew where everything was. One man knew the hiding place of the Ulunsu'ti. Somebody else knew the location of the ark. Before he died, the conjuror appointed the man he trusted to bury him and his medicine bundle in the grave he chose. The Suye'ta has to find all three before he can wake the Ulunsu'ti. We know where the bones and the ark are. Let's hope nobody knows where the Ulunsu'ti is. David Wayanettah can tell us some things we need to know about that."

"Is that why we're hauling around that tree stump behind the seat?" John asked.

"Lightning-struck buckeye," Walker said. "Dave will make

something pretty out of that. The man's a hell of an artist. But we're going to see him because he knows more about our history than anybody I know. He can tell us how much of the story of Kanegwa'ti is true and how much is myth built up over the years. He's a purist about our mythology. He strips off the layers laid on to make them more palatable to outsiders and gets to the old way. I want to hear his version of this one. And besides, I'd like to know about some things his grandfather might have told him before he walked over to the other world."

John decided to save the rest of his questions for later. Walker already volunteered more answers than he expected. He sat back to enjoy the drive.

Big Cove Community disappointed the few tourists who discovered it. It wasn't what they expected—no tepees or villages, just ordinary homes set back in the trees or in the middle of grassy lawns by the roadside, a lot like where the white folks lived.

The houses thinned out considerably by the time they came to Lightning Creek Road. A few miles more and the Wayanettahs' house stood beyond a narrow, one-lane bridge over Lightning Creek. The bridge rattled and swayed when they drove across. David was waiting for them, standing barefoot, holding the front screen door ajar. His long, black hair hung loose and tousled, like he just got out of bed.

John roused Wren from her nap and helped her out of the car. Yona took the porch steps three at a time and caught David in a casual one-armed hug, slapping him on the shoulder. The two big men were about equal in size and still looked as much alike as they had since they were kids. If John hadn't known them all his life, he would take them for brothers.

"Damn, I miss you on the crew, Wolf," Yona said. "You get to be such a big-time artist you don't need a job anymore, then we don't see you for weeks at a time."

"The price of success, old Bear," David answered. "Just don't have the time to enjoy working like a mule on a logging crew anymore."

Their camaraderie was familiar and comforting.

Walker made a more dignified entrance and Dave stooped to clasp his extended forearm. "Good to see you, Young Wolf," Walker said, using the English translation of "Wayanettah." "Looks like you've been plenty busy."

The porch, as well as the living room and the dining room beyond, held wood and stone carvings and works in bronze. John admired a carving in the early stages of creation. Under David's skilled hands, a buffalo began to take shape from a block of white alabaster.

"Wow."

Wren wandered around the living room, curious as a kitten as she examined each piece. "Come look, Daddy," she called. "It's the Nunne'hi coming out of Council House Mound."

John bent over beside her to get a good look at the wood carving displayed on a corner table. A seven-sided lodge grew right out of the wood, its walls blending into the carved mountainside so well he found it hard to tell where the mountain ended and the council house began, or if perhaps they were one and the same. The lithe forms emerging from an unseen doorway dressed in the old way and carried decorated bows and beaded quivers full of arrows. It didn't look like they walked through the doorway so much as just materialized from the mountain itself. The effect made it appear they stepped from another dimension into our own.

"It looks exactly like the real place, Daddy," Wren said. "Except I've never seen them there before. They look just like I thought they would."

"So, that's how you imagine them too?" David asked. "My great-grandpa claimed he saw a Nunne'hi woman there one time. Said she was the most beautiful being he had ever seen."

"There's something familiar about this piece," John said.

"Well, John, you've been all up and down the Cheoah, haven't you?" David asked.

"Uh-huh. Nearly every mile of it."

"Then you've seen the Council House Mound," David said.

"We were almost there last night, Daddy," Wren said. "When we were going to Degal gun'yi."

Another one of the old myths intruded on the real world. He knew this one. It only went back around five hundred years and told of the mound and the council house in the center of a Cherokee town. The people who lived there heard the voices of Nunne'hi calling on the wind, warning of the coming strangers who brought death and destruction to the land, ending the old ways forever. The immortals offered a plan for the town to survive and preserve their knowledge of the sacred ways. They must agree to be sealed inside the mountain and become like the Nunne'hi, the invisible, immortal beings who lived there. They listened. At the appointed time, they waited inside the council house.

"A whirlwind came and took the whole town inside the mountain, where all of the people still live in another dimension. The only evidence it ever existed is the shape of the mound. It looks just like the old seven-sided council houses." He told the story to Wren, mostly to let her know that he knew it.

"And the people are still there inside the mound, Daddy," Wren said. "You can hear them if you are quiet and listen. When I'm old enough, Mama Kate is gonna take me there at night so I can go to sleep. Then they can teach me in my dreams. That's why they agreed to do what the Nunne'hi asked. To preserve the old ways so they could pass them down to their children's children. That's how Mama Kate and Mama know so much. They slept on the mound. So did Uncle Yona and Grandpa."

John wished someone could teach him how to keep up with his kid. He'd be glad to sleep on the mound for that kind of dream. He didn't say it out loud, though, just muttered, "That's good, sugar. You do that," and followed David to the kitchen where he found Walker pouring himself a cup of coffee. Wren stayed behind, examining each sculpture. Her awed comments made it clear that she saw in them a visual telling of the stories she memorized.

David opened the refrigerator and took out a Coke and handed it to John. "The kid knows her stuff. Kate must be teaching her."

"A lot more than I can keep up with, Dave." John sipped on the Coke while he leaned against the door frame. "I don't know about her sleeping on Council House Mound, though. Sometimes Kate goes too far. It'd be a big disappointment to Wren to go to all that trouble and not have any of those dreams she's counting on."

"And what if she did have them? Who would be disappointed then?"

Another barb. "Hey, I don't mind her getting into her culture. But I guess it does bother me sometimes when I don't have a clue what she's talking about."

David said, "You know that town you told her about, where the mound is now? It used to be what your folks would call a 'medicine village.' It was a place of knowledge and healing, where holy people lived and taught. That's why the Nunne'hi chose it to be sealed off and protected. All the knowledge the elders held then is still there with them. That's what the dreams are about, passing down the wisdom. And it's one of the few places around here where the Nunne'hi are still seen."

"You've done it, haven't you, Dave? And did you dream?"

David picked up the coffee pot, got a cup from the cabinet, and strolled over to the table. "Yep," he said.

Yona took a seat at the table, admiring the way David made it from a single round slice cut from the trunk of an old oak that fell victim to the latest road-widening project on Highway 441. John remembered that tree. Must have been at least three hundred years old. David made good use of it.

John tried not to be impatient, but listening while they talked about the same old things got on his nerves. Did they forget the pile of human bones outside in the Blazer? David went on about tribal politics and building projects at the high school. Walker chatted about family and mutual friends on the Snowbird. Apparently several guys Yona's age got engaged, or married and had babies on the way.

Yona squirmed and changed the subject, tossing in a few anecdotes about guys who worked for the logging company. He sat bent over his coffee cup like he had something on his mind.

John understood why he didn't like it when talk turned to marriage and grandbabies. Yona would be married to David's sister, Meredith, if she hadn't decided to get a medical degree and complete her residency and internship before she settled down on the Qualla Boundary. Yona respected her decision and bragged about her all the time, but that didn't stop him from missing her. And it certainly didn't stop Walker from complaining about his delayed grandbabies.

When Walker got up to put the coffee pot back on the stove, Yona cleared his throat nervously. "Dave, what do you hear from Meredith? She said anything about when she's gonna be home?"

Sounded like they had another one of their fights. Nothing new about that. They went at each other like cats and dogs since they were kids.

"That's funny, Bear," David said. "She asked about you in her last text. In fact, she asks about you nearly every time I hear from her. She said to tell you hello, and ask you if you'd like to drive down to Georgia to see her. Said you know how to get to Atlanta just as well as she knows how to get here."

John felt sorry for his brother-in-law. Meredith wouldn't be moving back for at least two years, and Yona had a logging business to run now that Kate turned most of the management duties over to him. He couldn't go to Meredith and she wasn't coming home until she could set up her practice. Thank God Faron's business degree from Western Carolina satisfied her. John didn't think he could stand waiting as long as Yona and Meredith did.Yona slumped in his seat and looked like the loneliest man alive. "Grandpa, you wanna tell David why we're here so we can get on our way? We've got a lot to do today."

"Finally," John said. "I thought we might sit around chitchatting and drinking coffee until we turned into women. I took a day off work for this?"

The old man ignored him and took a long, slow sip from his cup. When he spoke, he said nothing about the bones. "David, I want you to tell me a story. The old version."

"That's the only version I tell," David said. "You won't get the sanitized stuff from me. I think we need to leave in the sex and humor, tell it the way our elders did. And speaking of our elders, Grandfather, I figure you know a lot more about our legends than I do. Between you and Grady Smoker, you must know everything that's happened in these hills since First Man and First Woman lived in the mother town."

"Never hurts to get a second opinion, son," Walker said. "I want you to tell me everything you know about Kanegwa'ti, and when and why and how he hid the Ulunsu'ti and the tools for using it. I need to know who's around today that might know about this stuff."

John felt the tension deepen in the room. Nobody said a word, like they were trying to wait each other out. David crossed his arms over his chest and stared out the window.

"You ask for a lot, Grandfather. You wanna tell me why you need to know things that, according to tradition, only one man at a time ever knows?"

"If you're not one of those men, you don't have to worry about telling any secrets," Walker said. "Just tell me the story."

Wren stood in the doorway, intent on every word, and John

couldn't do a thing about it. If only he had the balls to stand up to Faron and Kate, his little girl would be safe in her classroom at Robbinsville Elementary where she belonged, not listening to grown men talking about monsters.

David got up and went toward the living room. He hesitated at the door, still trying to make up his mind, then approached a locked cupboard built into the wall. Fishing for a key in his wallet, he unlocked it and swung the doors open. From their vantage point at the table, they could see a collection of sculpted figures.

Why would David hide them behind locked doors, rather than display them behind glass or on tables and open shelves like his other works? He had reason to be proud. Some of his work went to the Smithsonian, and some pieces sold for more than a forest ranger or a logger made in a whole year. The works in the cupboard looked more intricate than any of them, and more primal. They exuded energy, a force that could be felt, like needle-fine sleet against naked flesh. David took out a soapstone carving and carried it to the table.

"It's all here," he said.

Walker took the piece from David, placed it on the table, and scanned it inch by inch. John became so engrossed in the sculpture that he didn't think of Wren until he heard her awed whisper.

"Look at his hand, Grandpa Walker. He's holding it."

He couldn't tell if the figure was a man or a snake, or maybe a combination of both. John shivered when he looked into the white-fanged mouth. There was something familiar about it. In his right hand, the man-snake held a knife carved from an antler. At his feet, a rabbit's carcass, hardly more than a crumpled mass of fur, receded into the earth, all essence of life drained away. His left hand held an oval object that filled it the way a basketball would have filled John's hand. Life stirred in the object. John could see it as clearly as he could see the fear in the face of the man-snake. Life, and unbelievable power. John didn't realize he reached out to touch it until Walker stopped him.

He heard David say, "That's the only way it can ever be woken up. In the hand of the conjuror. He laid that on it before he hid it."

David and Walker sat looking at the figure, each waiting for the other to speak and neither wanting to say too much. Both of them showed signs of frustration, like something needed to be said and neither of them wanted to be the one to say it. John lacked the patience to sit around and watch the tension crackle between them. He and his little girl were involved in this too, and he wanted some answers. Maybe he could start by getting more information about the snake.

"As I understand it, the conjuror was what you call a 'skin changer.' He was a man who could turn into a snake. Right?"

David nodded.

"From what I remember," John continued, "Cherokee skin changers are usually the bad guys. Water Moccasin seems to be a hero. Why is that?"

David took a long time to consider his response. He glanced at Walker like he expected him to object. Walker didn't say a word.

"Well, for one thing, the conjuror wasn't a Cherokee. The Suye'ta never is. The chosen one is an outsider, same as the cottonmouth moccasin is an outsider around here. He is venomous, unlike our local water moccasins. The first outsider in the story was the Shawnee who risked his life and killed Uktena in the first place. The part of the story that gets left out these days is that the Ulunsu'ti was a bride price. The Shawnee loved a Cherokee woman so much that he put the woman and her people ahead of his own safety. She served as the bond that made him the Suye'ta."

John never heard that part of the story before, and Walker didn't seem to want him to hear it now.

"I think we know enough about the Suye'ta already," the old man said.

John disagreed. Getting actual answers to his questions was heady business, so he overruled Walked and asked another one. "Why is it that the Ulunsu'ti has to be brought to Degal gun'yi to be awakened?"

"It doesn't," David said. "In fact, that's the worst place for it to be. It has to be brought to the Council House Mound. It's safer there."

"Safer?" John asked.

David gave him a cold, humorless smile. "Yeah, safer, because that's a place of the Nunne'hi. The Suye'ta has a slight chance of surviving the first few minutes there if they help him."

Out of the corner of his eye, John saw Walker lift his left eyebrow in that signal he recently became aware of. The rest of the family responded instantly to his signal and shut the hell up. Apparently, David knew the signal too, because he stopped talking and became a dutiful host, warming up coffee cups and offering some bagels from a plastic Winn Dixie bakery bag. When only Yona refused, he sliced three in half and slid them into the toaster oven on the countertop, then opened a pack of cream cheese and served it on its own foil wrapper.

Wren stood on a chair in the pantry and took out a jar of homemade blackberry jam and brought it to the table. "I bet Meredith made this jam from the blackberries she picked with me and Mama last summer," she said.

Yona reached for the jar and smeared some on one of Walker's bagel halves he confiscated. "Your sister makes some good jam," he said to David, and his mood visibly lightened.

When they finished the last crumb, John helped carry the cups to the sink and clear away jars and wrappers and bottles. Wren returned to the living room. He watched as she stood in front of the open cupboard doors, gazing reverently at the sculpted figures.

David came to his side and nodded at Wren. "She understands what they are. She's okay. Now, let's see if we can get Walker to tell us why he's here."

Walker looked ready to talk. He headed toward the door. "Come out to the car, son. I want to show you something."

The three men followed him to the Blazer and stood aside while Yona lifted open the back. First, he took out the stump and handed it to David. "Lightning-struck buckeye."

"Grandpa found it down on Snowbird," Yona explained. "We thought you might like to have it for your artwork."

They watched while David examined it, wondering how he could see things in stone, wood, and even an old tree stump, that nobody else could.

David held the stump up, turning it so he could get a closer look at all its surfaces. "Looks like a beautiful lady in there to me. I think the lightning just parted her hair. I'd say she's one of the Nunne'hi. We'll see if Wren thinks so when I finish bringing her out of the wood." He walked to the porch and put the stump down and came back to the Blazer. "I don't think you guys drove all the way from the Snowbird on a workday to haul a tree stump to me. Now, you want to tell me what's going on?"

A piece of tarp covered the two gym bags. Yona folded the tarp out of the way and handed one of the gym bags to Walker. Walker opened it and gently removed some of the linen-wrapped objects and laid them on the carpeted floor of the Blazer. He unwrapped the first one, an ancient rattle, and gave it to David so carefully it didn't make a sound. David took it and ran his finger along the old terrapin shell. It gave off a soft rustle as he turned it, examining every inch of its surface.

"It's his, alright," David said. He pointed out the carving of the open-mouthed snake that coiled around the handle. John noticed the snakes then. Walker opened another bundle and lifted out a pipe and held it up for them to see. It was fashioned in the form of a snake, its open mouth serving as the bowl.

John watched as Walker removed the strips of sheet that wrapped the other relics and displayed them. He took advantage of the opportunity to do a close inspection.

A serpent image marked every item. The unfaded colors on a soapstone medicine bowl looked fresh enough to be mistaken for a recently formed replica from the local museum. John leaned into the Blazer to get a better look at it. A painted snake encircled the bowl, coiling around it from the base to the lip. Its vivid cottony-white mouth opened wide. Chills crept up John's legs. He didn't want to see anymore, but Walker had more to show them.

He took out a bundle wrapped in a nondescript old, blue jacket and sat it down beside the rest. He didn't release it. His hand remained possessively attached to it. They waited for him to untie the sleeves of the jacket and show them the last of his collection, but he just stood there. He made a move toward the sleeves, then pulled them tighter. The struggle to make up his mind showed in his face.

David asked, "Is it the ark, Grandfather?"

Walker nodded.

"Have you looked inside it?"

Walker picked up the bundle and clutched it to his chest.

David asked again, "Have you looked at it?"

The old man stammered, "N-no. I figured I needed another—another elder around. But who? I can't find Grady Smoker. He's not answering his phone and nobody's seen him. I had to talk to Kate about it. Some folks won't approve of bringing her into this, but I had to. She didn't feel right about me going to Grady."

"You told Kate?" David's tone bordered on an accusation.

Walker took out his handkerchief and wiped his face. The morning chill lingered but sweat beaded on his forehead. They waited, giving him time.

"I had to, Dave." With a sudden motion, Walker put the

bundle back into the Blazer. He lowered his voice. "Dave, I've got a bad feeling. A real bad feeling something's going on that's serious trouble."

"It must be bad, for you to bring an outsider into this."

Unbelievable. Did David Wayanettah actually scold the old man? And since when was Kate an outsider? Or was Dave referring to him?

Walker said, "This is something we've never had to deal with before. David, I wish your grandpa hadn't walked over. If Driver was still alive, he would be the one to handle this, but he's not, and I have to do what I think is right. I'm here because Kate felt like I had to come to you."

David acknowledged the wisdom of listening to Kate's feelings and reached into the Blazer to lift a fold of the jacket away from the ark, just enough to reveal a corner. He looked at it thoughtfully, then covered it up and said, "Pack it all up good. This is not the place. Be ready to go when I get back." He turned and bounded up the steps and into his house.

Walker slumped against the Blazer, his relief at turning the decisions over to David visible in the way his shoulders relaxed.

John stepped back out of the way and let Yona repack the duffle bag. This was not his problem and he didn't want anything else to do with it. The very air crackled with tension and uncertainty. Even Walker, who knew more about this shit than anybody in the tribe, didn't understand what was going on or what to do about it. John didn't plan to hang around, and he certainly didn't want Wren involved in some kind of creepy Indian mysticism that went beyond anything his snow-white culture had prepared him to deal with. Hell, his daughter was half-white. This looked more and more like a problem for the full-bloods to handle.

He worked up the nerve to call Faron and insist she come get him and Wren to take them home, when David reappeared in the doorway. He wore heavy hiking boots and a backpack hung across his right shoulder.

Wren tagged along behind him, looking like she knew what David had in mind and planned to go with him. John heard her ask, "So, where are we going now, David?"

John gave up on calling Faron. It wouldn't make any difference. Faron would side with Wren and he would be overruled. For all he knew, they had talked on the phone and agreed on the decision. Whether he liked it or not, he had to decide either to go on a hike with the rest or to let Wren go alone. He chose the hike. Faron would kill him if he let Wren out of his sight.

David lifted Wren into the backseat of the Blazer before he answered her question. "Honey, we're going to a place I never took anybody before. We're going to a cave up on the brow of Wolf Mountain."

Walker climbed into the front seat beside Yona. John and David got in the back with Wren between them. The Blazer felt crowded.

David directed Yona to drive up the narrow dirt road that curved along the backside of Lightning Creek and wound its way toward the foot of Wolf Mountain.

John hugged Wren to him and wished they were in Faron's Mustang going back to the Snowbird. Wolf Mountain rose ahead, its peak covered with clouds. The brow was a hell of a climb for a little girl. He felt Wren tremble as she cuddled against him.

Tuesday

Lightning Creek

They rode in silence past three small houses. David's aunts lived in the first two, a cousin in the third. A fourth house about a mile further down the road exuded an air of emptiness that reached all the way to the road. Two months ago he came there with Walker to say goodbye to David's grandfather, Driver Wayanettah. Driver died the next day. Now, an owl perched on the peak of the roof, standing guard.

David turned his head away as they passed the lifeless house. "Yeah, I wish Grandpa Driver was still here too. And it's not just because I miss him. I need him for several reasons. You know what I mean?"

Walker nodded. "Yeah, I think I do, son. Me and old Driver danced to the same drum."

"He told me," David said.

The exchange that passed between them resonated with meaning that went beyond John's understanding. Walker and David communicated something that gave a measure of comfort to both of them.

Walker glanced across at David and almost smiled. "I thought Driver might have had a talk with you," he said.

Whatever Walker needed to know, he got his answer. It showed in the way he relaxed against the seat, some of the tension gone from his body. Nothing else was said but Walker looked more peaceful. That made John feel easier. Wren relaxed against him. She knew too.

The road ended about five miles beyond Driver's deserted house. Yona downshifted and forced the Blazer as far as it would go up the rough path. The tires struggled to make it a few more feet up the slope, leaving the smell of burnt rubber on the morning air. When the underbrush got so thick the Blazer couldn't go any farther, Yona turned off the engine.

"Hope everybody's wearing good walking shoes," David said. "We've still got a ways to go, and it's mostly uphill."

Wren was solemn as she climbed down from the vehicle. She held Walker's walking stick until he joined her. "Are you up to this, Grandpa?" she asked.

Walker tweaked the bill of her cap. "Don't worry about me, sugar. I reckon you can tote me if I can't make it."

She giggled and said he was much too heavy. She wouldn't laugh if she was scared.

David went to the back of the Blazer and took out the duffle bag and packed the gym bags in it. When he started to put the ark in with the gym bags, Walker objected.

David said, "We don't have to worry about all these things being together. As long as the Ulunsu'ti isn't here too, we're okay. And we sure can't leave it here in the Blazer unattended."

David rearranged the contents until they fit just right, then tightened the cord and slung the bag across his shoulder. He hoisted his backpack and set his sights on a spot higher up the mountain. The backpack looked heavy. John briefly considered offering to carry it, but changed his mind. He might have to go along on this hike, but he'd be damned if he would lug around baggage. Why should he make it any harder on himself than it already was? Besides, David didn't look like he needed help.

"Where to now, Young Wolf?" Yona asked. He didn't offer to carry anything either.

"To a hiding place," David said. "A good one. My great-great-grandparents and all the family hid out there during the time of the removal. That's why their descendants are Eastern Band now and not living out in Oklahoma."

He looked around at the mountains rising to meet the smoke-like mist that veiled their peaks and gave them their name. "We're the lucky ones. This is where the spirit of our people lives. Like my grandfather, I'll do whatever I have to do to keep it here."

"Your grandpa would be proud, David," Walker said. "You're doing the right thing, just like Driver would have wanted."

"Nothing else I can do, Grandfather." David's jaw had a determined look. "We need to be sure at least one of Kanagwa'ti's hiding places is still holding up. The grave goods, the bones, and the ark have already been found. The only thing missing is what my family looks after, and Ulunsu'ti himself."

Walker stopped short. His knuckles whitened around the walking stick. "You don't have the Ulunsu'ti? I—we—always thought— What else? Dave, what else is there?"

John felt the chill of apprehension that began back in David's yard creep higher up his spine. What the hell was wrong with Walker? He hoped the old man wasn't as freaked as he looked.

He glanced at Yona and Wren and saw they noticed it too, and felt just as uncomfortable with Walker's unease as he was. Walker should be the one with all the answers. As the elder, they expected it of him. John found himself wishing Kate had come with them.

"We've got some walking to do, Grandfather," David said, picking up the pace. "We'll talk later." He took long, easy strides up the incline. Yona stayed close behind him. John and Walker hung back with Wren. When they lagged behind, David slowed to let them catch up.

John hadn't noticed when Wren slipped her hand in his, but now she gripped it like she needed to hold onto her daddy. They brought up the rear. Wren kept her eyes on David, careful not to let him get so far ahead that she lost sight of him. She didn't say anything, but she seemed to feel more secure with John than with Walker. John felt a perverse sense of satisfaction. He walked

114

taller, his little girl's hand in his.

Good thing they got an early start because they had a fair distance to cover and no trail that he could see. A few times, John wondered how David found the way at all. Once, when they stopped to let Walker lean on his walking stick and rest, John asked, "Hey, man, do you know where you're going? Looks to me like we're just wandering in the woods without a purpose."

David fixed his eyes on a place high up on Wolf Mountain where Lightning Creek began as a pond, bubbling up and spilling over the falls. The sun reflected off them in the distance. "Yeah, John. I've been there a few times. I just don't ever go the same way twice. It was Kanagwa'ti's idea, not to wear a trail that could be followed." He wiped his brow with his sleeve and walked through some scrub laurel. His boots cleared an easier path for them to follow.

Wren left John's side and walked beside Walker, her hand now tucked in his, John guessed more for Walker's comfort than Wren's. He saw her stumble, too tired to keep up any longer. Before he could pick her up, Yona stooped and swept her up to his shoulders.

Wren laughed. "I can see clear over the mountain from here. I hope I grow up to be as tall as you, Uncle Yona."

"Well, your grandma Kate nearly did, honey," Yona laughed back. "But I don't think you're gonna take after her."

"I wish she had come with us."

Nobody else expressed Wren's wish aloud, but the way they all fell quiet spoke her sentiments louder than words.

With the sun high in the sky and another hour of hiking ahead, David brought them to a halt beside a clear mountain stream. They flopped down on their bellies and drank directly from the clean, cold water, sipping as it flowed across their faces.

David pulled brown paper bags out of his backpack and spread them out on a flat rock. Wren helped him unpack a loaf of sourdough bread. He sliced it with a hunting knife and stacked the slices. "Not much time to pack a lunch, but I did the best I could," he said.

Wren opened a paper bag and took out two jars. She couldn't have been more pleased. Crunchy peanut butter and strawberry jelly on sourdough bread, her favorite sandwich.

It would have felt good to rest by the creek after their picnic, but David only gave them time for another long drink of cold, clear creek water before he had them on their feet again for the steepest part of the climb.

They left the tree line behind and trudged up a rocky incline sparsely populated with scrawny saplings and brush.

The mountain changed as they climbed higher. Granite protruded through gravely soil where scrub laurel grew in the few pockets of earth in the granite. An occasional pine found purchase and grew tall and gaunt. Giant boulders littered the landscape.

David stopped again. "Wait here. I need to check on something before we go any further." He didn't give them time to ask why, just took off around a big boulder and disappeared from sight before they could ask him where he was going. They sat down on the sun-warmed rocks to wait.

Where could he go, halfway up a mountain with nothing but rocks and scrub as far as they could see? Boulders big as a bus lay scattered about, looking like the sky opened up and dropped them from the above world. An unnatural silence hung over the terrain. Not the kind of peaceful quiet you usually felt in the Smokies punctuated with the sounds of life. No birds or crickets called. No rustling of the many critters that make so much noise you learn to tune them out. John mentioned it to Walker. The old man nodded and grunted.

Wren said, "Daddy, do you think this is a place where the Nunne'hi live? It looks and sounds and feels like it could be."

The familiar chill crept between John's shoulder blades. "I wouldn't know, honey." What else could he say? He thought of the Nunne'hi in the same way he thought of fairies, just a story you tell your kids. But this place had a weird feel about it. From the look on Walker's face, he felt it too. Was that where David went? If the Nunne'hi did live here, maybe he needed to get their approval before bringing visitors into their territory.

Wren got up to look around. If there were any supernaturals in the area, she could find them, invisible or not. John didn't want her to wander off alone, but as long as he could keep an eye on her, it wouldn't hurt to let her explore a bit. "Watch out for snakes, sugar," he called. "And stay where I can see you."

"I don't see any snakes, Daddy," she shouted from behind a heap of boulders. "But there sure are lots of ants. Their trail goes down behind these rocks."

Well, an ant trail couldn't hurt her. John sat back down beside Walker. With Wren out of hearing range, he took the opportunity to ask some questions he kept to himself while his daughter could hear. "Just where is David going, Grandpa? And what in the world does he need to check on way up here in the middle of nowhere? Does he think there really are Nunne'hi around here?"

Walker fiddled with the head of his walking stick. "Could be. I know bringing us here wasn't an easy thing for Dave to do. This might be as far as we go. At least I hope so." He looked scared.

His fear settled over John. He jumped like a rabbit when the lone pine dropped a dried-up pinecone on the rocks. "Damn, Old Man. You've got me freaked out, sitting there looking like we're waiting for the hangman."

Walker didn't answer. He kept looking in the direction where David disappeared around a pile of boulders.

"What if David comes back and takes us wherever he is now? Would that be so bad?" John asked.

"Very bad," Walker said. "It would mean there's no reason to keep Kanagwa'ti's hiding place a secret any more. That there's nothing left to hide."

Yona stood up and stretched his legs. "I'm gonna go see about Wren. Don't want her following her ant trail too far."

At that moment, her scream cut through the silence.

Tuesday Morning

Degal Gun'yi

Amy Locust murmured a sleepy "goodbye honey" when Buck told her he had to leave early, then promptly snuggled down to finish her night's sleep. She didn't need to be awake for at least an hour. He left a note on the fridge explaining why he had to leave before daylight: "Gone to check on a dieback Eli saw on the Cheoah before I go to the station. Be home at six."

He couldn't tell anyone, not even Amy the real reason he hurried off, or why he paced the floor most of the night, worried about what he might find on the backside of the mound at Degal gun'yi. The dieback Eli Smoker saw from the tower lay in the direction of the mound, and he intended to check it out, but he had a far more urgent reason for rushing off to that isolated corner of tribal land.

The fear set in when Walker Copperhead called about the duffle bag. Buck fought off the compulsion to go as fast as he could to a mound beyond the old burial ground. No one should know about the things in that duffle bag, or the places their protectors kept secret through the generations. His gut twisted into a tight knot when he considered the possibility the grave-robbers had found the place the Locust family guarded. As the hereditary guardian of the Cherokee Ark of the Covenant, the full responsibility for protecting it rested in his hands. Walker wouldn't tell him what the duffle bag contained, but he had to be sure the tunnel where the ark belonged remained intact.

He eased into the well-camouflaged turnoff as the first hint of daylight filtered through the leafy canopy. The road went a few miles into the forest but its condition made for a slow, rough ride.

The crushed weeds in the ruts and tire tracks in the damp earth didn't surprise him. John's Dodge Ram would have left these marks when he came to check on the dieback last night. But when he reached the rise at the end of the road, a second set of tracks brought him up short. Buck parked his truck and got out to take a look. John's truck didn't leave this trail. It would have climbed the incline easily and not left torn-up earth as evidence of spinning wheels. The second set of tracks were narrow, made by small tires, like on a compact car.

He bent over to examine them more closely. The tires that left these marks were so bald they barely had enough tread to leave an imprint.

Of all the people he knew who drove compact cars, only one came to mind who would know about this place. That would explain why Grady Smoker wasn't at his trailer last night. But what would he be doing in these woods?

His unease refused to be suppressed any longer. Buck Locust was very, very worried. He came to these woods alone so many times he could find his way in the dark, but this time something unfriendly permeated the shadows. He wished John was with him, but according to Walker, John had more important things to do than his job. It must be important for him to pull rank the way he did, insisting John needed time off to tend to something with him. If it had something to do with the duffle bag, Walker must have told him about it. John had no right knowing Snake Dancer business.

He slung his backpack over his shoulder. The shovel and hatchet made for an awkward burden, but he wanted to be ready for anything.

The silence of the forest felt unnatural. He listened for the flutter of night birds returning to roost, or the morning twitter of those ready to wake. Not a sound. The hint of daylight in the sky didn't touch the dark under the trees. The woodland lacked the welcoming feel he had come to expect. He clicked on his mag light and shined its beam ahead, braced for its reflection off multiple sets of eyes. Not even a raccoon crossed his path. He trudged ahead toward the mound. The trail he traveled at least once a month since Grandpa Del first brought him to the mound might as well be a strange land.

Why did Walker need John? The knot in Buck's gut twisted tighter. Fragments of conversations about Suye'ta and outsiders flashed through his mind.

The old burial ground they called Degal gun'yi, where the Ani'Kuta'Ni were buried, lay ahead. It always gave him the creeps, but never as much as this morning. He swung wide, keeping his distance as he passed it and continued on to the smaller mound beyond it. Few people knew of its existence, and the Locusts did their best to keep it that way. Until his grandfather explained what the mound concealed, he thought it an ordinary hill covered with pine trees and scrub brush.

The mound appeared intact as Buck approached, no different from the way it looked when Del Locust brought him here the first time. He circled the mound to reach the side his grandfather showed him that day when he pointed out the stone that blocked the entrance to the hidden tunnel. He didn't believe it when Del told him the great conjuror directed the first Snake Dancers to prepare the tunnel and shore it up with stout timbers, then entrusted the Locust men to guard it, but he did as his grandfather ordered and kept the secret.

Four years later, when he turned eighteen, he discovered his family guarded the Cherokee ark in that tunnel. When he learned the job would fall on his shoulders when Del Locust walked over, he didn't know whether to be proud or terrified.

Buck felt honored that Del trusted him enough to bring him into the circle at a younger age than was usual for a guardian. It made his resolve even stronger never to let the ancestors or the Snake Dancers down. He rounded the base of the mound, dreading what he might find on the other side. He hurried past the last stand of pines and stood at the foot of the mound, near the spot where Del Locust explained the role of a guardian and pointed out the flat slab of granite that covered the mouth of the tunnel.

Raw earth littered the hillside. The granite slab left a scar where it tumbled down to rest among moss and debris at the foot of the mound. A gaping hole remained.

He hung onto the faint hope that his ancestors' ingenuity saved the ark. They took precautions to secure the treasure they guarded, even if the tunnel itself fell into the wrong hands.

He sank down on the big stone with his head between his hands to wait for his trembling to subside. Del said the tunnel ended in a false wall sealed with earth and stone to give it the appearance of a dead end. They left a collection of grave goods and the bones of a dead relative to explain the existence of the tunnel, in case an intruder made it that far. No one else alive knew about it. But then, he thought only he knew about the tunnel.

The extra precautions his elders took seemed unnecessary when Del described them. With the tunnel well hidden and carefully guarded, they had no reason for concern. The tribe owned the land and the Snake Dancers maintained enough power in the council to make sure it, and other sites, remained undisturbed. He said a desperate prayer that the false wall and the burial satisfied the grave-robbers.

He examined the ground at the foot of the mound for clues to the identity of the interloper. Among the dried pine needles, a flash of red caught his eye. He picked up a sticky triangle of red wax. A quick sniff confirmed it to be the wax rind from a wedge of cheese. It didn't tell him who rolled the stone away, just that he took time for a picnic. It wasn't much, but it gave him something to go on. He looked at it for a moment, then slipped it into his jacket pocket with his cell phone.

A layer of leaves and pine needles covered the rocky soil, a poor surface for footprints. The only thing that looked out of place, other than the cheese rind, was a stout maple sapling, its bark skinned and scarred—the lever used to pry the stone away from the tunnel.

Buck took the shovel and pickaxe from his pack, laid his jacket on the stone, and climbed up to the gaping hole. He plunged inside, praying with every step to find the false wall intact.

His ancestors didn't consider comfort when they formed the tunnel. No more than four feet high, it forced him to inch forward in an awkward crouch that produced cramps in both his thighs. The mag light revealed a carved effigy untouched in a niche on the wall, just the sort of thing grave-robbers and pothunters looked for. On the floor, a collection of pots remained intact and undisturbed. The bones, blackened and crumbling, lay perfectly composed among a wealth of pots and artifacts.

Fresh marks on the ancient timbers that shored up the excavation told a story of recent disturbance. Someone knew to look for something more important than pots and bones. Farther on, a pile of rocks and dirt littered the floor. Over that, high on the side, a jagged opening lined with mortared stone ran behind a massive log. He shined the light inside.

Empty.

Generations of his family kept this place secure, and on his watch it ended. His mind refused to accept that possibility. The ark had to be here. Somewhere behind the logs or beyond the niche they concealed, protected by yet another of the conjuror's clever deceptions, he would find it.

He swung the pickaxe as hard as he could in the cramped quarters, smashing through rotting timbers and mortar. His attack revealed nothing but the packed earth behind them. Splintered logs and broken mortar littered the floor.

He dropped the pickaxe and leaned against the wall. The bones of his ancestor crunched under his feet.

He couldn't give up. As long as he was alive, he remained the guardian. He bore the responsibility for the ark. He had to find the thief and retrieve it. He willed his mind to clear and took deep breaths of stale air to settle his nerves.

He slumped to the ground amid the bones, his head resting on his knees. In the silence of the tunnel, he could think without distractions. He considered the tire marks on the trail. The wax cheese rind. He thought of discussions among the Dancers about the troubles of his people. Of the fear that the Nunne'hi were leaving and the need to do something before they were gone. He agreed, for he believed the legends of their coexistence with his people. When the Nunne'hi were gone, the Cherokee would follow.

Absorbed in contemplation, he took no notice of the first deep rumble far back in the mound. It began when he used the pickaxe on timbers already weakened by centuries of erosion and decay. They creaked and groaned until the noise broke through his distraction. Overhead beams shattered, releasing an avalanche of packed earth and rocks.

On hands and knees, Buck scrambled toward the tunnel's mouth. With a roar like a freight train, the roof collapsed behind him, filling the tunnel at his heels and sending plumes of dust and rubble toward the sunlight. He crawled in a desperate attempt to stay ahead of it. One end of a falling timber thudded across his back and knocked him flat. He kept his eyes on the light ahead and scuttled on his elbows. A few more feet to go. A sharp crack as dried ancient wood shattered above him. The heavy beam sagged, then fell across his back. Pain made it hard to cling to consciousness. He reached for the light that danced in the dust. The heavy weight across his body held him fast.

He struggled with all his might to pull himself forward just a few more feet. An intensified rumble rewarded his effort. A second beam cracked and fell, striking a glancing blow on the side of his head. Blood oozed warm down his face and neck. For a moment more, he struggled, then faded into darkness.

How long did he lie there before pain roused him? The throbbing ache in his head sparked an instant awareness of his predicament. The weight of the beam across his back pinned him to the ground. He flexed the muscles in his legs and wiggled his feet. The cramp that shot through his calf hurt like hell, but at least it signaled an intact spine. He tested his body and found he could turn his head and move his upper body.

He spit out dirt, wiped grit from his eyes, and tried to drag himself free of the beam. With his teeth clenched against the pain, he twisted toward the light at the tunnel mouth. Only a few feet to go and he would be out in the sunlight.

He did a push-up that lifted his head and chest off the ground, shoving his body up against the timber. A groan echoed above him and deep in the hillside. Panic gave him strength to push harder. The beam shifted.

He couldn't see what happened above him, but he didn't have to. He heard enough to know the beam on his back somehow connected with the last intact supporting structure of the tunnel. He weighed his choices. He could try again to get free and make a dash for the opening, or he could lie still and wait to die. The opening tantalized him with its nearness.

Focusing all his strength on the task at hand, he braced his feet against the ground and stiffened his arms under his chest. If he had to drag the whole hillside with him, he would, but he intended to make it out alive. With every ounce of strength he possessed, he lurched toward the light. He moved less than a foot when the beam above him sagged and released a shower of rocks and dirt. The rumble resumed, resonating through the hill and releasing a cascade of rubble. Buck cradled his face in his arms and lay still while the wreckage of the tunnel supports thundered down around him.

When the cave-in stopped, he lay in the dark, afraid to move. The beam across his back weighed heavier, pinning him firmly into place. Very carefully, he raked debris from the area around his face.

He could still breathe, but for how long? He tried to judge the space around him with an outstretched arm. He guessed there might be about two feet that wasn't full of dirt. That would give him possibly two hours of air, then he was done for. If he was going to live, he had to get out soon.

In the pitch darkness, Buck felt the weight of the mound crushing down. He shifted slightly. Even that small movement brought the supporting beam down by an inch or so, decreasing the air space.

Before he could control his panic, he yelled at the top of his lungs, calling for John or Eli, even the great conjuror himself, to come help. The mouthfuls of dust he inhaled convinced him of the futility of his shouts. It only used up his meager ration of oxygen, a senseless waste since there was nobody within miles to hear him.

He dismissed the fleeting thought that a quick death in the initial cave-in would have been better than what he looked forward to, trapped, alone in the dark, waiting for suffocation or thirst to kill him.

Panic almost got the best of him. It took every ounce of willpower he had to calm down and think. As long as life remained in his body, he was still the protector of the ark. He didn't have the right to die until he exhausted every means to live up to that obligation.

If Walker and John had the ark, Walker would know what to do. And John and Eli knew he planned to check on the dieback. They'd come looking for him when he didn't come home on time. They would find his truck and follow his trail. If he could stay alive until they got close enough to hear him yell, he might survive. He lay still, trying to make the air last as long as possible.

He counted minutes in his head. It helped settle his nerves.

He was still breathing long after he'd expected to run out of air. If anything, the air quality got better. The dust settled, and it didn't seem quite as dark. A pinpoint of light filtered through the rocks. Not enough to see by, but it gave him hope. If light could get in, so could air. This increased his chances of staying alive until John and Eli came looking for him—if he didn't die of thirst first.

He imagined he could hear the creek at the foot of the hill, taunting him with the sound of clear, clean water. Thirst tormented him, and it might be a long time before John came looking for him. And Eli was in the fire tower.

Buck closed his eyes and tried not to listen to the sound of the creek.

Tuesday

Wolf Mountain

The white man heard the waterfall, providing a hint at his orientation in the cave. He slowed to a walk, his hand against the wall to feel his way, his mind reeling on the edge of sanity. What possessed him to pursue the old man without even a flashlight to ease the darkness? He strained his ears for the echo of footsteps and heard only the roar of the waterfall.

Why didn't he pick up the flashlight before he tore off into the cave? It was right there on the rock. He remembered putting it there, still shining. If he retraced his steps, he could find his way back to the entrance. Hugging the wall, he inched along, praying he headed toward the cave mouth.

Over the noise of the water, he heard another sound. He flattened his body against the granite and listened. Footsteps echoed off the vault of the ceiling, coming closer. A dim glow in the distance drew nearer and grew brighter. He groped the wall with his fingers until they encountered a cleft in the rock. He squeezed his body flat into the fissure.

The light brightened and spread down the cavern. Had the old man somehow escaped him and gone back for the flashlight? He waited, watching the approaching light.

The light passed by, silhouetting the dark form of a man in its glare. He couldn't see the man's face, but his confident, purposeful stride and large stature told him this was a stranger who knew where he was going. He kept the man in sight and followed as close as he dared. The sound of rushing water got louder, obscuring the thud of boots on stone, his and those of the man ahead. He felt spray on his face.

The man with the light bent over to enter a cavern that ran

deeper into the mountain. The white man steeled himself against a threatened bout of claustrophobia and followed.

The sound of the water receded. The passage narrowed. When it squeezed down to a size that no longer allowed him to walk, he stifled a groan and crawled on hands and knees until he saw the other man lie on the floor and wriggle inside an opening barely big enough to accommodate his wide shoulders, stretch full length, and reach for something. When he found it, he brought it out, mumbling something about Kanagwa'ti's hands being safe, giving thanks to some ancient spirit guardian, then squirmed back inside to replace the object.

Grief for the one who lay dead outside, and rage at the man who threw the axe, retreated behind the knowledge that he now possessed the last piece of the puzzle. It belonged to him. He eased backward in the passage until he found a crevice big enough to conceal his body and stayed there till the light passed, then followed it back to the waterfall. He kept the light in sight, feeling the cave floor rise in the slight incline that led back toward the cave mouth. He knew where to find the hands, and the man who could lay his hands on everything else, was somewhere in the cave without a light. He had the advantage, and no reason for loyalty to a man who took an innocent life.

A wave of grief too great to bear stopped him in his tracks for a moment.

When he could move again, he followed the light to the angle where the cave branched off into the main cavern. His shoulder scraped against the wall. A trickle of loose pebbles showered down the wall and whispered to a landing on the floor. The flashlight swung his way. He ducked into the shadows in time to avoid the beam, waiting for the man with the light to resume his trek toward the world outside.

The light disappeared around a bend. He followed the upward slant until he caught sight of it again.

Unnerved at the short time in the dark, he kept closer to the light, careful to keep it in sight. They made a turn he didn't remember. It scared him to think of how easy it would be to get lost. The cave must ramble all through the heart of Wolf Mountain. No wonder the old man couldn't find the hands before.

He paid close attention to every detail outlined by the light ahead, mentally making plans to get his pack and flashlight and return to the cavern beyond the waterfall.

Then, he had to find the old man and make him pay for what he had done, after he took what rightfully belonged to him.

The darkness of the cave lessened, faintly illumined by daylight. He froze against the cave wall to wait until the man ahead got out of his way. Then he could ease out and get his pack and the flashlight.

The man stood silhouetted in the narrow opening. Faint voices reached him from outside. It sickened him to think of what they might find there on the rocks.

He ducked back into the shadows of the cave. A shrill, high-pitched scream from outside echoed in the recesses of the cave. The man ahead hesitated for a moment, then bolted from the cave.

Grief overwhelmed him. He sunk to his knees and sobbed silently until he regained control, then made his way toward the entrance and blinked in the sudden sunlight, waiting while his eyes adjusted. Beyond the boulder that concealed the cave, someone swore. A child cried. No risk in going for the flashlight now. They had other things on their minds. His pack sat there on the boulder where he left it. The flashlight gave off a weak glow beside it.

For a moment, he stood exposed, just long enough to get what he came for. The voices faded behind him as he fled down the dark recesses of the cave.

In the silence, he stopped to take stock of his new reality. One by one each piece fell into place, each puzzle was completed.

The preordained Suye'ta didn't need to seek out the Ulunsu'ti. It came to him. He could feel it reaching out to his mind, telling him he didn't need an old Indian calling the shots.

Cold rage empowered him. When he retrieved the conjuror's hands, the killer would pay for his crime and he could take his rightful place as Suye'ta. He was the outsider, with an Indian wife and child. And he knew everything he needed to know to control the Ulunsu'ti.

But, he no longer had the child.

The flashlight cast a weak glow against the gray stone. Best not to waste the remaining juice in the batteries. He could manage without the light for now. He knew the main cavern well enough to find his way with a hand against the wall until the slope in the floor steepened and the roar of the waterfall reached his ears. He trusted the forces available to the outsider destined to become Suye'ta to guide him. To spare the light until he needed it, he clicked it off and felt the darkness possess the cave. A surge of primal fear of the unseen tempted him to use the flashlight. He slipped it into his pack to remove the temptation, and felt his way along the wall.

His hands slipped into emptiness. He retrieved the flashlight and confirmed his fear. A passage he didn't see before angled off into the unknown. Using precious moments of light, he counted his steps back down the narrow corridor, carefully measuring out the distance from the angle to the branch that led to the waterfall.

He kept the flashlight in hand, using it when the oppressive darkness became too much to bear, and made his way inch by inch. The first whisper of the waterfall sent waves of relief through him. Every muscle tense, he followed the sound until spray dampened his face.

Almost there. The crevice with the hands lay within the sound of the falls and the feel of its mist. He stood still, listening to the pounding of his heart eclipse the noise of the falls.

It seemed farther to the opening than he remembered. He turned on the flashlight and searched the cavern until he found it in the weak beam, a deeper blackness in the cave. Lucky the guardian of the conjuror's hands came when he did to show it to him, or was it only luck? The Suye'ta could count on getting help when he needed it.

His confidence grew as he walked stooped over down the narrow tunnel, steeled against the oppressive confines of the passage. When he lay down, flat on his belly reaching into the hole, he knew what he would find. He felt around until he touched a ledge, and then the hard roughness of something round. He slipped his hand under it, carefully drew it to him and backed out with it clutched to his chest. His heart pumped so hard against his prize that it echoed like a drumbeat in the hollow vessel.

He scuttled out of the passage until he had room to straighten his back. Layers of cured hide protected his find. He chewed through the ties binding it and let the hide fall at his feet. The weakening light revealed an ancient clay pot. The image of a snake marked it, coiling around from base to rim, its head resting on the sealed lid—the snake marking that identified the treasures of Kanegwa'ti.

He stilled his breathing and doused the light. He still had to find the elder who could take him to the Ulunsu'ti and the duffle bag. Somewhere in the cave, he must be praying for rescue. When he understood the true Suye'ta had come, he would know better than to resist. The worm had turned.

With the pot tucked inside his jacket, he made his way back toward the main cavern. He counted his steps, measuring the distance. When he expected to break through into the main cavern, he checked with the light. Nothing looked familiar. He listened for the waterfall and heard nothing but his own blood rushing through his veins.

The flashlight dimmed to nothing and died. The darkness

failed to dampen his confidence. The powers that brought him this far would get him out of the cave. He remembered a little book of matches in his pack and formed a plan. Keep walking until he reached the main cavern. Light a match if he needed to get his bearings.

He took measured paces in the dark, counting each step, listening for the waterfall. The silence remained undisturbed. He ignited a match and laughed with relief. The brief flame lit the cavernous vault that had to be the main cave. When did he pass the waterfall? No matter. Perhaps the Ulunsu'ti led him to a better way out.

He set his feet to the upward slope, knowing daylight would soon appear. Pine pitch for torches abounded in the stunted tree stumps outside. He imagined them wedged into the cave wall, lighting his way when he returned to find the elder. His confidence grew by the moment.

Pain thudded up his arm when his outstretched hand met rock. How did he get turned around? No problem. One of his matches would give him enough light to get oriented—that's all he needed.

The brief flame flared, then died, leaving him shaken and confused. He struck another match. The cavern soared higher than the match's light could reach. The wall at his back was the only one he could see. Nothing looked familiar. The chamber looked much bigger than the one that led to the mouth of the cave. A trickle of fear nibbled at his confidence. He resisted it and kept walking, carefully feeling his way.

Another dead end, more matches, and nothing familiar, and the fear blossomed into terror.

With his last match, he set fire to the paper matchbook from Phillips Café, holding onto it until his fingers blistered before he dropped it and watched it flicker and die. The darkness was total now. Not a sound reached him except the pumping of his heart, his labored breathing, and the hesitant tread of his own footsteps.

How long did he wander? Perhaps night had fallen. He strained his eyes searching for the entrance, looking for a hint of moonlight. He tried calling on the powers that helped him find the conjuror's hands, but the Above Beings didn't listen. Doubt in their existence assailed him.

He stumbled in the darkness. An even greater fear worked its way into his mind. What if the Cherokee deities were real, and what if they were out to get him?

The craving for light gnawed at him like hunger, but not a ray reached the depths of the cavern. Darkness became a weight that crushed his soul. He staggered into one dead end after another.

When the floor began the upward slope that led to the outside, he didn't perceive it. He collapsed on the floor of the main cavern, too scared to go on, babbling to himself, or to the great conjuror, or anyone who would listen, but no one answered.

He sat on the cold stone, feeling the chill seep into his bones. Taking the pot from his jacket, he cradled it in his lap. Darkness pressed against him, roaring in his ears like the voice of something alive, something that caused him to whimper like a scared child and wonder if the cave was now his tomb.

Tuesday

The Scene of the Crime

The fear John tried to suppress all day surfaced with a vengeance when he heard Wren scream. He reached her first. She stood, frozen to the spot, staring at something behind the rock. A red stain on the stone led his eyes to the girl lying sprawled like a broken doll on the rocks. Blood matted her dark hair around a crushing wound. Her eyes stared at the sky, dull and lifeless.

John picked up his daughter and pressed her face against his chest, murmuring something dumb like, "It's okay, baby. It's okay." He couldn't take his eyes off the girl. He knew two things for sure at that moment. Nothing would ever be okay again. And the girl was dead.

He held Wren, stroking her hair, trying to comfort her, wishing he never brought her to this place. Why didn't he call Faron like he wanted to? They should be home now, back on the Snowbird where his baby was safe.

Walker and Yona knelt beside the girl. Walker closed her eyes and Yona spread his jacket over her face. What more could they do?

They came and stood beside John, looking helpless and saying the same sort of dumb things to Wren that he already said. John kept her face averted from the bloody mess on the rock.

David rushed from behind a great boulder leaning against the mountain. When Walker showed him the girl, David knelt and lifted Yona's jacket from her face.

"Thomas Smoker's daughter," David said. "Dead, but hardly even cold."

Yona made a visible effort to pull himself together and bent down at David's side. He stared at the blood, pooled in the hollows of the flat expanse of granite she lay on. It was just beginning to coagulate.

John looked over Wren's head at the girl's face. There was something familiar about her. With a sickening jolt of recognition, he remembered her. "That's the girl who was with Eagle Feather when he came to the station that time."

Nobody heard him. David's words left them stunned. He had called her "Thomas Smoker's daughter."

The words sunk in. "Who did you say she was?" John had known the Smoker family all his life. Eli Smoker was one of his best friends since they were boys. He would know if Eli had a sister.

It confused Walker too. "You're not making any sense, Dave. Eli is the only young'un Thomas has. If Grady Smoker had a granddaughter, I think I would know about it."

David stood up and turned away from the dead girl. "I'm sorry, guys," he said. "I should have said something before. I've seen her around with Eagle Feather. Buck found out who she was and told me yesterday. He's been trying to find Grady and see what he knows. I would have told you, Grandfather, but Buck thought we should keep it quiet until we talked to Grady. I'll tell you more later, but first things first. We've gotta report this and get Wren out of here." David went over to his backpack. He unzipped a side pocket, rummaged around, and pulled out a cell phone.

Walker stopped him before he could finish dialing. "Whoa, David. You're gonna have people all over this mountain. What are they gonna find? Have you thought about that?"

"Doesn't matter, Grandfather. The most they could find is an empty cave."

Walker's shoulders drooped. With a tone of sick finality in his voice, he said, "So they found it? Whoever killed this girl got it all. It's over."

David spoke quickly. "No, Grandfather. The cave's been searched, and good. Somebody even dug holes in the floor, but they didn't look in the right place. We're safe." He finished dialing and looked toward the cave while he listened to it ring. "Miles of cave wind around in there, all the way to the heart of Wolf Mountain. You'd have to know exactly where to search to find what the Wayanettahs guard. Nobody has found it in the last three centuries. I don't think we have to worry about that."

John sat down on a rock, cradling Wren like she was still a baby. Walker leaned on his walking stick beside them. Wren wriggled free from her daddy's arms and reached over and patted her great-grandpa's hand. "Don't worry, Grandpa Walker. He won't let anything happen. He's looking after everything."

Walker perked up. Wren had that effect on him. "You're right, honey. I never would have thought of bringing along a cell phone. Good thing David did."

"No, Grandpa. Not David. The conjuror will know what to do. He's the only one now. David doesn't know about everything. Some stuff has been forgotten by everybody, even you."

John heard what she said, and it scared him in ways he didn't understand. He didn't want her to talk about the conjuror anymore, but he had to find out what she knew. He asked as gently as he could, "And how would you know that, honey? If everybody forgot, even Mama Kate couldn't have told you. So who did?"

"He did, Daddy. Nobody else would listen to him."

John couldn't take any more of this. Now his little girl claimed to communicate with a man who died centuries before her birth. Lord help him, he almost believed her. That scared him even more. "That's it, Walker. I don't want her involved in this. She's just a kid."

Walker ignored him and caught Wren's hand between his. "You've got to let her talk, son. She might be right. The rest of us are getting old. We thought we knew everything. We wouldn't

137

listen to anything or anybody. Maybe it takes a child to pay attention to what he needs to say. A child would listen. Let her tell us what he said. It might be our only hope."

"It's true, Daddy," Wren said. "The conjuror needed to tell us stuff and nobody could hear him. I wasn't scared of him."

John knew when he was out-gunned. If Wren and Walker both thought Wren had some answers, he had to let her tell them. But he would be the one to control how far it went. He asked her, "What did the conjuror tell you, baby? And how did he talk to you? Have you seen him?"

"Thank you, Daddy." She sounded more annoyed at his resistance than grateful. "I saw him, but only in dreams. He was a big snake at first, but then he was just a man. I thought he was Grandpa Driver 'cause he had just walked over, and the conjuror looks a lot like him, but he told me his name."

"His name was Kanegwa'ti?"

She talked so fast John couldn't interrupt. "Uh-huh, Daddy. And he said Grandpa Driver gave David something important. You need it to wake up the Ulunsu'ti. The conjuror doesn't want the Ulunsu'ti to wake up. He's really scared of that."

John trembled, and couldn't stop. He looked into his daughter's innocent dark eyes and realized he couldn't even imagine what went on behind them. He didn't want to hear any more. Even Walker had heard enough.

David stuffed the phone into his backpack and zipped it closed. He turned to John. "I have to wait here, but y'all need to take Wren home. I'm gonna show you a way that will get you to a logging trail about an hour and a half away. I called my Aunt Lynelle and she's gonna pick you up and take you to my house. Stay there, and don't talk to anybody till I get home."

Walker crossed his arms over his chest and kept his seat when the others got ready to leave. "Dave," he said, "I don't like to argue with you, son, but I don't feel like I should leave."

"We could be stuck here awhile," David said. "And there's

no way off this mountain that doesn't include a lot of walking. It's gonna be pitch dark before we head down."

"Yeah, I know." Walker remained seated on the boulder. It didn't look like he intended to go anywhere.

"On your feet, Old Man," John said. "Faron and Kate will both skin me alive if I leave you here. Don't get stubborn on me."

Walker still didn't move. "I reckon they would tell you that the most important thing is to get Wren off this mountain and safely back on the Snowbird. Besides, boy, I've made up my mind and you can't change it for me."

John appealed to David, who just shrugged and said, "Don't waste your time, Johnny. You know better than I do how stubborn he is. I'll look after him. Just get Wren out of here before dark."

Yona made a stab at persuading Walker to come along. He didn't relish the idea of facing Faron and Kate and telling them he'd left his grandpa on Wolf Mountain with a dead girl. Walker held his ground and told them they better get started if they wanted to make it down the mountain while they could see the way.

"Well, we tried, John," Yona said.

John gave up on persuading Walker to go. He nodded toward the duffle bag. "You want me to take this with me?"

David said, "Just leave it here. Me and Walker will take care of it."

David walked with them around the boulders. Pointing out landmarks, he gave them directions for the quickest way down to the place where they were to meet his Aunt Lynelle.

"Now get going," David said. "Or else you'll be trying to find your way out of here in the dark."

John couldn't wait to get Wren home. It made him mad as hell that she had to be involved in such a nightmare. He offered to carry her down the mountain, but she shook her head. Taking her bearings from the landmarks David described, she set out in the lead toward the logging trail. His daughter must be made of tougher stuff than he. His stomach still clinched in a knot from the sight of Thomas Smoker's dead daughter, but it seemed Wren could put it aside to focus on getting home. Just like her mama.

They saw no discernible path and didn't expect to. They watched for David's landmarks and stayed lined up with a rock formation he pointed out, jutting from a peak in the distance. After nearly two hours of walking with no rest stops, they saw the logging trail below. Aunt Lynelle Wayanettah's Jeep Wrangler sat there waiting.

John greeted Aunt Lynelle and thanked her for coming to get them. He lifted Wren into the backseat and was about to climb in with her when something caught his eye. In the stand of hemlocks a few feet away, the setting sun sent a shiny reflection shimmering through the dark branches.

"Hang on just a minute, Aunt Lynelle," he said. "I think there's a car over there."

Yona followed him. For once, Wren was content to stay where she was. She had seen enough for one day.

The hemlock trees provided good camouflage for the dark green Mitsubishi Montero. The reflection off the rear window gave it away.

Yona pulled the low-hanging branches aside and looked the vehicle over. He knew who it belonged to. "Wonder if Mr. Eagle Feather was making an attempt to hide this thing or just trying to drive as far as possible," he said.

"Well, he couldn't get it much farther than this, even if it does have four-wheel drive," John said. "Must have been trying to keep it out of sight. Don't know why, though. Not likely anybody else would come around here."

They didn't notice that Lynelle followed until she spoke. "I don't know who this thing belongs to or why he hid it, but from what David told me, we'd better go call Nathan Axe and tell him about it. This is the sheriff's business."

John and Yona agreed. They all got into the Jeep and Lynelle turned around on the steep slope and headed toward her house. She didn't trust cell phones, and John and Yona had left theirs in the Blazer. Half the time cell phones didn't work in the mountains anyway, unless you had one of those fancy satellite phones like David's.

They got to Lynelle's house a lot quicker than expected. Apparently, Lynelle didn't mind driving at top speed on the narrow road. The Wrangler went airborne a few times, launched by the boulders and runnels left by a bad winter.

She wheeled up her driveway and left the motor running while she ran inside to make the call. In a couple of minutes she got back behind the wheel, her face set in an annoyed scowl.

"Nathan wasn't in," she snapped. "They said at the sheriff's office that we should wait till one of them gets here. We're supposed to keep an eye out to see if anybody comes around or drives off in the Montero." She shifted into reverse and backed out to the road and drove back toward the hemlocks and the hidden Montero.

John hugged Wren close and held on for dear life. His butt was already bruised and battered from the trip to Lynelle's house. The combination of hard seats with skimpy padding and a high-speed ride over what barely passed for a road made for a punishing journey.

They bounced along the rutted road for the five miles back to the hemlock trees. Lynelle Wayanettah parked behind the Montero and they sat in the Wrangler without a word, waiting for somebody from the sheriff's office to arrive.

John held onto Wren, just in case she might get bored and want to go explore again. If there was anything else to find, he didn't want her to be the one who discovered it.

Their wait proved mercifully short. Within twenty minutes, Sheriff Axe's deputy, Jimmy Hanks, wheeled up and parked beside them. John and Yona got out of the Wrangler and pointed him to the Montero.

Lynelle didn't give them time to describe how they found Eagle's Feather's vehicle. She gave an impatient beep on the horn and glowered at them from where she sat hunched over the steering wheel. John didn't blame her for wanting to be done with this whole mess and get back to her peace and quiet. Apparently, Jimmy didn't either. He apologized for keeping her waiting and told John the sheriff would want to talk to him and Yona later.

John and Yona got in the car. "Let's go, Aunt Lynelle," John said.

Lynelle spun the Wrangler around and tore off down the road, adding a few more bruises to John's butt. It didn't seem to bother Lynelle and Yona. Either the front seats had more padding, or Lynelle and Yona supplied their own. Lynelle came close to matching Yona's weight and most of it was in her backside.

At David's house, Lynelle didn't drive across the bridge. She dropped them off at the roadside and took off before they could thank her.

Wren rubbed her eyes and went straight to David's kitchen.

John went to prowl for food in the fridge. The peanut butter and jelly sandwich for lunch had worn off long ago.

Wren didn't go to search for dinner. She perched on the stool at the counter and reached for the phone. "I've gotta talk to my mama," she said. Her brave front disappeared the moment Faron answered. She cried quietly as she described finding the girl. "I was so scared, Mama. She was hurt so bad, and we couldn't do anything."

She dried her eyes with a paper napkin and listened. "Mama, I can't come home yet. David said we should stay here till he comes. We have to tell the law people about the girl. I don't want to, Mama. Can you and Mama Kate come? I'm really scared."

John listened to Wren's end of the conversation while he made her a bologna and cheese sandwich. He wanted to cry too. She took a deep breath as she hung up the phone and climbed down from the stool. "Mama and Mama Kate will be here as soon as they can," she said. "What have we got to eat?"

John put the sandwich on a plate and gave it to her. She found a bag of Doritos in the pantry and, ignoring the glass of milk Yona poured her, took a Coke from the fridge and went straight to David's easy chair in front of the TV.

John followed, watching her settle her dinner on a hassock. She found the remote control, turned on the television, then clicked through channels, stopping on one of her favorite shows, the episode where Bart falls in love with Reverend Lovejoy's daughter. He watched this "Simpsons" rerun with her more times than he could count. Now, she could enjoy her dinner.

When he came back to check on her, the episode was half over and the sandwich barely touched. Wren lay curled up asleep. John put a blanket over her to let her sleep until her mama came.

Tuesday Night

The Cave

Walker watched John walk away with Wren, praying to the Above Beings to keep his great-granddaughter safe. This whole thing unnerved him and he didn't know how to fix it. He needed Driver and Grady, but Driver walked over and he couldn't find Grady. The nervous feeling at the pit of his stomach got worse every time he thought about his old friend. Grady went away mad last time they talked.

Not long ago, he had a choice of elder Snake Dancers to call on, but most walked over leaving grandsons in their place. Yona waited to take his place when it came time, and Grady Smoker had Eli, but the two other elders neared the end with nobody to fill their place in the circle. Was Grady right to worry that the Snake Dancers, including the guardians of Kanagwa'ti's goods, would all die out and be forgotten?

Driver Wayanettah was the oldest one in the circle and the Principal Snake Dancer. When he walked over, the job fell to Walker. The responsibility weighed heavy on him, even before things started falling apart. Now, he needed help. A young dancer just brought into the circle was his only option. Good thing Driver believed in educating grandsons early. If he taught him well enough, they stood a chance.

The decision to break with tradition and talk with David about things he shouldn't breathe to a living soul didn't come easy, but he had to trust David. If David returned that trust, they might live through the week.

It was hard to ask a Snake Dancer to break the rules, but he had no choice. "Son," he said, "you and me, we're in a mess I don't think any Snake Dancer's ever been in before. We've both got information we're not supposed to have. That's a burden I don't like, but we're the only ones left to carry it."

David agreed fast, like he wanted to confide in Walker and didn't know how to start. "Driver said things would be different for me than for any of the other guardians, now or in the past. He said I should adapt and do what I knew to be right for me and all my generation. Looks like it starts now."

Walker kept his eyes on a straight pine tree at the edge of the cliff and remembered his last conversation with Driver Wayanettah. "We talked about that, and how hard it was already to keep people away from places they don't belong. There are just too many people. They've built a subdivision just a mile away from one of the last places where the Nunne'hi still live. That man who calls himself Eagle Feather set up a camp on the edge of a site that's more important than he can imagine." His voice dropped to a whisper, like it hurt to say it out loud. "The Nunne'hi are leaving. Driver knew it. Once they're gone, we're not far behind."

David echoed Walker's pain. "I know, Grandfather. I know." He hesitated. "Driver told me to trust you...but not anybody else. Not another Snake Dancer. Not even the other guardians."

Walker's eyes never left the pine tree. "He hinted something to me, son. I think he knew things he didn't want to say."

David sat silent for a moment. Walker gave him time to think things over.

David stood, paced, then came back to his seat. He'd made up his mind. "Grandpa Driver trusted you, and he said I should talk to you when the time came. He said I'd know when." He opened the duffle bag and took out one of the gym bags. "This is the one with his bones?"

Walker nodded and said the Cherokee word for "yes," which sounded like a grunt.

"Why would somebody want this old skeleton?" David

asked.

For a moment, Walker wondered if he overestimated David's knowledge. "Dave, you know how it goes. The Ulunsu'ti can only be awakened in the conjuror's hand. I figured we were thinking the same thing, that they dug him up to use his hand."

David lifted out the bundle of old bones and folded back the edges of the towel to expose them. He used a corner of the towel to sort out what had once been Kanagwa'ti's lower left arm, then the right. "Take a good look, Grandfather," he said.

Walker bent over the bones. He saw what David wanted him to see. His chest tightened. When he finally got his voice, he said, "Gone. They kept his hands." He looked closer. "Cut off. You can see the marks on the wrist bones. Cut off before the bones dried out. Who did this, David?"

David's answer shocked him more than the sight of the severed wrist bones.

"Kanegwa'ti cut off the left one himself with a knife made from Awi'Usdi's antler just before he died. Wanted to be sure it would get done in a way that bound Uktena to serve the hand. That's the one the Ulunsu'ti has to be held in for it to work. His son, the one he left the guardianship to, cut off the other one just to be sure, then he preserved both of them. Only he and those who inherited the guardianship after him knew about this, until now. You're the first one outside our family to hear this part of the story."

Walker couldn't speak. This brought everything he believed into question. From the time his grandpa, Tsali Copperhead, turned his guardianship over to him, he thought the hands lay in the grave with the conjuror. That's one of the reasons the Copperheads guarded the grave with such dedication. Not once did he suspect the hands were not there with the rest of Kanagwa'ti's remains. Nothing Tsali taught him prepared him for this. He gripped the head of his walking stick and leaned his head on his hands for a moment until he reined in his emotions.

When he spoke, his voice sounded so calm one would never know how this new information rocked him.

"That's what Driver looked after—Kanagwa'ti's hands? I figured he guarded the Ulunsu'ti."

"Grandpa Driver thought you had it till just a few months ago," Dave said, "when he found out who really had it."

"He knew who watched the Ulunsu'ti?"

"Yep. And he told me. He said I should tell you. When the time came."

Another surprise. Walker stared David in the eyes, the way it was impolite to do without good reason. "Has the time come, David?"

David didn't look away. "Yeah, Grandfather. For the first time, there will be at least three of us that know who holds it, and you and I know where the other keys are. Scary, huh?"

Walker turned his gaze back to the pine tree, took a deep breath, and exhaled with a sigh. "I've been scared shitless since Monday night, son—when I saw the ark and the conjuror's bones and grave goods right there within half a mile of Degal gun'yi."

"I've got a feeling it's gonna get worse, Grandfather. When they start killing off a Snake Dancer's family, that's a bad sign. Especially this dancer."

A commotion on the rocks where the girl's body lay got their attention. *Grady Smoker's granddaughter.*

A couple of crows inched too close. Walker picked up a pebble and chucked it at the crows. They scattered to reconsider their approach.

"Grady Smoker? He guards the Ulunsu'ti?"

"That's what Driver said."

"And you watch the hands?"

David answered "yes" in Cherokee. "Were you the bones or the medicine or the ark?"

Walker tossed another pebble at the crows. "I watched his grave. His bones and medicine were both in it. I always thought the hands were there too."

David nodded. "I figure Buck Locust for the ark."

"Good man, Buck. We're lucky to have you and him in the circle. He's covering for Johnny to be off as long as he needs too. Said he'd check on that dieback over at Degal gun'yi himself."

"Grandfather," David tossed a rock at the most persistent crow, "do you think it's time for Suye'ta?"

Walker felt sheepish, like a dark secret he'd tried to hide had been discovered. "I reckon if some damn fool managed to wake Ulunsu'ti, we'd sure need a hell of a lot more than we've got."

"They say only Suye'ta can wake it," David said.

Walker stirred the pebbles around with his walking stick and found a good big one. The crow squawked and backed off when he scored a fair hit. "They say only Suye'ta can control it, but the truth is that anybody with the keys, and with enough knowledge and stupidity to try, can wake it up. If that happens, only Suye'ta can keep the shit from hitting the fan. I figure we'd be better off if we called out a Suye'ta of our own, somebody we could guide along."

They stopped talking and watched the crows that had been joined by a couple of relatives.

After a few minutes David said, "If Faron knew what you had in mind for her husband, she'd kick your ass all the way back to Graham County."

Walker tried to grin, and almost made it. "Why do you think I'm so scared, boy?"

David laughed. "Yeah, what's some unleashed demon compared to the wrath of a Cherokee woman?"

The laughter died before it began. Only the squawking of the crows broke the grim silence as the sun sank lower behind Thunderhead. Walker threw a handful of pebbles at the flock that gathered, but it didn't faze them. David stood to pick up some bigger rocks. He was getting good at this since he stopped aiming to intimidate and started going for blood.

One by one the crows retreated to the big pine tree to quarrel among themselves.

David tossed his last stone and turned back to Walker. "Axe will be here in an hour or so. We need to decide what to do with the conjuror's bones and the rest of the stuff. Any suggestions?"

Walker threw a couple more rocks to make sure the crows wouldn't return. "The bones and medicine have to go back to Ataga'hi. We don't have a choice there. They have to rest in the conjuror's grave until the Suye'ta comes. As for the ark, I guess we have to talk to Buck about that. But you're right, Dave. We've got to do something. We can't keep toting it around in an old duffle bag."

"How much of a hike is it to Ataga'hi, Grandfather?"

"About an hour more than it took us to get here. I don't know about you, but I don't think I'm up to it tonight."

Dave walked over and picked up the duffle bag. "Come on, Grandfather. We're gonna stash this where it won't be found unless somebody blows up this whole damn mountain. We can take it where it belongs later."

Walker used his walking stick to pull himself slowly to his feet. "If you got that good a hiding place, I guess you're right. I won't feel easy till he's back where he told us to keep him, but with the law on the way to deal with Grady's granddaughter, we gotta do something, and I can't think of anything better. Lead on, boy."

David led him through the scrub and rocks. The ground and foliage lay undisturbed, like nobody ever set foot there before. Walker hoped they were too high up on the mountain for snakes because this looked like a perfect habitat for rattlers. He hummed the song that legend said announced him as a friend as he followed the younger man through the sparse brush, the only sign of life other than the crows.

He didn't know what to expect when David beckoned him

149

to follow, then climbed higher to a jumble of boulders. An overhanging slab of granite formed an alcove, but David didn't stop there. He stepped behind a concealing dolmen into the mouth of a cave and disappeared into the darkness.

Walker tried not to think of how much he hated places like this. David took a flashlight out of his backpack and shined it ahead into the depths of the cave. "This way, Grandfather."

After a few steps, the cave curved inward to the heart of the mountain and began a gradual downward slope. Walker stayed close on David's heels. He hated caves. The deeper they went, the less he liked it. A breeze touched him, light as a feather, redolent with the cold, damp breath of the mountain. From the distance, the faintest whisper of running water reached him.

The whisper built to a roar, and the spray reached his face. David swung the flashlight around, and even Walker had to admit the way the light sparkled off the clear water cascading over the walls of the cave and splashing into a deep crystal clear pond made it worth walking half an hour inside a mountain to see. They couldn't see where it went after that. It looked like the pool was the end of it, but when Walker listened carefully, he heard echoes of another waterfall far below.

"Lightning Creek," David said. "This is where it starts."

Walker stretched like his back hurt from the weight of the mountain over him. "I hope it ain't far to where we're going, boy, 'cause I'm not one for being underground any longer than I have to be."

David didn't say anything. Walker kept quiet and let him think. Finally, he turned around. "Grandfather, I've got a real important question. Kanagwa'ti's hands are not far from here. Driver told me the conjuror taught us to keep his hands apart from the rest of him so he could stick around to keep an eye on things. That if his hands and body are united, he's free to go on to the above world. If we get them too close to the rest of him, does that mean he's free to walk over if he wants to, or that he has to go whether he wants to or not? Or is the whole thing a load of bullshit?"

"Son, we always believed Kanegwa'ti haunted Lightning Creek. Remember a few years back when that bunch of great white hunters from Atlanta came up here to kill them a wild boar? They were diving in the pond down the mountain, the headwaters of Lightning Creek. One of them died from snake bite. The other three swore the biggest cottonmouth water moccasin they'd ever seen got him. Folks didn't pay any attention to them 'cause no cottonmouth could live this far north. I wondered about that."

David got the duffle bag from where he laid it on an outcropping of rock. "Weird shit, huh? But being who we are, I guess we gotta believe. It's probably best we don't get the rest of him any closer to his hands than we have to. We might need us a skin changer's ghost before this is over." He doubled back to another almost invisible passage and was gone a few minutes.

"It will all be safe there for the time being," he said when he reappeared. "If you want to go see where it is, just duck down that way. It's in a niche in there."

"I'm ready to get out of here, if you don't mind." Walker was already heading for the entrance. "This place puckers my ass." He needed to see the light of day again. Underground darkness was an almost tangible thing.

David laughed. "Aren't you supposed to be the head Snake Dancer now, Grandfather? I didn't think us conjurors, especially you elder guardians, were supposed to be afraid of anything."

"With what we know, son, we ought to be too scared to function most of the time. Who's got a better reason to be afraid than us?"

"You got a point there, Grandfather."

They emerged into fading twilight under the overhang at the mouth of the cave. They heard voices and listened long enough to identify them. Somebody bashed in that poor girl's head, and if her murderer came back, they didn't want to run into him.

Sheriff Nathan Axe's worried voice called David's name. They dreaded talking to anybody with all the secrets they had to keep, but it helped that it was Nathan. He was one of their own.

They told Axe what they had to, which wasn't nearly as much as he wanted to know. The sheriff didn't look too happy when David suggested that Walker needed to get started home. After all, he was old and tired and faced a long hike back to the Blazer. Walker obliged by acting as old and tired as he could until they were out of sight, then set a sprightly pace for David to follow. The walk down went fast.

Tuesday

Back in the Cave

The elder fought the spark of will that stirred him awake. The battle lost, consciousness returned with a sharp stab of pain that began with the gash in his head and worked its way down his body. He tried to stand but that only made it worse.

Physical pain was nothing compared to the despair that engulfed him, weighing heavier than the utter darkness of the cave. How long had he been there? An hour? A day? He had no way of knowing and didn't want to care. He longed to lie back down on the cold granite floor and wait for his spirit to ebb away, but something in him kept fighting, struggling to clear the fog from his mind. He had to think. Something happened that he needed to remember. It hung over him like the darkness.

An image of a sweet young girl flashed across his mind. She trusted him and the man who claimed her as his own after Thomas left her mother before he knew she carried his child. Now she lay dead and alone on Wolf Mountain. The agony of the memory took his breath away. He slumped back down on the floor. Dying would be the easy way out, but another recollection teased at his mind, something even harder to face than how he killed a sixteen-year-old girl he held in his arms as a baby. Salena, they named her, in honor of her grandmother. Sally didn't have to face the loss or know what he had done. He despaired at the thought of facing Salena's mother.

He struggled to his feet, craving death, knowing he had no right to die until he found a way out of the cave and let the Snake Dancers know where to find the conjuror's goods. He set into motion a chain of events that no one could stop but him. Once he set it right, only death would free him from guilt and grief beyond endurance.

He faded again and fought his way back from the fog. In the distance, the roar of the waterfall helped him get his bearings. If he walked away from the water, and not into one of the caverns that meandered off the main cave, he would reach the entrance.

His mind cleared as he stumbled in the dark. A plan took form in his mind. The duffle bag was safe, miles away under the hickory tree. He could leave it there for now. Walker Copperhead would take care of it when he knew where to find it, but first he must turn the Ulunsu'ti over to his grandson and make him the new guardian. When he filled him in on things only he could teach him, Walker could do the rest. And he might do a better job.

He leaned against the wall, massaging a cramp that seized his leg. Footsteps echoed in the cave. The white man? He flattened his back against the cave wall and trusted the darkness to hide him. He couldn't survive another encounter, and he needed to stay alive another day.

The sound of the footsteps came closer. He could hear two sets heading straight for him. He held his breath and pressed hard against the cold wall.

Just before their light reached him, the footsteps stopped. Familiar voices echoed in the cave. He didn't move a muscle or make a sound. The cramp in his calf made it hard to be still but he toughed it out and listened. He could trust these men. He toyed with the idea of going to them and asking for help, but too many reasons not to came to mind. Yet, it comforted him to listen to them talk, helped him focus his mind and made him feel less alone. And he needed to hear what they said.

In the glow of a flashlight, he could see what they carried. How could that be? The duffle bag was supposed to be under an old hickory log near Degal gun'yi. He stifled the urge to rush out and claim it. Then he heard what they were saying.

He didn't have to worry about the duffle bag and all the

relics it held. It was where it belonged, with men who took their duty as seriously as he once had. The only thing he needed to retrieve from it was the ark. He had to take it back to Buck Locust. Then, he would perform his last obligation as a guardian. He wouldn't be free of his sworn duty to the Ulunsu'ti until he turned it over to his grandson and revealed to him the secrets that a guardian had to know.

Before he could restore the ark to its rightful owner, or turn over the Ulunsu'ti to Eli, he had a more urgent problem. Somewhere in this cave, the white man lay in wait, and he knew enough to destroy them all.

He watched the two men, David and Walker. When David took the duffle bag, he followed him, staying in the shadows and taking careful note of where he went. He watched him stash it in a niche back near the waterfall. Everything in it but the ark belonged with them. Buck Locust needed that.

He followed David and Walker to the mouth of the cave, staying close enough to keep their light in view. Outside, he heard them talking to someone. He crept close enough to see Nathan Axe kneeling on the rock beside the girl. He prayed that Nathan would say she still lived, that they needed to take her down the mountain for help. Instead, they confirmed what he already knew. The girl was dead. Thomas would never get to meet his daughter.

A wave of anguish came too powerful to suppress. He couldn't live with it much longer. It hurt too much to endure. He had to find the strength to bear it until he repaired the damage he had done and earned the right to end his misery.

Nathan Axe's voice echoed in the recesses of the cave, cursing the soul of the monster who could do a thing like that to a poor innocent girl. The sheriff's words hit him harder than the fall that gashed his head. It sent his spirit reeling into the void between the world of the living and the land of the dead. His senses dulled; he still felt the pain, but it lacked the tormenting sharpness that made it unbearable.

No more than a shadow now, creeping, stealing behind boulders and scrub laurel away from the cave, he headed down the slope. One last look back at the girl's body, one quick prayer for her forgiveness, then on to the bottom of the mountain to the hemlocks where the Pinto waited. It offered sanctuary scented with gas fumes, age, and the lonely odor of fast food eaten on the run.

The last of his strength deserted him. Labored breath burned in his lungs. A sharp pain knifed through his chest and settled into a crushing ache under his ribs. Fighting for enough of a grip on his soul to make him care, he willed himself to bear it long enough to set things right.

Weakness lowered his guard, allowing images to drift across his vision. The axe as it flew toward its mark, the moment of impact. Her eyes as their light faded and died.

He deserved Nathan Axe's curse, and more. Death was too good for a man who did what he had done. He wouldn't fight it. When his spirit drifted free of his body to wander within that gray emptiness beyond this world, he let it go.

In an old yellow Pinto under a hemlock tree, an aged body slumped over the steering wheel. From a gray place between the worlds, the spirit it housed more than eighty years watched, taking on the anguish that would render the old form useless, willing strength into the empty shell.

The elder sat up behind the wheel of the Pinto. The guilt and grief lifted, leaving his mind clear. Everybody on Lightning Creek Road or Big Cove knew him and his car. They would be looking for him by now and he couldn't afford to be seen. He had time to wait under the hemlocks and rest. Later, when folks were in bed, the Pinto would be just the rattle of another old car in the night. Possibly some kid coming home from a date.

It was dark when he turned the key in the ignition. The familiar grinding of the starter almost brought him out of his trance, but he willed the numbness back and tried the starter again. When the Pinto sputtered into action, he shifted into reverse and backed out of the shelter of the hemlocks.

A few miles down the creek, he turned off the headlights and parked just before the bridge to the Wayanettah place. A soft pool of light from the porch illuminated a black Blazer in the yard. A lamp burned in the living room window. He knew that room well, but it offered no comfort for him tonight.

He continued on toward his home in the woods. Again, consciousness threatened to return when he found himself remembering Sally, wishing she had been there to keep him straight, regretting that he ever left his trailer that morning.

It surprised him to find the knapsack still around his shoulder. He took it off and left it lying on the threadbare seat. He would need it later to carry the crystal hidden in the niche inside his well.

He hurried past the houses along Lightning Creek, hoping no one saw him, trying not to think of the times he sat in those rooms sharing coffee and talk.

He was a dead man now, with no place among his people. Only the determination to right his wrongs animated his body.

One thing he could never undo, but the memory of that was so far away it had no power to hurt him. The image of the girl passed so briefly through his mind that he barely perceived it.

He drove slowly through the town of Cherokee with all the shops closed and the streets dark and deserted. Neon lights cast an eerie half-light that only accentuated the darkness. An occasional vehicle went by, its occupants in such a hurry to get home they paid no attention to the faded yellow car. Would they wonder why he wasn't home in bed like he usually was at this time of night?

He drove on, barely aware of the road. With the exception of the time he spent away during the war, he never lived anywhere else. If need be, he could make this trip in his sleep, which was a lot like what he was doing. His mind worked out what he had to do, and his spirit drifted so far away it wasn't even part of him.

He sensed that dreaded place of wandering lost souls. He hovered so close to it that he struggled against the desire to give in to its pull. The despair of the below worlds held less terror for him than the life he must endure long enough to set things right.

The days when he could face his people with an open heart, free of shame, were over. Now he slunk home like a fugitive, afraid to be seen by people as close as family.

He left the neon lights and souvenir shops behind. When he came to the highway, he drove into oncoming traffic without a glance. The angry shouts and blaring car horns barely pierced his awareness. Nothing mattered but keeping his wits about him long enough to finish this last obligation to his people.

First, the white man had to die. It was the only way to keep him from doing any more harm. With a stir of anticipation, he made the decision and plotted the deed. Should he look for another way, one that didn't call for murder? The question flashed through his mind like a thought that belonged to someone else. He didn't want to find another way. It was the white man's fault Salena died. He remembered the feel of the war axe in his hand, pictured it parting dirty-blonde hair. The thought evoked another image: Salena falling under the blow of the axe. Sickened, he fixed his mind on the white man who took away everything that mattered. He deserved to die, but not with the axe.

He almost missed the turn into his drive. Worn tires squealed when he stomped on the brake. Anticipation of what he had to do took his mind off driving and drew him closer to the darkness that hovered ever nearer. How easy it would be to let go and slip away. The gray world lurked at the edge of his mind, promising oblivion and peace. In the emptiness he could be free from it all.

The headlights caught the beech tree in their beams. He barely remembered the drive home. He parked under the ancient tree and sat in silence, reminiscing and saying farewell. He wouldn't be back this way again.

The plot of land he brought Sally to on their wedding day made a good home for them. Thomas could tear down the old house now, like he wanted to for a year or more. The memories the old house held meant nothing to him, or to anyone else. Thomas or Eli might build on the land, or sell it if neither of them wanted it.

High above him, a frayed rope dangled from a branch, the last remnant of a tire swing from his grandson's childhood. Memory tugged at his spirit but he resisted. He couldn't let anything make him feel. Not now. With the stub of a pencil, he scribbled a note to leave for Thomas. He needed to know about the safe in the well.

The night wore on and he had work to do. He wiped his eyes with an old, red bandana and got out of the car, then reached back for the knapsack. He'd need it to hold the Ulunsu'ti. And some ammunition.

Tuesday Night

David Wayanettah's House

John and Yona both went to the door when they heard Faron's Mustang drive onto the bridge less than an hour after Wren called her. Sheriff Nathan Axe arrived and parked behind her. Kate got out of the car and greeted the sheriff warmly with a lingering hug. John could see him blush from the door.

Faron had no time for anybody but her daughter. She ignored Axe's greeting and ran for the porch, rushing through the door John held open. He led her to David's easy chair where Wren lay curled up sound asleep. Faron didn't wake her, just bent close and stroked her hair away from her face. Satisfied that she slept peacefully, she let John take her outside to the porch.

"How did she take it," Faron asked him, "seeing that poor girl like that?"

"Not so good at first. She was shaking like a leaf when I picked her up, but she calmed down and handled it as well as the rest of us."

"Probably better than some of us," Yona said. "Made me sick as a dog to think somebody would hurt a girl that way and just leave her there alone to die."

"Oh, John, I just hate it that Wren had to see something so awful." Faron pressed her forehead against a porch post. "Mama Kate still insists we had to let her go with you, but I don't know."

John put his arms around her and held her close, for his own comfort as much as hers. "Honey, I don't know what's going on. Somebody murdered that girl. At first I thought she might have fallen, but she didn't get hurt like that from a fall. And what was she doing way up there anyway? We should never have let our baby go there today, no matter what she thinks her dreams said.

Hell, I don't want to be out there anymore myself."

Sheriff Axe and Kate stopped at the top of the steps. "He's right, Faron," Kate said. "Nathan just told me. That poor girl was murdered. Hit in the head with one of those old stone war axes like they have at the museum. They found it in the rocks with blood all over it."

"Who did that to her, Sheriff?" Faron asked. "And where's my grandpa and David Wayanettah?"

John and Yona greeted the sheriff. Axe tipped his hat and turned to Faron. "Evening, Faron. Walker and David should be here soon. They claimed they told me everything they knew about the dead girl, then they took off down the mountain. Said they'd walk down to Yona's car and drive straight back here."

"Was Grandpa alright?"

"He looked tired, but he seemed to be in good shape to me," Axe said. "I got a feeling he and David had something to do they didn't want to tell me about. I'll let it go for now, but I'm gonna need to talk to them later. If I didn't know them both as well as I do, I'd wonder what they were up to."

John echoed Faron's question. "Any idea who killed the girl?"

"Maybe so," Nathan said. "That big old SUV Lynelle called us about is registered to those Sacred Circle people. Back before they bought those mini-busses to haul their...*students* around in, they used that Montero. They were having meetings in the Holiday Inn on Highway 19 then. They'd drive the students off into the woods early in the morning and come back at night. Now they have those camps and a lot more people. I think Eagle Feather uses the Montero himself. Jimmy Hanks is checking it out."

John stroked Faron's hair. It was soothing to both of them. "Nathan," he said, "I've seen that girl before. She came to the station one time with that Sacred Circle man."

Faron stepped out of John's embrace and turned to Kate.

"Mama, is she the same girl you saw with him in town that day? Remember, we wondered who she was."

"You know, I bet she is the same one," Kate said.

"You saw the dead girl, with Eagle Feather?" Nathan asked.

"It must have been her," Kate said. "I tried to talk to her, but Mr. Sacred Circle rushed her off before I could find out anything. I think she's Cherokee, though. Just not from around here. She was as pretty as could be, just like a little doll."

She had Nathan's full attention now. "Real young?" he asked. "Say around fifteen or sixteen years old? Small frame?"

Kate nodded. "And I doubt she was more than five-feet-two. Tiny thing, and quiet as a mouse. I don't think she said a word."

"Sounds like the same girl," Nathan said. "I'm not sure how Buck Locust found out who she was, but if there's anything going on anywhere in our community, Buck's gonna know it. He called me a couple of days ago and wanted to talk about her. The weirdest thing is, he said she belonged to Grady Smoker's son, Thomas. Says he got worried when he saw a young girl with that weirdo and started checking on her. Buck ain't gonna let some flake take advantage of one of our kids if he can help it."

"I don't see how she could be Thomas's daughter," Kate said. "I've known Grady Smoker and his whole family all my life, and I would know it if he had a granddaughter. Thomas is a real horse's butt, but he's the only child Grady and Sally had. Thomas and his stuck-up wife didn't have any kids but Eli. You know how Grady dotes on Eli. He'd be unbearable if he had a granddaughter."

"I doubt Grady knew anything about her, Kate," Axe said. "Buck went over to Murphy yesterday and talked to Thomas. Seems like Eagle Feather told Buck who the girl was and he went to check it out. The white man married the girl's mother and adopted her when she wasn't much more than a baby. Grady's boy fessed up and said she could be his kid, because back when

162

he worked construction down in Mississippi, he took up with a Choctaw woman. Lived with her for nearly a year, till the job was up, just coming back home to his wife on the weekends. When he finished the job, he came home and didn't go back anymore. Never knew she had his kid till Buck told him about her."

"I always said that boy of Grady's was a sorry, no-account dog. Now I know he's worse than that." Kate wasn't one to hold back her opinions.

"Buck never has trusted Eagle Feather," the sheriff said. "He was afraid he would get to Grady and try to use the girl against him somehow. He went to Grady's house last night to talk to him about her, but nobody was home. Didn't see any sign of his car or anything. I sure wish Buck had found him. If only he'd had a chance to meet his granddaughter before—"

The sheriff took off his hat and ran his hand through his hair. "I should have done something. Maybe if we'd tried to get the girl away from that fake shaman, she might still be alive."

Sliding her arm around Nathan's waist, Kate snuggled against him. "Don't feel bad, Nathan. You couldn't know this would happen."

John interrupted, "How do you reckon Eagle Feather met the girl's mother?"

"He's got those camps down near the Choctaws," Nathan said. "He probably met up with her and she told him about Thomas. The girl must have come up here with him while she had spring break. They seemed real close from what Eagle Feather told Buck. She was learning to help him and her mom run the Sacred Circle Camp down in Mississippi."

Kate rubbed Nathan's arm. Sounded like he had difficulty breathing for a minute. John rescued him, whether he wanted to be rescued or not, with the suggestion that they go inside for a cup of coffee. He didn't like the look Kate gave him as Nathan disentangled himself.

"I could use a cup, John," Axe said. "And I need to use the

phone to call Sheriff Dorsey over in Graham County. He was gonna send somebody to look for Eagle Feather and to check around and see if anybody has seen Grady. I'd like to know if they've had any luck."

Faron said, "I'd sure hate to be the one to tell Grady about that poor girl and the way she was killed. It's going to break his heart, especially since he never even had the chance to get to know her."

John had every intention of making the coffee himself, but Kate took over. The sheriff sat on a stool at the kitchen counter, talking on the phone and jotting notes on a pad he took from his shirt pocket.

Kate worked quietly, you would think in an attempt to be courteous, trying not to disturb Nathan, but John could see she took in every word of the conversation on his end. By the time the pot perked on the stove, she gave up any pretense of ignoring him and stood across the counter from the sheriff, openly listening. Nathan didn't seem to notice.

"You talked to anybody that's seen him since Saturday?" Pause. "What about Buck Locust over on Snowbird? Anybody talked to him?"

Axe listened intently, a worried frown forming on his forehead. "When did Amy call you?"

Yona and Faron got out cups and brought them to the table. John added a carton of milk and the sugar bowl. They heard the sheriff ask a few more questions, then thank Dorsey for his help. He came to sit with them at the table to wait for the coffee to perk. "I don't like this a bit," he said, shaking his head. "People suddenly aren't where they're supposed to be…where they always are. It just beats all."

"Who's not where they're supposed to be, Nathan?" Kate asked.

Axe turned to John. "You didn't go to the station today, did you?"

"I had some things to do with Walker. Buck gave me the day off and said he would handle my work for today. He went up on the Cheoah to check on a dieback Eli saw from the tower. I was supposed to be up there all day, but Buck took over."

The sheriff squinted his eyes and stared at John for a moment. John didn't like the suspicious expression on his face.

"Where on the Cheoah?"

"Over on the south side, way off the road."

"Were you anywhere near that Sacred Circle camp, John?"

"Maybe," John said. "I'm not sure just exactly where the Sacred Circle camp is, but I reckon it's in that general area. I think Eagle Feather would set up close to a road, though. I doubt the folks who come to his camps are gonna want to hike in. A lot of them look like they couldn't walk far."

Nathan nodded thoughtfully. Nobody said anything. Kate brought the coffee pot over and filled the cups. Axe added liberal amounts of cream and sugar to his cup and took a long sip. After he savored the coffee for a moment, he said, "I called Dorsey and told him about the Montero y'all found. He went out to Eagle Feather's place to talk to him, but he wasn't there. Nobody knows where he is. He didn't show up at the camp today and his pigeons are worried. He was supposed to teach them to make medicine or something, and his daughter was going to teach them traditional chants. Dorsey said they were standing around with their hands full of crystals and dyed chicken feathers, looking like lost sheep."

"That's just pitiful," Kate said. "If he's gonna charge those poor people an arm and a leg and drag them up here to the mountains, he ought to at least show up and give them what they paid for. If he isn't the biggest charlatan in the state, he sure runs a close second."

John cleared his throat. "Well, Mama Kate. Like Walker said, they're just looking for some connection to Creator. If they can't get people who know something to teach them, like you for instance, then they have nobody to turn to but the charlatans. Ever think about that?"

Kate gave him a look that would freeze molten lava. It was what he expected. He knew she wouldn't acknowledge his comment, but before she could make a show of ignoring him, lights from the Blazer beamed in the living room window and they heard the engine shut off in the yard. It had to be Walker and David.

Kate and Faron ran to the door, anxious to reassure themselves that Walker was alright. Yona followed more slowly, but his relief at the safe arrival of his grandfather showed.

John waited at the table. He was in no hurry to talk to Faron's grandpa. He took a quick look to make sure the old man was still in one piece. Walker looked fine, maybe a bit tired and worried. He looked even more worried when he saw Nathan Axe.

"Sheriff Axe," David said with a nod. "Glad to see you made yourself at home. Sit down and finish your coffee."

Axe waited where he stood while David hugged Kate and Faron and responded to their inquiries about the health of his various relatives and told them how Meredith was doing in medical school down in Georgia. Then they all calmly trooped to the kitchen like they had nothing better to do than chat with the sheriff, except for Walker. He went to look for Wren.

John followed him to the living room where he bent over Wren, listening to her breathing. The sight made John soften a little toward the old man. Walker wouldn't ever do anything to hurt his little girl. He thought the world of his great-grandchildren.

"She's okay, Grandpa," he said. "Just tired out."

Walker tucked the blanket around her shoulders. "I just want to know my grandbabies are alright. Where's Diamond?"

John realized he hadn't even asked about his son. He and Walker went to the kitchen and sat down to the steaming hot coffee that waited for them. He took a sip and asked Faron who was looking after Diamond.

"Bonnie Locust is watching him for us," she said. "She's real good with the kids for a girl who's just turned thirteen. And her mama's close by if she has any problems."

Nathan put his cup down. "Faron," he said, "Amy Locust isn't at home. She's in Dorsey's office right now. Buck was supposed to be home around six o'clock. When he didn't show up, Amy called the station to see if anybody had heard from him. Nobody's seen or talked to him since he left the station early this morning. Eli Smoker and some of the men went up on Cheoah to look for him. Eli found his truck off up in the woods, but no sign of Buck. Amy's real worried."

Faron reached for her car keys on the countertop. "Honey," she said to John, "go get Wren. We've gotta go home."

Kate gave her a quick hug and told her goodnight. "You drive carefully, honey," she said.

John asked Kate, "You want to ride home with Yona and Grandpa or come with us?"

"I'll stay and make us some supper while Walker rests for a while. I think he could use a hot meal before we head for home," Kate said.

Faron rushed out the door without saying goodbye. John heard the car start before he could pick Wren up from the chair where she remained sound asleep. She didn't stir as he carried her out. As soon as they got into the car, Faron backed across the bridge, wheeled around, and took off for home. The people along Big Cove Road probably wondered who was in such an all-fired hurry when they heard her Mustang speeding toward the parkway.

John never saw her like this before. She knew as well as he that something was going on and she had no control over it. She didn't like it a bit. From the way she drove, she needed to get back to their house on the Snowbird as fast as possible. He didn't try to slow her down. He couldn't wait to be home, away from whatever drew Walker into something dark and malevolent.

Wren sat wide awake and secure in her seatbelt in the backseat. "Mama, it'll be okay," she said. "Mama Kate will take care of Grandpa and Uncle Yona."

"I know, baby," Faron said in a tight, controlled voice. She felt it too. "We can rest as soon as she gets them home and we're all where we belong."

John understood that. Sanctuary. That's what they found in their isolated corner of the world on Snowbird Creek. A place of refuge from the frightening things that happened to people beyond the protective circle of the Smokies. Out there young girls got murdered and old men went missing. Women had to worry about their husbands not making it home. But not in their house. Not on Snowbird, at least not until now.

Buck and Amy were like family. Now Buck was missing and a girl was dead—a young girl, one of their own, and they didn't even know her.

John put a hand on Faron's thigh and felt it tremble. She was scared to death. Something bore down on them, getting closer and more threatening with every minute. He could feel it too, and he had no idea what it was.

Faron never cried, but unshed tears glistened on her lashes. She held them back. She wouldn't want to scare him and Wren. He felt helpless in the face of her fear, but it was her stoicism that reduced him to complete impotence.

The knot in his belly tightened. The vague fear that dogged him all day grew stronger by the minute. But that wasn't the worst part. Seeing Faron hurting and knowing he couldn't do anything to help killed his soul. If she was the kind of woman who'd cry in his arms and let him hold her, it would make him feel like he was taking care of her, but that wasn't Faron's way.

"You okay, honey?" John asked her.

"Sure, darlin'." She smiled a tight smile and reached to squeeze his hand. Her hand felt cold as ice. "No problem," she said.

Tuesday Night

David Wayanettah's House

Walker watched the taillights of Faron's car disappear around the
bend. He went inside and closed the front door, feeling as tired
and old as he acted when he last saw Nathan Axe up on Wolf
Mountain. He sat down in Dave's easy chair, clutching the
blanket that still held Wren's warmth.

Axe came and perched on the arm of the couch. "Mr.
Copperhead, I don't think you and David had anything to do
with killing that girl, but I know you can tell me more than you
told me. I need you to help me out. I'm trying to make sure
nothing like that happens to anybody else's little granddaughter. I
want you to tell me what the hell y'all were doing way up on that
mountain today. Something's going on, and you know what it is
if anybody does."

"I reckon so, Nathan. But there are reasons why I can't tell
you much more than you already know. You're one of us. You
know how it is," Walker said.

Nathan Axe looked very uncomfortable. "Look, guys. I
don't like this any better than you do, but I'm just trying to do
my job. I don't know much about our spiritual ways. I leave that
to my mother. I've been a Baptist since I was twelve, and our
church doesn't approve of it. That works for me, because I like
things that make sense, and let's face it, our old ways defy logic. I
might not believe, but I respect your belief." His voice softened.
"Mr. Copperhead, my job is to find a murderer. I won't talk
about it to anybody unless there's no other way. Anything I learn
here tonight, I'll follow up on my own."

Walker leaned his head against the back of the chair and let
the blanket drop across his lap. Axe was watching him

expectantly. He could hear Kate in the kitchen, familiar homey sounds that usually made a man feel comfortable, but tonight it didn't have the same calming effect. David and Yona waited, like they expected him to know how to handle things.

Walker could see the sheriff's patience wearing thin. Tradition, and a lifetime of respect for the secret mysteries of the Snake Dancers' circle, determined how much Walker could tell the authorities, even Nathan Axe, who was a member of the tribe with a mother steeped in traditional ways.

Walker grinned like this was just a friendly visit from an old family friend. "Nathan, you know us elders have a lot of old-fashioned ways you young men don't think much of. That's all it is. These boys just try to humor me sometimes. That's the only reason we were up there."

The sheriff didn't buy it. Walker's explanation made him mad. "I hoped you would do better than that. You might pull something like the superstitious elder bullshit on Dorsey, but I thought you had more respect for the son of one of those elders."

Walker held his temper. He watched Nathan Axe grow up in one of the most traditional families on the Qualla Boundary. The boy knew enough to understand when it was best to leave things alone. Couldn't he take a hint? He tried turning the questions aside with small talk. "Speaking of your mother, Nathan, how's she doing these days? Mighty fine woman, Maddie Axe is. You tell her how much I appreciate how she taught Kate ever since she was just a girl."

"You see my mother at least once a week, Mr. Copperhead. You know how she's doing as well as I do. Now, no disrespect intended, but let's cut the crap. Tell me why you guys just happened to be in a place you had to hike three hours to get to, and you find a dead girl there. Then tell me why you think it is that two of your good buddies and that weird-assed white shaman have turned up missing. Any connection with that secret society you elders belong to?"

171

The sheriff went too far. Walker's voice dripped icicles. "Nathan, like you said, you're the son of an elder. You know there are some things we'd be better off not airing to the world. I suggest you settle for what I tell you. Just accept that we were teaching Wren a history lesson. David helped us out by showing us the place where some of our people hid out during the removal. You've done the same thing yourself for some of the kids. It makes it more real to them if we take them to the places where it happened."

Nathan leaned toward Walker. "That's the story I'll put on the book if you want me to, but only if you tell me the truth, as much of it as you can. The sooner we work this out, the better it will be for all of us. I doubt that you want this to drag on with a lot of people prowling around the crime scene."

That put a damper on Walker's anger and made him apprehensive. He glanced at David. "Boy, what do you think Driver would have said about this?"

"He already said it, Grandfather. Things are a lot different now. We have to find our own way."

Walker stared at Nathan a while and then grinned slightly. "I reckon you'd have to answer to Miss Maddie if you didn't keep your mouth shut."

Nathan nodded. "Talk to me, Mr. Copperhead. I've got a lot to do before I can get any sleep tonight."

Walker didn't see any way out. An innocent young girl lay dead, and whoever killed her was out there somewhere. And Wren wasn't far enough away to be out of danger. If telling the sheriff enough to help him catch the killer would protect his granddaughter, he had to do it. At least Nathan Axe was Cherokee. That made it easier.

First he spoke to Yona. "Listen up, boy. You're gonna need to know this too." He told the story in the same way the elders passed it down through the generations. The monster serpent Uktena and the powerful crystal Ulunsu'ti, taken from his head

172

by the outsider. He described how the conjurors of old controlled the crystal and used it for good until the fame of its power brought greedy men who tried to steal it away. The last great conjuror, Kanegwa'ti, the Water Moccasin, hid it to await the Suye'ta who would use it again to help the Cherokee people.

Neither Nathan nor Yona interrupted. When Walker finished, Nathan said, "We've heard the story before. What does it have to do with that girl getting killed?"

Walker asked, "You mentioned a secret society. What do you know about a society made up of the descendants of the conjurors of old? A society that's responsible for looking after certain objects that could give a man the same kind of power the old conjurors had?"

Axe said, "I've heard rumors."

"The rumors are true," Walker said. "I'm a member of that society."

"I figured you would be." Nathan turned to David. "And Driver, was he in it too?"

David grunted a yes. "The two Cherokee men you can't find are members too. I hold Driver's place, since he walked over."

Nathan asked again, "Can you tell me what that has to do with the dead girl?"

Yona said, "Go on, Grandpa. I'd like to know that too."

"I'm getting to it," Walker said. "It could have something to do with the things the society protected. Powerful objects, well hidden by the first guardians long before the removal, each in its own place, each with its own protector. Nobody knew the whereabouts of anything except the thing the guardian and his descendants guarded. Yesterday, that changed. We found a duffle bag full of almost everything we've been guarding for nearly four hundred years. All of it in one place."

Nathan leaned forward. "You've seen them, and know for sure they're real, not just another old story?"

David let the sheriff know what he thought of that remark. "These old stories are the only way we have of passing our heritage down. Everything our ancestors put in writing has either been destroyed or stashed in a museum, where none of us can get our hands on it. The little we have left is encoded in the stories we tell. People like you, who've turned more white than Indian, might be surprised at how much truth the stories have in them when they're told right. If you had listened to your mother, you'd know that. Miss Maddie knows."

Walker felt a surge of pride in David. Driver left his place in the circle in good hands.

The sheriff looked sheepish. "Sorry, David. In my line of work, you tend to get a little cynical." He turned back to Walker, all business now. "Now, Mr. Copperhead, tell me what was in that duffle bag." He took out a notepad and pen, ready to write down whatever Walker told him.

"Put that away, Nathan, or I won't say another word about anything. None of this has ever been written down and I aim to keep it that way."

Axe reluctantly put the notepad back into the inside pocket of his jacket. "Okay, Mr. Copperhead. Have it your way, but I need to know what you saw and why it's such a big deal."

Walker already told him more than he wanted to. Only the thought of the dead girl, and the need to help Nathan catch the man who killed her before he hurt anyone else, made him go on. He leaned forward. "Nathan, would you understand what it meant if I told you that duffle bag was filled with Kanagwa'ti's medicine, his bones, and the Cherokee Ark of the Covenant? And that we found it within a couple of miles of the Council House Mound?"

"I'd appreciate it if you'd go on and tell me what it means, Mr. Copperhead."

"It means, at the very least, that somebody robbed the conjuror's grave. And that they stole the ark from where it had

174

been safeguarded for generations, then they brought everything they stole to the only place it can safely be used to wake up the Ulunsu'ti. It means they might also have the Ulunsu'ti, and they are just waiting to get their hands on the only other thing they need to wake him. That last thing is just a few yards away from where that girl got killed. If they have that, we can just stick our heads between our legs and kiss our ass goodbye."

Walker sat back and looked the sheriff in the eye. "You wanna write all that down in your notebook and tell it to the folks down at that church you go to? Wonder what they'd have to say about your superstitious Indians then, Nathan."

Nathan stood and walked to the window and looked out into the darkness for a moment, then came back to his perch on the end of the sofa. "Is the Ulunsu'ti real, Mr. Copperhead? Can it really do what the stories say it can?"

Walker wished he could say no. "Yeah, son. It's real, and it can do more than you ever heard about. If it gets into the wrong hands, and the wrong person tries to use it…well, we don't want that to happen. Kanegwa'ti went to a lot of trouble to prevent it."

Nathan asked, "Don't they say somebody is supposed to come along and be able to use the Ulunsu'ti's power for the good of the tribe? Could it be that he's the one who gathered up all the stuff you found?"

"If the Suye'ta was here, the Snake Dancers would be the first to know. We would have spent a lot of time preparing him and making sure he didn't bring on more harm than good. No, Nathan, it's not the Suye'ta, but it's somebody who knows a lot of things they shouldn't. That, or…"

"Or what, Mr. Copperhead?" Nathan asked.

Walker couldn't bring himself to say it.

David answered for him. "Or one of us has gone crazy."

"One of the Snake Dancers?" the sheriff asked.

Walker nodded.

David said, "Most of my generation had a hard time

175

believing what our elders told us when they first brought us in. Doesn't take long to be convinced, though, once you've seen a few things you never thought possible. But those things have always been enough to keep us on the straight and narrow. It's possible they didn't make that big of an impression on everybody. Could be that somebody hung around to learn all they needed to know to—"

"No, Dave." Walker couldn't let him say such things. "In all these centuries, that never happened. I know all the others. Not a one of us would even think about it. Somehow, somebody found out. It had to be an outsider. No Cherokee would dig up the conjuror's grave."

"I know it wasn't easy for you to tell me all this," the sheriff said, "but it'll help me figure out who killed the girl, and I'll keep it to myself."

Walker nodded his approval. "I appreciate that, Nathan."

The sheriff knitted his fingers, stretched his arms out, and cracked all his knuckles at once. "Mr. Copperhead," he said, "tell me about the Suye'ta. If I remember right, he would be an outsider. Right?"

"Yeah, he would. But we've always believed he would be someone we brought in. Someone we had to bribe with a prize that made the well-being of the tribe more important to him than his own safety. He would be like the Shawnee who killed Uktena so he could have the Cherokee woman he loved."

"What if a man wanted the power of the Ulunsu'ti the same way the Shawnee wanted a Cherokee wife?" Nathan asked. "What if that power was important enough that he would put it ahead of his own safety? There are lots of people like that in the world, possibly even in your society. I hate to do this, Mr. Copperhead, but I'm gonna have to ask you to give me the names of the other members."

David jumped to his feet, but Walker raised his hand in a quieting gesture before he could say anything. He was as mad as

David, but anger wouldn't accomplish anything. Walker stood and pointed to the door. "Nathan, you'd best be getting to work. Like you said, you've got a lot to do tonight, and you've got all you're gonna get around here."

Nathan didn't have time to object before Kate appeared at his side, all smiles. "Nathan, honey, I do wish you had time to eat some supper with us, but I understand." She took his hand and led him to the door. "I cooked almost everything David had in the house too, even if it was just a few trout from the freezer and some frozen French fries. I made a bowl of hushpuppies to go with it. You'll have to come over to Snowbird real soon and I'll make it up to you. How does next Sunday sound? You could bring Miss Maddie over for dinner with us. Would you like that?"

She practically purred. Axe was so busy blushing and fidgeting with his hat, he hardly noticed when she edged him out the door.

"Why, sure, Kate, but I do need to talk to Mr. Copperhead just a minute longer."

Kate laughed. "Lord, Nathan, you men will have plenty of time to socialize later. Right now, Grandpa needs to eat and get home to his own bed. You run along now, and we'll see you Sunday." She kissed the air at him and shut the door.

"Supper's ready," she said to her men folks. Walker motioned to Yona and David and they followed Kate to the kitchen. A woman like Kate made life easier. She knew how to handle things.

Supper was good, although dark thoughts kept Walker's mind occupied as he ate in silence. It surprised him he could eat at all, but he finished every bite. As soon as the last morsel of crisp fried trout disappeared from his plate, Kate cleared the table.

When she went to the sink with a load of dirty dishes, Walker spoke in a near whisper. "Boys, we've got some talking to

177

do, but I need to think awhile first. Why don't you take over and clean up, so Kate can go home. If she's gonna be on the road by herself, I'd like her to head out soon."

"She kinda figured on you and me going home with her, Grandpa," Yona said.

"I know she did, son, but we've got too much to do right here on Lightning Creek. Dave, hope you don't mind if me and Yona stay the night with you."

"Sure, Grandfather," David said. "I've got plenty of room here since I've been living alone. Yona, you're familiar with Meredith's room. I doubt she would mind if you bunked in there."

Walker grinned at Yona. "So, you've been coming over here to hang out with Dave, huh? I noticed you haven't been over here much since Meredith went back to Atlanta."

"Lay off, Grandpa." Yona reddened. "If I'd said anything to you, you would have had us married and cranking out grandbabies by now. Meredith's not ready for that."

"When do you reckon she's gonna be ready, boy?"

"When she's ready, Grandpa," Yona grunted. "You ask her when that'll be." He took the rest of the dishes to the sink.

Kate came to the table and planted a loud kiss on top of Walker's head. "I need the keys to the Blazer," she said. "I guess David can bring you home when you and Yona finish whatever you've been whispering about."

"You're not gonna fuss about it or nothing?" Walker asked.

"Would it do any good?"

"I reckon not, Kate." Walker almost wished she would insist that he come on home, or just tell him he was way too old to go trudging around through the Smoky Mountains. He watched her walk out the door. It sure would feel good to be heading home to his own bed.

It gave him a measure of comfort to think of her safely on Snowbird. Faron and John and Wren should be almost there by now. He didn't have to worry about Wren any more. Tomorrow night he'd be there with them if things went well. If not, then who knew if he would ever go home?

Sounds echoed the way they do through an empty house. The closing of the door. Kate's footsteps on the porch. The rattle of the bridge under the Blazer's wheels. The resonance of things unsaid, hanging in the evening silence.

Walker sat in David's easy chair, listening to the clatter of dishes while Yona and David cleaned up, and thought about what he had to do. By the time they joined him, he was ready to talk.

"Boys," he said, "you've heard how the stories say the Suye'ta has to be an outsider. I think you know what I had in mind, don't you, David?"

David nodded. "About John?"

Walker looked at Yona. "How about you, son? We've talked about Suye'ta being an outsider with a strong connection to the tribe. David caught on that I had John in mind and was rightly pissed. How about you?"

Yona stopped pacing and faced his grandfather. "I know something's been going on, but I don't know what. Reckon you could fill me in, Grandpa? I'm getting just a bit pissed myself. Just following along, keeping my mouth shut when I don't know jack-shit about what's up. You been throwing me hints as long as I can remember. Don't you think it's about time you...bring me in, or whatever?"

"Whoa, boy. Don't get ahead of yourself." Walker hadn't expected that.

David leaned back in the chair across from Walker. "Grandfather," he said. "I don't see that Yona is getting ahead of himself. Driver claimed if you had your way, you'd try to hang on till Diamond gets old enough to take over for you. I'd say we can't afford to take that chance. With things the way they are, Yona needs to be able to step in if anything happens to you."

179

"Does it look like I've been holding back on Yona? He's heard a lot in the last two days."

"He's heard next to nothing, considering all he's gonna have to learn. Grandfather, the last thing Driver said to me was that he wished he hadn't waited so long. He walked over knowing he wouldn't have time to teach me all the things he needed to. I'm looking to you to take up where he left off. Yona and I will have our hands full. We need to work with you as long as we can, and you're not getting any younger. Buck's grandpa brought him in early. They had years in the circle together. I wish I'd had that with Driver."

Walker tried to come up with some sort of objection before he lost control of a situation that he thought he planned well.

Yona stood and stretched to his full height. "It's late and I'm worn out. Grandpa, why don't you get some rest now? You and I have to get up early in the morning and take the conjuror's bones and medicine back to Ataga'hi. That's a good place to start, I reckon. We can do what we need to do then. It's about time I was a Snake Dancer." He went to Meredith's room without a backward glance.

"Looks like it's been decided, huh, Grandfather?" David said.

Walker didn't answer. He knew he should have started preparations for Yona's initiation long ago. Why did he wait so long? Driver asked him that question last time they talked. True, it did make him face his own mortality, but then, at his age, that lurked around the corner whether or not he admitted it. He talked about it with Grady. They both had grandsons ready and waiting, but for some reason, they both stalled.

He could hear Yona getting ready for bed. He would be glad when Meredith Wayanettah finished her residency so she and Yona could marry and have him some more grandbabies. But Yona needed to stay alive for that.

It's like Grady said when they talked about Eli and Yona.

The Snake Dancers would be right in the line of fire. That was a hard place to put somebody you loved. It looked like the new Dancers had to deal with the very thing they feared.

This generation of Dancers would have their hands full, and the elders wouldn't be around to help much longer. He and Grady both knew they didn't have many more years in the world. Driver Wayanettah and Del Locust already walked over. Walker leaned back in the chair and said a prayer for the grandsons. It would all be up to them soon. Very soon.

Wednesday Morning

Qualla Boundary

The trailer no longer offered comfort. Even the old house, once filled with memory and love, was nothing but a hulking shadow against the darker shade of the mountain. He didn't bother to hide his car behind the laurels this time. The only mortal he feared wandered through the cave, probably still searching for the conjuror's hands, or for him. Next time they met, he would be the hunter, not the prey. He wearied of running from a man who already cost him everything that mattered. The chance to undo the harm kept him on his feet. He wouldn't let that go.

With time running out, he had a lot to do before he was free to walk over to the other world. He parked the Pinto under the beech tree and walked to the old house. He stopped for a moment on the front porch and leaned against one of the sagging posts, allowing memories of better days to flash through his mind. Faces and voices of people he would never see again reminded him of all he lost. At the edge of his mind, the darkness drew him in. He slipped into it, away from the pain.

He could think better this way. His mind remained sharp, as long as he stayed in that place where pain and remorse couldn't reach him. It seemed strange to watch his worn-out old body from that gray, empty void, to see it wander through the memory-haunted rooms of the house and out to the back porch. To watch it stoop down and wiggle the stone loose from the well.

His hands reached in and lifted the crystal from the safe and cradled it against his body. The weight of it drew him back to reality. It felt heavier than he remembered. It filled his arms and compelled him to look into its core. Did he imagine a fiery radiance awakening there? With an act of will, he turned his eyes away and dropped the crystal into the knapsack.

Opening the back door of his old house, he breathed in the smells of age and decay. The house no longer held the welcoming sense of home, only the echo of a life that belonged to somebody else. The man who lived here couldn't kill, no more than he could betray his people.

Memories flooded his mind and wrenched him back from the shadows. The weight of all the generations he dishonored bore down on his soul. He couldn't blame anybody but himself and his own foolish pride. If he had listened to the other Snake Dancers, they would have stopped him, but he thought he knew better than his brothers.

The white man who called himself Eagle Feather took the place of his own son in his heart when he found out Thomas abandoned the Choctaw woman who carried his baby. Eagle Feather brought her to this old house and placed their baby granddaughter in Sally's arms. Sally cried when they told her she had her name. Little Salena never left her stepfather's side. Their shared love for the little girl who shared her grandmother's name bound them together. Now, she was dead.

He didn't linger in the old house. What he needed wasn't there. He hurried through the house, across the yard, and into the backdoor of his trailer. In the kitchen the coffee pot still sat on the stove, the grounds emitting the smell of stale coffee. He tried not to think of the gentle, trusting girl who poured his last cup from that pot, but the memory washed over him before he could stop it. Grief knifed through him until he found his way back into the gray world. There, the pain numbed and became a raging desire for vengeance. It allowed him to think again.

He remembered an extra flashlight in the pantry and took it to replace the one the white man took from him. He put in fresh batteries, then grabbed a second flashlight from his bedside table. He didn't dare risk getting stranded in the dark again.

A long time ago, when wild game sometimes meant the

difference between hunger and a full belly, he hunted for meat. He never did it for pleasure, so he didn't have fancy rifles like his son. From the bedroom closet, he pulled out his only firearm. The old double-barreled twelve-gauge shotgun seldom got fired anymore, but he kept it polished and ready. Living out here in the woods, he never knew when he might need a gun.

Only two shells remained in the box. He put them both in the knapsack and went back to the car. From that place where cold couldn't touch him, he watched his body shiver in the damp air.

Just before dawn, he pulled out onto 441. Thick, dark clouds hung low in the sky and made it feel more like the dead of night. He cranked up the heater in an attempt to dispel the bone-deep chill in his body, but it didn't help, just fogged up the windows. He turned it off and drove on, back up to the head of Lightning Creek.

He needed to see if the Montero still sat parked where they left it yesterday. As he crossed the bridge, the Pinto coughed. He looked at the gas gauge. Empty. With everything on his mind, he neglected to fill it up. The remaining few drops of gas served to get the car off the road, beside the creek where it coughed one last time and died.

Slinging the knapsack over his shoulder and cradling the shotgun in the crook of his arm, he set off back up Wolf Mountain. His head throbbed. He touched his wound and winced at the pain. Blood still oozed from the gash. He ignored the pain and kept walking. Nothing he could do about it anyway.

A damp, cold wind blew against him, slowing his steps and chilling him to the bone. He shivered and considered it small penance for his evil deeds.

His discomfort helped to keep his mind focused on the task at hand. When he grew so tired he didn't think he could take another step, he willed his legs to keep moving.

Near the crest, his body gave out. Ahead he saw the

boulders that marked the entrance of the cave. He could afford to rest a few minutes, but not out in the open. For all he knew, the white man lurked somewhere up there in the rocks waiting to finish him off. He sunk down under a clump of scrub laurel and rested long enough to catch his breath and regain some strength in his legs.

When he caught his breath, he breached the shotgun and loaded both barrels. The briefest instant of clarity flashed through his mind, a voice that reminded him of the years Eagle Feather cherished Salena, taking care of her, teaching her, and giving her the love Thomas denied her. But, that only brought on an unbearable guilt. He retreated to the gray world where he didn't feel anything but rage and blame.

He pulled himself to his feet and kept to the cover of bushes and boulders, making his way to the overhang at the mouth of the cave, and listened. Not a sound reached his ears. He peered as far as he could see into the cave and saw no one. Was Eagle Feather lying in wait to ambush him, or wandering lost in the darkness?

With the flashlight in one hand and the shotgun in the other, he entered the cave. A few feet past the entrance, he stopped and flashed the light ahead. Nothing moved and only his labored breathing broke the silence. Adjusting the knapsack across his shoulder, he plunged ahead. The Ulunsu'ti's weight pressed heavy against his body.

Early Wednesday Morning

Lightning Creek

Morning broke gray and way too cool for this time of the year. Walker must have been really tired to sleep in long enough to let the boys get up before him. He heard them in the kitchen. The smell of coffee motivated him to join them. David poured him a cup when he got to the table. A pan of bacon sizzled on the stove, and Yona scrambled the last dozen eggs in the fridge. He put half a loaf of buttered bread in the oven to toast and set a jar of Meredith's blackberry jam on the table. The aroma from the kitchen promised a good start for the day.

Walker let Yona and David serve him, one of the privileges of being the old man of the family. He hurried through breakfast but David and Yona took their time, like they planned to linger over coffee and enjoy the morning. He gave them a nudge.

"Boys, I'd like to get on the trail as soon as we can," he said. "I want to put things back where they belong. Kanagwa'ti's bones and medicine ought to have a good resting place before nightfall."

"As soon as we finish breakfast, Grandpa," Yona said. "Then, Dave and I will go back up Wolf Mountain to get the stuff we left there. You can wait here while we do that. Then I guess you and I have to go to Ataga'hi alone. From what I've heard, I figure we'd have to kill Dave if he knew where we dug the grave."

Walker didn't laugh. "Yona, some things we don't joke about. You need to remember that."

"Well, Grandpa," Yona said, "to be honest, I wondered if it was true. The way you guys talked, sounded like you'd do just about anything to protect your secrets."

Walker sipped his coffee and didn't say anything.

David chuckled. It sounded strained, like he worried he just might end up dead if he learned the Copperhead's hiding place. "No problem. One mountain a day is enough for me to climb. You two are on your own when we get back from the cave. I'll be busy finding a new place to hide the hands. I don't think it's a good idea to leave them in the cave."

"And you don't need our help for that?" Yona asked.

"I'll have to handle it without you," David said. "Can't have you Copperheads knowing where they are. A tough old dude like Walker would be mighty hard to kill, but I reckon I'd have to do it somehow. Snake Dancer rules."

Walker got up and took his plate to the sink. "Forget it, boys. You're not leaving me here. I'm ready to go. No reason for me to hang around the house doing nothing all morning."

Yona and David exchanged glances. Yona shrugged in resignation. "Well, Dave, we tried."

David looked for a moment like he would argue, then echoed Yona's shrug and finished the last of his breakfast.

They left their dishes in the sink and piled into David's pickup. The closest route to the cave was the path off the logging road past Aunt Lynelle's place. The ride gave Walker time to start Yona's education. He finally admitted to himself that it was long overdue. Both of the boys needed to know about the history of the Snake Dancers and the duties that fell to them now that the elders no longer had things under control.

He told them about the Ulunsu'ti, not the stories they heard all their lives, but real things it could do and how it could be used. And he told them the truth about Kanegwa'ti, how he was an outsider adopted into the tribe. As the Suye'ta of his day, he risked possession by Uktena, the serpent spirit of the Ulunsu'ti, in order to use its power for the good of the people.

"With the white people taking everything else, Kanegwa'ti knew it was only a matter of time before they found out about the Ulunsu'ti and wanted it too. You boys are part of a long line of Snake Dancers Kanegwa'ti appointed to protect the Ulunsu'ti and its medicine. You're descendants of men who hold the knowledge of where each object is."

Yona said one word under his breath. "Damn."

David grinned in sympathy. "Hang in there, Yona. It's a lot to ask modern guys like us to accept, but I've learned enough to believe it's all true."

"You sure this isn't a load of bullshit, huh, Dave? He's not just putting me on, like some sort of initiation or something? Is he just testing me to see how gullible I am?"

"No, man. There's more, and it gets weirder," David answered.

Yona pointed out that he didn't know where or what anything was. "I've been kept in the dark until now. Nobody tells me anything until things get messed up and I'm expected to help fix it."

Walker apologized to Yona. "I was wrong to keep things from you for so long. I don't know why I did. Me and Grady talked about it once. He never told Eli anything either. We had a feeling this generation was going to have a hard time, and we hated to put that burden on our grandsons. Now, if we can't find Grady, we'll have to take Eli in too."

There wasn't time to fill Yona in on the details of his guardianship before they reached the trail. David parked his pickup near the hemlocks where they found the Montero.

David slung his backpack across his shoulder and picked out a path toward the cave. Walker tried to keep up with the younger men, but he didn't feel as strong as he let on. The rain that started with a drizzle about the time they left home came down in heavy, cold drops now. He wore a plastic poncho he found in a hall closet at David's house. Judging by the powder blue color, he figured it was one Meredith left behind. It gave him better protection than the windbreakers and baseball caps Yona and

David wore. He tried to warn them, but they were convinced the rain would let up. The weatherman on TV said so. They'd learn.

The wind picked up, leaving them all chilled. Walker couldn't stop shivering under the poncho. When he lagged behind, David and Yona waited for him to catch up. His teeth chattered and he couldn't stop it. David and Yona looked worried.

"When we get to the cave, we'll build a fire to thaw you out," David said. "It's not far now. Can you hold out a while longer?"

Walker lied and said he was fine. A fire would feel good. That motivated him to find the strength to speed up a little. By the time they came in sight of the rocks where Grady's granddaughter died, he felt chilled to the bone.

The granite overhang at the mouth of the cave sheltered them from a fine, cold drizzle that looked like it could go on all day. Walker hunkered down against the rock. "Where's that fire you promised me, Dave?" He shivered uncontrollably and every joint in his body felt stiff with cold. He clenched his teeth to stop their chattering.

A few crows still crouched forlornly in the tall pine tree.

He watched David take a nine-inch hunting knife from his pack and go at an old stump beside the tree. The boy should be able to hack out enough pitch to start a fire. It would burn hot even when wet. Yona gathered up some dead branches and hurried back to him.

Walker sat hunched over under the poncho. It didn't offer much warmth. His shivering was getting out of control. Yona dropped the branches on the ground and looked him over. "I don't like the way you look, Grandpa."

David looked up from the small flame he teased out of the pine pitch. "He's turning kinda blue. We better get him warmed up. He can rest awhile before we head back. If the rain lets up, it won't be so bad." Walker huddled against the rocks, drawing the poncho around him.

"Too much easy living, Grandfather," David said. "In the old days, a man your age would still be in his prime. Here you are, shivering like you're gonna freeze to death." He laughed, but the laugh came out strained.

"Yeah, I'm getting soft from easy living. Just get the fire going, boy, if you don't want to tote my carcass back down the mountain." Walker tried to laugh too, but started coughing instead.

The flame danced from the damp pine pitch and crackled to life. Yona's hands shook as he piled on the wet pine twigs. Walker wasn't the only one getting chilled to the bone.

Dark, pitch-scented smoke spiraled up toward the crack in the rocks and disappeared out into the drizzle. Walker leaned toward the fire and watched David take a thermos from his pack. The boy thought of everything. He took the coffee David offered and cupped it between his palms, enjoying the warmth. His teeth finally stopped chattering.

"You think you gonna make it now, Grandpa?" Yona asked.

"I reckon I just might, son. I'd sure like to dry out some, though. I can't remember it ever being so cold this late in the year."

They passed the coffee cup around and all took a swig, then David refilled it.

"Hey, Dave," Walker said, "any chance of you pulling a helicopter out of that knapsack of yours? You seem to have nearly everything else. I could use a ride down this mountain."

"You had your chance to stay home warm and dry, Grandfather. Reckon you'll have to make it home on your own two feet, just like the rest of us." David put the thermos down beside Walker and stood up. "You stay here and get warmed up. Me and Yona will go get the stuff. If I recall, the pucker factor is a bit too high for you in the cave anyway."

Walker leaned back against a rock and tried to get

comfortable. He poured the last of the coffee into the cup and sipped. "You're mighty right, son. I'd just as soon stay here." He waved them off and watched Yona follow Dave into the cave, hoping they were as strong as they looked. It wouldn't be long now before their generation would be on their own. He and Grady were the only elders left, and they were both too old to handle a guardian's duties. If he'd had any doubts about it before, he didn't now. The exertion and cold left him so weak, he wasn't worth a crap. He was practically dead on his feet, right in the middle of the biggest crisis the Snake Dancers had ever faced.

If he made it down off this mountain, he had to find Grady Smoker. The two of them needed to get the boys ready and turn things over to the next generation of Snake Dancers. He hoped they were up to it.

Wednesday Morning

The Cave

He heard the white man's voice before he saw him staggering toward him at the edge of the light, calling out to him, praising his wisdom and thanking God he came back.

Eagle Feather hurried toward him, talking fast. "I found them. We can do it now. Just like you planned. It will work."

He didn't dare risk allowing the white man to convince him. Eagle Feather couldn't control the crystal. "It won't work," he said. "It has to go back to the Snake Dancers. All of it."

Eagle Feather came closer. "No, I won't let you give it back. We've come too far to quit. I have them. Look." He reached inside his fringed jacket and brought out the bowl, holding it out to the elder like a gift. "See. We have everything we need now. I *am* the Suye'ta." His voice came low and sincere, but his eyes locked on the knapsack.

He swung the shotgun up and rested the stock against his shoulder, his finger gripping the trigger. Eagle Feather didn't take his eyes off the knapsack. He couldn't let him get his hands on the crystal.

"We have to do it for her," the white man said. "Salena would want us to. We can't let her death be in vain."

The sound of her name from the lips of the man he blamed for her death was a sacrilege he couldn't bear. He nestled the stock against his shoulder, pointing the long barrel at the white man's head, shouting at him to stay back.

It didn't stop him.

His finger tightened on the trigger of its own volition. The explosion that followed reverberated in his head. The force of the recoil slammed the gunstock hard into his shoulder and knocked him off his feet, sending him reeling against the cave wall. A sharp protrusion in the rock caught him high on his back, tearing through muscle and flesh.

He sagged to the floor and lay limp, afraid to open his eyes. Echoes of the blast resounded in the deep recesses of the cave and died away. He called the white man's name, straining to catch any sound. The silence was absolute.

He groped around him for the dropped flashlight. The shotgun lay somewhere on the cave floor.

His right arm felt numb. He checked the shoulder that took the brunt of the shotgun's recoil. It hurt like hell, but the skin wasn't broken. Still, something that could only be blood spread warm and wet through his shirt.

A diffused glow illuminated a spot a few feet away. He pulled himself to his feet and took a couple of halting steps toward it and tripped over the knapsack. He fumbled inside for the extra flashlight and felt the smooth surface of the Ulunsu'ti, warm and pulsing with life.

The flashlight shook in his hand as he searched the nearby floor. He needed the gun. If Eagle Feather came for him, he had to be prepared. When he found it a few feet away, he clutched it under his arm, his finger on the trigger ready to fire. He panned the light around, searching for the white man.

He saw the blood first and followed the trail to its source. The flashlight cast a faint, eerie glow lying beneath the body.

The elder stared down at the body. The shotgun blast at close range took off most of his face. He searched for some trace of guilt or grief but felt only relief. Now, he could finish what he had to do without worrying about the white man interfering.

The pain in his shoulder intensified past his ability to ignore it. Blood trickled down his arm and soaked his sleeve. He remembered falling against something sharp when he fired the shotgun. He took a red bandana from his pocket and fashioned a makeshift bandage, applying pressure to staunch the flow of blood.

The flashlight revealed shards of pottery scattered on the cave floor. He swung the light around, searching. A bundle wrapped in deerskin nestled in one broken half of a bowl.

The white man said he had the conjuror's hands. Could it be true?

He picked up the half of the bowl and inspected the bundle. Walker and Dave would know what to do with everything in the duffle bag, but how would he get the hands back to David?

He peeled away the protective wrappings one layer at a time, hoping against hope that the white man lied, that this was just another one of his tricks and the hands remained safe where they belonged. With the last layer removed, he saw that Eagle Feather told the truth. The ancient, mummified pair of hands lay there in the broken bowl, so well preserved they could have been the shriveled, aged hands of a living old man.

This complicated his plan, but it didn't change anything. As long as he got them back to David Wayanettah, it would work out. And if he put them in the duffle bag with everything else, Walker would make sure David got them. He had to hurry. Pain and blood loss took a toll, leaving him weak and dull-witted.

He eased the hands into the knapsack. Something flashed in his mind, something about why he shouldn't do that, but he couldn't think about it now. He had a lot to do while he still could walk. He slung the knapsack over his wounded shoulder, ignoring the pain its weight caused. It was lighter than the shotgun, and he needed that in case anyone tried to stop him. One shell remained in the chamber. It would come in handy to end his misery.

He staggered down the cavern toward the sound of the waterfall where he watched David stash the duffle bag. He found it tucked under the crevice where Driver's grandson hid it.

Just one more look at the conjuror's treasures, to assure himself he had it all. He propped the flashlight on a ledge and pulled the duffle bag out of the crevice.

The ark rested at the top of the bag, right where he put it. The beauty of it endured through the centuries, and its power vibrated in his hands. He went to a lot of trouble to get it out of the Locusts' tunnel. Buck got careless when he let him find it. A man who couldn't take better care of his guardianship than that didn't deserve the job. Buck Locust couldn't be trusted with something as important as the ark. And David let Eagle Feather find the conjuror's hands. Could he be trusted with the responsibility of the hands that could revive the Ulunsu'ti?

He opened the first gym bag. The medicine pouch tempted him. He reached into the bag to touch it. One brush against his fingers made him recoil. The pouch felt dangerous, like it could hurt him. He didn't want to touch it anymore. The sense of threat lessened when he closed the gym bag on it.

He stuffed the gym bags back into the duffle bag and set the ark atop them. If he put it back in the crevice, David and Walker would take care of it. And he could give the Ulunsu'ti to his grandson and be done with it all. But he felt tired now, too tired to make it down the mountain.

He clutched the knapsack against his bleeding shoulder and leaned against the cave wall to rest. With a few minutes of rest, his mind cleared and reason returned. Perhaps he knew a better way. He proved he could outsmart the Snake Dancers. He learned the identity of all the guardians and found what they protected. Carelessness on their part made it possible. And the white man with his grandiose ideas about controlling the Ulunsu'ti lay dead on the cave floor. Not as smart as he thought he was.

He remained alive, and in possession of the Ulunsu'ti and everything he needed to wake it. He stood up and stretched, feeling stronger than he had in years. Why should he leave it for

David and Walker when he knew what to do?

The duffle bag didn't feel so heavy when he lifted it to his good shoulder. He hugged the knapsack against his side, took the shotgun, and set out toward daylight.

Eagle Feather lay sprawled where he left him, his body outlined in the darkness by the flashlight he fell on. He stopped and looked down at the body for a moment, searching for some emotion that would tell him he remained human enough to feel remorse. The sound of a brief, harsh laugh startled him until he realized it came from his own throat. He moved on, troubled that he found pleasure at the sight of the dead man.

Blood soaked his shirt. He saw its red stain on the knapsack. The saturated bandana no longer functioned to staunch his wound. Blood loss threatened his newfound strength. He needed a better bandage.

He heard rain as he approached the cave mouth.

He found a ledge for the flashlight near the entrance and stripped down to his undershirt. Tearing strands of plaid flannel from the tail of his shirt, he fashioned an inadequate dressing and secured it with strips of flannel. Blood dampened it but it would have to do for now. He put his bloody shirt back on, took up the duffle bag, knapsack, and shotgun, and would have hurried outside had not familiar voices brought him up short.

He listened, torn between the urge to ask the men for help and the perverse desire to hide from them. He gave in to the latter and ducked out of sight when two of the men entered the cave. With his body against the wall, he knew he should call out to David, turn the hands over to their rightful guardian. But Yona Copperhead was with him. He had no right to know about the conjuror's hands.

Without a word, he watched them go by, heading into the cave to retrieve the duffle bag they wouldn't find. He couldn't let them see him. What if they wanted the Ulunsu'ti too? It belonged to him, and his grandson. Nobody else could be trusted with it.

When the two men disappeared into the recesses of the cave, he stepped outside. The smell of smoke stung his nose. Through the cloud of smoke, an old man huddled by a smoldering fire, calling his name. He could stop now, leave the duffle bag, and go on his way to be free from it all. That's what he intended to do, but the old man rose to his feet, looking at the knapsack just like Eagle Feather did.

He crept away from the fire, but Walker Copperhead followed him, still eying the knapsack. He wanted it—not just the relics that belonged to him, but the crystal too. He wanted it to give to the white boy his granddaughter married.

He tried to get away, but Walker kept coming at him, grabbing for the knapsack, prodding him with his walking stick. He took the walking stick from the old man but he wouldn't stop. He swung the shotgun and felt it connect. Walker crumpled to the ground.

Remorse hit him with the force of a blow. What had he done? First the white man, now this, a friend and fellow Snake Dancer. He left him lying in the rain and staggered away.

A voice in his head whispered that Walker deserved what he got. Anybody who got in his way would get the same thing. He liked what he heard. The voice got louder. The elder, who only wanted to help his people, listened and knew he was lost. He lacked the power to resist, not in the body of a man who could strike a friend. He let his spirit slip away into a gray, hopeless world far beyond Wolf Mountain.

From the shadows of that world of the lost, he watched an old man stumbling down the trail, clutching the bloody knapsack to his side. He remembered a time when he was a good man, a man everybody trusted. Now, only a wounded, worn-out old body crept away down the trail.

Nothing else remained of him. The good man who had walked in it for more than eighty years was gone now, watching from the gray world where he could do no more harm.

Wednesday Morning

Back Into the Cave

"Damn, man. What is this? Journey to the center of the earth?" They were less than fifty yards inside and Yona already decided he didn't like it much.

"Still got a long way to go," David said, laughing. "You don't like this any better than old Walker does, do you, brother?"

"Let's just say you're right about the high pucker factor." Yona started to say something else, but then David suddenly stopped and knelt on the cave floor. Something in his attitude said, "Be quiet." Yona stopped and kept his mouth shut till Dave waved him to his side. David pointed to the cave floor. A wet footprint stood out against the gray stone.

"You think it's yours? Or could it be Grandpa's from last night?" Yona asked.

"Wasn't it raining last night? It would be gone now anyway. Somebody's been here recently, within the last few minutes, I would say." David spoke in a whisper, but his words echoed in the stillness.

He stood and cast the light ahead, finding several more dark spots on the dry stone. He didn't take time to check them out, just signaled Yona to feel his way to the cave wall, then snapped off the light and started walking.

Yona could barely hear Dave's footsteps even though he stayed right behind him, trying to walk just as softly as he did and not think about the possibility that someone else lurked ahead with his own light turned off. Darkness closed around them, so thick he swore he could feel it, like cold water. He reached for David and held onto his shoulder. David was the one who knew his way around in the cave and Yona didn't want to risk getting separated.

It felt like they walked for miles. Yona thought he discerned a slight downward slant, as if the cave floor sloped deeper into the mountain. It unnerved him. He stumbled against David. David reached back to steady him, then kept walking. Silence hung as thick as the darkness.

When the smallest ray of light appeared in the distance, Yona thought he must be imagining it. Just his brain's way of giving him some hope when he had stood all he could of the total absence of light. But if he was hallucinating, David was too.

"Do you see that?" David's whisper was barely audible.

"I think so," Yona whispered back.

They inched forward, hardly daring to breathe. The light drew nearer but not much brighter. Yona could hear his heart pounding as they got closer to the dim, eerie glow. He stepped away from David and focused on the light. It was at his feet when he stepped on something that felt so out of place in the cave, he yelled before he could stop himself. He knew it was a body. Nothing else would give quite that way under a hiking boot.

David clicked on the flashlight, then yelled louder than Yona had. "He's dead!"

"Shit!" The only word Yona could say echoed through the depths of the cave.

"What the hell have we got ourselves into, man?" David said.

"A damn sight more than I signed on for. Shit!"

The dead man's face lacked anything that would identify him. It didn't matter, though. They both knew who he was. Hell, most anybody around here could identify him even without a face. But he was the last man on earth either of them expected to see in the Wayanettahs' secret cave.

David got his wits about him enough to keep his voice down. "Looks like we need to let Nathan Axe know he can stop looking for this guy."

A thick, blonde braid tied with a beaded leather thong trailed in a pool of blood. In the ear that remained, a silver feather hung from the lobe on a stud shaped like an eagle.

"Shit!" Yona yelled.

David flashed the light away from the bloody mess and swept it in an arc along the cave floor. The light fell on an empty red shotgun shell casing a few feet from the body. Yona bent over and looked at it, remembering not to touch it. It was evidence.

Beyond the shell, shards of a broken pot lay scattered on the floor. David moaned, a primitive sound of despair, and fell to his knees beside half an ancient clay pot. He made a desperate inspection on hands and knees, sweeping the floor with his hands.

"What are you looking for, Dave?" Yona asked.

David didn't answer. A wadded pile of old deer skin met his searching fingers at the edge of the light.

"Dave, what's wrong?"

David stood up with the deerskins in his hand, tearing through their brittle folds. The skins crumbled and fell at his feet. He watched them fall in hopeless resignation. "They're gone, Yona. They're gone."

"The conjuror's hands?"

David turned and tore off down the cavern, taking the flashlight with him.

The glow from the light beneath the dead man illuminated the bloody fringe on his jacket. Yona needed light. The echo of David's footsteps resonated deeper into the cave. He rolled the dead man off the flashlight with the toe of his boot and grabbed the light, wiping it on the dead man's pants to clean as much blood off as he could. The mingled odor of blood and gun powder hit him hard when he stood up. A wave of nausea caught him off guard and he lost his breakfast a few steps away from the body.

If the killer with the shotgun lurked somewhere in the cave, he already knew he wasn't alone. No need to try to be stealthy now. Every living thing on this mountain had already heard them.

Yona ran after David, bellowing his name as loud as he could. When David didn't answer, he kept running, straining his eyes ahead into the darkness hoping to see David's flashlight.

"Shit!" He didn't know why he kept saying that. It didn't help. Maybe it's the one thing you can say when you're so scared your brain turns to jelly. He said it again, a few more times, then fell silent when he saw a speck of light in the distance. Hoping it was David, he waited until it got close enough that he could be sure. "Just don't be the man with the gun," he prayed under his breath.

David's shoulders slumped in despair. He held fragments of buckskins and sinew in his hand. "Yona." His voice came out as a hoarse croak. "They got the hands. The hands and all the rest. It's all gone."

Yona didn't know what to say. He reached out and David gave him the buckskin. He searched through them trying to find the conjuror's hands among the ancient, brittle folds. The dried fragments crumbled. He handed them back to David. David kept looking through them, as if he couldn't believe the hands weren't there.

"Dave, we gotta find whoever did it. We'll get Nathan Axe and anybody else who can help and tell them anything they need to know. We gotta find him, and the hands. It's our job now."

David dropped the buckskin fragments and slapped the cave wall with the flat of his palm. He turned back to Yona and took a deep breath, reining in his emotions. "We need Buck. He's been a guardian for a while. He'll know what to do." He sounded almost calm.

What if they couldn't find Buck? At the risk of setting David off again, he blurted out his fear. "What if Buck is somewhere with *his* face blown off? And Grady, what if he's gone? We don't know where he is, and Eli ain't got a clue about what's going on. He won't be any help. What are we supposed to do, David?"

David drew himself up and sounded cool and calm. "We have to take good care of your grandpa, for a start. He's the only one we've got who might know how to handle this. We gotta look after him good now."

David picked up the fragments of buckskin off the cave floor and stuffed them into his backpack, then broke into a trot back toward the mouth of the cave.

Yona fell in behind him, relieved to see him taking charge. Walker waited alone outside, and someone with a shotgun had already killed one man a few feet away.

They hurried past Eagle Feather's body, trying not to step in the blood.

Several yards beyond the body, David stopped and yelled, "Oh, shit!"

"What the hell?"

David pointed the light down at the floor and turned back toward the body, scanning the cave with the light. He paused every few steps to get a better look. "See this, Yona?"

He pointed out a trail of footprints, dark and perfectly formed, like tracks of boots just in out of the rain. But it wasn't water that wet those boots, and the tracks didn't lead into the cave, but toward the entrance where his grandpa waited alone and unarmed.

"Shit!"

Yona forgot everything but Walker and the marks on the floor near the entrance. Bloody footprints that led toward the only guardian they knew to still be alive.

David kept the light trained on the trail of footprints, growing fainter at first, then clearer and darker. Yona stopped running and knelt beside a dark stain.

"Hey, Dave, wait."

David came back and squatted down beside him.

"Look at this," he said.

With obvious distaste, David touched a fingertip to the stain. "Still wet." He rubbed his finger on the stone to wipe away the blood. Wet blood framed a partial print of a worn-down boot heel on the cave floor.

"It's fresh," David said, "like he just stepped in it. But Eagle Feather is way back there. This is not his blood."

Yona looked closer. "Looks like the blood is pooled up beside his shoe. Like it just dripped down and he stepped in it."

"You think it could be the killer's own blood?" David asked. "Maybe Eagle Feather went at him with that bowie knife he carries, before he got shot."

"He might be hurt, but he's still on his feet with a shotgun, and Grandpa's out there by himself." Yona rushed past David in a hurry to make sure Walker was still alive.

David caught up with him, every few feet pointing out another splotch of blood, sometimes outlining a bit of boot print. When the gray light beyond the cave broke through the darkness, Yona would have rushed out to check on Walker but David stopped him, pointing out the path of bloody footprints that veered off toward the wall.

A spent flashlight lay there among a few shreds of plaid flannel. Wet blood stains marked the cave floor.

"The man who killed Eagle Feather," David said, "he must have stood here and bandaged his wound, and it wasn't long ago. The blood is still wet."

Yona's heart beat like a hammer. An armed man, who already killed once today, had passed within a few feet away from his grandpa, one of the last guardians alive. He ran toward the entrance yelling Walker's name, urging David to hurry.

At the entrance where they left Walker, the fire still smoldered. The empty coffee cup and thermos sat beside it.

Walker no longer sat beside the fire. Yona ran out into the misty rain, calling to his grandfather. Something blue lay crumpled on the rocks near the tall pine. He yelled for David and bolted toward it, afraid of what he would find.

David hurried to his side, where he knelt beside Meredith's blue poncho and the motionless form it covered.

"Grandpa!" Yona cried.

He heard David on the cell phone. "Walker Copperhead is down with a bad head wound. Eagle Feather is dead with his face shot off, and somebody is running around with a shotgun up here on Wolf Mountain where we found the dead girl." He stuffed the phone in his backpack. "Nathan Axe is not there. Jimmy Hanks will take care of things."

Yona swabbed at Walker's temple with the corner of the wet poncho. With the blood wiped away, he could see an ugly purple lump.

Walker moaned, opened his eyes, and began to struggle until he recognized his grandson. "Grady," he mumbled, "get Grady," and pointed weakly toward the trail down the side of the mountain, then he slumped in Yona's arms.

David reached for his wrist. "His pulse is faint and thready, but he's got one."

"Help is on the way, Grandpa. We'll get you out of here." Yona felt on the verge of breaking down and crying like a little baby. He cradled Walker in his arms and pleaded with him to hang on. "Who did this to you, Grandpa?"

Walker's head lolled to the side.

Yona looked helplessly at David. "What kind of person would do this to an old man?"

David said, "The same kind of person who would split a young girl's skull with a stone axe, or shoot a man in the face with a shotgun."

He looked closer at Walker's wound, dabbing at the blood with the sleeve of his shirt. "Somebody hit him hard. Probably with the butt of the same gun that killed Eagle Feather. He might have a concussion, but he's not bleeding. This isn't his blood."

"Damn. Whoever's blood it is, my grandpa's hurt bad. We can't just sit here, Dave. Call Nathan Axe's office again and tell them to send Cherokee Rescue Service up the way he came last night. We can carry Grandpa down and meet them on the way. We gotta get him to a hospital, fast."

David got out the phone and dialed. Jimmy Hanks answered this time, and David filled him in on Walker's condition and told him where to send the rescue team. When he hung up, they didn't waste any time. Yona already had his arms around Walker, lifting him to carry like a child.

"Wait, man," David said. "Remember that fireman's carry we learned? Let's do it like that." He put an arm around Walker's back, and Yona shifted his hold to conform to the position they learned when they joined the volunteer fire department. It worked much better.

Walker's weight surprised him. For a scrawny old man, he felt solid.

With Walker between them, they set off down the mountain in a near trot.

Once, Walker stirred and opened his eyes. "Go get Grady," he mumbled, then went limp, drooped his head against Yona's shoulder, and passed out again.

"Yeah, Grandpa. We'll find Grady as soon as we get you to the hospital," Yona said.

"Grandfather," David pleaded. "Stay with us, Old Man."

Walker just moaned.

They did their best to hurry down the steep, rocky trail, but with Walker a dead weight between them, they didn't cover much distance. Walker opened his eyes a couple of times and mumbled Grady's name, urging them to find him.

"Don't worry about Grady Smoker, Grandpa," Yona said.

"We'll find him after we get you to the hospital."

Walker's occasional bout of struggling toward consciousness made him an even more awkward burden.

A shout from below came as the most welcome sound all day. When the Cherokee Rescue Team got close enough to identify, they laid Walker down on the grass and waited.

The rescue squad worked fast, checking Walker's airway, doing initial first aid, then getting him secured to the litter.

Nathan Axe arrived before the rescue squad left with Walker. Yona and David intended to stay close to Walker, but Nathan wouldn't hear of it.

"Wait here a minute, boys. Mr. Copperhead's in good hands. I need to talk to you right now, and I don't want any bullshit about some secret society." He sent the rescue squad on their way with the litter, leaving him alone with Yona and David.

Yona said, "He's right Dave. We don't have anything to hide anymore."

The sheriff got out his little notepad. "Go on. Start with what you're doing here."

David said, "We are way out of our league with this one. We're ready to tell you anything we know. We're here because we hid something up on the mountain that we couldn't allow to fall into the wrong hands."

"If it does, we could all be in a hell of a lot more trouble than a few murders. We were trying to prevent that from happening because…because it's our job." Yona knew when he said it, it meant he had to be willing to risk his life to fulfill his duties to the Snake Dancers, and to the conjurors of old.

"We tried to protect it, but we failed," David said. "The stuff is gone. The man who stole it is probably the same guy who blew Eagle Feather's head off. The only ones who might know what to do now are Walker, Grady Smoker, and Buck Locust. Walker is out of the picture. Buck and Grady are missing. If you got any suggestions, Sheriff, we're listening."

"Damn! You're telling me two people have already been killed because of something out of an old story. I don't want to hear that bullshit. My job is to figure out who is killing people, and I expect you to help me do my job by telling me the plain, down-to-earth truth. You Snake Dancers are welcome to handle the supernatural stuff. I want you to, but you've gotta fill me in on everything you know about what's happening right here and now."

They told him, and didn't hold back anything. The story tumbled out with both of them talking so fast that Nathan had to ask them to slow down. The information came quicker than he could scribble it in his notepad.

When they got to the part about Grady's dead granddaughter, Nathan interrupted. "We don't have to feel bad anymore about Grady not getting to know the girl. According to Martha Waits at the bank, he's been sending a check to the girl's mother on the first of every month for years, addressed to a Mrs. Carl Johnson. They had a college fund set up for her. Sounds like he knew about her long before Thomas found out he had a daughter."

That news should have made Yona feel better, but it left him too stunned to speak. One look at David's stricken expression and he knew it hit him just as hard. This could be bad news for so many reasons. The understanding of what it meant scared him more than the dead bodies. Betrayal of this magnitude could cause damage beyond repair.

Nathan gave them time to recover from the blow his news delivered. "I take it this is part of the problem?"

Yona told him the part about the outsider Suye'ta, who used the Ulunsu'ti for the good of the tribe because he loved a Cherokee woman.

They spilled the whole story, the guardians and what they guarded, the duffle bag with everything in it and where they found it, and the fact that only the Ulunsu'ti remained unaccounted for.

"We can't find Grady Smoker, and I'm pretty sure he guarded it," David said.

Nathan closed his notepad and slipped it back into his pocket, satisfied they told him all they could. He gave them bit of information that eased Yona's mind. "I called Mr. Copperhead's house to let Kate know what happened. She's gonna go tell Faron, then head over here. Now, if you'll tell me how to find the dead man you found, you can go on and catch up with Walker."

The cave held no more secrets. With no reason to hide it anymore, David told Nathan how to find the entrance. From there, he could follow the trail of bloody footprints to Eagle Feather's body.

Two of Nathan's men waited down the trail for his signal. He beckoned them to follow and they set off up Wolf Mountain to check out yet another dead body.

Yona passed them without a word, anxious to reach Walker's side.

David yelled, "Slow down, man! You'll kill yourself if you don't watch where you're going."

Yona stumbled on the rough trail. He grasped a branch from a stand of laurels to get his balance and waited for David to catch up. He wiped the dampness from the laurel on his pants.

"What's that?" David asked.

He looked at his pants and at the stain on his hand. Blood.

More blood smeared the laurel leaves. David followed the trail of broken branches and vegetation and saw another splotch a few feet away. A boot print in the damp earth was a twin to the prints in the cave.

"Your grandpa's in good hands with the rescue squad. They'll take care of him. We need to follow this trail."

Yona took one last look down the trail to a flash of color through the trees. Cherokee Rescue could do a lot more for Walker than he could. He had to find the man who hurt his

209

grandfather. He plunged into the wet laurel thicket behind David.

The hunt was on.

Tuesday Night

Sanctuary on the Snowbird

Faron sped up the unpaved driveway and over her new bridge and braked to a stop at the edge of the yard. John felt the tension lift from his body. The house on the Snowbird offered safety for his wife and kids.

Bonnie rushed to the car as soon as Faron's Mustang came to a stop. "Diamond's asleep, Aunt Faron," she said. "I've gotta go home now."

John wanted nothing more than to go inside with Faron and his kids and lock the door, but he and Faron both knew he couldn't do it. Buck was in trouble. He sent Bonnie to wait in his truck and kissed Faron and Wren goodbye. "You know I have to go look for Buck, don't you, honey?"

Faron didn't try to stop him. She trembled when he held her and clung to him for a full minute before she let him go. Not a word about her fear, but he knew. He let her go and carried Wren to the house. She hugged him when he put her down and made him promise to be careful. Just like her mama.

"My mobile phone is in the truck. I'll keep in touch." He kissed them again and shut the door behind him.

Bonnie climbed into the Ram without a word. The poor kid looked worried to death about her daddy, and with good reason. Buck always came home when he said he would, or called to let Amy know he might be a few minutes late. Midnight neared, and nobody heard from Buck since before daylight that morning.

"Your daddy's gonna be just fine. We'll find him in no time. Nothing to worry about." John didn't believe a word he said, and it didn't reassure Bonnie one bit. They both knew it would take something serious to keep Buck from calling home.

Amy Locust waited for them on the porch. She hugged Bonnie close. "You find Buck and bring him home," she said to John with tears in her eyes.

"Amy, you know I'll do my best. I'll call you as soon as I have any news."

He drove as fast as he dared, straight up the Cheoah to the place where Eli found Buck's truck. Eli would be somewhere around there too. He could count on that.

He kept his eyes peeled for the cutoff that took him close to Degal gun'yi. Strange how Eli and Buck both knew about it. Sometimes he wondered just how much they knew and couldn't tell him. He considered information Walker parceled out to him since Wren found those gym bags. Perhaps he knew a thing or two even Buck didn't know.

The Council House Mound where the wisdom-keepers of old kept the knowledge alive was somewhere near. How many of his friends slept on it and had dreams like David? Would it help him keep up with Faron and his kids if he tried it?

The slope under the pines looked like a parking lot. He expected to see Buck's pickup, and Eli's behind it. The Bronco with the Graham County Sheriff's Department logo came as a surprise. He pulled up beside the Bronco and parked.

He took out his cell phone and considered calling Buck's number but thought better of it. Amy tried that since six-thirty until she gave up. He punched in Eli Smoker's mobile phone number and almost instantly heard a frantic, "Hello," at the other end, along with the yip-yip of the Chihuahua.

"Where are you, man?" John asked.

"I'm just east of the burial ground. You know the one. Degal gun'yi."

"Anybody seen any sign of Buck? I just left Amy and Bonnie and they're about worried to death."

"Ain't seen hide or hair of him, Johnny. I found a partial footprint back a ways. It might have been Buck's. I don't know.

212

Dorsey wants to wait till morning to start a search. Says we can't see well enough to hunt for him in the dark, but I think we need to keep looking."

"You're right, buddy, but the sheriff's probably smart not to get a search party out tonight. Any tracks Buck might have left would get destroyed. I'll head your way. Keep in touch. And, hey, if that barking rat you've got in your pocket ain't scared to get his little feet dirty, see if he can sniff out a scent or something."

So, Eli shared John's intuition that tomorrow might be too late. They needed to find Buck tonight. Then they could look for Grady Smoker. Come to think of it, Eli probably didn't know about the dead girl, or that Grady was missing too. Amy said she called Eli first, as soon as Buck didn't answer his phone, and sent him to look for her husband. He'd been in these woods since around six-thirty.

Scanning the ground for footprints and the bushes for signs of disturbance, John made his way toward the burial ground. It felt like the right direction. Eli must have thought so too. He didn't know where the owner of the Bronco was, but he appreciated the fact that somebody from the sheriff's department stayed behind to search for Buck.

He oriented himself with landmarks that would help him find the way back to his truck and ducked into the thick, pathless stand of pines, taking note of a rock that protruded from the ground, a dead tree ready to topple over, anything that marked his trail. Here and there he came across a broken twig or a scuff mark on a patch of moss, but not much else to indicate anyone passed this way. He found enough to prove to himself the trail led him toward Degal gun'yi.

He bent down to examine what he thought might be a heel mark when his phone buzzed against his hip.

"Hey, John, where are you?" Eli asked before John could even say hello.

"Heading toward you, I think. You still around the burial

ground?"

"Yeah. And somebody's been here recently. You know this ground ain't much good for holding tracks, but I've found a couple of fairly clear ones. I think they might be Buck's."

"And I'm following a trail right for you. You wanna stay where you are and I'll catch up with you?"

"No problem," Eli answered. "I'm not too crazy about being in this old graveyard by myself in the middle of the night. Gives me the creeps. I could use some company."

John didn't need to look for tracks anymore since Eli already tracked Buck as far as the burial ground. He went straight toward the burial ground and, within a few minutes, he saw a light ahead. Eli must have gotten spooked and come back to meet him. John didn't blame him. Something about this place weirded him out even in broad daylight. In the dark…well, he just tried not to think about it.

When he heard Eli calling, he nearly jumped out of his skin. After so long in the dark with no sound but the nightlife, a human voice shattered the stillness. He ran as fast as he dared, closing the distance between them.

Glad as they were to see each other, they wasted no time on greetings. "How far have you trailed him?" John asked.

"Me and Yippi looked around some since I talked to you. We found two prints just beyond where Degal gun'yi slopes off into the woods. There's a narrow stream that runs by there and it looks like somebody jumped over it. They're two real good prints in the mud, one on each side. I figure they're Buck's tracks."

The bloodhound duties must have been a real strain for the Chihuahua. John saw his tiny round head and forepaws hanging over the pocket of Eli's jacket. The poor thing trembled like he was scared to death. He wasn't usually *that* nervous.

John followed Eli for a while, debating with himself whether he should say anything about the duffle bag and what was in it. Walker said not to talk about it to anybody but family, but the Smokers seemed like the kind of family that really mattered, like Buck was. With all that happened, he didn't want to keep secrets from his friend. Besides, if he talked about this first, he could stall about other things he had to tell Eli. Like, a young girl in the Swain County morgue who was his blood kin. And that nobody knows where to find his grandpa.

John kept his voice as casual as he could. "Eli, what do you know about a blood-drinking crystal called Ulunsu'ti, from a big snake's head?"

Eli slowed down. "Are you asking just because you remember the stories we grew up on, or do you have some other reason?"

"Let's say, some other reason. So, what do you know about it?"

Eli stalled, trying to decide how much he should say. John lost patience with all the secrecy. "How about it, Eli?" he demanded.

Eli spoke slowly. "For some time now, Grandpa has been dropping hints about telling me something important when the time comes. His hints were broad enough that, combined with some snooping and keen observation, I've probably learned more than he suspected."

When he clammed up again, John prompted him, "Care to let me in on it?"

Eli gave him one of the half-assed answers John had learned to expect. "I probably know more than I'm supposed to, but not as much as I need to. Why are you so interested in something that might not even exist outside of legend?"

John told him everything. After all, nobody swore *him* to secrecy. "Because, yesterday evening just before dark, when I came up here with Walker and Wren to check on those trees you were worried about, Wren found something hidden under a log that freaked her and Walker out. They said it was all the stuff that some conjuror needed to bring the Ulunsu'ti back to life, and the best place to do it was at that mound that looks like an old council house, which was very close to where we found the stuff."

"Good God, man," Eli said. "Who all knows about this? Has Walker told my grandpa?"

"Well, buddy, that's something else I wanted to ask you about. When's the last time you talked to your grandpa?"

"It's been a couple of weeks," Eli said. "I don't know what's going on with him lately. Buck told me he's been hanging around with that weirdo white man who claims to be a shaman. The one with those camps all over the place where he rips off other white people. He says the white man has been seen with a young Indian girl. Buck didn't like the looks of it. You know how he is. He won't rest until he finds out every detail, especially if it involves one of our kids."

Eli didn't even suspect the identity of the girl. John had to tell him, but how? He fell in behind Eli, heading for the stream where he and Yippi found the footprints. Once they got there and began the search for Buck in earnest, he wouldn't have time to tell Eli what happened up on Wolf Mountain and why Grady might be hanging around with the girl. He needed to know.

"Eli, you know I didn't go to work today, and that's why Buck came up here checking things out instead of me?"

Eli grunted an affirmative and kept walking.

"Well, I didn't go to work because I went with Walker and Yona and David Wayanettah up to a cave on the side of Wolf Mountain. I don't understand why we had to go, but Wren found something else up there that was real bad. Worse even than what we found here in the woods."

"Yeah? Sounds like your kid's real good at finding bad things, John. What did she find this time?"

"That girl you were talking about. The one with the white man. We found her body. Somebody killed her and left her lying there in the rocks."

Eli stopped short and almost dropped his flashlight. "Damn!

From what Buck said, she wasn't much more than a kid. Who'd do a thing like that?"

"I don't know who did it. Nathan Axe is trying to find out. There's more, Eli. Something you should know."

"Go on."

"Okay, buddy. But it's bad. You ready?"

Eli stopped and turned to face John. "Go ahead."

"Buck found out who the girl was. He talked to Nathan Axe and David Wayanettah about it. It started back when we were kids and your dad went to work on that construction job down in Mississippi and was away so much."

"That was years ago," Eli said. "What's that got to do with the dead girl?"

John had to just spit it out. There was no way to make it easy. "Seems like your dad took up with a Choctaw woman down there, and she had a kid. The white guy that calls himself Eagle Feather married the Choctaw woman and adopted the kid, a little girl."

Eli stopped him. "You can't be saying…no!"

"Damn, Eli. I wish it wasn't true, but it is. It's her. The girl that was killed belonged to your dad and the Choctaw woman."

Eli's arms dropped limp to his side and the flashlight fell from his hand. He walked off into the darkness. John grabbed the light and went after him. "Wait," he called. "I'm sorry, man. Just slow down."

Eli stopped and leaned against a tree. When John got there, he held Yippi snuggled under his chin. The dog whimpered and licked his face. John wasn't sure what to say, so he just waited until Eli looked ready to talk.

After a couple of minutes, Eli asked, "When did you find this out, John?"

Eli sounded calm, like it hadn't sunk in yet, or he realized he didn't have time to get emotional. He just learned he had a sister, and that she was dead. But he also had a good friend who was lost and in trouble. That had to come first.

"I didn't know till this evening. Seems like it started when Buck checked on the white guy and the girl. David knew too. They tracked her down to Mississippi. That's how they found out about your dad. Buck told David he talked to Thomas yesterday. Buck went to tell your grandpa last night, but Grady wasn't home and nobody has seen him. Buck got worried about your grandpa and called Nathan. Seems like nobody knows where Grady is."

"I wouldn't be too worried about Grandpa," Eli said. "He's gone off on his own before, but he usually lets somebody know. Soon as we find Buck, we'll look for my grandpa."

"I'd feel better about it if Buck was here to help us. I hate to drop all this on you and then tell you to get over it until we have more time, but that's what we gotta do. We can't leave Buck wherever he is much longer. I have a gut feeling our buddy's in big trouble."

"You've been living with the Copperheads too long, John. You've developed a sixth sense, just like the rest of them. And I think I might have picked it up from you, because I know you're right. Knew it the minute Amy called me. That's why I dropped everything and took off out here. Amy said he was going to check on that blight, or whatever, for you."

They heard the stream long before they saw it. With their flashlight beams trained on the ground, they searched every inch the light illuminated for signs that Buck had passed by. They saw nothing until they came to the tracks Eli already found on the muddy banks of the shallow brook. Exposed rocks above the water provided a crossing. They picked their way across the rocks to the opposite side. A broken branch on a honeysuckle bush a few feet away and some trampled weeds reassured them.

"He's somewhere close, Eli," John said. "I know he is."

Eli shouted Buck's name as loudly as he could. Nobody answered.

"What if he's hurt and can't answer?" John asked.

"Then we gotta find him, John. Let's go."

John pulled the cell phone out of his jacket pocket. "You know, Buck always has his phone with him. He likes to keep in touch with the station, and with Amy and Bonnie."

"We've all tried calling him and he doesn't answer. His voicemail box is full," Eli said.

"Don't expect him to answer," John said. He dialed Buck's cell phone number and walked slowly ahead, listening. He gave up when he heard nothing. They followed an ill-defined path through trampled weeds, toward a hill that looked out of place.

Eli dialed Buck's number. Somewhere in the distance came the soft sound of Doc Watson singing bluegrass. Buck's ringtone.

They ran toward the sound. Around on the far side of the hill, their lights found a scattered pile of rocks. At the bottom of the hill a big flat stone looked out of place. Draped across it lay a jacket they both recognized. Doc Watson's voice came from the pocket.

"He's around here somewhere, John." Eli picked up the coat and took Buck's phone out of the pocket.

John swung the flashlight around, looking at the pile of rocks scattered around the big, flat stone, and followed their trajectory up the scarred hillside to the gaping hole in the mound. Something happened here. With sudden clarity, he knew what. Yelling Buck's name, he ran for the wound in the hillside.

A muffled voice responded.

"Buck! Where are you, man?" Eli yelled.

"He's in here," John said, and attacked the jumble of rocks and dirt that blocked entry to the tunnel, seeking a way to reach his friend.

"Easy!" Buck yelled. "Nothing holding this hillside off me but a rotten timber. Don't blow it for me."

"Jesus!" Eli said. "He's inside there. How are we gonna get him out?"

219

Buck hollered his answer. "Very carefully! This thing's been trying to fall in on me all day. By the way, think you could get some light in here so I can see what's happening?"

Eli played the beams from his flashlight across the landslide, hoping to find a place where the light could leak through to Buck. He steadied the light when Buck called out, "There you go. Now hold it there."

John's hands shook when he got out his phone. The only number he could remember at that moment was his own. Good enough. Faron could get help here as fast as anybody, and she would know exactly where to find them when John told her to send help to that funny-looking hill out east of Degal gun'yi. He put the phone in his pocket and called to Buck, "How does it look?"

"About as bad as it gets. I'm in a hole here with a beam right above my head that's holding up the roof, and it's bent almost double. Wouldn't take a hair's weight more to break it. If that happens, I'm in big trouble."

"Think it would help if you had something to support that beam?" John asked.

"Sure couldn't hurt. But how you gonna get anything in here?"

"We'll figure it out," John said and turned away with his light. Eli followed him.

"Damn. It's dark in here," Buck called.

"We need the light more than you do right now. Chill out," John called. Then, on second thought, he said to Eli, "See if you can find exactly where the light was getting in. Try to make a bigger opening there without caving in the place."

John left Eli at work creating an opening and went to search for something to shore up the beam over Buck's head. He needed a tree branch or sapling sturdy enough and yet not too big to maneuver into the tunnel. He found one that looked promising and went to work trimming branches with his pocket knife when

Eli came running. "John," he said. "I don't know how we're gonna do this. Looks like he's got a big log lying right across his back."

John dropped the branch and climbed back up the hill.

Eli showed him where he found the miniscule crevice between the stones, then carefully eased away one stone at a time till he could look in. He directed the light to shine in on Buck. John's heart almost stopped when he saw the fix he was in.

Eli said, "He's gotta be hurt bad, John. What are we gonna do?"

John pushed him away from the opening. No need to let Buck know how scared they were. "Keep calm. We've gotta figure it out in a hurry. Help me find something to shore that hole up till we can drag him out."

Their combined weight broke a couple of limbs from a maple. They stripped the branches off as best they could, ending up with two rough-looking poles.

"John," Eli said just before they were in Buck's hearing range, "what if his back is broken and we pull him out? He could be paralyzed."

"And if we don't, he could be dead," John said.

John carefully enlarged the opening until he could stick his head inside. Then he said as calmly as he could, "So tell me about it, Buck. What are we dealing with here?"

"Well, it's like this...," Buck copied John's forced casual manner. "I've got this big heavy thing laying across my back. I think I could get out from under it and dig out of here myself, only it must be holding the beam over my head in place. Every time I try to wiggle free, the roof falls down a little."

John said, "We're gonna hand some saplings in to you. See if you can use them to prop up the roof beam. Think you can manage that, man?"

"It's better than anything I've come up with all day. Give them to me one at a time. I'll see what I can do."

It was pure torture, easing the poles in so slowly when they knew every second counted. But one mistake and Buck would be under tons of earth and rocks. They'd never get him out alive.

They kept the light on Buck and listened, holding their breath, jumping at every sound. They heard a dull creak, then the old beam sagged. Falling earth and splinters rendered the light useless. A curtain of dust cut Buck off from sight. Sick at heart, John counted the seconds while he and Eli dug with their bare hands, afraid of what they would find.

When the noise of falling rubble abated, they listened. Buck's muffled, "I'm still alive so far," gave them hope.

"You got the beams propped up yet?" John yelled.

"I'm working on it," Buck grunted with exertion. "Got the second one up. I think it's gonna hold."

John pulled Eli away and shined the flashlight through the cloud of dust. Buck had the last sapling in place. The supports looked like toothpicks bending under the big beam above his head. The beam creaked and groaned, releasing another shower of earth. A rumble came from deep inside the mound.

"Now or never, Buck," John yelled. He reached in as far as he could. "Let's go."

Buck gave a mighty grunt, straining to break free of the timber that held him down. The beam above him shifted and settled against the poles. They bent under the weight. One cracked and splintered, useless now.

John reached deeper. He heard Eli yelling, "Oh Jesus," as he got a firm grip on his ankles. His fingers connected with Buck's. With a yell, Buck lurched toward him and latched onto his arms. He gripped Buck as hard as he could and yelled to Eli, "Pull!"

Thunder rumbled inside the mound. One last desperate heave and the three of them were hanging onto each other, tumbling down the hillside in an avalanche of rock and earth.

When they came to a stop, John stumbled to his feet. His

body ached in a hundred places, but he could stand. Eli lay across Buck a few feet away. John helped Eli sit up. Buck groaned and turned over. He needed help to stand, but as soon as he got on his feet, he stumbled toward the creek.

Before he reached it, they heard shouting from the edge of the woods.

Eli said, "Hey, Buck, we're okay now. The pros are here to rescue you."

Sheriff Dorsey and a deputy ran toward them, wanting to know if Buck was hurt.

Buck said, "Don't have time to talk to you now, guys. I'm gonna go drink that creek dry."

John and Eli helped him limp to the stream. When they let him go, he dropped down on his belly with his face in the water.

John crossed the stream and gave Dorsey a terse account of what happened. He used the excuse that he and Eli wanted to get Buck to the emergency room to have his injuries looked after, to give them a chance to make a quick getaway. One look at Buck and they believed John. Abrasions and contusions covered his face, and his torn shirt revealed a bloody laceration across his chest.

Dorsey offered to take him.

"Tell you what, Sheriff," John said, "if you'll get in touch with Amy and let her know Buck's okay, Eli and I will look after him. We need to go now. It's gonna take him awhile to get to my truck. Buck's walking kinda slow." He didn't mention they had cell phones and could call Amy themselves.

John bent down beside Buck and made a show of helping him to his feet. "Let's go, guys," he said.

Buck leaned on him heavier than he expected. John supported him while they walked out of Dorsey's hearing. Unless Buck's injuries were life-threatening, they had no time to go to an emergency room. When he felt sure they were alone, he stopped and propped Buck against a tree. "We've gotta talk,

Buck. Wanna tell me what you were looking for in that hole?"

"What makes you think I was looking for something?"

"Well, for one thing, if you came up here to check on those trees, I don't think they were under that hill. For another thing, I know Walker told you what we found Monday night. I figured there was a good chance you might be worried about that."

"Did you assume I might wonder about an old, hide-covered box?" Buck asked.

"That's what you were looking for, huh?" John asked. "Would it make you feel any better to know it's safe? That Walker and David Wayanettah have it?"

Buck seemed to forget all about his wounds. "You gotta tell me everything. Walker wouldn't give me any details. Did you see what all he found?"

John told him to lower his voice. Dorsey and his deputy could still hear them. Speaking barely above a whisper, he said, "I just know enough to confuse the hell out of me. Walker and David are keeping something from me and Yona. I saw a pile of bones. Walker said they belonged to Kanegwa'ti. Then there was a whole shitload of medicine stuff, like a bowl, a pipe, rattle, whistle, and other stuff like that. Everything had a snake on it in some way. Then there was the box. Walker grabbed it before I got a good look at it, and said something about that crystal thing."

"Where's the ark now, John?"

"Last I saw of it, Walker and David had it up on Wolf Mountain. That's where we went today."

"Did Walker get in touch with Grady?"

John figured Buck must still be worried about Grady, since he couldn't find him last night. Eli answered for him. "No. Seems like nobody knows where Grandpa is. I'm uneasy about him, after what John told me earlier." He looked at John. "Tell him about the girl. I don't think I can."

John didn't know where to start, so he just plunged in.

"Nathan Axe says you were checking up on Eagle Feather and the Indian girl with him."

Buck interrupted, "Wait, Johnny, there's something I need to talk to Eli about before you get into this."

"No need, Buck," Eli said. "John already told me who she was."

Buck forgot to keep his voice down. "Something's wrong there. I don't trust that Eagle Feather. I wanted to talk to Grady about the girl. I don't like her hanging out with that creep."

"You don't have to worry about that anymore, Buck," Eli said. "John can tell you that part, but if you don't mind, I'd just as soon not listen to it again." He went on ahead.

John stopped Buck when he wanted to go after Eli. "Let him go. He's just now learned about the girl. He didn't even have time to get used to the idea of her being his half-sister before she got killed."

Buck swore. "The girl's dead? Damn, man. What happened?"

"We found her body today up on Wolf Mountain. Somebody split her head open and left her to die. David called Nathan Axe and he met us up there. They found an old stone axe near the body. It was all bloody, so he figures that's what they killed her with."

"She was a kid, man. Damn. Did Nathan Axe pick up that Eagle Feather guy? He had to be the one that did it. Son of a bitch."

"The sheriff can't find him," John said. "Dorsey sent a man up to his camp to look for him and he wasn't there. Nobody's seen him all day. Can't seem to find Grady either. I told Eli we'd go looking for him as soon as we saved your sorry ass. You up to it?"

Buck ran his hands through his hair, shaking out a day's accumulation of dirt and debris before he answered. "John, what if Eagle Feather killed the girl and Grady found out? If he knew who the girl was, do you think he would go after the man that killed her?"

"I don't know, man. I figure Grady for the kind of man who would come to somebody for help. He never was one to go out on his own with anything. Grady would have called on Walker. He always came to him when he had troubles."

"And Walker hasn't heard from him?"

"Not a word. I've been with him all day, and he didn't know where Grady was. We left Walker at David's house this evening. He was gonna ride back with Kate after supper. I'm sure he's at home now. In fact, I bet he'll be back at your truck along with Amy waiting to see you when we get there. He's been worried about you."

Buck's back seemed to have loosened up, and his limp improved with every step. "I hope he does show up here. I need to talk to him bad. Him and Grady."

John hustled to keep up. It was a wonder Buck could walk at all after what he'd been through. Every muscle and joint in John's body ached from moving the rock pile. Bruises and scrapes covered most of his body from the landslide that tumbled him to the bottom of the mound. He didn't dare complain. Buck had been through more than he, and Eli just as much, but neither of them said a word about their injuries.

Eli tagged behind. They let him have his time alone to think. Lord knows he had plenty to think about.

Amy came running as soon as she caught sight of the flashlights through the trees, crying with relief and hugging her husband until he had to pull away to protect his battered body. She wanted to rush him straight to the emergency room of course, or at least take him home and get him cleaned up, but he wouldn't hear of it.

"I'm just fine, honey. I got caught in a little cave-in, that's all."

Amy insisted, and might have dragged him off to the

hospital by force if Kate hadn't rescued him. "Honey, if Buck was hurt all that bad, I doubt he would be on his feet. He looks fit enough to me."

Buck put his arms around his wife and held her while she settled down.

John took the opportunity to ask Kate why the women came alone. "Where's Walker?" Buck joined them in time to hear her answer. "Last I saw of him, he was at David Wayanettah's house. I left him and Yona there last night."Kate turned to Buck. "If I was you, I'd go on over there and see what they're up to. Far be it from me to poke my nose in your business, but I figure you're in this up to your eyeballs."

Amy objected. Kate put an arm around her shoulders and pulled her toward the car. "Johnny and Eli will be with Buck. Don't you worry about your man. They'll look after him."

"You keep an eye on him, John, and get him straight to the ER if he has any problems," Amy yelled as Kate stuffed her into the car.

Lights approached through the woods. John's truck gave them the best shot at getting away before Dorsey and his deputy reached them. They made a run for it, determined to avoid Dorsey's questions about how Buck got himself trapped in the tunnel, and how John and Eli managed to find him. They didn't have time to explain to the sheriff.

They followed Kate and Amy out of the woods, making sure that by the time Dorsey got there, he saw two sets of taillights disappearing down the trail.

John's gas gauge registered better than half a tank of gas. Good thing, since he didn't know of an open gas station for miles. The dash clock read 4:28 A.M., when he should be snuggled up beside Faron in bed. He gave her a call to let her know about Buck. She answered on the first ring, wide awake like he knew she would be.

She didn't object when he told her he, Buck, and Eli had to

227

go look for Grady, but she couldn't keep the worry out of her voice. "Make sure Grandpa is okay," she said.

He told her to try to get some sleep, even though he knew she wouldn't close her eyes until he came home. He thought he heard Wren in the background, asking if that was Daddy. He hung up before he decided to bail out and go home.

The town of Robbinsville seemed sound asleep when they went through. They drove through town in silence and, for the second time in twenty-four hours, John found himself driving across Stecoah in the wee hours of morning.

"Let's go by Grandpa's place first," Eli said. "Maybe he's home now. I'd sure like to know he's okay."

"You and me both, buddy," Buck said. "Grady might be able to settle my mind a whole lot if I could talk to him. You know, he was seen with Eagle Feather more than once lately. I'd like to know why. If he knew about the girl, that would explain a lot. He could have been spending time with her. I'd feel better about that than to think he took up with Eagle Feather."

"If he knew about her, why didn't he tell Dad and me? We had a right to know," Eli said.

"Maybe he kept it to himself because of your mom. She'd bust your dad's head if she found out," John said. "Grady wouldn't want to cause trouble between your folks, but no reason for him not to tell you that you had a sister. This whole thing is weird."

They made use of the time it took to drive over Stecoah Mountain to talk and speculate about Eagle Feather, the dead girl, and their elders. Yippi snoozed in Eli's lap, worn out by his night in the woods. The atmosphere in the truck became tense when Buck started asking John a lot of strange questions, questions that got even stranger every time he answered one.

Buck wanted to know if Walker told him the story of the Suye'ta, and how he had to be an outsider. Then he asked if Walker mentioned that the Suye'ta would wake the Ulunsu'ti, because something or someone in the tribe mattered more to him than his own safety.

John thought of all the times he wondered if he read too much into what Walker said. All too often lately, he suspected Walker hinted at things he couldn't say directly.

His discomfort level reached the max when Buck mentioned how everybody knew he loved Faron and his kids enough to do anything for them. He made it sound like a compliment when he remarked, "For an outsider, you're real connected to the Cherokee people."

John caught on. "Hey, wait a freaking minute! I've done a lot of things I don't understand. And my own family says that I'm more of a Copperhead than a McLeymore, but if you think that I'm gonna have anything to do with some crazy-assed plan to rule the world with a damn blood-drinking crystal, think again, man!"

Buck tried to backpedal, telling John to calm down.

John couldn't calm down. "Don't think you're gonna drag me into this shit. I'm already way more involved than I want to be. Soon as we find Grady, I'm out of this superstitious crap." He drove much too fast for the curves, and only occasionally wandered into the proper lane. Buck and Eli had to do some smooth talking to get him settled down.

"John, I'm not asking you to do anything, especially that," Buck said. "It's just that I have reason to suspect Walker might be thinking about it. My grandpa told me one time that Walker brought it up to him."

"Jesus, Buck!" Eli said. "Your grandpa walked over four years ago. You mean they were talking about this way back then?"

"They've been talking about it for years, ever since Fontana Dam got built," Buck said. "People will never know what was buried under that lake. Since then, it's been one thing after another. They say there won't be any sacred places left if things keep going the way they are. And we need some of those places more than most people will ever know. Even the homes of the Nunne'hi have tourists crawling all over them. The immortals are mighty scarce around here these days, and the elders say once the Nunne'hi are gone, we're not far behind. Some of the men feel like the Suye'ta and Ulunsu'ti are the only way to stop it."

"Well, they can damn sure do it without me," John said.

"Don't blame you, man," Buck said. "It's not the way to go anyhow. The time for conjurors is passed. We need to handle things in a different way now. To tell you the truth, I've been kinda worried that Walker might talk you into something crazy. I should have come to you about it a long time ago, but...well..."

"But you Snake Dancers aren't supposed to talk to outsiders about your private mojo," John finished for him.

That shocked Buck and Eli both. "Walker told you about the Snake Dancers?" Eli asked.

"No, but all day long I've been listening to him and Dave and Yona talking some weird shit. I reckon Grady must have told you, Eli."

Buck said, "Hold on. Last I heard, neither one of you knew anything about the Snake Dancers. There's been some complaining about how Grady was waiting too long to bring you in, Eli. And John, according to the way I was taught, you never were supposed to know, unless you are the Suye'ta."

"It's not like I give a rat's ass. I could have lived my whole life without knowing any of this crap, but looks like Walker's been hauling me in behind my back. He even dragged me down to the river about twenty-four hours ago. God only knows what that was all about."

"Walker took you to water?" Buck asked. "The whole deal, with the puking and praying?"

"And the fasting, and the freezing my balls off in the cold water. And that was after the funky smoke that gave me hallucinations of a cotton-mouthed water moccasin crawling up my legs. Damn. That was spooky."

230

"John," Buck said. "You know we don't use hallucinogens. If you saw a snake, it wasn't from the smoke."

John became very subdued. "I would rather just go on believing it was the smoke if you don't mind, guys. That was the weirdest thing I've ever experienced. It could be a carry-over from all the snake dreams I keep having—that is, when I get a chance to actually sleep."

"Jesus! I hate snakes more than Indiana Jones does," Buck said. "If I'd thought there was a chance of snakes being in that tunnel, it might have saved us all a lot of trouble. I don't know that I could have gone in there. How long have you been having these snake dreams?"

"Ever since I married into a nest of Copperheads," John snapped, "and the head Copperhead started trying to turn me into the living dead or something. Don't you reckon that might be about enough to give a man nightmares?"

"Yeah. That would do it for me," Eli said. "You see now why I married out. There's something to be said for dull in-laws. Hilda's folks are just as happy not to get me too involved. Wonder what they'd do if I offered to start going over to Murphy every Sunday to the Episcopal Church with them?"

That mental image brought a laugh to all three. It helped John's stress level. "Don't do it, man," he said. "They just might take you up on it and you'd be stuck. Of course, they'd want you to cut your hair and get a suit. Think you could go that far just so you could get white man's religion?"

"Oh, I might look sharp in a suit. Might even try it someday, but the hair stays. Hilda likes it just the way it is. Besides, we got married in that church. I figure I've been there enough."

The talk kept John alert for the rest of the drive. Thin, brief streaks of lightning intermittently flashed across the gray morning sky, disappearing so fast he couldn't be sure he really saw them at all.

"Looks like it's gonna rain," he said.

"Good day for a drive in the Smokies, huh, guys?" Eli said.

Buck stretched and complained of the pain in his back. "Yeah, if I'd listened to Amy, I could have spent the day in a nice, warm, dry emergency room."

They fell quiet after that and watched as the rain commenced a steady drizzle on the windshield. After a while Buck broke the silence. "You sure it was the ark, John? And you know it's safe with Walker and Dave?"

John was glad the conversation had picked up again. In the silence, it was hard not to think of the dead girl, or worry about Grady Smoker.

"Wren seemed sure of it, and she knows more about this stuff than I do," he said. "Last I saw of it, it was all in a big duffle bag that Walker hung onto like it was welded to his arm. I think you can rest easy about it. He ain't gonna let anything happen to your conjure crap."

Buck said, "I can't rest easy till I have it in my hands. I have to find a place where it will be safe. It's my responsibility until I have a male heir to turn it over to. Besides, I want to get it away from Walker before he manages to turn you into the Suye'ta."

"Damn, man. Don't even joke about that," John said. "Makes me want to kick Walker's ass for even thinking about it."

Buck didn't laugh. "One thing I agree with Walker about, if we wanted to bring in a Suye'ta, we couldn't do any better than you. When this is over and everything is back in its place, we have to leave you out of all the Snake Dancer business. I kinda hate that. None of us ever kept secrets from each other, except this. I'm glad you understand why it has to be this way."

John hunched over the steering wheel. "Don't let it worry you one bit, ol' buddy. Feel free to leave me out of as much of this bullshit as you want to. I've had about all of it I can stand."

"That's fine for you, John," Eli said, "but I've been left out long enough. As soon as we can find my grandpa, I'm gonna choke as much information out of him as I can. I know enough to understand that the Snake Dancers need me now."

Buck agreed. "We'll both be needed in the circle, Eli. We've gotta find Grady."

For some reason, John stopped thinking about the dead girl or worrying about Grady Smoker. All he could think of was Walker. This had to be another one of those *feelings*, like the Copperheads got. He had a bad one about Faron's grandfather. He tried to put it in the back of his mind and concentrated on driving.

Visibility became increasingly poor. A steady, cold drizzle settled in well before they reached Grady's trailer. Early spring came as a traitorous time here in the mountains. One day it would feel like summer had arrived, then cold wind and rain would dash that hope and make you think winter would stay forever.

This felt like one of those winter days.

He parked under the beech tree. Buck limped as they ran to the trailer's front stoop and huddled in its shelter while Eli knocked and called. When Grady didn't answer, he tried the door. "I'll be damned," he said when it opened. "Grandpa never leaves the door unlocked."

They trooped in while Eli kept calling, "Hey, Grandpa. You in here, Grandpa?"

The trailer felt empty, like nobody had lived there in a long time. John remembered how the Smoker home smelled like hot gingerbread and chicory coffee before Miss Sally died. Now, the coffee pot was cold and there didn't appear to be anything to eat in the kitchen but the leavings of a round of hoop cheese on the countertop beside a smoothed-out wrapper from a hamburger. Buck ignored the piece of paper, concentrating on the cheese. He reached in his jacket pocket and pulled out a red, waxy piece of cheese rind.

He showed it to John, then called, "Come look at this, Eli."

233

The three of them looked at the cheese rind, waiting for Buck to tell them why. He laid it down next to the round of cheese. "Think it matches?" he asked.

"Man, are we gonna look for my grandpa or stand around playing games with cheese?" Eli turned to walk away.

"Wait a minute, Eli. You want to know where this rind came from?"

"I figured it was laying there with the cheese." Eli looked concerned. "Where did it come from, Buck?"

"Yesterday morning, when I got to the hill where you found me, this was lying there on a rock. It wasn't mine, because I sure didn't take time for a snack. My guess was that somebody had a picnic out in the woods."

John understood. "Probably the same person who opened up the tunnel and stole the ark."

Eli looked like he had been kicked in the belly. "Guys, I can't listen to this anymore. When we find Grandpa, he'll explain. We've gotta find my grandpa." He ran out of the trailer. John and Buck followed him to the front porch of the old house.

Eli sat on the steps, his back against a sagging post and his chin on his knees, like he did since they came here as boys. They squatted beside him. "Remember how we used to sit out here listening to Grandpa tell us stories?" he asked.

John remembered, "Used to scare the crap out of me. I only came up here with you guys because of all the cookies and gingerbread your grandma used to make us."

Eli looked up. "It was a beautiful view, before they put the trailer there. When I'd stay over, we'd sit out here and watch the sunset. It was peaceful, listening to Grandma and Grandpa talk in our language. Made me feel good."

They sat, quietly talking about the old days until a commotion in the side yard interrupted them. Expecting the worst, they eased around the corner. Sally's old cat sat crouched over her kill, spitting at them. She didn't like it when her breakfast got disturbed. The chipmunk she prepared to dine on would have appreciated it if they had come along sooner. Eli braved her teeth and claws to pick her up and carry her back to the trailer's kitchen. John and Buck followed. They helped him search through cabinets and found one lone can of cat food. Eli dumped it into her dish. She was generous enough to share it with Yippi.

"That lazy cat never hunted in her life," Eli said. "They always fed her canned cat food. She must have been half starved to go kill a chipmunk."

John said, "Grady's not here, Eli. He would at least have fed his cat if he was. Let's look around the place. Then I think we should go talk to Walker."

They spread out to search the grounds. Back near the laurel thicket, Buck bent down to check out a set of tire tracks made by narrow, nearly bald tires.

John stooped beside him. "You know something, don't you, Buck?"

Eli came around the clump of laurels. Buck said, "I'll tell you about it later. Let's go to David's and see if they've heard from Grady."

Eli heard the last part. "I don't know where Grandpa is, but I'm afraid he's in some kind of trouble. If it has anything to do with that Eagle Feather creep, I want to be ready for him when I see him."

John didn't know what he meant by that, but Eli turned and went back to the trailer. He and Buck followed.

Eli went to Grady's bedroom and opened the closet door. After he rummaged around a while, he announced, "It's gone."

"What's gone, Eli?" John asked.

"Grandpa's shotgun. He always kept it here."

The three of them stood staring into the closet like that might make the shotgun reappear, until Eli closed the door and hurried out to the truck. John and Buck climbed in after him.

Again, John drove much too fast for the rain-slick mountain road. They didn't need to discuss what they feared. The same thought plagued them all. Grady knew who killed his granddaughter. He took the gun to make Eagle Feather pay for what he did. If they caught up with him first, maybe they could keep Grady from committing murder. They needed to find him first. "Walker can talk to Nathan Axe and tell him about Grady and the shotgun," John said. "He'll know how much to say."

"Then we should check out Eagle Feather's camp. Grandpa would probably go there to look for him," Yona said.

They fell quiet, listening to the rain on the windshield. John had things he wanted to say, but he didn't feel like talking. Nobody did. Hell, it hurt too much even to think.

Eli broke the silence when he couldn't take it anymore. "Eagle Feather. He killed the girl and Grandpa found out. Eagle Feather was probably using her to control Grandpa. That's the only way my grandpa would do what you're thinking he did."

"Grady Smoker is as good a man as I've ever known, Eli," Buck said. "All I'm thinking is that he's in trouble and we need to find him and see what we can do."

John wanted to comfort his friend, but he had enough trouble dealing with his feelings about Walker. The old goat had no right to suck him into something as weird as that Suye'ta business. And he went right along with it, just like he did with everything the Copperheads came up with. Well, not anymore. When he got hold of Walker Copperhead, he'd let him know just what he thought of his plans. What right did Walker have, dragging him into his schemes? And calling him an "outsider" after he spent his whole life in the bosom of the Copperhead family?

Even as he relished the thought of verbally ripping Walker a new one, a sharp stab of concern shot through him. He'd sure hate to see anything happen to the old man. He punched his speed up a notch. They needed to get to the Wayanettah place fast and make sure Faron's grandpa was okay. That bad feeling got stronger every minute.

He drove across the narrow bridge to David's house and parked in the empty driveway. He looked for Yona's Blazer until he remembered Mama Kate drove it home last night. He didn't see David's truck.

Buck got out and knocked on the door to make sure, but they already knew nobody would come to the door.

"Where do you think they went, John?" Eli asked.

"I don't know why, but I figure they went back up there where we found the girl. If not, I'd say they took those bones and grave goods to Ataga'hi." John shifted into reverse when Buck climbed in. "We'll go see if David's truck is parked up on the trail. If it's not, we'll go to Thunderhead."

Nobody could come up with a better plan.

They drove past Lynelle Wayanettah's house and saw her standing by her mailbox. She waved them down and John reluctantly stopped and backed up. She might have information they could use, but it was more likely she wanted to ask about the girl's murder. Lynelle liked her privacy, but if anything went on in her neighborhood, she needed all the details.

Without wasting a moment for polite exchanges, she began firing questions at them as soon as John lowered the window. "What in the world is going on around here this morning? Between the Cherokee Rescue people and Nathan Axe and his bunch, looks like everybody in Western North Carolina is tearing up and down my road. A body needs peace and quiet in the morning."

John leaned across the seat and yelled back, "I guess Nathan's looking into what happened to that girl. Did you see David go by here this morning?"

"I haven't seen anybody but the sheriff. I came down here when I heard the rescue boys with their siren wailing, like anybody around here needed to hear that. Nathan went by about the time I got to the road. But I heard a couple of cars go by early this morning. There's been more traffic on my road the last two days than I usually see in a week. Body might as well just move to town, with all this racket."

John's bad feeling really kicked in when he heard about the rescue squad. The sheriff must have gone back up the mountain to continue his investigation, but who needed to be rescued? His last shred of anger toward Walker melted into a sick dread that Faron's grandpa might be the one in trouble. He pulled away, yelling out the window, "We'll go see what's happening, Miss Lynelle, and let you know something later."

"Something's wrong, guys," he said. "Bad wrong."

Buck and Eli agreed.

"They might have found my grandpa," Eli said. "If he's hurt, that would explain why he's missing."

It made sense. And with the Cherokee Rescue Squad there, they figured he was still alive. John couldn't talk about it anymore. He'd stopped worrying about whether or not they ever found Grady Smoker. He needed to know Walker was okay.

The tire tracks left the story of spinning wheels making their way up the muddy logging trail. Someone else came this way earlier. Three vehicles sat parked beside the trail. David's truck was first, then a Cherokee Rescue vehicle. Behind that was Sheriff Nathan Axe's car.

"What the hell?" John said, braking to a stop.

Buck jumped out of the truck. "Surely they're not all here to bring the girl's body down. They would have done that last night."

"I'm sure they did," John said. "We brought Wren down before the authorities got there, but I don't think they would have left the girl up there all night. It wouldn't be respectful."

"No, they're here for something else," Eli said.

They set off up what was now a well-defined path.

John forgot all about being tired and ignored the aches and

pains in his bruised body. Buck and Eli had their work cut out for them just to keep up with him.

When he saw men up ahead with a litter, he left the others behind and ran.

"Oh, Jesus." Walker lay still as death, his eyes closed. Not a trace of breath stirred his chest. The men carrying him paused long enough to let John get a look. He felt Walker's neck for the carotid artery, then choked back a sob of relief. The pulse beat weak but steady against his fingers. Whatever made that big purple lump on Walker's head didn't kill him. As long as the tough old goat still breathed, he would pull through. He had to.

Something felt wrong. It took a moment for it to sink in that Walker didn't have his walking stick. He knew with sickening certainty, Walker didn't willingly leave it behind. He never let it out of his sight, and if somebody else had it, they took it by force.

"Where's his walking stick?"

One of the men answered him, "He didn't have it when we got to him. And we didn't have time to look for it. They're waiting for him at the Swain County emergency room. Sheriff Axe is up the hill. He can tell you what happened. Ask him about the walking stick."

John bent close to Walker. "Hang on, Old Man. We'll take care of things now." He waved the litter-bearers on, then with Buck and Eli in tow, trekked up Wolf Mountain. Within half an hour, they spotted Nathan and a couple of men ahead.

The sheriff stopped to wait for them when Buck called him.

"Good to see you in one piece, Buck," Nathan said. "Dorsey said you were going to the emergency room."

"Didn't need to," Buck said.

"What happened to Walker?" John panted from exertion. "Was he up here alone? Have you seen David and Yona?"

Nathan didn't try to hide his impatience. "Mr. Copperhead was here with David and Yona. Somebody knocked him in the head. He couldn't tell us who did it because he was out cold. We think it was the same person that blew Eagle Feather's head off in a cave up there where the girl was killed. You got anything to tell me that might help me find out who that was?" He looked straight at Buck.

"Eagle Feather's dead?" Buck asked.

"Considering the shape he was in, he's better off that way," Nathan said. "I hear he took a shotgun blast from close range, right in that pretty face of his."

Eli made a choking sound like he was trying to say something, but John didn't give him time to get the words out. "Anybody know where Grady Smoker might be?" It was probably better not to mention Grady's shotgun to the sheriff.

"I've got Jimmy looking for him. Yona told me Mr. Copperhead asked for him right before he passed out." Nathan cocked his head, looking suspicious. "Seems to me Grady's taken off without saying jack-shit to anybody for years, and nobody thought a thing about it. Now he's gone a couple of days and folks are worried. Is that because he was seen with Eagle Feather, or does it have something to do with the Snake Dancers?"

That question surprised John. From the looks that Eli and Buck exchanged, they didn't expect it either. Nathan shouldn't know about the Snake Dancers. They glanced at each other, then back at the sheriff. Since they couldn't think of an answer that would help without giving away something they weren't supposed to reveal, they said nothing.

John watched the three of them trying to stare each other down as long as he could stand it. "Nathan," he said. "I don't know about all that crap. I just know Walker is hurt and I'm gonna have to face Faron and Kate sometime today and tell them what happened. What can I tell them?"

"I've called Kate to let her know about Walker. She'll be here to meet him when they get him down the trail. All I could tell her was that Yona and David found him at that cave with a

240

Holly Sullivan McClure

knot on his head. By the way, why didn't you ask Yona and David about the walking stick when you met them on the trail?"

"What do you mean, met them on the trail?" Buck asked.

"They stopped long enough to tell me what had happened, then took off like scalded dogs to catch up with Mr. Copperhead and the rescue team," Nathan said.

John didn't wait for anything else, just yelled at the sheriff to keep an eye out for Walker's walking stick and started back down the mountain. Buck and Eli ran to catch up to him. Buck shouted for him to wait but John didn't slow down.

When they caught up close enough to talk, John asked, "Where were they, guys? We know David and Yona weren't with Walker, but it would take a damn good reason to make them leave him when he was hurt. I aim to find out what that reason was."

Buck agreed with John. He and Eli scanned the trailside for some sign that told them where David and Yona veered off. Even Yippi sniffed the air like he could smell something he didn't like. Buck saw the splotch of blood on the laurels first. From there, tracking them came easy. David and Yona left a well-marked trail in the rain-softened soil.

When John spotted the first blood stain on the muddy ground, the search took on added urgency.

"They can't be far ahead," he said. "Whoever they're following must have been important to make them leave Walker. It has to be Grady, and he's hurt."

"What's happened to my grandpa?" Eli asked.

"We'll know when we catch up with David and Yona." John hurried to a rock outcropping that gave him a view of the terrain below. When he spotted movement through the foliage and recognized his brother-in-law's form, he gave a shrill whistle to get Yona's attention and broke into a run.

Yona and David waited for him. John and Eli barely got a greeting. Buck got all the attention. They clapped him on the

241

back, hugging him and telling him how glad they were to see him.

"Jesus, Buck," Yona said, "we were afraid the guy with the shotgun got to you too. And man, we needed you to be alive. We're in way over our heads."

"The same guy who shot Eagle Feather? Do you know who he is?" John asked.

"Don't know yet. Haven't seen him, but he's hurt. He's been bleeding since he was in the cave," David said. "He's gotta be the one who shot Eagle Feather and slugged Walker. But it's worse than that, John. Lots worse."

The words came out strangled, as if Buck could hardly speak. "Did he find what he killed for?"

"Everything that was in the cave, and that was all but the Ulunsu'ti. If he has that, he can do anything he wants, if he lives."

Buck propped against a tree and rubbed his bruised hip. He stared at the ground to keep from looking at Eli. "If it's who I think it is, he's had the Ulunsu'ti since his grandfather turned it over to him. I'd just like to know how he got hold of the rest."

David said, "Walker and I thought it would be safe in the cave. We stashed the medicine and the ark, and even Kanagwa'ti's skeleton. I hid everything myself where I thought nobody would ever find it. Yona and I went to get it this morning. We built Walker a fire at the mouth of the cave, and he stayed out there trying to warm up. We found Eagle Feather dead in the cave. The things we hid, and what I guarded—all of it was gone."

"What you guarded?" Buck asked.

"The hands of the conjuror. They weren't buried with Kanegwa'ti. They've been in my family."

Buck's whole body slumped like the life had just drained out of him. "So, a man who has killed two people, and tried to kill Walker Copperhead, has the Ulunsu'ti and everything he needs to use it."

John listened as his friends talked, thinking about Walker, half dead on his way down the mountain, and the girl alone in the rocks with her head split open. Somebody killed her and tried to kill an old man, and they fretted about some old relics. He wanted to find out who killed the girl and hurt Faron's grandpa and make sure he couldn't hurt anyone else.

They didn't see him leave. He could move quietly when he wanted to. He heard them calling as he ran into a stand of pines, but he kept going. He had a better chance of sneaking up on the man than if all four of them tried.

John didn't need a trail. He no longer even looked for one. Relying on instinct alone, he closed in.

When he first caught sight of the man, he only saw a shadowy form moving between the tree trunks. He knew, even before he saw his face, that this would be harder for Eli than learning about his sister.

He crept closer, careful not to give away his presence. His caution proved essential when he saw the twelve-gauge shotgun the man carried. If a man killed once, he would do it again.

He got as close as he dared, torn between self-preservation and the disconcerting impulse to help when the man stumbled and almost fell. After all, this was one of the elders he'd looked up to since childhood.

The elder stumbled again under the weight of that heavy-looking duffle bag and the blood-soaked knapsack. He carried the shotgun under one arm and steadied himself with a sturdy walking stick almost as tall as he was.

He'd know that walking stick anywhere. Son of a bitch. He choked back his outrage and kept out of sight. Grady Smoker knew how much that walking stick meant to Walker. What else did he know about it? What would make him hit his oldest friend in the head and take away his most prized possession?

That walking stick had to be part of the story. Something

worth killing for.

He followed quietly, waiting for his chance to strike. The incongruity of it made it hard to think. No plan came to his mind.

Grady picked up the pace. He walked much steadier now. John got a good look at the knapsack and wondered why he thought it was bloody. It didn't look bloody now, and neither did Grady's shirt.

It got harder to keep up. Grady stood tall and moved through the scrub brush like a twenty-year-old athlete. John found it more difficult to keep him in sight.

Grady walked with the sure stride of a man who knew his destination. That confused John. Unless he veered off in another direction, their path led straight toward the pond where Lightning Creek began.

His path didn't change. John could hear the waterfall ahead. Around a bend in the path, he caught sight of it cascading down the cliff to form a crystal-clear pond.

John crouched behind a clump of boulders when Grady stopped and propped the shotgun against a rock.

With Grady unarmed, he could take him by surprise. He had a plan now: restrain Grady and march him down the trail to Lightning Creek Road.

An aura of danger radiated from the old man, even without the gun. John hung back and watched. Grady put the duffle bag down and took out the gym bags. He lifted out a bundle still wrapped in the jacket. The Cherokee Ark of the Covenant.

He took out bundles one by one until everything in the gym bags lay in a pile on the boulder.

John bided his time, watching, waiting for his chance. Grady kept the gun close by, close enough to reach in a hurry. This wasn't the same nice old man he knew all his life—the way he moved, the way he lifted the duffle bag like it didn't weigh as much as his cat.

John stayed out of sight and listened for the guys to come up behind him, wishing they would hurry. What the hell was keeping them? He counted on Eli to know what to do about his grandfather.

When he heard voices on the creek bank below, he stood up before he could stop himself. Kate and Wren stepped into the clearing and looked into the pond, unaware of Grady.

Grady didn't seem surprised to see them. He called to them like it was the most natural thing in the world for the three of them to meet halfway up a mountain where few people ever came.

John resisted the urge to run to protect Kate and Wren. It seemed smarter to ease back behind the rocks out of sight. He had no reason to think Grady would hurt them, but it scared him to death when he took a few steps toward them.

He forced himself to stay behind the rocks and wait. That bad feeling that began as a tickle at the back of his mind spread like an ache through his whole body. If he didn't handle this right, Kate and his baby girl were going to die there at the head of Lightning Creek.

Early Wednesday Morning

Snowbird

Wren lay still beside her with her eyes closed, but she didn't fool Faron. She couldn't sleep either. Diamond snuggled next to her in the big king-size bed where John should have been. She wanted her kids close where she could watch over them all night.

Wren stirred. "You awake, Mama?" she whispered.

"Shhh, baby. Go back to sleep."

"It's too scary, Mama. The dream is too real. It's like the man-snake is right here in the room. He says Daddy needs me and I should go to him."

Faron rolled out of bed and drew Wren into her arms. "Let's go downstairs, honey," she whispered. "We don't want to wake Diamond." She felt Wren trembling.

They tiptoed down the stairs.

"Where's Daddy?" Wren asked. "Has he called anymore?"

Faron spoke sharper than she meant to. "Daddy's with Eli and Buck, looking for Grady Smoker. You heard what he said when he called. Let's not worry. He'll be okay."

"Mama. The conjuror talked to me again, like in a dream. He's afraid for Daddy too. He says I should go to him. I think Daddy really needs me."

Faron opened the kitchen window curtain. A faint twinge of dawn lit the sky and she hadn't even closed her eyes. "Daddy's okay. You'll feel better if you eat something."

If only she believed it. Faron didn't need a dream to know John was in trouble. And some long-dead conjuror giving her daughter nightmares only made things worse. She poured two bowls of cornflakes and sat down, pushing her cereal around with her spoon till it became a soggy mess. Wren didn't touch her bowl. Faron gave up on breakfast and dumped it into the dog's dish on the back porch.

Wren opened each of them a cold bottle of Coke when she got back to the kitchen. They sipped from the bottles. At least they would have something in their stomachs while they talked."Okay, Wren, tell me what's on your mind."

Wren put her Coke down. "Did Daddy say where they were going to look for Uncle Grady? Because I think he's at the creek where Kanegwa'ti lives."

Faron had all she could take of Kanegwa'ti. The men let this get out of hand, and now her family paid the price for their mistakes. "I don't want to hear another word about the conjuror. Kanegwa'ti has been dead hundreds of years. Daddy probably went to Grady's house to see if he came home yet. Or he's talking to some of the Smokers or their friends. There's no reason he'd be way up on Lightning Creek. Where did you get such an idea?" Before the words left her mouth, she regretted raising her voice to her daughter.

Wren didn't back down. "Kanegwa'ti told me. I know he's supposed to be dead, but even if he is, he's still at the creek. He can't leave as long as he's responsible for the Ulunsu'ti, and I think he will always have to watch over it."

Did Kate tell her that? Faron didn't want her to believe it. "Honey, remember how the story says the conjuror turned the Ulunsu'ti over to his descendants to guard? Whoever his living descendant is, he has to take care of it now. It's out of the conjuror's hands."

"No, Mama," Wren said. "He was responsible for it till he turned it over to somebody else. He never did, so he's still tied to it."

"Why do you say that, honey? The stories all say he gave it to his grandson, who was the war chief of his day, and his family is still watching over it."

Wren shook her head. "No, Mama, he just gave them the

crystal. The thing that lives in it and makes it strong is the spirit of Uktena. That's what gave the conjuror his power. He never turned Uktena over to anybody. That's why he still lives at Lightning Creek. You have to cross over it to get something important. You can't bring Uktena's spirit to life without that important thing, and the man-snake is supposed to keep anyone from getting it."

"How do you know this? Did Grandpa tell you? Or Mama Kate?"

"No, Mama. I just know it. I think I might have learned it when I dreamed about the man-snake. I think he's the conjuror. Anyway, he's the one that said I should go find Daddy."

Faron didn't know what to say. She couldn't let Wren go back up there, not when she already found the poor murdered girl on that mountain. But what if John did need her?

She got up and wiped the spotless countertops with a sponge. John was in danger. She knew it even before she left David's house. That's what scared her so much. And not just for John—for her little girl, and Walker too. In the pit of her stomach she knew she could lose all three of them, and she felt completely helpless and out of her depth. She needed Kate's help with this.

"Wren," she said, "I don't understand any of this. Let's hope your grandma knows what to do. We'll call Mama Kate."

Wren nodded and handed her mother the phone.

Faron entered the number and Kate answered on the first ring, her voice strained and anxious.

"You're already up, huh?" Kate said. "You'd think we'd all be asleep, since it was nearly daylight by the time we got to bed."

"Mom," Faron said, "I'm scared. I haven't heard a word from John since they left for Grady's house, and I've got a bad feeling about Grandpa. To make it worse, Wren had another dream about the conjuror. Now she says he wants her to go look for her daddy. I don't know what to do. Something's happened, something bad. I can feel it, and I just can't let Wren go back up there."

Kate said, "You're not the only one who has a bad feeling about John and Walker. I've had one for the last two days. And honey, when I get a bad feeling, you can take it to the bank."

"What are we going to do, Mom? Do you think John is in danger? Is that why Wren is having these dreams?"

"I don't know, but my gut's kicking in real heavy about him. Strangest thing is I can't seem to get any sense at all about what's going on with Walker. Walker and John aren't blood kin to me, but we're close enough that I usually know if they're in trouble."

Faron asked, "How about Grady Smoker? Any idea about what's going on with him?"

"Not the slightest," Kate said. "But I'm not too surprised that my instincts don't pick up anything on him. He's not really family. But Walker's different. He's been like blood to me since I married his son, and I'm worried to death about him. Only thing I know to do is to pay attention to Wren's dream."

Faron felt betrayed. "You can't mean that, Mom. Wren's already been through too much. I want her left out of this from now on. She's staying right here with me, and we're not going to talk about this to her. She's only eight years old."

"Listen, Faron," Kate said. "I called Maddie Axe the minute I got home last night. I was hoping she could help us out, but she says there's not much we can do. It's something the men have to handle but they've screwed up. All we can do now is just look after our men and kids, like we've always done, and we need to use whatever we've got to do it with. Right now, all we have to go on are Wren's dreams. If we can get some insight from them, we have to listen to her."

Faron felt more conflicted than before calling Kate. This put Wren in danger and Kate wanted to get her more involved. But what if it would help John? Sometimes she envied the McLeymores. If they couldn't see and touch something, it didn't exist. They would just dismiss Kate's feelings as woman's intuition at best. And Granny Mac would treat Wren's nightmares with a cup of chamomile tea. She toyed with the idea of calling John's mom. Granny Mac wouldn't send her granddaughter out on a wild goose chase where one girl had already been murdered. She should hang up on Kate and dial the McLeymores' number, but of course she didn't do it. Like everybody else in the Copperhead family, up to and including Walker, she listened to Kate.

Kate ended the phone call with instructions. "Get Wren dressed. I'll be right over and we'll talk about what we're gonna do."

The relief that usually came when her mother took charge evaded her. Faron grilled Wren about her dreams, hoping for something that suggested an answer that didn't include sending her little girl into danger, or making the choice between keeping Wren safe or looking after John and Walker.

When Kate's Trans Am roared over her new bridge twenty minutes later, she still had no answer.

Kate marched in, dressed for business in a sweater and a pair of jeans that fit like a glove. Sturdy hiking boots and a leather jacket completed her outfit. Her long hair hung in a thick black ponytail stuffed through the back of a baseball cap. She entered with news that couldn't wait.

"Nathan Axe called just as I was walking out the door. Grandpa's been hurt."

Faron dropped down on the nearest chair, her knees suddenly too weak to support her. "How bad?"

Kate hugged her. "Nathan has talked to John, and he's okay. And Cherokee Rescue is bringing Walker down off Wolf Mountain. I want to be there to meet him."

"What's wrong with Grandpa?" Wren heard every word.

Kate opened her arms and Wren stepped into her embrace. "Nathan didn't see anything but a lump on his head that didn't look all that bad. The paramedics say he's out cold. They suspect he had a concussion. They'll take good care of him."

Wren choked back tears. Kate tried to comfort her. "Grandpa's gonna be okay," she said. "He's in good hands with the Cherokee Rescue Squad. They'll get him to the hospital in no time. I'm gonna leave now and be there to meet him. I'll make sure he's taken care of."

"I'm going with you, Mama," Faron said. "We'll take Wren and Diamond by the McLeymores. Granny Mac will look after them."

"No, honey. John would want you to stay here where he knows you and his kids are safe. I'll let you know as soon as I lay eyes on Grandpa."

Wren got her yellow slicker and kissed Faron's cheek. "Bye, Mama. I have to go with Mama Kate."

"No, Wren. Absolutely not. I can't let you go back up there."

Wren's lip trembled. It didn't come easy for her to defy her mother but she continued to put on her slicker and get ready to go.

Kate bent down to help her. "You know I'll take care of her. We'll be home as soon as we see about Grandpa. We're just gonna meet him and make sure he gets to the hospital alright. I'll call you from there."

Wren looked far more grim and determined than any eight-year-old girl should. "We better get going, Mama Kate," she said.

Faron tried one last time. "Mom, please."

Kate gave her a quick goodbye hug. "I swear I won't let anything happen to her, but we need her insight. If the conjuror is getting through to her, it might be all we have to fix this mess. You call Amy Locust and tell her what's going on, and try to keep her calm till we can get her man home."

Wren ran outside and got into Kate's car before Faron could stop her.

Faron asked, "Mom, do you know what's going on with the men? Is John a part of it now?"

Kate said, "Honey, you know I've suspected Walker was keeping something from me. Not just about the Snake Dancers. That's none of my business. But there was something else he didn't want me to know. I know it involved Johnny, and that worries me. That husband of yours gets on my nerves sometimes, but he's your man, and he's good to you. If that old goat does anything that gets him hurt, I'll put another knot on his hard old head."

"The outsider story? Is that it, he wants John to be the Suye'ta?"

"It better not be that crazy nonsense. Walker knows better than to pull that crap." Kate took off without another word.

Faron stood on the porch with Diamond in her arms, waving as Kate drove across her new bridge. It felt like months ago when they built it, not just last Sunday. Strange how your whole world can change in three short days. She didn't like the changes at all.

Shivering in the cold, she watched the Trans Am until it passed around the bend in the driveway and out of sight.

Faron heard Diamond crying. She brought him downstairs and held him a little too tightly while she fed him his morning oatmeal.

Wednesday Morning

Leaving Snowbird

Wren shivered with cold and asked Kate to turn on the heat.

Kate set the heater on high. "It is awful chilly for this time of year, isn't it? The thermometer says fifty degrees, but it feels more like thirty. It's probably the dampness that makes it seem so cold."

Kate drove so fast the wheels squealed on the turns. It scared Wren, but it meant they would get to her daddy and Grandpa faster. When she warmed enough to stop shivering, she asked, "What did Mr. Axe say about my daddy?"

"I told you, sweetie. He's with Buck and Eli and they were all just fine. They look out for each other, so don't worry."

But Wren did worry. In her dream she didn't see anybody looking out for her daddy. He was on his own. The only one with him tried to hurt him, and she didn't understand that at all. Grady Smoker was a real nice man. He and Miss Sally used to bring her frosted cupcakes when they came to visit. She liked them. Maybe Granny Mac told the truth when she said dreams didn't mean anything. Worrying about her daddy caused her to dream such a dumb thing about Grady. She almost convinced herself of that when Kate asked her about that nightmare.

"It was really scary, Mama Kate. Grady Smoker was hurting people. He was big and strong and Daddy was afraid. The snake tried to help him, but it couldn't."

"The snake?" Kate asked.

"Yeah, but it's not always a snake. Sometimes it looks sort of like Grandpa Driver, but it isn't."

"Wren, Sheriff Axe will help us take care of your daddy. I don't know what your dream means, but Grady Smoker wouldn't hurt a fly. He's like one of our family."

Wren always paid attention to what the grown-ups said, even when they didn't think she heard. "If he's like one of the family, how come we didn't know about his granddaughter until she turned up dead?"

Kate didn't try to answer.

Wren leaned her head against the back of the seat and closed her eyes. Mama Kate didn't understand this anymore than her mama, and that scared her more than anything. Mama Kate usually knew things. She expected Mr. Axe to help her daddy, but he didn't keep Grandpa Walker from getting hurt and he couldn't stop the girl from getting killed. Wren glanced at her grandmother. Mama Kate looked like a woman who intended to take care of her family, and she could do it too. If Grady Smoker or anybody else messed with her, he'd be sorry. But Mama Kate looked scared too. The way she gripped the steering wheel and took the curves so fast gave her away. As much as she tried to act brave, waving at people she recognized as they drove through Cherokee, she still looked scared.

They went through the main drag without any traffic problems. "If only it could stay like this. In a couple of months, this place will be crawling with summer tourists." Kate talked too fast, trying to keep Wren thinking about something other than her daddy and Grandpa Walker.

Wren played along. "A blessing and a curse, Grandpa calls them. Bringing their money and leaving their pollution." He didn't like the casino or the bingo hall. She didn't either.

They left the town behind and turned onto Lightning Creek Road. The porch light was still on at the Wayanettah house, the only sign of life. "David's car is gone," Wren said.

"Nathan said he saw it parked on that logging road past Aunt Lynelle's house," Kate told her. "He figured David brought Walker and Yona up there." Then she added, "Those two had better have a good explanation for why they let Walker get hurt."

Wren wouldn't want to be in Yona and David's shoes when Mama Kate got hold of them. "Looks like the rain is letting up," Wren said.

"That's a mercy," Kate said, easing the car onto the bridge over Lightning Creek. "Now if it would just get warmer. I hope they don't let Grandpa get a chill."

Something caught Wren's attention off the side of the road, a flash of dull yellow in the bushes beside the creek. "Mama Kate, stop the car." She rose up on her knees to get a better look. "Somebody ran off the road."

Kate pulled over to the side of the narrow dirt road and stopped. Wren jumped out and ran through the weeds. She heard Kate calling but kept running. Kate sloshed through the wet weeds after her. They both recognized Grady Smoker's car. He drove the same old yellow Pinto for more years than Wren had been alive. It looked like an abandoned wreck with both front wheels almost in the creek. They looked inside. The little picture frame dangling from the keys in the ignition displayed a photo of Miss Sally smiling at a little girl on her lap. A few fast-food containers lay crumpled on the floor.

"Mama Kate, where's Uncle Grady? Do you think he's hurt?"

"I don't know, honey." Kate looked around for signs that Grady might be injured somewhere in the bushes. "I don't understand how he could have accidentally run off the road there. My guess is that he finally got tired of this old wreck and just drove down here and left it."

Wren no longer listened to her grandmother's voice. She had a feeling the snake wanted to talk to her. She felt him calling her, drawing her toward the creek. She let it pull her toward the water. The surface of the stream broke and a snake's head emerged, its snowy white mouth catching the light behind gaping fangs. Now Mama Kate had to believe her.

"Look, Mama Kate," she called.

Kate ran to her side and stared into the water. The snake ducked its head under the surface. Wren pointed to a dark, undulating form beneath the water. He blended so well with the shadows that they couldn't see him until he lifted his head to stare at them unafraid. Fangs longer than Wren's fingers gleamed in his cottony mouth. His thick body whipped wavelets in the creek. Wren bent over close to the water.

Kate tried to pull her away, but Wren needed to see the snake. She struggled, but Kate picked her up and set her down a few feet away from the creek.

"That's not natural," Kate said. "This creek is too cold for him, and there's no sun to warm his blood. Cold-blooded reptiles can't live like that. What's he doing here? He should be holed up in his den, or at least so sluggish he wouldn't have the energy to move like that."

"He's got plenty of energy." Wren slipped out of Kate's grasp and ran alongside the creek, searching the water for the snake.

Kate yelled for her to stop.

Wren didn't want to disobey her grandmother. She never had before, but this time she had no choice. She needed to follow the snake. She could see him now, just beneath the surface, swimming against the rapids.

Kate stayed on her heels. The snake didn't scare Wren. She knew him from her dreams when he tried to help her daddy. The bad man wanted to hurt them all. She needed Mama Kate with her if she saw him.

"Slow down, honey," Kate called.

Wren panted for breath. The climb over the rocks and boulders that lined the creek taxed her endurance, but she didn't dare slow down.

"Please, Mama Kate. We have to go with the snake. He'll take us to Daddy."

She reached back and took Kate's hand and felt it trembling.

It would be easier if Mama Kate could be brave.

"Stay close to me, baby," Kate said, and let Wren lead her over the rocky banks toward the pond at the head of the creek.

Mama Kate would know what to do when they found Daddy. She heard the waterfall at the head of the creek.

The rain let up and the air felt warmer on the creek bank. The snake waited up ahead, his huge head protruding above the water. Wren could feel him urging them to hurry. She pulled on Kate's hand, telling her to run.

Kate held back. "Wren, we're supposed to meet the rescue squad with your grandpa. Can't we come back later and look for the snake?"

"Come on, Mama Kate!" Wren shouted. Her grandmother gave in and scrambled over the rocks behind her.

She lost sight of the snake in the rocks where the water spilled from the pond and rushed down the mountainside. Kate tried once more to get her to turn back. Wren didn't have time to explain why they had to keep going. She knew where she had to go. The snake called her on, urging her to hurry.

When they broke through the thick green bushes beside the pond into a rocky clearing, Grady Smoker stood there waiting for them. He never scared her before. Grandpa Walker called him almost family, so why did he seem like the scariest thing in the world, and why did he come out on such a cold, wet day with nothing to keep him warm but a ragged old flannel shirt? His unblinking eyes stared right through her. Wren could tell by the way Mama Kate's hand turned cold, and clutched hers so hard it hurt, that he scared her too. She didn't even scold him for coming out without his coat.

Grady grinned at them, like he knew a secret they didn't know. But his eyes didn't smile. They looked dead.

Mama Kate grabbed Wren and ducked behind a boulder. Wren pressed her body against the rock, trying to keep out of Grady's sight, trembling so hard she couldn't be still.

"Why didn't I listen to your mother and leave you at home?" Kate whispered in her ear.

"'Cause, I had to come," Wren said.

Minutes passed and Grady didn't make a sound. Kate signaled Wren to be quiet and eased out from behind the rock.

Wren peeked from behind the boulder, wishing she could pull her grandmother back. Grady just stood there, less than three feet away, with that weird grin on his face.

She understood when he turned away. Someone had hurt him. His torn shirt hung off his shoulder and revealed a gash so deep it probably went to the bone. It should have been bleeding but the wound didn't have a drop of blood in it. It looked whiter than the snake's mouth. Grady needed help.

Mama Kate took a step toward him. He turned to stare at them again and Kate stopped.

Her grandmother always helped hurt people, but Wren didn't want her to get any closer to Grady. She didn't like the way he stared at her, like a hungry dog at a pork chop. And he didn't act like his hurt bothered him. In fact, he looked like he felt real strong.

She couldn't leave Mama Kate alone with him. She inched from behind the boulder and went to stand beside her grandmother.

"Why is he so blue?" Wren asked.

"Oh, Lord. He sees you." Kate tried to push Wren back behind the boulder.

Wren clung to her grandmother's jacket and choked back a whimper.

Grady came closer and they backed away. He was a good man. Everybody said so. Why did he want to hurt them? Wren looked toward the pond, hoping the snake would come to help. The snake didn't appear. She and Mama Kate had to manage alone, if Grady Smoker didn't kill them.

"Do you think he killed that girl, Mama Kate?" she asked.

"I'm afraid he did," Kate said.

Uncle Grady Smoker was the bad man in her dream, the one who wanted to kill her daddy. He looked like he wanted to kill her and Mama Kate too.

Wednesday

The First World Below

Walker Copperhead didn't move a muscle, strapped to the litter, vaguely aware of the men who carried him. A couple of times they stopped and checked to make sure his heart was still beating. Once, when they couldn't find a pulse or see any sign of respiration, he heard them give him up for dead.

They talked about how they hated to face Kate Copperhead at the foot of the trail and tell her Walker died. Walker drew breath and willed his body to stay alive. Dying served no purpose, and it might leave him stuck in the world of lost souls with nothing to come back to.

He heard their relieved comments through the fog that separated him from the world in which they walked. While they carried his motionless body on their litter, another part of him wandered far from Wolf Mountain to a gray, cold place where a man could get lost and never find his way home. He traveled there before, but long ago and never alone. Driver Wayanettah always waited to guide him back into the world of light. Driver wouldn't be there to rescue him this time. If he failed, he and Grady would both be left to wander the wastelands, two lost souls trapped in the first world below.

As the last spirit walker alive since Driver Wayanettah walked over, he ventured beyond the land of the living into the darkness with no one to rescue him if he failed. Walker's grandfather, Tsali Copperhead, taught them both to walk the worlds below and retrieve lost souls. Tsali honored his grandson with the title "Ai'da" when he proved adept at navigating places where living men seldom choose to go. It meant "spirit walker," but Tsali shortened it to "Walker." Only he and Driver knew what he endured to earn the name.

He advanced with great caution, trusting the rescue team to take good care of his body back on Wolf Mountain. He counted on the thread of life that connected him to his physical form to draw him back to the living world. If it broke, he and Grady would both be stuck here—not just a lifetime but, as far as anyone knew, forever. Nobody wanted to spend eternity in the first world below.

When he last walked the void, rescuing the spirit of a boy more dead than alive from a drug overdose, youth and physical strength served to pull him back even without Driver to guide him. Now, the frail old body on the litter had such a minor claim on him that he couldn't find it. Grady had even less of a tie to his flesh and bones. He fled so far from it that he didn't know what now walked in his form, using it to do things Grady would never do.

Old Tsali's teaching laid a duty on him and Driver. A spirit walker took vows, agreeing to venture into this land to retrieve spirits lost before their time. They did it together many times after they talked it over and couldn't find another way. Not even the conjurors wanted to go there, and nobody asked to be trained to walk the below worlds anymore. With Driver gone, only he remained to teach a new walker to replace him. If nobody took on the duty, the path died with him.

This time, Driver wasn't waiting in the physical world to call him home. He counted on his walking stick to show him the way, as it had generations of walkers before him. The only Snake Dancer left to help now walked the dark lands as a shadow, his body inhabited by an evil so old no one knew where it came from. He risked everything when he shoved his walking stick in Grady Smoker's hand, calling his true name and demanding he keep the walking stick with him. The thing in Grady's body didn't like that. It made Grady hit him with the shotgun, but it couldn't make him drop the walking stick.

The voices of the Cherokee Rescue Squad faded into silence as he sent his spirit into the gray world, calling Grady's true name, the one they knew him by in the circle. As long as his spirit existed, he would answer to that name. He had no choice.

No answer came through the void. He called again and reached out to feel for his walking stick, shaping his hand around the eagle image he conjured in his mind. When he perceived the faintest pull, he let it draw him, planting his feet on an imaginary path taking one step at a time, watching, sensing his surroundings, cautious of the denizens of the wasteland who traveled with him. Tsali described those beings, hungry, angry spirits who fed on the life force of the living who entered their world. He drew his consciousness into the void and trudged on, alert, ready to present a defense against the kind of beings his presence attracted. The surface of the gray land sucked at his spirit legs like wading through knee-deep mud.

The pull of his walking stick tugged at his mind. He moved toward it, calling Grady's name. Something other than Grady answered. He didn't call out anymore, just reached out for his walking stick, knowing nothing here wanted to touch the shade of the real thing.

Thick, viscous mist swirled around his face. Forms moved in and out, blending with the mist until he couldn't tell where he ended and they began. The part of him that walked the first world below consisted of less substance than the mist. He waded through it like trudging against the rapids of an icy trout stream, going nowhere. He needed a stronger presence, even if that meant withdrawing even further from the shell of himself he left behind on Wolf Mountain.

Aware of the dismayed rescue squad pounding his chest, urging him to breath, he drained his spirit from it, drawing it away to the first world below. Even the weak beacon of energy he counted on to guide him back dwindled down to a trickle.

The possessed man who carried his walking stick held the key to his survival. If he put the walking stick in his flesh-and-blood hand at the right time, they both stood a chance. Without it, nothing could bring him out of the first world below.

Grady would know what to do—if he survived.

Maybe his family could find a way to get the walking stick into his hand if Grady didn't make it back. Years of humoring him conditioned them to please him. In some ways, he carried almost as much weight as Kate. They didn't have to know why he needed it, just that he liked having it within reach. Even John understood that.

Grady's spirit presence called to him. The carved eagle touched his palm and stirred to life. He risked calling Grady's true name, softly so only he could hear. The answer came as an agonized wail that tore through the darkness. It rose above the ever-present, hopeless keening of the disembodied lost who wandered these hopeless lands. In the world of doomed souls, the cry of physical pain carries a shattering force. Even here, Grady couldn't escape what happened to his body in the world of form and substance.

Walker Copperhead waded toward Grady's voice, trying not to think about the depth of torment that could make one of the toughest old soldiers he'd ever known yell like that. He couldn't hope to save Grady's life, and it became harder to stifle the fear of what would happen to his soul. If he failed to retrieve his spirit from the below world, his old friend would be stuck there without hope. He couldn't even give Grady an easy death, but if he reunited with his body long enough to atone before he left it for good, they stood a chance of removing the peril he unleashed on the world. Hiding out in the below world promised oblivion and spared Grady the price he must pay for betraying the guardians, but he couldn't allow him to claim that way out.

Walker turned his will toward the physical world on Wolf Mountain, searching for the substance of the walking stick he thrust in Grady's flesh-and-blood hand. With the first brush of his mind against it, scorching heat ran through him, seeking out his body and driving his consciousness back into the world below.

He couldn't risk contact with the body that walked down the trail toward the waterfall. Even in his spirit-walker form, the serpent reached out from Grady's body searching for him. He didn't dare lead him to the frail old carcass on the litter.

Wednesday Afternoon

Lightning Creek

Grady Smoker's fear faded. He found himself at peace in a dark, empty place. Emptiness, where only cold reached, made him forget the wound in his back or the throbbing gash in his head. Guilt no longer tormented him and his mind was at rest. Even the dead girl didn't matter. She existed in his thoughts, still alive, his only granddaughter. The white man lay dead in the cave where he couldn't cause trouble for her or their people.

Memories didn't hurt anymore, so he allowed his mind to drift across the years, remembering when the girl's mother came to Robbinsville with Eagle Feather, looking for Thomas Smoker. She found Grady first, the baby girl in her arms. How Sally's face lit up when she held their granddaughter, but she understood the threat to their son. If Thomas's wife found out, she'd take Eli and go back to her folks in Oklahoma. The Choctaw woman only wanted security for her baby, so she listened to them. A father married to another woman offered less than a pair of loving grandparents who looked after them both. Eagle Feather promised her and the baby a home and family.

He kept their secret from Thomas, the only way to prevent his daughter-in-law from taking Eli away. The next guardian of the Ulunsu'ti needed to stay in the homeland where he could learn his duties. He started Eli's education early, with stories that prepared him for the real mysteries.

The Choctaw woman became the daughter Sally always wanted and the baby girl her pride and joy. And Eagle Feather looked after both of them.

Somewhere beyond the fog, a voice broke through his reverie. His name echoed in the darkness. Shame gave him the strength to resist, and guilt made him flee deeper into the mist.

If Walker's spirit entered the below world, he must be dead. Walker called again, saying the name that compelled him to answer. It forced him to face the truth. Even death lacked the power to condemn a good man to the world below. Walker Copperhead entered the gray world to bring the vengeance of the Snake Dancers to the one who betrayed them. Not even here could he hope to escape them. They sent the only spirit walker in the circle to get him.

The voice called again, speaking the name he couldn't ignore. Walker came so close he could feel him reaching for the walking stick. Why did he have the walking stick in his hand?

The memory teased at his mind, the butt of the shotgun connecting with Walker's head, Walker forcing the walking stick in his hand as he crumpled on the ground. It called to Walker, giving him away. Though just a shadow of the real one, its power still connected the worlds. He couldn't hide in this world or any other. The Ai'da would find him.

Before he could answer Walker's call, another hand joined his on the eagle's head. The voice that spoke held no anger and no pity, just a commanding force that gave no quarter and left him no option but obedience.

Walker called his warrior name, the name only the Snake Dancers knew.

"Look and see."

He lacked the power to resist. When Walker spoke again, he stood beside him, directing him to observe the thing that took control of his body on Wolf Mountain. Shadows in a shadow world, they stood side by side, watching an old man staggering through a grove of pine trees. Even as they watched, the old man stood taller and walked with firmer steps. Strength flowed into him from the knapsack on his wounded shoulder, a dark strength

266

that writhed through him, eating into his mind.

He watched it from a world away until loathing overpowered him. The face he saw held no trace of remorse. The eyes looked at the world with wonder, pleased with everything they saw. The thing that looked out of his eyes and snaked through his body emanated raw hunger and power that reached all the way to the world below.

He turned away, but Walker insisted, "You must go back and reclaim your body."

The serpent that snaked through his body reached out, searching for him, mocking his weakness. He couldn't go back to that.

"You must return," the shadow beside him said. "You must see with your mortal eyes and hold a part of your spirit in your mortal form."

He watched, imagining how it would feel to walk once more as that man. How strange to look through the mist to see himself so solid and real, holding the eagle-headed walking stick in his flesh-and-blood hand. Walker's voice reached him like cobwebs against his mind, urging him closer to the body that walked on the mountain, yet holding him in the shadow.

He reached out with a thread of thought and let it touch the mind of the man on the trail. Serpent hunger snaked through him like fire through his soul. An alien consciousness touched him when he tried to pull away. It held him there with an intensity that trapped him in a body no longer his own. He could feel it worming through his memories, seeking the way into all he knew.

Walker's voice held a trace of kindness when he said, "He won't like the walking stick, but don't lose it. It will take us home."

He took comfort from that. He had a way home. That's why Walker made him take the walking stick back at the cave. He didn't have to do this alone.

Grady could feel his body now. The movement of his legs. The weight of the duffle bag and the gun. And the thing that lived with him in the body. A cold, hungry mind snaked against his, tasting his presence. It wanted him there but promised nothing but pain if he stayed. He could feel it exploring his memories and relishing his fear. Walker still whispered in his mind, helping him hold on when fear threatened to overwhelm him.

The walking stick. The serpent spirit didn't like it. It wanted him to leave it beside the path. Walker made him close his hand tightly around the eagle head and hold on, even when it burned into his flesh.

He let his spirit settle into his body and looked out at the trail through his mortal eyes. Blood still oozed from the wound on his back and ran down into the knapsack. That stirred a vague fear of something important he must remember. The hands and the Ulunsu'ti, both in the blood-soaked knapsack.

The serpent mind swept away his thoughts of the conjuror's hands cupped around the crystal in the bloody knapsack.

Walker's voice spoke his warrior name, the name only he could hear. "He wants to go to Degal gun'yi, where he is safe from the Nunne'hi. Think of that and nothing else."

He emptied his mind. No more thoughts of the pool at the head of Lightning Creek, where the immortals were strong and Kanegwa'ti waited. Thinking only of the mound of the Ani'Kuta'Ni, he made himself see the image before his eyes and said aloud, "This is where we are going."

He felt satisfaction from the serpent mind. It liked the image. There, where the Ani'Kuta'Ni were buried and the Nunne'hi never came, he could wait and gather strength.

From the shadows of the first world below, he and Walker guided Grady's body to the head of Lightning Creek. Only a day before, he still thought he could go to the Council House Mound and feed the Ulunsu'ti just enough blood from a rabbit to give it life, but not enough to bring it to full power. The tools in the duffle bag would help him control it, and the eagle bone whistle would call the Nunne'hi if the serpent spirit became too strong. Now, the crystal feasted on the blood of a Wolf Clan warrior, and the Council House Mound was miles away.

The waterfall at the head of Lightning Creek lay ahead. No bird or insect sang there, and no sound other than the water and the wind could be heard. The doorway to the world of the immortals was a silent place.

Holding the image of Degal gun'yi in his mind, he watched his body emerge from the pine grove and walk toward the waterfall. His mortal eyes saw only the image he held before it of the burial mound at Degal gun'yi.

The thing in his head was pleased.

More than eighty years of living in his body should have made him feel as if he belonged there, but it wasn't his anymore. The gash on his shoulder that caused him so much pain no longer hurt. He still carried the knapsack, but it was almost clean, the last traces of blood drained away. Fresh tendrils of life spread from it into his blood. He could feel it, eating into his mind and seeking out his soul.

He couldn't bear it any longer. His body was a trap that held him for the serpent to feed on. Walker spoke the name that made him listen and ordered him to stay, telling him to look at the thin shining cord binding him to his body. It made him part of all that happened to it as long as it lived. That could be a very long time if they failed. As long as the serpent needed his body, it would still walk and breathe, and Grady Smoker would always be there with him.

When fear weakened him, Walker's voice painted a picture of Degal gun'yi in his mind. He used all his will to build up the image and keep it in the serpent's thoughts. His body walked toward the falls at the head of Lightning Creek, but the serpent saw the mound of the Ani'Kuta'Ni. It urged him to hurry.

269

Tentacles of fire writhed from the knapsack and into his veins. Without Walker's commands to hang on, he couldn't have endured the pain. When agony weakened him, Walker gave him the strength to keep walking toward the falls and keep the image of Degal gun'yi strong.

Walker's voice spoke his warrior name, calling him to stand for his final battle.

In the shadows of the first world below, the spirits of two old Snake Dancers watched Grady Smoker's body laboring under the heavy load he carried.

Grady couldn't tell anymore whether he observed the trail from his shadow form or from his physical eyes. His body grew stronger with every step. Age and weakness dropped away. He stood straight and strong and strode down the mountain like a young man. He felt excitement and power, and not the slightest twinge of the remorse that drove him to the dark world of lost souls. Even the memory of the dead girl lying on the rocks brought no anguish, just a vague stirring of hunger.

Grady stopped struggling to distance himself from his body and settled into his familiar form. He wasn't this strong, even as a young soldier. Sensations surged through him that he never knew before, and he liked them. Something nagged at him to fight it, but he didn't want to.

Why did he feel such revulsion for the Ulunsu'ti? He never actually looked at it before, and he couldn't remember why. Gazing deep into its core, he saw the glow of life. Fire danced through it, consuming the blood it drew from the knapsack. He watched the last traces disappear into the living fire. It was a good and proper thing. Strange, reptilian beauty made him reach in and caress the surface, as smooth and warm as flesh.

A serpent whisper told him this was all he needed. Walker's voice whispered in his thoughts, reminding him of work only the guardian of the Ulunsu'ti could do. He ignored it until it called the name he had to heed. Walker made him struggle against the tendrils of the serpent mind that threaded through his thoughts.

Uktena walked in his body, but he must fight to hold his mind and spirit free.

He and Walker kept the image of Degal gun'yi before his eyes. The serpent, pleased with the vision, seemed unaware that Grady walked straight toward the waterfall at the head of the creek. Grady listened through ears as sharp as when he was a boy, but heard no noises—not a sound, as if every living thing had fled or gone to ground.

Like a hunter with senses alert for game, he observed the world. Long unsatisfied hunger stirred in his body as he scanned for anything that moved. Not so much as a bird flew over. His eyes looked out on a strange land. The contrail from a jet overhead didn't register as familiar, and his clothing felt odd against his skin.

Grady walked on toward the image of Degal gun'yi. There, the duffle bag and all the hateful things it held could be destroyed. The weight of it slowed his steps and clouded his thoughts. It was dangerous. The old conjurors used the things inside it to make him weak so they could hold him prisoner. When they were gone, he would be free of them forever. Then, neither the Nunne'hi nor the conjurors could control him.

He was aware of the walking stick he carried. It was even heavier than the duffle bag, and almost as much of a threat. He would have left it beside the trail, but a voice in his mind said it should be taken to Degal gun'yi to be destroyed with the rest. He held it and walked on.

In the below world, his shadow hand gripped the shade of the walking stick. Walker held it with him, giving him strength to bear the fear, forcing him to view everything that happened, and get ready. The two old Snake Dancers watched through the mist as the form that once housed Grady Smoker walked toward the head of Lightning Creek.

The serpent saw only the mound of the Ani'Kuta'Ni before

271

him and grew stronger with each step. The tentacles spreading through the body pushed aside the scrap of Grady Smoker that still inhabited it. He could hear it exulting in the knowledge of imminent freedom. He tasted the memory of how it lived before the Shawnee warrior came with his fire.

The image of Degal gun'yi held true, rising before him real enough to touch. He climbed to the top of the mound and opened the duffle bag. First, he took out the gym bag that held the bones and shook them out atop the mound. How shattered and dry they had become, as if they would soon be no more than dust. He felt the serpent's fear when he opened the other bag. His body shuddered when he reached in and lifted out the medicine bowl.

For only a moment, the serpent's hold on his mind lessened. Grady Smoker seized the chance to crack the cover of the medicine bowl against the stone. The pungent fragrance of a powerful preparation of herbs and tobacco spread through the clearing, but the serpent spirit didn't detect it. He was occupied with placing something even more threatening to him on the pile. The medicine pouch held the eagle bone whistle. It wasn't capable of hurting someone as powerful as he, but it would call beings who could.

The rattle came next. He moved slowly, careful not to allow it to make the slightest sound. The ark, he left in the duffle bag and set it beside the boulder out of his sight. He didn't dare touch it until everything else was destroyed.

When the conjuror's medicine lay stacked on top of the bones, he put the knapsack beside the pile. It didn't look bloody at all anymore. Grady saw the last trace of red disappear into the glowing thing inside, feeding a burst of heat that built and spread through the clearing.

The knapsack glowed red, then flames consumed it, leaving nothing but ashes. Within the ashes, the Ulunsu'ti lay, a pulsing, glowing mass of life.

The dried, ancient hands of the great conjuror curved round it while white fire licked at them. They remained whole until the crystal drew them inside itself.

The heat increased until it seemed the mound would catch fire and burn.

From the shadow world, the two Snake Dancers fought to hold the image of Degal gun'yi, enhancing it with the vision of the fire. They couldn't let themselves think the truth, that the bones and relics lay untouched on a great boulder beside the creek. The effort of holding the illusion sapped their dwindling strength, but they couldn't rest yet.

The serpent mind was satisfied. The hated tools of the conjurors would soon be ashes. The crystal that held the power to make him whole lay amid the flames.

Grady reached into the fire. The Ulunsu'ti belonged to him now, and now he could claim it. The illusory flame had no power to burn him, but the touch of the Ulunsu'ti seared his flesh. His agonized cry echoed through the worlds below. He struggled to draw his hand away from the crystal, but the efforts of the two most powerful conjurors in the world couldn't resist the will of Uktena. He had grown strong, and his power increased with each moment that passed.

Grady no longer controlled his body. In spite of the pain, his hand plunged deeper into the molten heart of the Ulunsu'ti. It was the serpent's will that lifted the crystal high above his head in triumph. He could only watch helplessly as his hand writhed inside the Ulunsu'ti, struggling to escape the torment.

Grady had no more fight left in him. The serpent controlled his body and devoured the last of his will. His struggle ceased. His mind and body belonged to the serpent. In the shadows of the below world, the odor of charred flesh added its stench to the mist. The wall between the worlds posed no boundary to the evil that claimed Grady Smoker. It had a home in all dimensions.

The fire that consumed Grady's flesh feasted on his mind.

Serpent thoughts spoke in his head and tormented him even more than the fire. It delighted in his pain and fear, and gloated that it would consume his being as it had his blood. Memories surfaced as Uktena drew them from him. The serpent devoured them and knew all that he had ever known.

The battle ended. He lost. Grady's eyes still looked out at the world, but the serpent chose where those eyes would stare. They saw through rocks and trees, far into the world beyond the mountains, looking in wonder at all they observed.

He could see the woman and child, staring at him from behind the rocks where they retreated. He saw John, silently closing in behind them, and other men beyond in the trees. He knew them well. They had once been important to him but now they were nothing. He watched them, savoring the taste of their fear.

Why did Kate and Wren stand there watching him? Did his face betray his agony? Could they see that he was on fire inside? If they did, they couldn't imagine how the fire strengthened him, burning power into his flesh and swelling his mind until it encompassed all things and all time.

Blood flowed from him into the Ulunsu'ti and back through his heart as they became one being. His memory awakened to all Uktena knew down through time. He felt its rage against those who enslaved it, and the rage became his own. Hunger born from centuries of sleep imprisoned in the Ulunsu'ti gnawed in his belly. He felt an awareness that someone fought against the force within him, even as it grew, telling him to move away from the boulder.

For a moment Grady Smoker found the strength to stumble away like a man wading against a swift current. He clutched at the trunk of a water willow, leaf buds swelling with new spring greenery. The tree burst into flame at his touch and in seconds disintegrated into a pile of ashes.

He wouldn't struggle any more. His surrender was

274

complete. The new mind that thought with his brain held full sway. Memories not his own flowed in his blood, promising him that anything he wanted was his. No one could stop him. Not this time.

He felt Uktena's hunger gnawing through his body. Hunger, as painful as the fire. The blood and being of one old man was enough to awake the crystal, but not enough to sate centuries of deprivation. The woman and child were not what he needed, not after so long a fast. They offered no more sustenance than the rabbits and woodchucks the old conjurors fed him while they enslaved him.

He remembered warriors, strong and powerful in their bloodlust. They came to him in great numbers, but that was before his last sleep, when he had to subsist on nothing but those frightened animals. Just enough to give him the strength to do what they asked of him and no more. Now, he was free of them. The last one who could bind him was gone.

He watched John lurking behind the boulders. The others who followed him would be here soon. He could wait awhile longer. What mattered a few minutes when he had waited centuries?

The child stepped from behind the rocks and walked toward him. She hid her fear well, but he saw through her pretense at courage. He smiled at her. No need to further frighten the little girl.

"Uncle Grady," she said. "Kanegwa'ti won't like what you've done. You're gonna be in big trouble if you don't put his Ulunsu'ti back where it belongs."

She posed no threat or served any purpose, but the man hiding behind the boulder wouldn't want his child to come to harm. No man fought more fiercely than when he battled for the life of his child. This was good. A warrior's blood to give him strength.

Did John McLeymore think he could hide from him? His

thoughts thundered as loudly as his labored breathing. He could hear him wondering how an old man could withstand such heat and not be consumed. Grady relished the taste of fear that came with thoughts of his daughter. A father who would die for his child. Yes, this was good.

He watched John walk toward him, trying to act casual, like it was not unusual for him to meet up with his daughter and an old man in the middle of nowhere. Kate couldn't hide her thoughts either. She was scared, not as much for herself as for her granddaughter. Wren surprised her, stepping out into the open that way. Some part of him remembered that Kate was like family to him. That part diminished almost too small now to hear, swallowed up in another mind that laid claim to all he had been and drank it up, just as it drained the blood from his body.

The spark of Grady that clung to consciousness felt the power of the awakening Uktena as it marveled at the knowledge it tasted in his blood. Its memories from centuries ago, of warriors who came with spears, bows, and arrows, and even the one who slew its serpent form with fire, paled against images Grady spent a lifetime trying to subdue. It tasted suppressed recollections of a warrior past, of blood and horror beyond words. Of weapons more powerful than anything that existed when he lived before. It feasted on visions of war that laid waste to whole lands and left multitudes slain, a war that had touched the entire world.

The serpent's hunger grew. It savored the first taste of what it was becoming and poured strength into the body it claimed. The old warrior's body had strength, but his spirit wandered in the below world where it offered no resistance. Soon, he would absorb the last spark of Grady's life, just as he had absorbed the being of others before the conjurors enslaved him.

Thoughts and images flowed within the blood it now shared with the old warrior's body. A strange and wondrous world came to be since he slept in the darkness. He craved that world and all the wonders it promised.

Drinking deeply of Grady's mind and memories, the serpent tightened his grip on Grady's being. Something pushed against him, trying to keep him from going any further. The old man lacked the power to resist on his own. Someone else interfered, lending Grady strength to defy him. He couldn't allow that. A thread of consciousness connected Grady to his source of strength. The serpent followed the thread to the warrior he sensed. There was nothing to fear from him. He was even older and weaker, lying like a dead man, his mind closed and unreachable. The serpent could snuff him with a touch, but this one was a warrior too, with more knowledge, like that of the one whose memories he tasted. The men who carried him could bring him to the serpent.

He sensed confusion from the men from the Cherokee Rescue Squad as they veered off the path to the logging trail and carried Walker Copperhead toward the falls. Walker didn't move or show any sign of consciousness. The serpent drew them closer. Weak though it was, he sensed a spark of life in the old warrior.

The serpent turned his attention back to John. Something in his thoughts disturbed him. He thought Grady should have known better than to show himself with Walker Copperhead's walking stick in his hand. It meant nothing. The serpent dismissed the trace of fear the thought aroused.

John, Kate, and Wren all pretended they saw nothing wrong. They would be amusing for a while until he came into his strength.

"Morning, Johnny," Grady said. "You picked a bad day to take Wren for a hike, with all the rain we've had." He kept his left hand behind his back, out of sight.

"Yeah, Grady, I guess I did," John said. "Where have you been keeping yourself? Eli's been worried about you."

"Eli?" That stirred a memory. "Eli? My grandson? He's worried, is he?"

John came closer. "Yeah, Eli's been looking for you. If you'll come with me, I'll take you to him."

Grady knew without seeing her when Kate reached for Wren. He knew the plan that formed in her mind: pick up the child and run away. He heard John silently urging her to hurry. His desperate hope that she would take his little girl to safety overshadowed fear for his own safety.

The serpent waited until Kate reached Wren, then he turned to her and smiled, a parody of Grady, her trusted friend. She faced him, still trying to pretend she believed him. The strength he sensed in her tempted him. Like a war woman of legend, she challenged him, prepared to fight for the child as fiercely as the man. He studied her as she clutched the child in her arms.

"I'd better get Wren home now," she said, forcing a smile. "I don't want Faron to worry."

He lifted his left hand so they could see. The child didn't pretend anymore. She screamed loud and long. Yes, she understood about the crystal. She knew it could make Grady do anything it wanted him to. Kate called Grady's name, begging him to shatter the crystal on the rocks and free himself.

Grady took a step toward her, his hand still raised. John ran at him behind his back, almost reaching him before he turned around. "Leave them alone!" John yelled. "Can't you see you're scaring them?"

John held a tree branch in his hand, raised to strike. Grady touched it with the crystal and it burst into flame and turned to ashes in an instant.

John pleaded now, begging him to let Kate take Wren home.

Wren whimpered aloud, unable to control her fear any longer, but the serpent sensed something in her thoughts that worried him. He saw fear, but not surrender. Images from a dream swam in her thoughts. He saw himself in the dream, and

John. Another image surfaced in the child's mind. He saw the last man who enslaved him, heard him speak to her.

A trace of fear weakened him for a moment. The conjuror who made him sleep within the crystal talked to the child in her dreams.

Kate reached for Wren but she pulled away and shouted, "I have to find the thing that will stop Uktena. The conjuror wants me to give it to Daddy."

The trace of fear faded. Nothing could stop him. All the conjuror's tools burned away to ashes. Only old men and frightened weaklings challenged him without the weapons the conjuror created to use against him. He was Uktena again.

John yelled at Kate, "Take Wren and get the hell out of here. Go!"

Wren wriggled out of Kate's grasp. Kate froze in place, watching while Grady got closer. She pleaded, "Grady, try to get free. Please."

Wren reached the big dome-shaped boulder. She screamed, "Daddy, I can't find it!"

"Wren, go with Mama Kate," John yelled. He almost sobbed with relief when Grady turned his back on Wren and Kate and turned on him.

John backed away. This wasn't Grady Smoker, but a bloodless mockery of the grandfather who told stories when they were boys. Heat poured from him, so hot it scorched John's face as he got closer. It emanated from the thing that encased Grady's hand all the way to his wrist, like a basketball-sized diamond. Its facets shimmered and flowed with life. Inside it, John could see Grady's hand, blackened and shriveled but still moving.

Grady knew he saw it. He raised the crystal above his head for all to see, then extended it toward a boulder the size of a bus. The boulder melted like lava and flowed down the slope.

John could do nothing but watch and wonder if his mind played tricks on him. After all, this was just Grady Smoker, a nice old man almost like kin.

Wren screamed again, pleading with Kate to help her.

Kate didn't move. She stood like stone, staring at Grady. Wren scampered behind the dome shaped boulder, scrambling among the rocks scared to death, and her normally protective grandmother didn't help her.

"Kate," John yelled as loudly as he could, "look after Wren!"

Kate didn't hear him. His little girl needed him and he didn't dare go near her. That thing on Grady's hand could burn her to a crisp. And Grady, or whatever it was that possessed his body, looked like he would enjoy watching her die. It watched him, moving every time he took a step. Like a helpless mouse under a cat's paw, he tried to draw attention to himself and away from Wren. Grady toyed with them, waiting.

Wren ran to the creek. She leaned over the water and called out something in Cherokee. John could make out the word, "Kanegwa'ti." Did she think the conjuror would hear her and come to help? Every instinct cried out that he had to get her away from here, but how?

Grady looked past John into the thick undergrowth on the slope. A herd of buffalo would have made less noise than David, Yona, Buck, and Eli trying to sneak up.

Yona broke through the bushes. John tried to keep the fear out of his voice. "Yona, take Wren home."

Yona took one look at Grady and walked toward the creek where Wren bent over the water, calling for the conjuror. He almost reached her when Grady stopped him, greeting him as pleasantly as if meeting him on the main street of Robbinsville. "Osiyo, Yona. Where's the rest of the Copperhead family? I doubt Walker is far away."

Yona forgot all about Wren.

John raised his voice. "Yona, Wren needs to go home." Yona didn't move. He stood staring at Grady, spellbound.

"What have you got there, Uncle?" Yona pointed at Grady's

hand.

Grady held his crystal-encased hand up, wriggling his fingers as if he didn't understand how they got there. The sleeve of his shirt burned away, leaving the smell of scorched cloth to mingle with the odor of seared flesh.

Something changed about Grady's face. His eyes blinked and cleared. The real Grady, the man John remembered, appeared. The familiar features contorted in agony. His lips cracked open when they parted in a scream. Then the mask slipped back into place.

That brief moment of respite released Yona from the serpent's control. He rushed to John's side. Wren ran from the creek to the big dome-shaped boulder. Kate dove for her and pulled her out of sight behind it.

But Wren wouldn't stay there. She scrambled among the rocks that littered the ground at the base of the boulder. John watched, trying not to draw Grady's attention to his daughter. He heard her crying, "Mama Kate, I don't know what to do. He's gonna hurt Daddy and I can't find the ark."

John yelled, "Kate, get her out of here!" He and Yona might stand a better chance if they didn't have to worry about Wren. "Go call Nathan."

He heard Kate plead with Wren, "Come on, baby. We need to get help for your daddy."

"Go with Mama Kate, Wren," John yelled. "Go get help."

"No, Mama Kate," Wren cried. "We have to take Daddy the ark. It's his only chance, just like in the dream."

Kate knelt down beside Wren, giving in to her pleading. John knew neither of them would listen to him now. Scared half to death, knowing what stalked them in Grady's body, they still intended to fight and he could do nothing to change that.

Grady circled Yona now, making odd comments about how strong Yona looked. Yona backed away and Grady followed. John edged toward Kate and Wren.

"Okay, baby. What's in the ark and why do we need it?" Kate asked.

"I don't know, but it's something that will help Daddy."

"Then, we have to find it." Kate yelled, "John, go help Yona." She took Wren's hand and ran.

Helpless to stop them, he followed Yona and Grady, praying Wren found the ark. If something in it could control the Ulunsu'ti, it might be their only hope.

Wren disappeared behind the boulder. Kate stood at its base, looking up toward the top of it. He followed her gaze and saw thin tendrils of smoke and fragments of charred canvas scatter in the wind. If Grady burned the duffle bag, the ark burned with it.

Grady tormented Yona with a parody of conversation. John joined Yona, feigning interest in what Grady said. If they could keep him distracted until Wren and Kate found the ark, perhaps they could figure out how to use it to control the thing on Grady's hand.

Grady rambled on about his days as a soldier in World War II. He'd never talked about those days before. When they were boys, they'd begged for war stories and he refused. Now he embellished descriptions of death and devastation so graphic it made John shudder.

Grady Smoker wasn't a big man, and well into his eighties. John and Yona both kept in good shape. They shouldn't be afraid of an old man. If they could just talk to him about the crystal attached to his hand, he might listen to reason. As a Snake Dancer, he knew what it could do. If they could make him remember his duties as a guardian, he would know how to escape it. It was worth a try.

"Uncle," John said, "do you know what's happening to you? I want to talk to you, Grady Smoker, the Snake Dancer. Can you hear me?"

"I hear you just fine, John." It was Grady's voice, but he

seemed distracted, like his mind was somewhere else.

John came a step closer. The crystal didn't emit as much heat. John shook like a leaf for fear he'd say the wrong thing and rile him up again, and risk getting melted like the rock. Damn, he wished Walker was here. He'd know how to handle this.

"He's on his way," Grady said. "Ought to be here in a few minutes."

John froze. "What? What do you mean?"

"Walker Copperhead, he's on his way."

Yona lost it then. "What do you know about my grandfather? He's nowhere near here."

"You are right, and you are wrong," Grady said. "He's as close as I am, and as far away."

John heard footsteps on the rocks. Did David, Eli, and Buck circle around to sneak up on Grady? His heart almost stopped when he saw the men from the rescue squad step into sight. Walker lay still as death on the litter.

Grady didn't look surprised at all to see him. He ordered them to put Walker down and they obeyed. He stooped and looked Walker over, curious, examining him like he almost remembered, but couldn't be sure. When he reached out to touch Walker's face, John's reflexes took over. He lunged at Grady in helpless rage, unable to restrain himself.

One of the men from the rescue squad reacted quicker. Before John could reach them, he put his hand on Grady's shoulder to push him away. Grady lifted the Ulunsu'ti and touched him. The man opened his mouth to scream but no sound emerged. A brief flash blinded them for an instant, then ashes lay piled around the smoldering soles of his hiking boots. Nothing else remained of the would-be rescuer.

The crystal pulsed and glowed brighter. The three remaining members of the rescue squad turned and walked away, like sleepwalkers, leaving the litter and the unconscious Walker Copperhead on the ground.

Wren screamed again. She saw what Grady did, and still she wouldn't leave. The urge to pick up his daughter and run overwhelmed him. But where would he go? Was there anywhere they could be safe? If Grady could make them bring Walker here, he could find them and bring them back. The Ulunsu'ti could give him that power if the old stories were true. He no longer doubted that they were.

"Don't let him touch Walker," Kate yelled at him.

What did she want him to do? Why didn't Buck or David come to help? They could at least buy some time. John never felt more alone and helpless, torn between wishing his friends would show up and feeling terrified for their safety if they did.

Grady squatted down beside Walker. Walker didn't stir or show any sign of life.

John bent down and closed his fist over a smooth, round rock. Not much of a weapon against a man who could incinerate him with a touch, but he had nothing else. He inched closer, talking softly. "He's your friend, Uncle. You don't want to hurt Walker."

Grady bent closer to Walker's inert form and called an unfamiliar name. Walker's warrior name? When it brought no response, Grady looked annoyed and prodded Walker in the ribs with the walking stick. He didn't get a chance to withdraw the walking stick. Walker came to life so fast it caught them all off guard. He grasped the walking stick and leapt to his feet, brandishing it like a weapon. Even the thing that controlled Grady reacted with a start. He took a step back, then pasted a distorted smile on his face.

So relieved he almost cried, John leapt to Walker's side, still holding the rock in his upraised fist. "Don't trust him, Walker. It's not Grady."

"I know who it is." Walker shielded them both with the walking stick and shouted out a name. Grady went still.

"Call this name, John. It'll give Grady the strength to fight the serpent." Walker yelled it again.

John tried to fit the unfamiliar syllables to his tongue, shouting it with all his might.

For an instant the Grady Smoker he knew looked at him and pleaded for help. "You are the only one who can take it off me, John," he groaned. Then the serpent took control.

"Stay close to me, John," Walker said. "Until he gets his full strength, the walking stick is one of the tools that can still hurt him. Don't let him near you. He'll want a stronger body than Grady's when he's ready."

A travesty of Grady's voice spoke through his cracked lips. "I hear what you're thinking. It's good that warriors still come to me. One is near who has a body that will serve me well, when I am ready." He extended his crystal-encased hand toward Walker's chest. Walker swung the walking stick, shouting Grady's warrior name so loudly that it tore through the air with the force of a blow. The walking stick sliced the air, connecting with the charred arm that wore the Ulunsu'ti.

The cry of pain came from Grady, not the serpent. Walker raised the walking stick to strike again. Grady cowered in agony.

The old man who told them stories on the porch under the beech tree pleaded for mercy. John caught Walker's arm. "No, Walker. You'll kill him. It's Grady Smoker."

Walker pushed him away in a fury that made John fear the old man would turn on him with the walking stick, then spoke through clenched teeth. "Killing him would be a kindness. If I could do it, I would. Uktena will keep him alive as long as there's enough flesh and bone left to serve his purpose. Grady will be the one who feels the pain."

Grady's agonized voice begged for release from the pain. "Help me, John. Hurry."

Walker yelled, "John, we need Kanagwa'ti's medicine. You've gotta find it before Grady loses his hold."

Walker talked to Grady, calling him by his warrior name,

urging him to hang on. John rushed to the boulder where Wren looked for the relics and grave goods. Wren climbed up to the pile of ashes and crumbling bones atop it. Frantically she searched through the pile and found the ragged medicine bag and tossed it to him.

"Give it to Grandpa," Kate said. "He'll know what to do."

John ran to Walker with the ragged medicine bag.

David, Buck, and Eli picked that moment to break through the underbrush. They joined Yona and Walker to form a circle around the pitiful specter that used to be Grady Smoker.

Eli pleaded, "Please, Grandpa, tell us what to do."

Grady's features twisted in an effort to speak to his grandson, then the mask of Uktena slipped back into place.

Buck shouted at him, "No, Eli. Get back. It's not your grandpa anymore."

But it was Grady for a few seconds at a time before he became absorbed into the hunger that was Uktena.

He appeared to hear when Eli called to him, "Grandpa. How can I help you? Please, talk to me." Grady's mouth worked like he tried to speak, but only an anguished moan escaped.

John came close enough to Walker to slip the medicine bag into his hands. It fell apart when Walker opened it to take out the eagle bone whistle.

"Now," Buck yelled. "Blow it."

Walker brought the whistle to his lips and blew. John heard a thin, sweet note, so soft it drifted away on the wind. He didn't wait to see what happened. Wren called to him from atop the boulder, "Here, Daddy, take this." She tossed a rattle to him.

He caught the rattle and took it to the circle around Grady. Walker blew a barely audible tone from the eagle bone whistle. "Shake the rattle, John," he shouted.

John did as Walker told him. He raised the rattle and shook a rhythm from it. It produced a sound no louder than the whistle. Grady screamed a loud, keening wail of pain. When he couldn't bear it anymore, John silenced the rattle and called out to Grady. Grady pointed his crystal-encased hand at Eli. It glowed white hot. Walker blew the whistle and John followed his lead and shook the rattle harder. Eli covered his face against the heat and yelled, "No, Grandpa!"

Grady reclaimed his body and answered him, his whole body convulsing with the effort to pull the crystal away from his grandson, his rasping voice a mere whisper. "Run, Eli."

With all his strength, he drew the Ulunsu'ti against his chest. The few rags still remaining of his shirt flamed and burned away from his charred and blistered flesh. His features twisted in a struggle against the serpent's grip on his mind. "Run now, Eli."

Eli took a few steps away, then stopped and stood his ground. "No, Grandpa. I can't leave you like this." Grady stumbled toward him.

John yelled, "Get the hell out of here, Eli, before he burns you to a cinder. That thing is using you to get to him."

Eli didn't move. John lunged toward him, intending to shove him away from the crystal only inches from his face. A force brought him up short like a dog on a leash. He couldn't lift a finger. Heat from the crystal raised blisters on his skin. He tried to back away but paralysis held him where he stood. He heard Buck yelling at Eli to get out of the way. He tried to tell Buck that he and Eli were both trapped, but he couldn't speak. He felt the life draining out of him and remembered the man from the rescue squad and how quickly he burned to ashes.

A shadow passed between John and Grady, breaking the invisible bond that held him fast. He lurched forward, crashing into Eli. Eli crumpled to the ground and lay there, still and cold. John shook him and he flopped like a rag doll.

A strong hand closed around his arm and lifted him to his feet. Buck? No, Buck stood beside Walker, Yona and David a few feet away spreading out to encircle Grady.

Eli lay motionless at his feet.

The man helped him to his feet and knelt down beside Eli. When he stood up, Eli stirred and opened his eyes. The man sent him to take his place in the circle that formed around Grady.

The strange man turned to Grady. Slender as a reed, he stood as tall as David and Yona and wore buckskin leggings under a beaded tunic. A strip of sky-blue linen wrapped like a loose turban around his head, with black hair escaping beneath it to hang almost to his waist. Smooth, unlined skin looked youthful, but something about him suggested he had lived longer than they could imagine.

He moved closer to Grady, only inches away. The Ulunsu'ti blazed white hot but left no mark on his skin.

John's doubt disappeared. The immortal Nunne'hi existed, and one of them stood in their presence. Awe took the edge off his fear. He became a believer. A week ago he compared his kind to dragons and fairies, but this was not a myth. The Nunne'hi come in answer to the call of the whistle and rattle to help their people in time of great need. He watched, expecting the Nunne'hi to take the Ulunsu'ti off Grady's hand and set everything aright.

The immortal did nothing but stand between them and Grady.

Grady howled in agony, fighting to hold his spirit in what was left of his body. The Nunne'hi made no move to intervene.

"Help him," John yelled. "He can't take it much longer."

"You have to act fast, boy. Grady's trying to help, but Uktena can drink up his soul if we don't hurry. Then he'll be too strong for us," Walker said.

"I don't know what to do." Was he supposed to try to kill Grady? The look of helpless terror in the old man's bloodshot eyes told him Grady remained very much alive and aware in the pitiful husk of his body.

Eli saw it too. He tried to get close enough to his grandpa to ask him what to do. Smoke rose from his hair and clothing.

John pulled him away for fear he would burst into flame. The crystal blazed white, driving them all back behind the rocks.

The immortal stood his ground.

Buck and Walker called Grady's name, pleading with him to hang on. From blackened lips, Grady's voice croaked, "Free me."

The Nunne'hi looked straight at John, like he expected something of him. But what? Everybody here knew more about these things than he did. What could he do? He was the outsider. But then, only an outsider could control the serpent force that inhabited the Ulunsu'ti. In spite of the heat emanating from the crystal, charring trees and bushes for yards around, he felt chilled to the bone.

"Walker, we need the ark," he yelled. "You said it would control the Ulunsu'ti."

Before Walker could reply, Kate shouted, "John, it's here."

He saw Wren dragging the duffle bag from behind the rocks. "Give it to Mama Kate," he yelled.

Wren whimpered in fear and stumbled toward him, the heavy bag in tow. Kate caught up with her and picked up both Wren and the duffle bag and ran to John. John took the duffle bag and looked inside. Grady's jacket was the first thing he saw. He took it out and untied the sleeves, revealing the ark, so old and fragile it couldn't possibly be effective against a force as powerful as the Ulunsu'ti.

"Now you get out of here," he ordered Wren. "I mean it. You've done all you can."

This time she listened. Kate held Wren tight and ran. A weight lifted off John when they disappeared through the underbrush. He rushed back to the Nunne'hi holding out the ark. The Nunne'hi ignored him and continued to speak to Grady in an older version of the language. Grady listened, and held on in spite of the agony it compelled him to endure.

Walker said, "You have to do it, John. You're the only one

who can."

Do what? Why couldn't Walker, or Buck or David, or Yona handle this? They looked at him, expecting him to know what to do, even the Nunne'hi.

He sank down and put the ark on the ground in front of him. With shaking hands, he felt around the edges until his fingers connected with the fangs of the snake. Something inside could save them.

He pulled the fangs apart, opening the serpent's mouth. He felt the lid give way and worked the box open.

When he looked inside, he groaned in despair. "Oh, God, what do we do now?" Somebody must have taken the weapon that was supposed to be there, because he didn't see anything. The ark was empty.

Walker squatted beside him and pulled the lid back so he could see under it. From a slit in the doeskin lining, he drew a sliver of a knife. The five-inch-long pale ivory blade looked as thin as paper and too fragile to cut hot butter without breaking. John's desperation deepened. He laid the knife across his palm and showed Walker. "What the hell are we supposed to do with this?"

"Save Grady and send Uktena back to sleep," Walker said. "You'll have to figure out how. It's Awi'Usdi's antler. That makes it stronger than it looks."

Awi'Usdi. The little white deer he always thought as much a myth as Santa Claus, and he was supposed to use a sliver of his antler to control the thing burning Grady Smoker alive. This had to be a nightmare.

John rose to his feet, his legs trembling so he could barely walk. The Nunne'hi stood a foot or so in front of Grady but didn't touch him, or do anything except shield the rest of them from the life-threatening heat of the crystal. He looked at John, waiting for him to do whatever it was they expected him to do.

John edged closer to the Nunne'hi, the tiny knife gripped in his fingers, hoping the immortal would show him how to use it. A dart of heat from the Ulunsu'ti touched him and weakness shot through his body. The immortal passed his hand between John and the crystal and broke its hold. The Nunne'hi spoke two words to him in English. "Do it."

The miniscule knife balanced weightlessly across John's palm. He looked for Wren, afraid that she might escape Kate and come back. His daughter had seen things that could scar her for life. He didn't want her to see him die. The Ulunsu'ti would surely kill him if he threatened it with the sliver of antler he held.

The Nunne'hi wanted John to come closer, to stand beside him, there where the thing in Grady's body could reach him. The thought of it turned his insides to jelly. Walker urged him to go on, to do what he had to do. John took a step toward the immortal, then another.

"Go on, John," Walker said. "It's up to you now."

John raised the knife. Oh, Jesus. They wanted him to kill Grady. He couldn't do it.

In a hoarse whisper, Grady begged for release. "Now, John. Please. I can't hold on any longer."

Choking back his horror, John brought the knife down across Grady's throat and felt it connect, slicing cleanly through flesh and bone. When he staggered away, he thought it was done.

Walker shouted, "Look out, John!"

John turned. Grady lurched toward him, pulled by the crystal. The bloodless gash across his throat did nothing but cause him more pain.

Heat took John's breath away until the Nunne'hi stepped between him and the crystal. The fire died when it touched the immortal, leaving him unscathed. The Nunne'hi moved away and John stood alone. No trace of Grady remained in the body that advanced on him. The serpent was in full control. He raised the knife to defend himself, but the Nunne'hi signaled him to stop, then called out Grady's true name.

The scent of burning herbs wafted from the boulder. Kate stood there alone, fanning smoke toward them with her jacket. How did she know to light Kanagwa'ti's medicine bowl? Something about the smoke strengthened him and gave him courage.

The smoke wafted across Grady's face. He breathed deeply of the scented smoke. The voice that spoke through the charred lips belonged to Grady. "Now, John. Hurry."

The Ulunsu'ti glowed even hotter. John watched it and saw something slither within the flame. It coalesced into a dark, writhing mass as smoke from Kanagwa'ti's preparation in the medicine bowl drove Uktena's spirit back into his prison inside the crystal.

Grady drew in deep, rasping breaths. The Nunne'hi called his name, speaking to him in the old tongue. Whatever he said gave Grady the will to hang on. Uktena still fought him and raised the crystal for one last attack. Grady grasped the Ulunsu'ti in his right hand, drawing it down to send the heat into the ground. John saw the hand inside it blacken.

"Free me, John," Grady croaked. "Please. Use the knife."

John looked at the open gash on Grady's throat. Pale, bloodless flesh and bone showed through. It was more than enough to kill a man, yet he still lived. What would it take? He looked at the Nunne'hi for guidance, but whatever the immortal said was of no use to him. He could understand enough Cherokee to recognize the language, but the old form he used meant nothing to him.

Walker shouted a translation: "Cut him free, John."

John looked at the crystal. The writhing shape inside it took a serpent form. Smoke from the medicine bowl swirled thick around them now. Grady inhaled deep gasps of herb-scented air. With each breath, the form in the crystal grew, becoming darker and more solid.

Understanding dawned. The smoke drove the Uktena from

Grady's body back into the crystal, still trapped on his hand.

John choked back nausea and dove for the Ulunsu'ti with the knife. Scalding blood poured over his arms, gushing not from Grady's severed wrist, but from the crystal. Heat and life poured onto the scorched soil. Within Grady's blood that drenched the ground, a black and shriveled hand twitched and then lay still. For a moment Grady kept his feet, then swayed and collapsed in a heap, face down beside the Ulunsu'ti.

John heard himself crying and didn't try to stop. The blood that soaked his shirt and stained his hands belonged to Grady Smoker, a good man who was like family. And he killed him. "I'm sorry Grady. I'm sorry," he kept repeating, knowing Grady couldn't hear him.

The Nunne'hi man stood impassive, watching. He held the Ulunsu'ti out to John, expecting him to take it. A wave of rage cut through John's grief and guilt. "Get that damn thing out of my sight."

The Nunne'hi lowered the Ulunsu'ti and said something in Cherokee. Walker translated, "You killed the Uktena. The crystal belongs to you now."

The Nunne'hi spoke again. John understood one word, "Suye'ta." He looked at the antler knife in his hand, then threw it at the immortal. He caught it easily and tossed it to Buck.

They used him to kill Grady. The blood still drenched his shirt and stained his hands. He swallowed the nausea that rose in his throat and swore at the Nunne'hi, at Walker and all the Snake Dancers, blaming them all for Grady's death and for what it had done to him and his family. Not one of them said a word, just listened like they were humoring him.

With an outraged yell, John made a run for the pond and lunged into the icy water. He tore off his shirt and watched it drift away, leaving red stains in its wake. The water eased the pain in his scalded hands. He rubbed hard enough to break blisters and scour away tender skin, disregarding the pain. He had to cleanse away the blood. When he was clean enough to face his daughter, he swam toward the creek bank. He wanted to find Wren, go home, and forget all about the Ulunsu'ti and the Suye'ta business.

The Nunne'hi waited, squatted beside the pond, talking to someone John couldn't see. He followed the immortal's eyes to the water and saw the snake. The water moccasin whipped his enormous body in a graceful motion and came to John. The cottonmouth gaped wide as the serpent curled around John once then slid away into the creek and disappeared.

He heard the Nunne'hi tell the snake goodbye.

The immortal waited for him to get out of the water. John faced him. "Why didn't you save Grady?" His rage faded into grief too great to bear. Someone owed him an answer. "You had the power. Why didn't you save Grady?"

The Nunne'hi spoke in perfect English. "Only the Suye'ta could save him. I shielded you and the guardians until it was done." He turned and walked away.

"That's not an answer," John called. The immortal disappeared into the hillside without looking back.

Wet and cold now, John stood alone on the creek bank. Kate came through the underbrush. "Wren?" John asked.

"She's okay, waiting for me down the trail. I'll take her home. You look after Walker and make sure he gets back to Snowbird." She left him to go take care of Wren.

John sloshed back to the others, bare-chested in soggy jeans. The hardest thing he had to face now was Eli. What could he say? He lost his nerve when Eli came toward him. At first, they just stood there mute, staring at each other.

"I'm sorry, Eli." Hollow, empty words that couldn't possibly convey the depths of regret John felt. He killed Eli's grandfather. He could never atone for that.

Tears streamed from Eli's eyes. "Walker said you freed him. He was dead already."

John felt warm tears on his face.

Walker cut short their exchange and drew their attention to the pines beyond the rocky clearing. Flames leapt through the trees. "The Ulunsu'ti set fire to the woods trying to get to us. We've gotta clean up and get out of here."

John saw the smoke, but with the rain-drenched woods and a thin drizzle still falling, the fire didn't pose a great threat. But smoke quickly attracted firefighters. They couldn't leave the conjuror's medicine and Grady's body for them to find.

"What now, Walker?" he asked.

Walker handed him the sleeping Ulunsu'ti. "It would have gone to Eli. Now I guess you have to decide what to do with it."

"Don't start that Suye'ta shit with me again, Old Man." John handed the crystal to Eli. "Your grandpa would have passed it on to you. Figure out a good place to hide it and look after it like you're supposed to."

Buck and Yona hurried over, both carrying bundles wrapped in shirts and jackets scented with the herbs from Kanagwa'ti's medicine bowl. Walker instructed them to take Eli to the truck and sent John back to help David.

Smoke billowed thick now. John bent low to the ground to stay below it and went to Grady's body where David waited. "Do we have to carry him down the trail?" John hoped David came up with another way.

He did. "We'll leave Grady in the creek till we can come back for him. His body needs to be in a grave with his medicine. The Snake Dancers will keep doing what we've done since the conjuror started the circle."

They wedged the body among the rocks under the creek bank to protect it from the fire. David picked up the blackened hand, wrapped it in his handkerchief, and put it in his jacket pocket. "I'm still the guardian of the last hands to hold the Ulunsu'ti," he said.

Kate waited alone at the road. "Wren needed her mama,"

she said when John asked about his daughter. "Lynelle Wayanettah is taking her back to Snowbird. I wanted to make sure you and Walker were okay." He thanked her for everything. Kate hugged him hard.

"You're one tough old gal, Kate," he said.

Kate had no more time for John. She pushed him away and got busy fussing over Walker, insisting he get in her car so she could take him home.

Walker stood firm. "I can't leave yet. I'll try to be home tonight. You have to go now, Kate."

It surprised John when she agreed. "Faron and I have to do payroll anyway," she said. "Loggers work hard for their wages and they'll want to get paid, no matter what else is going on." She turned to John. "You'd better not let anything happen to the old man."

They watched her wheel the Trans Am around and take off for Snowbird.

John looked back up the mountain where black smoke still rose above the trees at the head of Lightning Creek.

"The fire service is already on the way," David said. "The fire will probably die out before they get here. If anybody asks, lightning started another fire. They'll figure that's what killed Grady too."

John didn't mention the man who died trying to protect Walker Copperhead from something he didn't even understand. There was nothing left of him to recover but the soles of his boots. He would always remember the man's courage.

He wondered about the other men from the Cherokee Rescue Squad.

Walker said, "I doubt they have any memory of what happened after Uktena got into their heads and made them bring me here. I'll give them a good story about how I came to and took off."

They walked to their trucks at the logging trail in silence.

John didn't expect them to discuss the hurt they all felt. It wasn't their way. He had his own dark thoughts that would be with him for the rest of his days. He'd have to learn to keep them to himself. This was only the beginning of something that would go on for generations yet to come.

For the first time in his life, he really wanted to go to water. Not just to please the Copperheads, but because he needed to be clean of all the evil and pain. He couldn't wait to get to the cleansing flow of Big Santetla.

He even asked Walker if they could go straight there. Walker said, "I don't think we need to wait that long, son. I've got something closer in mind."

As soon as they reached the trucks, Walker got them organized. "Boys, there's a place on the Oconoluftee where we can purify ourselves and figure out some things. John, you and Eli and me will go in your truck. The rest of you follow us."

John watched David walk away, glad they weren't riding together. He couldn't get the image of Grady's shriveled hand out of his mind. He started the truck and drove down Lightning Creek Road, turning at Walker's instruction onto a graveled road. After that, Walker rode with his head lowered and his eyes closed, so quiet John worried that the head wound was acting up.

"You alright, Grandpa?" he asked.

Walker opened his eyes. "Just thinking, John. I'm the only elder Snake Dancer left. In spite of what you boys have seen, you've got a lot to learn and nobody but me to teach you. There's more to the guardianship than the Ulunsu'ti and the relics that control it. Lots more."

John stopped him. "That's not something I need to know about, Grandpa."

Walker gave an expressive grunt and continued. "You five boys are in for some interesting times, different from anything the ancestors could have prepared you for. But to tell you the truth, I don't think there could be a better choice of guardians.

297

I've got a world of confidence in every one of you."

John tried again to shut him up. "This is all stuff I'm not supposed to know, Old Man. I've already heard and seen more than I want to. So I suggest you wait till I've gone home before you tell the guys about this Snake Dancer stuff."

Walker went on like John hadn't said a word. "There's Buck. He's always behaved like he was born to keep an eye on everybody in the Eastern Band, or anyone that had anything to do with us. Not much ever got past him since he was just a boy. And David has a greater love of the old ways and knowledge than anybody I've ever known. He'll make sure they live for the children's children. Eli knows every inch of our land and has dedicated his whole life to looking after it. Yona makes sure the resources of the land are protected and used wisely. He and Meredith Wayanettah will have some fine kids one day to keep things going."

John took a curve way too fast. Eli swore, the first word he said since they got into the truck.

Walker said, "I know you don't want to hear this, John, but you might as well listen. You're the wild card. It's gonna take you a while to accept where you fit in, but the truth is, you don't have much choice. You're already in too deep to get out now."

John said, "You're dreaming, Old Man. I don't want any part of this bullshit."

Walker paid no attention. "Sure, it might take some time, John, but you'll come around. You might learn to like being the Suye'ta one of these days."

John let him know in words that he could never use with Wren in the car that he could forget that idea right now.

Walker leaned back and got comfortable. "Well, you'll have to learn to accept it. Not much you can do about it anyway. John McLeymore, you're the first white Snake Dancer, and for sure the first white Suye'ta."

John gripped the steering wheel and tried not to look at

Walker's smug face for fear he might punch it if he did.

Eli picked that moment to put in his two-cents worth. "Yep. We're in for some interesting times, John. Might as well get used to it."

Epilogue

Friday Morning

Yellow Hill

The sun collected morning fog from the valleys and drew it higher into the hills and mountains. It drifted like dragon's breath toward the pale blue sky. Under the canopy of hardwoods, newly opening dogwood blossoms gleamed so white they looked like snow on the trees.

John turned his eyes away from the scenery and took his place with the five other pallbearers who carried Grady Smoker's body to his final resting place. Drums called through the trees, the heartbeat of the earth calling the old soldier home. Thomas and Eli began the procession. The Choctaw woman, her head bowed in grief, walked beside Thomas. He supported her with an arm around her waist. Eli's mother said her goodbyes as soon as she learned about the Choctaw woman and her daughter, and left for her long delayed return to her family in the west. Just as well. She never liked living on the Snowbird. Her melancholy infected the Smokers, causing a darkness in their home.

The Choctaw woman knew the way to the grave. They came here with her a day ago to lay her daughter to rest beneath the mound of newly turned earth beside Sally. John stood at the casket then with Thomas and Eli when they saw the girl for the first time. That's when Thomas took the Choctaw woman in his arms, and they knew she never left his heart. He traded love for duty and came home to a wife and son who needed him.

The Choctaw woman pleaded with Thomas and Eli to forgive Grady and Sally for keeping her secret. They did what they had to do to keep Eli's mother from leaving for Oklahoma and taking her son with her. Eli gave in when he saw how much the woman loved his grandparents.

The grave lay open, welcoming an old man to his rest. The pallbearers positioned the coffin on the frame that would support it until time to lower it into the dark earth. John lingered a moment to say a silent goodbye, then joined the crowd who came to bid farewell.

A quartet of elder women broke into song. They sang in the Cherokee language, but everyone at the grave recognized the hymn and knew the words. *Amazing grace, how sweet the sound.*

Walker Copperhead came forward and laid a hand on the coffin, then turned away to face the four directions, calling on the guardians of each to guide his friend through worlds above to his dwelling place. While he prayed, Yona and David walked among the people offering shells of smoking sage. Mourners drew the cleansing comfort of the smoke to themselves with feather fans or bare hands.

Eli returned to Hilda's side. His wife clung to his hand, her blue eyes brimming with tears. Her parents stood behind her, looking uncomfortable and out of place. The deep respect they held for their son-in-law's grandfather brought them here. The young priest from the Episcopal church in Murphy stood with them to lend support. He stepped up to the grave and read a prayer from his book.

Drums beat a rhythm and a singer took the priest's place. He sang not for the living, but for the journey of the one who walked over to the other world. The Cherokee people at the grave understood.

The song resonated in John's heart. An image of Grady and Sally, standing together under a giant beech tree, danced before his eyes and vanished when the singer fell silent.

Eli and Thomas came forward to add their prayers. They sang them together in the tongue of their forefathers, asking the ancestors to look with kindness on a man who had suffered to right his wrongs.

The empty grave showed no evidence of what lay beneath it. Yona and Walker came in the dark of night to bury it there in the best place they could think of to conceal the replenished medicine bowl and all the rest of Kanagwa'ti's grave goods. Few safe hiding places existed in the wilderness anymore. Here, on the grounds of the Baptist church, pothunters didn't prowl like they did in the old burial grounds. The conjuror's medicine would be safe until the right person and the right time came along.

They told John where they secreted the conjuror's goods away, as if he cared what they did with their Snake Dancer business. They insisted he had a right to know as the Suye'ta.

They looked from the grave to the rise beyond as seven riflemen lined up at parade rest. At the command, "Firing squad, attention!" the riflemen snapped to attention.

"Port arms." They brought the rifles into position.

"Lock and load," the squad leader called.

In unison, bolts snapped back and the first round dropped into the chamber.

"Prepare to fire salute."

"Fire."

Rifle fire cracked in the stillness. Three seconds to reload, then the second volley, and the third. A salute to a fallen hero.

Echoes resounded off the far hills. "Order arms." The squad brought their weapons to the position of attention.

"Present arms," and rifles snapped vertical before the riflemen's chests.

The squad leader's hand salute signaled a lone soldier who raised a bugle to his lips. The bugler's mournful refrain called an old soldier to his final sleep. The last note still hung in the air when the next order came.

"Order arms."

"Right shoulder arms."

"Right face."

"Forward march." The squad marched away over the rise.

The six soldiers who came forward to remove the flag from Grady's coffin folded it into the tri-corn shape. The squad leader presented it to Thomas on behalf of a grateful nation.

They stood in silence then, watching dark-suited strangers from the funeral home lower Grady's coffin into the grave.

Thomas and Eli each scooped up a handful of black earth and dropped it in. The Choctaw woman knelt, holding a shiny gold locket shaped like a heart, and released it to fall atop the coffin. A gift, she said, that Sally and Grady gave her daughter. Thomas lifted her to her feet. She buried her face against his chest and let him hold her.

The funeral was over and done, but they couldn't go home yet.

John and Eli directed the crowd away from the grave, guiding them to a circle prepared in the meadow over the rise. Eli had asked for a giveaway. Usually that came later, but Thomas let Eli have his way.

Walker went to the center of the ceremonial circle to bless the drum with sage and tobacco. John joined him to walk the circumference, consecrating it with smoking sage bundles and prayers, while Grady's family and friends gathered at its outer edge. He felt awkward, performing a ritual better handled by one of the Indians, but Walker insisted.

Even the birds fell silent, the only sound being that of the drum beating that deep, regular rhythm, the heartbeat of the earth. Mourners swayed gently to the healing song of the Mother's heart.

When everyone found their place, lined side by side around the circle, a different rhythm emerged. The drum thundered and singers raised their voices in an ancient primal song that lifted the Cherokees to another place and time. There, they were one with the ancients who lived here before the white man came, those who journeyed west or left their bodies along the Trail of Tears, or sacrificed to stay behind and preserve the precious fragment that remained of their ancestral land—even with those who left the community but still remembered who they were.

They were Cherokee. Behind closed eyes they gave themselves up to the ache and joy of being who and what they were. One People now, they entered the song, lifting voices that blended and united. It stirred their spirits and called them into the circle. John felt the call. His feet moved and his body swayed in union with the dancers. Other white people stood awkwardly outside the circle, like he always did before, but now he belonged with his people.

Faron danced at his side, matching his rhythm. He could feel her there, though his eyes stayed closed. The dance was a prayer, a covenant and a source of power, and he understood. No longer an outsider who married in, John was Cherokee.

He saw Walker, Buck, and David leave the circle and pride welled in his heart. They would return as warriors. He had looked up to the Cherokee Warrior Society as long as he could remember.

A few more songs and dances, then the dancers snaked from the circle and took their place in a ring around it. Only Eli and Thomas remained inside with the drum and singers. The last deep rumble of the drum hung in the air then faded into stillness.

Through the silence, Eli's voice rang strong and proud. "My grandfather was a warrior. In World War II, he received a battlefield commission for an act of courage that saved his platoon and gave his people another reason to be proud of our warriors. When this was our own land, our people fought to defend it. When America goes to war, Indian people are among the first to go and the first to die, and often the last to be recognized, but our warriors do their duty. Today, my father and I hold this giveaway to honor Lt. Colonel Grady Smoker, a soldier in the American Army. His courage was as great as any hero of the past. His final battle will be sung by only a few, but it will be remembered through all the generations of his children."

The drum came alive, rising with the power and passion of a warrior's dance. Women gave voice to a tremolo that ignited war cries from young men. The circle parted at the eastern side and, with great dignity and bearing, Walker danced in, carrying in one hand the totem banner of the Bird Clan, and in the other, his walking stick. He wore the uniform of the U.S. Marine Corps. A badge on his sleeve proclaimed him a member of the Cherokee Warrior Society. A single hawk feather and a strand of red yarn adorned his long braid. Behind him came others clad in parts of uniforms they wore in their own service to their country: Army, Navy, Air Force, Marines, a couple of Green Berets. Two elder women wore Army Nurse Corps uniforms from the same vintage as Walker's garb. Women and men alike added something of their Indian regalia to the military dress. All danced to honor a fallen warrior who would no longer dance in their circle.

Clan banners and totems from all the seven clans lifted proudly above the marching, dancing warriors as they traversed the circle. They formed an arc behind Thomas and Eli and came to a halt.

David and Buck stepped out of the line of warriors, each in uniforms worn during their service in the desert. David laid a blanket before Thomas and Eli, spreading it out on the ground to reveal a collection of items that belonged to Grady.

On a white blanket that lay waiting, Buck carefully placed a tunic and leggings, the ceremonial regalia Grady treasured and wore only on the most important occasions. Sally made it for him soon after they married. Every bead and feather on the beautifully worked buckskin spoke of the skill and love with which she fashioned it. Today, it would be passed on to the one who took over any unfinished tasks he left undone, carrying on his place and duty in the world.

305

One by one, Eli and Thomas held up an article that belonged to Grady and called out a name. The old Barlow pocket knife he carried with him for years went to Hilda's dad. He blinked back tears and struggled to maintain his Anglican dignity when he took it from Eli's hand.

A turquoise pendant went to Bonnie Locust. She stood straight and proud, lifting her hair for Buck to fasten it around her neck. Hilda's younger brother choked up when he went into the circle to take the keys to the old Pinto. He would be old enough for a learner's license in a few months. With a few repairs and a new set of tires, it would serve him well. The deed to Grady's land went to Eli. Thomas took a quilt Sally made and laid it across the Choctaw woman's arm. She held it against her breast and silently cried. An old book of poetry went to John. He leafed through it, noting scribbled comments in the margin that revealed a sensitive, philosophical side of Grady he wished he knew about sooner.

When nothing remained but Grady's regalia, Buck picked it up on its blanket and laid it across Walker's arms. Walker signaled with a nod for John, David, and Yona to stand with them when he made the presentation. With a lump in his throat, John listened. Walker spoke loud enough for everyone to hear, but the depth of meaning in his words was meant for Eli and the four who flanked Walker.

"You stand in your grandfather's place now, son. What he would have done, you must do. What he has forgotten, you must remember. Keep his words to pass down to the generations of his children. Honor his spirit as long as you live and keep your duty to him until you leave it in other hands that you trust to keep it well."

Lowering his voice, he continued, "Eli, you are the grandson and heir of the last guardian of the Ulunsu'ti. Until the Suye'ta calls for it, it is in your care. In your grandfather's stead, I will stand with you until I walk over to be with the ancestors.

306

Grady did wrong, but he atoned for his offense in the only way he could. It's up to you to set it right. We'll be with you, Eli."

Walker laid Grady's regalia across Eli's outstretched arms and stepped back and bowed his head. John and the others followed his lead. The clear, sweet melody of a lone cedar flute sang the old warrior to his rest.

When the last note faded, the drum took up the slow, solemn rhythm of the heartbeat. The Cherokee Warrior Society danced out of the circle.

John looked across the hill where they left a new unmarked grave behind. Grady Smoker no longer existed in this world. He silently thanked him for a lifetime of stories that prepared them to get through the past week alive. Other than Grady's son and grandson, only Walker and Yona had reason to remember where his bones rested.

Yona walked away without a backward glance. Meredith Wayanettah slipped her arm through his and fell into step with him. She wouldn't be leaving until Monday morning. They needed time alone to make the most of her visit home. John counted himself lucky not to be one of the men working with Yona on Monday. His brother-in-law was grumpy as hell when Meredith left for Atlanta.

He resolved to remind Eli again that Meredith was doing the right thing for all the right reasons. One day soon, when she came home and set up her practice, the waiting would be worthwhile. They could start that family and make Walker happy.

Yona waved goodbye over his shoulder.

John watched them go, anxious to leave the cemetery and go home. Back on the Snowbird with Faron and the kids, he could put the last few days out of his mind. The only Lightning Creek in his future was his band. Saturday night meant singing bluegrass with the boys at the Round House, and this time Faron planned to come along. Kate offered to spend the night with the kids, so they could stay out as late as they wanted to.

"Ready to go home, Johnny?" Faron took his arm. It would be easier if he could tell Faron everything, but Walker said he had to keep the Snake Dancers a secret from her, if he could.

Walker waited up ahead, leaning on his walking stick and looking frail and tired. It made John feel guilty for some of the things he said to the old man to make him shut up about initiating him into the Snake Dancers Circle. How else could he get it through Walker's head? No way in hell he intended to become a Snake Dancer. It created tension between them, and it hurt both of them.

John made an attempt to mend the rift. He didn't blame the old man for doing what he thought best.

"You want to ride home with us, Old Man?" He clapped a hand on Walker's shoulder.

"Sure, son." Walker grabbed Diamond's arm as the boy tore past him. "Your son's getting as independent as you are lately. Thinks he can get by on his own without any help from anybody. It'll take time, but he'll learn we're all in this together."

Diamond broke into a run, dragging Walker along with him. As usual, Walker got the last word.

Kate said goodbye to Nathan Axe with a brief kiss and left him to join her family. Wren took her hand and stood looking toward the grave. "Mama Kate, are you sure he's in that grave?"

John waited for Kate's answer, not at all happy with the dark circles under his baby's eyes. The poor kid probably hadn't slept a wink since that morning on Wolf Mountain. No wonder. He'd had a couple of nightmares himself.

Wren asked again, "He's in there, isn't he, Mama Kate? The real Uncle Grady?"

"That's just his body, honey," Kate told her. "Grady walked over to the above world."

"But it's him, isn't it? Not the thing that made him a bad man?" Wren needed to be sure.

"Honey, that bad thing can't hurt anybody anymore. Uktena is asleep again inside the Ulunsu'ti. I think the men know better than to try to use it again. Let's hope they learned something from this." She shot a meaningful glare in Walker's direction.

"Mama Kate," Wren began, "why do the men keep that thing? Why don't they just try to find a way to break it and make it go away?"

John kept quiet and listened. He wondered about that more than once.

"You know the stories about the good things the old conjuror did with it, and the others before him who controlled it. When it's used in the right way, by the right person, the power of Uktena is good to have on our side."

"Mama Kate, do the women have anything like that? Some kind of thing that gives us power?"

Kate smiled, a faint, mysterious smile. "No, Wren," she said. "We don't need it. We do just fine without any crystal."

For the first time in days, Wren smiled. "Let's go home now, Daddy," she said.

John picked her up and held her like he did when she was much younger. Faron slipped an arm around his waist. Kate went to help Walker try to keep Diamond under control till they got to the car. They were less than an hour away from home.

"Yes, baby," John said, "let's go home now."

The first white Suye'ta took his family home to the little house on the Snowbird.